Charle

D

U. S.

Marshal

1879 - 1906

"The story of one man's lifetime of service with the U.S. Marshal force"

Linda Pool Anderson

Cover: Designed by Phillip Sandgren

Charles Barnhill Deputy U. S. Marshall

For more information, please write:
Linda Anderson
linda.skymama@gmail.com

This book is a work of fictionalized history. Real locations and public figures are mentioned. The events described in this book are as reported in newspapers and letters of the period.

Manufactured in the United States of America.

To my family and all the
Barnhill Descendants, especially my son,
Tony who stands tall like his ancestors.

Enjoy this true story of
three brave lawmen,
Linda Pool Anderson

Acknowledgements...

I would like to offer special thanks to those who assisted me in my research, especially my husband, Meredith I. Anderson, who accompanied me on many research trips to Fort Smith, Arkansas and my sister, Delores Butcher, who instilled in me a love of family history; to the staff of the Fort Smith National Historic Site, who answered my questions with patience and offered suggestions on the available resources pertaining to the history of the Western District of Arkansas Judicial Court and its officers. The staff at the beautiful, modern Fort Smith City Library showed me the microfilm records of the court they had in their genealogy department along with years of the Fort Smith Elevator during the famous court's era.

The professional service of the National Archives and Records Administration in Fort Worth, Texas which is the repository of the case files for the prisoners who were arrested, arraigned and convicted, cannot be over-stated. They gleaned out and copied the dozens of cases that I requested. Though Charles and Abe Barnhill were involved in several hundred arrests, I chose to present the more important cases of murder, of which there were dozens, along with some sensational ones such as the arrests of Belle Starr and Jim Cook.

My personal gratitude goes to Mr. Edward (Jerry) Akins, a volunteer from the Fort Smith National Historic Site, who worked in the Site's library and allowed me access to the resources and files. Without his help many details would have been lost

The family descendants of the Barnhills were most encouraging. These include Stephen Barnhill, great-grandson of Charley, who provided the initial family genealogy and LaVerne Barnhill Wallace Barnes , daughter of Tony Barnhill, who gave me wonderful insights into her grandparent's lives, having spent many years of her childhood with her Grandmother Irene. Sandy McKim, a cousin, added deputy oaths to the data. They provided from their own family histories tidbits of information that I was able to use as a starting point to locate and substantiate the facts. Any family story that I could not find mentioned in a public record was not included even though it may have been interesting and probably is true. Research has to be concluded at some point and this is a story that could be researched for another decade. I had to limit how many family members to include because this is a historical biography, not a genealogical one.

All persons named with first and last names are historical figures except two, Jim Slater and Dan Griffin who were created by the author as a prototype to glue the story together. This is a work of fiction based on known facts. Public records were followed where ever they were available. Conversations are, of course, of the writer's creation unless sited in newspaper reports or trial documents but in every case they are based either on real situations or situations which are typical of time, place and condition.

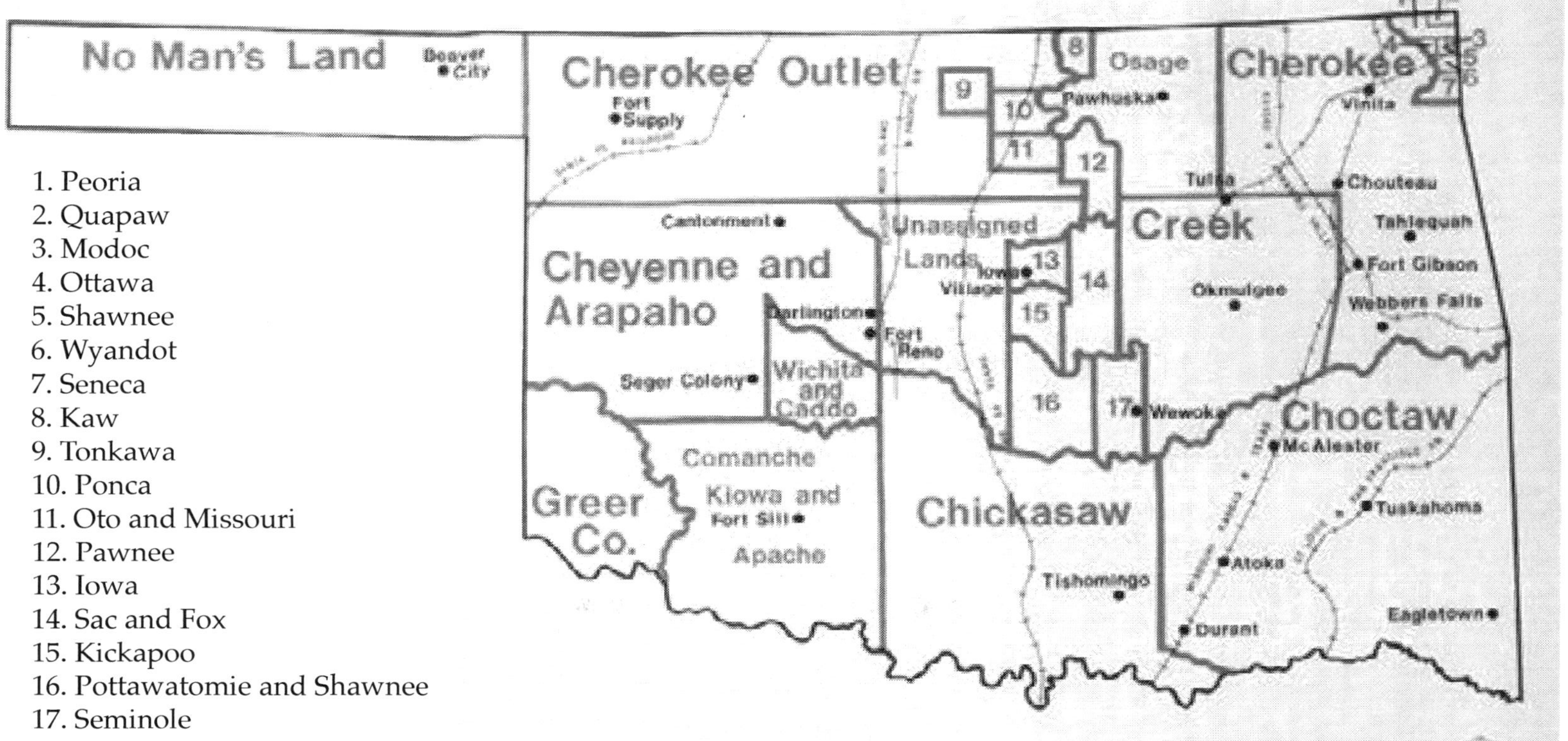
No Man's Land
Beaver City
Cherokee Outlet
Fort Supply
Osage
Pawhuska
Cherokee
Vinita
Tulsa
Chouteau
Tahlequah
Fort Gibson
Webbers Falls
Creek
Okmulgee
Unassigned Lands
Iowa Village
Cantonment
Cheyenne and Arapaho
Darlington
Fort Reno
Seger Colony
Wichita and Caddo
Wewoka
Choctaw
McAlester
Tuskahoma
Atoka
Durant
Eagletown
Chickasaw
Tishomingo
Comanche
Kiowa and
Fort Sill
Apache
Greer Co.
1. Peoria
2. Quapaw
3. Modoc
4. Ottawa
5. Shawnee
6. Wyandot
7. Seneca
8. Kaw
9. Tonkawa
10. Ponca
11. Oto and Missouri
12. Pawnee
13. Iowa
14. Sac and Fox
15. Kickapoo
16. Pottawatomie and Shawnee
17. Seminole

Oklahoma Indian Territory 1869 - 1889

Chapter 1

Vendetta

Charley's friend, Jim Slater was a fighter. He rushed the rider, his hands grasping for the bridle. "That's my horse! Give it to me!"

At the sound of his friend's shout, Charley turned. Charley felt the heat on his face before he could recoil from the pistol that shot flames out its barrel just inches from his head. He watched Jim crumple into the dirt of the street without a sound, his left hand still clutching his Bible. His eyes, wide with shock, clouded over even as Charley knelt beside him. He heard the oath of the rider as he pulled the horse around and kicked it in the flanks, disappearing around the side of the general store.

This is all wrong. He attempted to wipe away the warmth from his face and, in that moment, realized it was his friend's blood moving in a free-flowing stream down his hand. Seconds ago while walking to the church in the square of the little town, Jim had complained of the loss of his horse during the night. Charley had picked him up in his ranch wagon and they had headed into town for a meeting of the church elders.

"Where's the doctor? Get the doctor?" He looked up into the faces of the crowd that had gathered silently around the lifeless form. A woman with a hand to her throat, the store clerk from inside the general store, a loose gathering of Indian boys, the pastor and elders from the church.

He felt a hand on his shoulder. The pastor spoke. "He's dead, son. No need for a doctor now."

Charley stood and looked around for his wagon, the team still tied to the hitching post in front of the church. "Help me put him in the wagon."

His friends from the church stepped forward to help pick up Jim's body. Charley had never lifted a corpse before. He tried not to stare at the lifeblood that had stopped running out on the ground splattering into the dust. *Ashes to ashes, dust to dust.* The men struggled to the wagon bed with their burden. No one spoke for several seconds.

"Here, mister. He dropped this." One of the street urchins handed him Jim's Bible, smoothing the dirt and blood off of it with his sleeve. "I'm sorry about your friend. I know the fella who was riding the horse. His name's Terrell. He's a friend of my pa, and a mean man. I saw him kill his dog one day just because it wouldn't get out of his way fast enough."

"Thanks, son. Where does he live?"

"Outside of town just past the creek."

He placed the Bible underneath Jim's arms which were beginning to grow cold and stiff and crossed them on his chest. He buttoned his jacket over it to keep it in place and smoothed Jim's long golden hair underneath his hat, laying his head with tenderness onto the hard wood of the wagon bed.

The pastor stepped forward.

"Charley, let us take your friend home. You need to go find the law."

He went through the motions of handing the reins of the team to the pastor, his mind racing back to the feel and sound of the bullet whipping past his face and the look on Jim's face as he fell. Without thought he shifted his hand to his Winchester rifle in the corner of the wagon box, a symbol of the West - justice of the gun, not justice of the law.

Their wives were such good friends. He knew Salina would comfort Jim's Betty, but who would comfort Salina when the terrible news was delivered if he was seeking his own justice? But this time he could not step back and let someone else do what he knew he needed to do - kill a stranger named Terrell.

He looked at the clerk "I need the marshal. Where can I find him?"

The clerk's hands shook as he pointed to the center of town.

"He's at his office down the road by the courthouse. I saw him when he came in for a cigar about noon."

The marshal, having been summoned by the street urchin, rode up and stopped at the back of the wagon. He stared at the body for a long minute and then spat into the dirt.

"I'm United States Deputy Marshal Ayers. Who wants to ride posse after the killer?" Several men in the crowd stepped up. He turned his steady gaze on Charley, his eyes flicking to his fingers wrapped around the rifle barrel.

"What's your name, boy? You know how to use that Winchester?

Charley barely heard his reply spoken through his drooping moustache.

"Charles Barnhill, sir. Yes, I can shoot as straight as anyone." He removed the rifle from the wagon box and pulled his cartridge belt from under the seat.

The marshal smiled. "Now, young man, you got a horse to ride?"

"Take mine, Charley," the pastor offered, "over in Bishop's livery."

He struggled to keep up with the withering pace of Deputy Ayers, who pushed them up and down gullies and into rock- strewn hillsides. The horse under him heaved to cross a five foot jump over a stream. He felt the saddle creak with the effort. The foam-flecked withers of the pastor's horse mirrored his companions' mounts. Everyone, man and beast, needed a break.

Ranging out half a mile ahead keeping up a fast trot on foot, the Indian trackers dismounted now and again to examine the tracks of the fleeing murderer. The veteran lawman pressed his pack onward toward the setting sun. If they did not catch the killer by night fall, he would escape.

The prairie spread out before them as they topped the ridge above the Canadian River. At this time of year it was a mile wide and only a foot deep. Their leader stopped his horse at the water's edge and swung down.

"Take five minutes to rest and water up. Check your ammunition and make sure your guns are ready to go. The scouts are hot on his heels."

The men stood beside horses, loosening straps and tightening saddle girths for the final pursuit. Charley bent down and scooped up a hat full of water before his horse could muddy it up. It felt cool and refreshing to his dust-parched throat. The rest he just dumped on his head when he replaced his hat. He pulled out the Winchester and gave it a quick look before inserting it back into the saddle holster.

Numbness from the hours of riding could not cover the grief and hate he felt warring inside him. His mind played back the scene in the street, the sounds, the blood, the shock. He had never even hit a man in anger and now he wanted to kill one. Would the marshal give the man a chance to surrender? From what he knew of Ayers, he would. He did not shoot first and ask questions later as some deputies did.

Adrenalin raced his pulse as his thoughts were interrupted with a Cherokee war-whoop, one you never forget if you have ever heard it. The shrill high-pitched screech set his hair one end but he knew what it meant. The prize was at hand.

The pursuers splashed through the river to the opposite shore as the scouts came sliding down an embankment on their ponies The older one pointed up and toward the south, gesturing to Ayers with sign language. Charlie had picked up this skill over a period of years living amongst many tribes who used it to communicate. The hands flew indicating a cage with no escape.

Without a word, the marshal mounted up to follow his two blood hounds. Their pace was fast, but the horses kept them well insight until they came to a deep fissure in the side of the river. Dense foliage along the high bank offered concealment from the exposure of the prairie.

Before they could dismount, a rifle shot kicked up dirt near the trackers. The Cherokees took cover in a position slightly to left of the outcropping. Ayers pulled his men into a recess of boulders built up from years of erosion along the riverbed.

"That fella could hold out until dark and then escape if we don't flush him. Charley, you go with my brother, Ben, here and circle around behind him. We will keep up a hot fire until you get into position above him. I'll give you ten minutes."

"What do you want us to do when we get up there?" Ben asked.

"Make his life miserable and he'll come out sooner or later. I want him alive if possible."

In his position, slightly above the concealed killer, Charley waited for the sound of Ben's rifle. When it began, he jerked the Winchester levering mechanism as fast as he could sending shot after shot into the foliage. He could not see his target and spread the pattern of his fire along the top of the trees.

As he fired, his mind raced. What if I just happen to fire lower? Maybe a skunk gone to ground will come out. Or maybe a lucky shot will finish him off? He has no right to live for what he did.

He reloaded the rifle and poured more lead into the area. Tree leaves flew and bullets whined as the culprit returned fire in both directions, up toward their position and down toward the river bank.

This will go on until someone runs out of ammunition he thought. Then he saw it, the arcing slice of a burning torch flying up from the position of the scouts. An old Indian trick, burn our your adversary. Why waste time? It landed in the top of a post oak tree which began to smolder and then burn fiercely. The smoke drifted along the embankment moving with the wind. Soon Charley could not see clearly enough to continue firing, but he did not need to.

A coughing, sputtering figure emerged from the foliage with flames licking at his heels, his rifle still up and firing wildly. Blinded by the smoke, he took a tumble and rolled down the embankment to stop on his stomach, his rifle underneath him.

Ayers came out of the boulders, gun pointed at the man's back.

"Get up and raise 'em high, Terrell."

By the time Charley and Ben got to them, the prisoner, wearing handcuffs, stood between the two scouts.

Overcome by emotion, Charley did not stop as he approached but cocked his rifle and placed it under the man's chin, whose eyes widened in fear.

"Now you know how it feels to look down a barrel just before you die." He moved his finger onto the trigger while the man's mouth opened to beg for his life.

"Please, Marshal. Don't let him kill me."

The two scouts stepped back and waited, as did Ayers and the others. Charley had every right to want this man dead, but could he murder an unarmed man? If he did, he would be no better than Terrell. It was his choice. He felt the immense power to take a life or give it; but he also felt the revulsion of pushing aside God's wrath. *Vengeance is mine, saith the Lord.* The anger that had driven him to the brink of murder smoldered but it could not force his finger down on the trigger. He lowered the steel barrel, its imprint leaving a red indention in Terrell's neck.

"You're not worth a good bullet. I'll wait to see you hang from the Fort Smith gallows."

Ayers came to him and placed a hand on his shoulder.

"You've done your duty now. Just help me get him to Fort Smith."

As Charley turned away, he spoke again.

"After this is all over, come see me. I need a good posse man."

Charley hesitated and faced the marshal. His blood still raced and his hands clenched to keep them from shaking. "Man-hunting is not for me."

Chapter 2

The Decision

A solitary fence line of crossed timbers protected a garden from the open range. A pull at the canteen hanging across the fence next to his shirt cleared his throat but not the confusion in twenty-eight year-old Charley Barnhill's mind. He had called out to God for direction during the painful days after Jim's death. When tragedy strikes, it focuses your thoughts on darker fears of more loss. He knew nothing was sure now, not even the safety of his wife and children in this outlaw-infested territory. His thoughts pulled him back to the lonely hillside surrounded by a grove of trees. The hollow ring of dirt on Jim's coffin had buried not only his friend but their childhood dreams to become prosperous cattle ranchers.

Pulling off a work glove and throwing it down in frustration, he inspected the tender bruise the shovel handle had left on the base of his palm. He raised his head from the wound to watch two riders on the public road which was only a wide dirt trail. As they emerged out of a dust cloud, he reached for his shirt. His mama had taught him to never be caught in public improperly dressed. He recognized the younger man, Deputy Ayers.

Ayers spoke first. "Say, your name is Barnhill. Didn't know you lived out this way."

"Yes, sir. What can I do for you?"

The other man sat tall in the saddle: gray, almost white hair under a wide brimmed hat, neatly trimmed beard, weathered face and warm blue eyes. He shifted in the saddle to push his dust covered slicker open revealing a silver star.

His voice was soft and smooth. "I'm Texas Ranger Wilson. We're looking for a fella riding a paint horse. You seen anybody like that come by here in the last couple of hours?"

"Yes," Charley said, " There was a man here just before noon. He was asking 'how far' to Fort Smith." He leaned his slender frame against the fence and removed his other glove. "This man you're after, is he a real bad man?"

"He's wanted in Denison, Texas for murder and horse stealin'," Ayers explained.

"Texas? That's a far piece to chase a man, isn't it?"

"Not for a Ranger," Wilson replied. "I once trailed a man all the way to Montana."

Ayers tipped his hat. "Thanks for the help."

The two men turned their horses and were about to ride off when he got off a last question. "That offer you made me last month, is it still good?" The words spilled out of his mouth before his mind had a chance to stop them. *What am I thinking?*

Ayers turned and examined him. "It is. I need a man who can put personal motives of revenge behind him. He needs to have his wits about him and be able to handle a gun."

Charley's heart pounded in his throat with each word. "I know I was rude to you the last time we spoke, but I've had time to think. I can give you a proper answer on your offer after I speak to my wife."

"Come and see me in town and we'll talk."

He watched the riders until they were out of sight, only a cloud of dust remaining to mark their presence. What had he just done? He was no gunhand; he did not even own a pistol. He had only a few minutes to compose his thoughts before arriving at the barn. He deposited the shovel in the tool locker inside and closed the door, leaning against it for a few seconds to collect his racing mind.

Bounding up the steps to the back door, his words spilled out. No control there. "Salina, darlin', come quick."

His wife, a petite young woman of twenty-five, poked her head out of the kitchen. He thought the ten years of their marriage just made her more perfect. Her brunette hair was fastened tight in a bun at the nap of her neck accenting soft cheeks and pretty eyes.

He wiped his face with his bandana before he continued. "I just met a Texas ranger and the deputy marshal who caught Terrell. Ayers says his offer for me to posse with him still stands."

She smoothed her hands on her apron as she stepped towards him. "What would possess you to think of such a thing? Marshals hunt bad men and you're always hearing of them getting killed."

This was not encouragement. He had to make her understand. "With Jim dead, I've lost all interest in ranching. I'd like to try something else."

"I don't like it, Charley." She would not budge. "What about our three children? They need a father at home and I need a husband."

He took her in his arms and kissed her rose-colored lips. "Nothing is going to happen to me. If those two I saw today are any example, a lawman can stay in the job until he has white hair." Surprised to see tears welling in her eyes, he pulled her close again. "I understand your fears," he mumbled with a quiet drawl. "How about this afternoon I ride over and consult with my father? He'll be able to give me the truth about this offer."

The gray-haired figure looked up from the Bible that lay across his knees, the evening breeze ruffling the pages. His fluffy white beard gave him the appearance of a congenial village elder. In childhood Alford Barnhill had developed a love of the Bible and ecclesiastical studies. With forty years of service as a Free Will Baptist minister, he was well-known by the families of the Indian Territory where churches were few and far between.

A Tennessee emigrant and widower with three sons, in 1841 he had married Sarah Ann Fletcher, an Indian girl from Georgia. Of their ten children, only four sons survived to adulthood. *The Lord giveth and the Lord taketh away.* Now sixty-nine, he spent the hot afternoons in the shade preparing his next sermon for the Choctaw people whom he lived among and loved.

He squinted at the horseman approaching in the evening sun. The silhouette was familiar - his son, Charley, the aspiring rancher: slim frame slouched in the saddle, hat settled on his head, the long tie string cinched up under his chin, a bandana hanging loosely around his neck, positioned for easy placement. He detected a wide grin on his son's face. *Good news? Perhaps Salina is with child again?*

The dusty rider swung down from the saddle, inserted the reins through the hitching ring and pulled the leather tight. "Howdy, Pa. How you been keepin?" He swatted down his pants, the dust momentarily making him cough and rub his eyes.

Rising from his rocking chair, Alford sat his Bible on the smoking table beside the chair. "It's good to see you. How's your family? Can you stay for supper?"

"Yes, I might. I've come for some advice." The young man shook his father's hand and slid into the chair next to his rocker.

Pastor Barnhill lit his pipe and looked across the bowl at his son's face. "Mighty sorry about your friend Jim. At least you caught the murderer."

"That's what I've come to discuss. Ever since Jim's death, I've felt uneasy. Serving with Deputy Ayers made me realize that a quiet life in this Territory is possible only with the toil of lawmen to keep it that way. No man is safe without a pistol on his hip."

His father nodded but did not speak. He knew there was more to be explained.

"Ayers and a Texas Ranger came by the ranch earlier today on the trail of a fugitive, tracked all the way from Texas. Ayers has made me an offer of a job with him and he said it's still open." He paused to catch his breath.

The family patriarch thought for a few moments before replying. "God expects us to be useful, peaceful men; carrying a gun for the law is another matter entirely."

Charley tried another argument. "Yes, I understand, Pa. But remember the turmoil of the War and how we were forced from our farm by bushwhackers. The violence has followed us here and our Indian friends are helpless."

Alford reflected on these words, his eyes pouring over the eager face before him. His wife's Cherokee family had been driven from Georgia under similar circumstances, hostile men with guns overpowering the innocent and powerless. It was happening again here with outlaws flooding in from all over the country to hid and seek their fortune stealing and robbing. "You have my blessing, if that is your choice." He extended his hand. "And may God's protection surround you."

Sarah Barnhill poked her head out the front door. "Supper is served, if you two are hungry."

As they entered the house, Charley gave his thirteen year-old brother, Jimmy, a bear hug with a wrestling arm lock. They both laughed.

To his mother he gave a peck on the cheek. She was so short that the top of her head barely came to his chest. He playfully pulled at her gray hair fixed in a tight knot at the back of her head. She slapped his hands away in fun.

Through a mouthful of chicken, Charley praised the cook. "Your cooking's the best, more than worth a fifteen mile ride. But I can't stay. Salina is anxious to hear what I've decided."

Alford waved as his son slipped out the front gate thrusting a drumstick in the air.

"What's the hurry? Couldn't he at least sit down with us to eat?" Sarah asked.

"He has plans for a new life. Come inside and I'll explain."

He allowed the rhythm of the horse's easy gait to settle his mind. What would Salina say? He did not want her to be left alone on the prairie, but marshalling would be a lot better way to provide for his family than his day to day existence.

Approaching the comfortable log home with the large porch, he saw Salina and all the children lined up at the horse railing: the five year-old twin boys, Henry and Joseph and three year-old little Minnie who held onto her mother's skirt tails. Holding the reins in his hands to hide his excitement, he composed his tone and words so as to sooth and assure his wife.

"Hello, Darlin'. I see you have a greeting party. I talked to Pa for some time and had a bite of supper with 'em. He's supportive of whatever decision I make. If I don't like it or it's not what I expect, I can always go back to ranching." He attempted to give her a gentle hug.

To his disappointment, she pushed back and broke down in tears, sobbing out words of fear from her heart. "Please, honey. This is so sudden. You've never spoken of this before now. I need to think on it."

This was not what he wanted to hear, but he swallowed and held her close. "Alright, sweetheart. I will be patient but I must talk to the marshal soon." Trying to console her and the children who watched with wide eyes, he winked at the twins and rumpled Minnie's long curls.

Salina took Minnie's hand and motioned to the twins to go back into the house. Her sobs lessened with each step, but her eyes were still pools of panic.

He bowed his head and closed his eyes momentarily. His mind was filled with scenes he could not untangle; his friend's body laid out in the front room of his humble home; Slater's wife and children huddled together in the corner as friends and neighbors came forward to counsel them; the killer with his silent stare and unflinching hate as rough hands tied him to Slater's horse, the object of the whole affair. One man's life for a good horse. Another man's life to be forfeited in payment.

This was not what he had in mind when he had asked God to open the door. But open it was and he could not go on being a by-stander in this rough land. The blood of his friend cried out from the dirt street of Kully-cha-ha as Abel's had cried out to God when slain by Cain. Tomorrow he would go into town and talk to Deputy Ayers. *God, if this is a door you have opened, help me to step through it. Otherwise, close it quickly.*

Chapter 3

The First Star

Deputy Will Ayers sat at the desk, cleaning his .44-40 Colt Peacemaker with a pig bristle brush and soft cloth. He took every opportunity between trips to make sure his equipment was in perfect condition. A jammed gun could mean his death. He slicked his hair back from his forehead and scratched the side of his long thin moustache, the fashion for young men that had displaced the long beards of the Civil War era. Now in his early thirties, he had been a United States Deputy Marshal for almost a decade.

Nearby sat Dan Griffin, the man who drove chuck wagon on his trips. Half Choctaw by birth, he had taken the offer of Ayers to cook for him and his prisoners after his children were grown. After rubbing an oil cloth across a harness trace, Dan spit into the can at his feet, replaced the match stick he was chewing and mumbled, "Got a new posse man yet?"

Will eyed his pistol as he slid the fifth cartridge into the cylinder and rotated it so that an empty chamber was under the hammer, a safety precaution. "Talked to young Barnhill again. He seems favorable to the idea. I liked what I saw in him when we went after Terrell."

A knock on the office door brought them both to their feet. Nodding at Dan to stand by, he swung the door open and immediately recognized the tall, dark-haired young man, moustache drooping down either side of his pleasant face.

The visitor took off his hat. "Hello, again, Deputy Ayers. I've spoken to my wife. Is the posse position still open?"

Will nodded his head. "Of course - Charley Barnhill, the ranch hand who wants to be a lawman! Come on in, this here's Dan Griffin, my cook."

"Nice to meet you, Dan," the young man said as he extended his hand. Then turning back to the deputy, he continued. "Jim Slater's murder has been a real blow. He was a life-long friend and I can't set idly by anymore."

As he hesitated, Ayers spoke up. "We're sending the killer to Fort Smith today when the deputy brings out the arrest warrant. I hear Slater had a family and all. That's too bad."

Charley's eyes fixed on the deputy's face as he spoke, his eager words tumbling out. "I got to thinking about what you said. I know how to handle a gun and how to track. I've lived in these parts for some time and know the people and their ways."

The lawman massaged his chin, a positive sign to those acquainted with him. "I need to talk with people who know you and see if you fit what I need. Can you read and write?"

"Sure thing. Completed the eighth grade. You can start with my neighbors: Mr. Goodnight, the postmaster from Poteau, and the folks at my Pa's church up near Skullyville."

Ayers raised an eyebrow in surprise. "A preacher's kid, huh? Alright, I'll visit with 'em. Come back this time tomorrow. I need to form my posse and leave in three days." He stopped a second and thought of what else he needed to tell his potential new hire. "The pay is pretty good for posse men, $3 a day. You would assist in arrests and help the guards see that the prisoners don't break custody. We might be out a few days or all month. I plan to go as far as Fort Sill on the next trip."

His new hire glanced toward Will's pistol laying on the desk. "I understand the risks, but my wife is really worried about my safety. "

"As she should be. No woman wants to be made a widow. To keep down the danger, if a man is expected to be violent, I double down on posse men and try to outsmart them. Do you have any other questions?"

"No, sir. I'll be back same time tomorrow."

Will shook Charley's hand and walked him to the door. There was something about this young man that made him feel good. This youngster would be a welcome addition. The men he had were good enough, but some were getting too old for the demanding pace of the marshalling life. He turned to face Dan as the door closed.

"This kid will need his wits to survive an early grave."

"Maybe you shoulda' mentioned that," Dan drawled.

"He has stars in his eyes. It wouldn't matter. Wait until he sees a few men shot up then, he'll understand the danger."

Charley rode home with his head full of questions. These wouldn't be Sunday school boys but men so ruthless even their own people shunned them. He bowed his head as he rode. *Lord, protect me and my family. Help me be your tool of justice.*

The Eastern journalists who romanticized outlaws should try riding the road from his home at night. The click of a hammer being pulled back on a Colt or Winchester was the only warning before the bullets started to fly.

His eyes examined his home in a new light as he thought of having to leave it soon. Making his way to the front door, he opened it to the greetings of his children, "Daddy." They all had grubby faces and hands from building dirt castles and forts.

Henry, who was always ready to eat, shouted, "Pa, supper is ready. It's your favorite: fried chicken, boiled potatoes, collard greens and corn bread."

He reached over and ruffled the top of son's head. "Let me give your Ma a kiss and I'll go wash up for supper."

Salina stood at the cook stove, her hair tied up in a ribbon, thin wisps escaping at her neck and ears. She brushed the hair from her eyes and lifted a heavy metal pan out of the oven, placing the corn bread on a trivet.

He had hoped for a smile and a soft greeting, but he felt her stiffen as his hand went for her waist. This was not going to be easy for either of them.

"Hello, Darlin'. Ayers wants to hire me. The pay is good and most of his warrants are for liquor selling or theft; I shouldn't be gone but a week or two."

"People always tell you the best side of something until they get you involved."

He nuzzled his lips against the top of her head which smelled of rose water and lye soap. "We'll be prepared for them."

"Then why have so many deputies been brought home dead or seriously wounded?" she asked.

"They didn't take proper precautions. The deputy I'm riding with has plenty of experience."

She turned back to preparing the dinner and sniffed a little sigh. "Wash up, please."

He did not rest well that night, conflicting thoughts of Slater's killer and Salina's worried look pulling him in opposite directions. Finally, he fell into a restless sleep knowing he would never be content until he gave the offer a try.

Next morning he rode into town where Will greeted him. "How's my new posse man today? Have a seat." He pulled out a chair and placed it beside his desk.

Charley sat down after removing his hat holding it in his lap.

The lawman pulled out a stack of tri-folded papers from his desk drawer. "I can't make an arrest unless I have a writ from the court or I witness a violation. That's what these are." He handed one to Charley and pointed at the front. "Each one has the name of the fugitive and the charge on the front and then a space to fill in the date of capture and location. That's because, in addition to the arrest fee of $2, I get paid for each day a prisoner is in my custody to cover feeding him in addition to mileage to go out to the point of arrest and back to Fort Smith. Posse men are paid per day only. You'll have to fill out a voucher for that when we return to Fort Smith. "

He nodded his understanding and handed the writ back to his new boss who continued.

"We bring in prisoners alive because we don't get paid for the dead ones. Once in a while, in a case of a really mean robber or murderer, Judge Parker will issue a 'dead or alive' warrant."

Charley, who had been taking in the instructions, glanced at the rifle case behind the desk. "I believe the court should be the executioner and the gun a last resort. What should I bring? I have a Winchester and a shotgun."

"You'll need a pistol for close in work. Just let Mr. Craddock over at the store know you're my posse and he'll give you a discount. He has some Colts for seventeen dollars, a bit pricey but worth it for the reliability."

On hearing that, the young posse man rubbed his chin. *Where am I going to get seventeen dollars? That's almost two months' wages for a top cowhand."*

"The chuck wagon will provide the grub for us and the prisoners. Bring clothing for all types of weather. Extra supplies such as medical needs are up to you. Pack well. There'll be few trading posts along the route."

"When do we start?"

"Tomorrow at sunrise. We need to reach the Missouri-Kansas-Texas railroad line, a good two days' ride, as soon possible. That's when the real work begins."

"I'll be here," Charley said as he turned to the door.

"Oh, you might need this," Ayers said as he opened his outstretched hand, revealing a shiny posse man badge, with the U.S. FEDERAL MARSHAL emblem on it.

"I have these made up special for my men. It gives them a distinct identity when confronting the people we have to deal with. You should wear it at all times when you are on duty."

He took the badge and pinned it on his vest pocket then walked across the street to the general store. The smell of leather and seeds wafted in his face.

"Hello, Mr. Craddock? How are you, today?" He found himself talking to the back of the old gentleman's head.

The shopkeeper turned away from the tall shelves to greet his customer. "Mr. Barnhill, I'm fine, and yourself? What's that on your shirt?"

"Got a new job since Slater was gunned down out in the street. I'm going man-hunting with Deputy Ayers."

"That was terrible. Such a nice young man."

"My best friend. I can't believe he's gone. I expect anytime to hear him call my name and try to catch me in a bear hug."

"What do you need from the store?"

"A pistol like what Ayers carries, a good Colt .45, but I don't have the cash right now."

"You've been trading with me for some time so pay me when you get paid. The 1871 model is the best because it's shells are compatible with your Winchester so you only have to buy one type of ammunition."

"Much obliged." He bent over the case and pointed to a model that had a long barrel and a carved walnut handle. "How about that one?"

The proprietor brought it out and handed it to him, handle first. He weighed it in his right hand, checking the balance. *Very good.* The motion was effortless even though it weighed seven pounds.

"This one's perfect. I need a holster and cartridges too."

The owner took down three boxes of shells along with a fine leather holster. As he placed them on the counter, he looked Charley straight in the eye.

"It's one thing to shoot at bottle and cans, but another thing again to have your sights on a man's belt buckle. This gun will see you through whatever happens. "

"I appreciate that, sir. What's my total?"

"Seventeen for the revolver and holster and a dollar for each box of shells, so twenty dollars."

"Thanks. I'll be in to pay you as soon as I get back."

He put the Colt in the holster to see how it fit. It would take a few pulls to wear down the newness of the leather. He rolled the belt around the gun and picked up the boxes of shells. Outside, he stuffed the new purchases in his saddlebags and mounted for the short ride home. *What will I do when I have to draw down on an armed man? I'll find out soon enough.*

Chapter 4

Learning the Trade

The next morning, Charley pulled his big gelding to a halt in front of Deputy Ayers' office. His horse had been transformed into a beast of burden, laden with rifle, shotgun, canteen, bedroll, rain slicker and two saddle riders full of clothes and extra food. He tied his well-burdened horse to a railing and walked toward a heavy wagon containing a large crate and canvas tarp and decorated with bold lettering, *U.S. Marshal*. He had heard about the jail wagons but never seen one up close. This sight would become so familiar that he could not imagine the time he had not ridden beside one.

Deputy Ayers appeared from the barn. "You're looking bright and alert this morning," he said. "Put everything into the wagon except your canteen and your Winchester."

Charley pointed at the side of the wagon. "What's with the four iron rings on the sides?"

"We shackle the prisoners to them while we travel. They have to walk unless injured or ill."

"Oh, right."in

The lawman flipped open the lid of a long wooden box under the wagon seat and dropped his own ammunition belt into it. "We keep this locked box for extra ammunition, so put your shotgun belt in here," he said.

Charley did so as three other men shouldered their way up and dropped in their ammunition belts along with extra boxes of cartridges. All of the men met at the back of the wagon and the deputy made his introductions.

"Fellas, this is our new posse man, Charley Barnhill. "

Charley extended his hand as Will pointed to each man.

"This is Tyner Hughes."

A young man with tanned features, fresh shaven face and twinkling eyes smiled. "My friends call me Tyne."

Will continued."Ben Ayers, my brother, you already met. William Moody here is my brother-in-law. Everyone calls him Zack. It's kinda' a family affair this trip." Ben and Zack shook his hand in welcome.

The deputy paused with a big smile as he nodded toward the grey-haired

Choctaw standing at the end of the wagon. "You've already met Dan. He gets a little grumpy now and then, but he's the best cook and trail guard you'll find in the entire territory."

"Who you callin' old?" Dan replied as he shook Charley's hand.

Will and Zack led out, with Charley and Ben behind them. Dan on the wagon followed with Tyne in the rear.

Standing in his stirrups, looking around as they moved out onto the open prairie, Charley said to Ben, "Hey, shouldn't the junior man ride behind the wagon."

Ben leaned across his saddle horn as his horse walked at an easy gait. He spoke in a soft tone. "Tyne's not riding back there because he likes eating dust. He's back there because he's the best."

Charley strained to turn in the saddle to get a better look at the man following the wagon forty yards behind. He appeared about the same size and age as himself, his hands folded on the pommel of his saddle, his reins trapped under a right thumb. He was slightly hunched in the saddle as if he were about to fall asleep, but at the same time his head seemed to be in motion, slowly taking in all of the landscape from one side to the other.

"He's not goin' to be there all the time you know," Ben said. "He'll be fallin' back a little further as our rear guard. If we didn't have him back there, some outlaw could come up behind us and get us all before we had a chance. That kind of thing has happened you know?"

Not wanting to seem too naive, Charley nodded, turned his head to the front and relaxed in the saddle. A good man was watching his back.

Charley had taken in the lay of the land during their progress, eager to learn every canyon, river and settlement. He had never been more than a hundred miles from home in his whole life. Two days passed and soon they were deep in the Choctaw Nation at a place called Roberts. Their camp site had a stream of fresh water, prairie grass for the horses, tall stands of shade trees and an open space for setting up the tents.

While the rest of the men set up the camp and hobbled their horses, Tyne continued to range out in a large circle about a quarter mile away.

"He's securing our perimeter," Will said, as he pounded in the last stake anchoring the front tent flap. "You fellas get something to eat and turn in. We'll be going out to get a few bootleggers tomorrow. They are the most dangerous creatures in this forest."

"What do you mean?" Charley asked. Not being a drinking man, he had never had much contact with the fringes of society that provided the illegal whiskey to the Indian Territory.

"They're often men who have been chased out of the surrounding states.

They're gambling that we won't catch 'em. When cornered, they fight like wildcats. I try to outfox 'em and get the drop on 'em."

The following morning after a restless night, he and the other posse members met with their deputy over breakfast.

"We're going up Black Fork on the Poteau River into the Palean Mountains," he said. "About nine miles up, there's a moonshine operation run by three white men, the Dodson brothers, and a half-black Choctaw named Harris. There's bound to be more, maybe four or five."

"Will we be arresting everyone we come across?" Charley asked.

Tyne spoke up. "I'll say." He set the coffee pot back onto the fire grate. "When you walk into a den of rattlers, you don't get the big ones and let the little ones slither away."

Charley glanced at the Colt on his waist. "How do you know when to pull your pistol? Do we go in at the ready?"

"I'll give you a briefing when we get the layout," Ayers explained. "Don't worry. You'll know when to use that iron."

At that moment, Dan came from behind the wagon with a bucket of water. "It would be nice if I had some idea as to how many I'll be feedin' tonight," he said.

"Let's say seven, more or less," Will said. "That's not counting us."

Seven! Charley felt his stomach sink in fear. *Seven against five. We'll be outnumbered.*

The five men wound their way up a barely visible wagon track into the Palean Mountains. Charley resisted the urge to keep rechecking his rifle and pistol. They were cleaned, well oiled and fully loaded. He had to leave them with the assurance they would fire when he needed them. About high noon by the sun they dismounted near their quarry. He could see a light wisp of smoke playing over the pine trees just over the ridge ahead.

"Okay, men," Ayers said. "We'll split up here. I'll give you time to get into position and then I'll come in through the front door. They will have a guard posted. Tyne and Zack, take him in then give me a hand signal. I don't want a sound to tip these fella's off."

The two men went around to the left searching for the guard, while Ben moved out to the right. Charley, crouched near the side of a log cabin, could see three men working with a large liquor still in the front of the cabin. As he glanced across the porch of the cabin he saw a rifle leaning against the front wall. That would be his first objective, keep it out of the hands of the whiskey-runners.

Presently, he saw Tyne waving his hat above his head. A man cuffed and gagged stood beside him. *That was certainly quick work.* He passed the sign on to Ayers who was watching from just inside the trees surrounding the house and still.

The fearless deputy rode in, his horse at a slow walk. He was now upon the men busy bottling the alcohol as it ran from the pipe. One of them looked up in confusion and started for a rifle laying against the still, but stopped as he saw the long-barreled shotgun across the stranger's lap.

"Are you fellas the Dodson brothers?" Ayers asked.

The younger of the three men said, "Who wants to know?"

"U.S. Deputy Marshal Ayers. Put your hands in the air and stand real quiet," Ayers said. "You're charged with 'illicit distilling' and you've just been caught red handed."

At that moment a large black man came out of the cabin, his arms full of glass quart jars. Seeing his friends held at gunpoint, he dropped the jars, glass shattering and settling on the porch. As he leaned down and turned to grab the Winchester from against the wall, Charley stepped from his hiding place, the double barrel of his shotgun four inches from the man's face.

"I wouldn't try that if I were you," he said.

The wide-eyed man came erect, his hands in the air.

"Is your name Harris?" Charley asked.

"It is."

After a quick look inside the cabin, he pointed to the group in the center of the yard. "The deputy has a paper for you too. Move along."

As he walked his prisoner to the center of the yard, Charley heard a scuffling in the wood pile off to his left. He ran forward and shifted his shotgun in time to see Tyne prodding another man with his shotgun and dragging the bound and gagged sentry in tow by his cuffs. "This one tried to hide in the wood pile," he said.

From the other side of the yard, Zack and Ben approached, a young Choctaw walking between them. In short order, the seven prisoners were shackled and their weapons locked in the long box.

That went pretty well. This is going to be easier than I thought. Charley shouldered his shotgun and turned to follow the others to their horses.

His boss called him back. "Your Pa is a preacher isn't he?"

"Yes, why?"

"You see all this distilling equipment and those bottles of liquor? It has to be destroyed, and I can't think of a better person to take care of it than you. We'll see you back at camp when you get the job done."

He pulled an axe from the wood pile and swung at the large metal tub and curled copper tubing. He figured he had gotten this job because he was junior, but he would do anything to learn this trade - even to smashing a few gallons of liquor.

Today, they were searching for a gang who had held up a train south of Muskogee, killing a railroad agent and a passenger. Three of the men had been reported by spies to be in the vicinity. Ben had stayed behind to help Dan guard the seven prisoners. Presently, they came into a clearing where the trail divided, one path going up a hill and the other showing horse tracks going into a ravine.

Will stopped. "Tyne, take Charley and head downhill. We'll check the hillside."

The trail turned into briar bushes and scrub oak, almost impenetrable on horse back. *Where are the horse tracks?* Charley dismounted to check for any signs.

Tyne pointed to the ground. "Look at the bent grass and upturned dirt; they went further into the ravine, but where? There must be a secret entrance into this mess."

"We can get through this easier on foot," Charley said.

"Alright. Let's go."

Charley was encouraged by the genial disposition of his new partner. He never once belittled him for his suggestions and treated him as a veteran manhunter, at the same time showing him new things, like the bent grass and scuffed dirt.

They stooped and made their way through the undergrowth. After covering only a hundred yards, Charley felt his hands scratched raw from the brambles. As he reached for the gloves in his back pocket, Tyne halted abruptly. "There's something ahead to the left."

Charley heard the sound as they drew closer - moaning. They crawled on their bellies until he could see a lean-to made of logs and brush. A man stood in front of a fire pit before the lean-to, the moaning coming from within.

Tyne rolled over on his back, pulled his pistol and checked the chamber. "Spread out so we come into the clearing about twenty feet apart. Keep your gun trained on the fella at the fire. Whoever is in the lean-to might be armed. I'll get over there before he can try anything."

As they burst into the clearing, the man at the fire grabbed for his pistol.

Charley yelled, "Hands up! Don't even think about it." The man raised his hands high above his head.

He covered his prisoner as he watched Tyne reach the lean-to and kick the entrance covering aside to expose a man lying on a pallet, a make-shift bandage around his chest; his hand reached for a pistol beside him. Tyne put his boot on the man's wrist. Pain and hatred mixed in the outlaw's youthful face.

Tyne said, "Get up and don't try anything."

The train-robber was shot in the back and could not move. When his captor attempted to lift him by the arm, he groaned and sagged to the ground.

The man Charley covered was a lean-looking predator, the kind that would make a sensible man run for cover. He had gray eyes set close together under a head of long black hair.

Charley shifted his gaze toward the struggles inside the lean-to. He felt the predator move before the huge fist slammed into his wrist, knocking the pistol from his hand. It was only then that he saw the knife in the man's right hand as it slashed toward his chest. He fended off the thrust with his left arm, the blade cutting into his forearm. A hand move toward his throat and the flashing knife raised again. Before it could fall, Charley put all his strength into a right upper cut to the jaw that sent the attacker reeling backwards.

Tyne had reached them by then and had his gun levelled at the attacker, who hunched his shoulders and spit out a mouth of blood, the knife still in his right hand.

"Drop the knife. You even twitch and I'll cut you in half," Tyne growled. "Are you alright, Charley?"

"Yeah, just shook up some. He got me on the arm."

"Get you pistol and cover him while I bundle him up. Some of these fellas you can't look at sideways without inviting an attack."

His hands shook as he fumbled for his gun in the dirt. His new pistol had been of no use against a crafty outlaw.

Tyne pulled out his handcuffs, took the knife and forced the prisoner's hands together. "That'll keep you still. You're lucky I'm not prone to shoot first and ask questions later."

The man grunted and spit more blood.

Tyne wiped his hands on his trousers and turned to his attention to Charley. "Let me tie up your arm with my bandana. That should hold it until Dan can look at you."

Charley winced as his friend pulled up the shirt sleeve to reveal a long slash that extended from his wrist to his elbow. He was lucky this time. The wound did not appear to be serious, just painful. He slumped down on an overturned tree stump the robbers had placed before the fire and wondered why he had not seen the knife coming until it was too late. Another mistake like that could leave his family fatherless. From now on he would trust no one.

After locating the outlaw's horses tethered in a clearing, the wounded youth was supported on his horse by the shackled prisoner who rode behind him. Tyne led the extra horse ahead of the prisoners and Charley took up the end of the procession. They met Will and Zack Moody with another prisoner, a gaunt man with bad teeth and a crooked smile. He had made a fight of it as evidenced by the red stain on his gun hand which was wrapped in a bandage.

"Good work, three birds in the hand. We'll bring down a hefty reward for these guys. The railroad has a bounty on their heads," the deputy said. "What happened to your arm, Charley?"

"Knife wound. This fella here thinks he's Jim Bowie."

"Dan'll clean you up."

After cleaning and bandaging his wound, Dan served him a good stew prepared using dried beef, potatoes and onions. Corn bread, the traditional

Indian food, topped it off.

Charley ate the stew washing it down with steaming hot coffee. *What else can a man want?*

After the prisoners were all fed, the rest took turns eating while Tyne and Charley watched the prisoners. Ayers eyed the proceedings from his seat at the campfire, smoking his pipe and drinking a cup of coffee.

"You two did a fine job today. I'm going to recommend to Marshal Upham that you be given deputy commissions when we get back to Fort Smith," he said.

Charley looked at Tyne. "Did you hear that, partner? I started this trip with no plans for the future and now Deputy Ayers has made them for me."

"Yup, he sure is persuasive. Isn't he?" Tyne said.

Charley tried to sleep that night but was too excited about his new vocation. He had no second thoughts and was eager to learn all he could from this veteran team of men, not suspecting that two in this group would lose their lives in the future on what was considered "simple" arrests.

Chapter 5

End of the Line

Five horsemen rode in single file to the Arkansas River ferry across from Fort Smith. Dan's wagon and a hired wagon followed with twenty-two prisoners. The ferryman hurried to disembark a farmer with a wagon of cotton and four horsemen. It would take him three trips to convey the entire party across.

Charley took the opportunity to get down and stretch. It did not last long. Will rode up.

"Go with Dan and his prisoners. Shackle them on the long chain from the bed. If they need to be freed in an emergency, pull the main pen. I don't get paid for drowned prisoners."

Doing as he was instructed, Charley dismounted and, while Ben covered the prisoners with his shotgun, he began to unshackle them from the wagon and attach them to the long chain. He was done in a few minutes.

He walked over to Will who was speaking to the driver of the second wagon. "McCoy, when it's your turn, Zack will release your prisoners' handcuffs and cover them while he rides over with you on the next ferry. When you get to the other side, take them straight to the jail."

He turned in the saddle and addressed Charley. "Give this paperwork to the jailer. I'll be along as quickly as possible."

"Tyne, that leaves you and me to handle the ones on horseback," Will continued without taking a breath. "Release the leg chains and rope all the horses together. You take up the rear. If any one tries anything, shoot 'em."

"Sure thing, Boss." Tyne patted his shotgun resting across his lap.

Charley waved to the group as he guided his horse onto the ferry. His big roan, Billie, did not like the rolling feel of the planking but under his master's firm hand, he settled down with flattened ears and rolling eyes. The ferry chugged across the broad river on a heavy steel cable pulled by a steam engine on the other side. He was surprised at the smooth ride; the shrill call of the steam release valve when activated by the attendant on the shore made Billie prance, his rump against the side railings.

He and Ben herded the prisoners up the bank from the ferry landing, Dan yelling and cracking his whip over his teams' ears, the men secured to the long

Fort Smith Jail after remodel in 1886

chain scurrying to keep up. It was only a stone's throw to the jail.

Dogs barked and little street ruffians with dirty faces appeared from nowhere as the party swung onto the dusty street. By the time they had covered the couple hundred yards to the jail, a crowd of townspeople had gathered. In 1875 President Grant had made one of his better appointments by sending Judge Isaac Parker to serve as the federal judge for the Western District of Arkansas. Parker had begun the successful roundup of outlaws in the Indian Territory. Yet, even now, four years later, the spectacle of a prison wagon never ceased to draw crowds of townspeople who wanted to see what "famous" outlaw had been captured or, in some cases, an acquaintance.

Charley had ridden by the old infantry fort many times when he had lived in Fort Smith during the War of the Rebellion. It had been abandoned for a decade after the war before the U.S. Marshal and the court had started using it. All that remained was the old commissary building and the infantry barracks; one side of the main floor of the barracks housed the Court and the Judges Chambers, the other half the U.S. Marshal, Clerk and other court officers. The basement housed the jail, known as "Hell on the Border." It was claimed by inmates and yellow journalists to be worse than the legendary "black hole of Calcutta".

Eying the structure with new interest, he dismounted and tied Billie to the hitching rail. A young man in a business suit approached him, writing tablet in hand. "Sir, sir. I'm a reporter for the Fort Smith Elevator. Can you tell me the names and something about the capture of these prisoners? Our readers await our court reports every week."

Disregarding the list in his breast pocket, Charley said, "You can get that from the jailer when he's finished compiling his log." These court reporters were pretty accurate and the jailer was the best source for such information.

"Much obliged." The young man tipped his bowler hat.

Charley approached the jailer who was watching the wagons from the front steps of the jail. The old veteran's beard hung down to the second button of his vest. Atop his gray crown he wore a short-billed hat, similar to an infantry soldier's, with the insignia U.S. Marshal on it.

"Here's the paperwork for this crowd. Deputy Ayers wanted you to have it right away. He'll be along after he gets off the ferry."

The jailer spit out his chew and took the papers. "How many you got?"

"Twenty-two."

"Where am I going to put them? I already have men sleeping elbow to elbow down there." Charley said nothing. The old fellow just needed to let off some steam.

The jailer shifted the list to his left hand and extended his right hand. "Thanks, kid. What's your name?"

"Charley Barnhill from Kully-cha-ha. I'm Deputy Ayer's new posse."

Charley listened to the people gathered around as the jailer and his assistants led the prisoners into the jail.

"Say, that looks like the guy who sold me a horse he didn't own. I never thought they'd catch him," one said. "I might get my money back after all."

Others commented on the appearance of the prisoners.

"Oh, he looks so young. What's he done?" This question was directed toward a young Creek Freedman that they had picked up for assault with intent to kill. *Give that kid a gun and you'll find out how young he is*, Charley thought.

When the second contingent appeared, Zack looked around in surprise at the crowd outside the old jail.

"Doesn't anybody in this place have a job?" Zack asked the jailer.

The older man lifted his hat and scratched at the top of his receding hairline. "You guys are a circus sideshow, getting the reputation of always getting your man, no matter how long it takes."

Presently, Will and Tyne rode up with their four mounted prisoners. Tyne dismounted and unhooked the chains freeing his prisoners to dismount. Their horses would be put into the livery until disposition was made to family or friends.

"Wait for me out front," Will instructed as he walked up the steps to the jailer's office on the first floor.

As the guards escorted the prisoners down the steps and through the door below the porch, Charley approached a jail attendant. " Can I come inside with you?"

"Sure, leave your pistol up stairs with the clerk."

He came down the steps behind a couple of the prisoners and entered the dim interior. He had never been near enough to the jail to observe it. Now that he was, he didn't like what he saw, a claustrophobic area divided into two sections giving the appearance of a medieval dungeon The ceiling of the jail cell was only seven feet high and each section was thirty by sixty feet, a connecting opening allowing movement from side to side. The only ventilation came through the windows underneath the porches located at either end of the building.

Some kind of over-whelming putrid smell gagged him as he entered. Both areas teemed with prisoners sitting, standing or lounging on straw mattresses on the flagstone floors. Each prisoner had a single blanket. Some were fortunate enough to have a pillow. A few men played cards in the center of the room. Two fireplaces at opposite ends of the two sections held the lavatory buckets. *Where do they put those in the winter?* He could not imagine staying in this hell hole for any length of time.

"You get used to the smell after awhile. Kind a' like living on a pig farm," the guard said.

Charley walked up to a man who wore a solemn frown. He looked to be all of nineteen, if that. His long hair was greasy and his face covered with a thin beard.

"How long you been here? What are you in for?" Charley asked.

"I been here two months awaiting trial for larceny since I have no money for bail," the youngster replied.

"How's your care?"

"Now that it is warmer, it's comfortable at night. We don't get any exercise though. The food is real good and we get plenty of it. It's the best I've eaten since I left home. "

"Do you have a lawyer?"

"Yes sir. But I've only seen him once since I been here."

"When do you wash?"

"They allow us buckets of soap and water once a week for everyone to wash off as best we can. There's no privacy and if you take your clothes off, you have to ask a buddy to watch them so they're not stolen. We're allowed one change of clothes each week so that the prison laundress can wash our clothes, but we have to pay her a fee. Some of the men can't afford it and stay in their dirty clothes for months."

Charley gave the jail attendant a farewell wave. "Thanks for letting me come down here." He tried to put his mind on the promise of a bath and soft bed to blot out the stink and the shock of what he had seen.

Will waited in the half-circle driveway, his eyes examining Charley's face as he neared the group. Charley could not contain his disgust at what he had seen. He grabbed the deputy by the arm. "Something needs to be done to alleviate the crowding. The men barely have room to turn over in their sleep."

The deputy spat into the dust and swept his eyes over the old building. "Congress does not give the court enough money to run itself properly let alone build an adequate jail. Maybe if we get a new president who cares about the Indian Territory that will change."

Charley remained silent, staring at the structure. Would he be able to bring men to this hell hole? There was no other choice for now.

Will turned to his group of helpers. "The Marshal's office will have your money ready in the morning. Turn in your weapons to the Marshal's office. We can't walk around Fort Smith armed to the teeth. If you leave those things in a hotel room, they might get stolen."

After the chief deputy checked in Charley's weapons, he handed him a ticket stub. "Bring that back to get your things. If you loose it, I still have your name in my weapons log."

He pocketed the stub and followed the group to Will's favorite establishment, a hotel on Garrison Avenue a short walk from the jail. As Will entered the lobby, a big man with a handlebar moustache and slicked-down hair parted in the middle rushed to his side. "Deputy Ayers, you ole rattlesnake. Cheated fate again, huh?"

"Yup. How you been, Sandy?" Ayers greeted his friend. "We've six hungry bellies to fill. Give us your best table."

The man led them to a large round table where they gave their orders to a young man in an apron, ordering as if they had not eaten in a month.

Will explained the layout of the hotel. "This hotel is attached to a bar and a dance hall, so a respectable woman cannot work in the dining room. The women hired for the dance hall and bar cannot tend the dining room. So we have Louie here as our waiter."

Charley felt uncomfortable. Bars and dance halls were off limits for most people in his circle of family and friends. He looked around to see if he was the only one showing any signs of discomfort. The others seemed at ease and ready to eat, but they were all older men except Tyne and Zack.

Will ordered. "Let's have a drink to celebrate our successful trip. Barkeeper, whiskey all around please."

Now he was trapped. If he refused the drink, the others would cackle at him as a momma's boy; he decided to accept the shot glass and nurse it all evening. When the drinks came out, the others gulped them down and Will ordered more. By the time the meal came, three glasses sat in front of him.

"Charley, ole buddy, have a sip; it won't hurt you and it will help you sleep," Tyne said, his voice already beginning to slur.

Charley took a sip. "I'll catch up. I'm just so hungry, I'm getting the shakes. Don't want to spill any of that good whiskey." The whiskey taken straight seemed to go right through the blood stream to his brain.

Will stuffed a large piece of steak into his mouth. "Let's eat."

Charley felt better as he stared at his cleaned plate. This good meal made the hard ground, cold rains and rough trails he had ridden worth it.

His leader wiped his mouth and belched. "I'm heading to the barber shop for a bath, shave and hair cut. Anyone want to join me?"

"If I show up home looking and smelling like I do, my wife'll make me sleep in the barn!" Dan said.

Will pulled Charley and Tyne aside as the others filed out. "Remember, I want you two as deputies. I've talked to Marshal Upham. He's expecting you to come in first thing tomorrow for an interview."

They headed to the barber shop across the street. Before he knew it, Charley sat in a steaming tub full of soapy bubbles. He laid his dirt-ridden clothes on a chair outside the room for the Chinese attendant to pick them up, launder them, and deliver them to the hotel in the morning. He pulled the one change of clothes he had left out of his saddle bags.

He could hear Tyne singing at the top of his lungs in an adjoining room. He settled into the bath luxuriating in the feel of the warm water. His head felt light and dizzy from the tiny bit of whiskey he had sipped.

An hour later, he met Tyne to walk downstairs for a shave and a haircut. Charley's hair stuck out from underneath his hat in all directions. Tyne wore a beard that covered his face. Only the most fastidious person managed to shave while on the trail.

After the barber had done his best for Charley, Tyne surveyed his partner. "You look pretty good now that you are shined up a bit," he teased Even though this was their first trip together, they seemed drawn to each other in friendship.

"You don't look so bad yourself."

"I want to show you around town." Tyne said. "You need a tour of something other than the general stores. This town has thirty saloons plus all kinds of other entertainment."

"I better pass on that. Salina asked me to save all the money I earned so we can get some things for the children and the place. I'll get her a little present, in the morning. She has had to tend three children alone while I've been gone."

"I'm a newly wed myself. Mattie's still getting used to having a husband who is gone most of the time. She knew that when she married me and has put up with it so far."

"Well good night then." Charley extended his hand to the man who was now his new friend.

Tyne slapped Charley on the shoulder. "You don't know what you'll be missing."

The sounds of the night drifted in the window: passing horses and rigs; people's shouts and greetings; hawkers with their sing-song rhythms. He tossed about on the mattress, his exhausted body fighting the sleep he needed. *What an adventure. This is harder than I thought, but it's something I could do for quite a while. Thank you, Lord for the opportunity you have given me,* Charley prayed as he drifted to sleep.

"Hello, wake up. Mr. Barnhill, wake up." The pounding on his door continued as he sat up to rub the sleep from his face.

"Who is it?" Charley said from his bed

"It's the desk clerk. You need to come quick. Two of your friends are in a ruckus downstairs."

He slipped on his clothes as quickly as he could in the dark and stepped to the door. When he opened it, the night clerk pointed down the stairs.

"They're challenging six toughs in the saloon. If they start busting up the place, I'll have to call the town marshal. I don't want to see any federal posse men hauled off to jail."

Charley followed him down the stairs two at a time and turned into the saloon through the adjoining double doors. He would have to use his wits on this mess.

"Get your fists up and defend yourself. I'm going to whip you, you lying son of a bitch." Tyne stood nose to nose with a mean-looking riverboat hand, whose long unkempt beard reached to his belt. Ben stood beside him, swaying slightly in the gas-lit interior. Behind the deck hand stood five others, all with knives in their scabbards.

"What's going on here?" Charley stepped between the two men.

"Charley my ole' buddy. Come to give me a hand?"

"Nope, I've come to get you out of here in one piece. What's this about?"

"This low crawling son of a snake has called the marshal force a bunch of cowards. He says we only go after defenseless whisky peddlers trying to make an honest living and run from the murderers and thieves."

Charley turned to the big man with the sullen eyes. "I think there's been a misunderstanding. My friend doesn't know when youall are joking. He takes his job real serious. Can I buy you a drink?"

The man shifted his eyes from Charley to Tyne and back. He shrugged his shoulders and replied, "Sure, why not. At least your money's good enough to buy whisky. Come on, fellas. Get to the bar."

Charley threw the bartender a five dollar gold piece. "Buy them as much as they can drink and keep the change." *Well, there goes Salina's present.*

"Come on, you two." He turned Tyne toward the door and motioned to Ben to follow.

The two young men staggered out the door, Tyne muttering to Charley. "I could've whipped them all. They don't know anything about bringing in prisoners. I think we ought to let them loose in the jail over there and see what they think."

Charley patted his friend on the back. "They're just riverboat men. What do they know about anything? " It wasn't the last time he figured he would lose sleep over this friend.

Hand and leg irons of the period

Chapter 6

Homecoming

Charley had ridden several hundred miles in the past three weeks. For all of that effort he had ninety dollars in his back pocket, minus the five paid to the barkeeper in Fort Smith. The incident of the knife wound had been the subject of his only short letter to Salina posted at Muskogee two weeks ago. What would her reaction be when she saw him? They had never been separated for any length of time in their marriage. He had not realized how much he enjoyed her care until he had suffered all kinds of weather, the ground for a bed, aching joints longing for a warm hearth. He took a deep breath, filling his lungs with air as he dismounted and swung around as the front door opened. A pair of heads with dark brown unruly hair appeared.

"Papa!" exclaimed his four year-old twins, Henry and Joseph. They scampered down the steps, bare feet barely touching the last step as they jumped into his arms, little Minnie teetering down the steps in an attempt to get in on the hugging and kissing. He reached down and lifted her up, making her squirm as he rubbed her check with his rough hands and gave her a resounding kiss on the forehead.

"Where's your Ma?" Charley questioned as he untied his saddlebags and dropped them across the twins' shoulders. The boys struggled under the load as they carried the bags to the house, one supporting each side of the pouches.

Henry, the talkative one, spoke back over his shoulder. "Oh, she's cooking dinner to celebrate your homecoming. A man came by a couple of days ago saying you were on the way home. She wants everything special, like a birthday surprise."

As he reached the door carrying his shotgun and Winchester, he was met by his wife who rushed to him and lifted her face. Placing the weapons down on the porch, he had no need for words as his eyes met hers and his arms encircled her waist. She had a fresh spring morning scent that made him even more aware of his horse- smell-covered pants and sweaty shirt front. His lips met hers in a tender, warm kiss. There was something amiss in her pale face and deep penetrating eyes. He drew back in concern as her fingers roved over his head, face and chest, testing to see if he was still in one piece.

"Honey, what's wrong?" he asked, holding her at arm's length. Her smile could not disguise the taut skin over her hollow cheek bones.

Ignoring his question, she touched his left forearm where the knife had ripped at his flesh. "Are you alright?"

"Yes, Darlin'. My arm is all healed and I've been well-fed and other than saddle-weary, I'm as fit as the day I told you good-bye. But you did not answer *my* question. What's wrong?"

She slipped her arms from around his neck and squeezed his hand. "Nothing, I'm fine. Supper's about ready. You can wash up and after dinner I'll get you a bath heated on the stove."

"No need for that bath. I had one in Fort Smith last night when we got in."

Relaxing as he sat down on the bed, the springs squeaked as he shifted his weight. It would be good to be able to sleep on something other than the hard ground with his saddle as a pillow. He lay back on the bed, experiencing the softness and warmth. His thoughts turned back to the too quick assurance she had given him. There was something she was reluctant to tell him, but what?

Salina's gentle voice penetrated his dream, her face within inches of his nose. "Sweetheart, wake up. It's time for you to wash up." He focused his eyes and realized he had fallen soundly asleep.

"I must be more tired than I realized.," he apologized as he rose from the bed.

At the supper table, the children were lined up on the benches on either side of the long trestle table. Their eyes sparkled with anticipation of the food and an evening with their father.

The little family bowed heads as he prayed. "Dear Lord, Thank you for the provisions of this table and for the care and concern that has gone into its preparation. Thank you for the blessings of health and safety that you have provided for us during this past month. In your son's name, Amen."

He examined Salina as she passed the first course to him, a slight tremor in her hands. Forcing himself to turn his attention to the various choices, he marvelled at what was before him. He had gotten used to dried meat, biscuits and coffee for breakfast and dinner. For supper Dan sometimes added a boiled potato or corn mush for variety. The Indians he had been living amongst had a delicious dish called pepper pot soup: beans, corn, venison and onions. He hoped Salina would know what he was describing when he told her about it. It had warmed all their stomachs on the cold nights they had to sleep under the stars.

The children ate ravenously making him thankful for their full bellies. He had seen a lot of want amongst many Indian children, who were neglected by parents overcome by the firewater they bought from illegal bootleggers.

Henry and Joseph stuffed their mouths full of biscuits. Slight in build, their little muscles were like iron when he tried to tickle them.

As Henry put the last piece into his mouth, his father asked, "What have you been doing besides driving your mother crazy bringing home snakes and toads?"

"Oh, Pa. I just leave those critters in the house for a little while. Joey and I have a dam built out behind the barn to raise catfish in the pond. I bet we can have catfish stew or such every week."

He smiled at Joey who was smaller than his twin and had a paper thin complexion. He suffered from something in his lungs the doctor could not rightly figure out - no treatment was offered except warm sunshine and rest.

"Ok, Joey, it's your turn. What've you been up to?"

The freckle-covered face lit up in excitement. "I want to raise a pig. Mr. Thomas has a litter for sale right now. Can I get one, Pa?"

"We'll see about that before I have to leave."

Little Minnie eagerly waited her turn to speak. Her excited jabber of words ran together in haste, her dark eyes glittering in seriousness as she tried to describe something. Her long brown hair which was tied back with a pink ribbon at the neck moved in joyous bursts of energy as she gestured and bobbed her head.

"Papa, I've a new dolly Mommy made me. You want to see her? Her name is Maggie."

"Sure, Sweetie. I'll look at your new dolly right after supper."

"How about you, Darlin'?" he asked his Salina. "Did you get the letter I posted at Muskogee?"

"Yes, I just got it last week. I was so worried. The children and I kept you in our prayers everyday. While you were away, I've managed to put up most of the garden produce that has come on so we will eat well this winter.

It alarmed Charley again when she added, "I've been feeling a little tired, lately, though."

What did she mean? He knew he would have to speak to her privately after the children were in bed. "Now that I'm home for a while, let me take the little ones with me on my errands during the day and you can get some rest."

"That may help." She looked relieved that he didn't ask more questions. She picked up the dishes from the table and sat them beside the sink. "You boys get ready for bed. I'll be in to tuck you in after a few minutes. Be sure to visit the outhouse, then wash your face and hands and anything else that is covered with grime, including behind you ears." She took the iron kettle off the wood stove and poured hot water into the washbasin in the back hall.

"Ok, Mommy, can we hear one of Pa's stories first. Just a short one?" Henry asked eagerly tugging at her dress sleeve.

"Ask your father. Minnie, you may go in the bedroom and play with Maggie for a few minutes before you have to go to bed."

"Pa!" Henry exclaimed as he raced across the room to the fireplace where Charley sat. "Mommy says you can tell us a short story about your trip before we have to go to bed."

"Alright, children. Gather round and I'll tell you about a doctor of medicine from Yale and Harvard who turned into an outlaw."

"Where are those countries, Pa?"asked Joey.

"Well, son, they are not countries but very fine universities back East where all the wealthy families and country leaders send their sons for education. They are the best schools in the country."

"Oh, do you have to be really smart, too?"

"Yes, that helps. This outlaw's name was Dr. Henri Stewart and he lived not far from here. But he did not like the honorable profession for which he had been trained. So he became an outlaw and a member of a notorious gang."

"What happened to him?' asked Henry wearing a solemn, wide-eyed expression.

"As happens often to most bad men, he and a wild cousin, named Wiley Stewart, got arrested for introducing and selling liquor. They appealed to another doctor friend, Dr. Jones, to post their bond. When he refused, they had it out for him. Dr. Stewart fired a pistol and struck the other doctor in the hand. Then the cousin came up and used a shotgun on the helpless man. Dr. Stewart was caught and stood trial while I was at Ft. Smith. He was found guilty of murder and is scheduled to be hung in August."

Now it was Joey's turn to ask the questions. "Are those the kind of people you have to chase down, Pa?"

"Yes, Joey. But don't worry. I am working with some very fine men who know how to handle the outlaws we catch. Now, off to bed with you."

He gave each boy a hug and sent them to their bedroom which was at the back of the house, across from the kitchen. Little Minnie still slept in a small frame bed in the corner of her parents' bedroom in the front of the house.

Salina tucked the covers up around Minnie's face and smoothed her hair down around her nightgown. "You want to say your prayers now?" she asked.

"Yes, please. Dear Lord, thank you for my daddy's return. Help me and Maggie have a good night with nice dreams."

Salina adjusted the bonnet on the doll's head as Charley came in and sat down on the bed beside them. She stood and wiped her hands on her apron. "I'll be in the kitchen straightening up."

"OK, sweetheart, " he said as he lowered his face to Minnie's level. "Tell me about your new dolly,"

"She has a special dress and bonnet that Mommy made for her that matches my dress and bonnet. That way, when we go to church, we can be like sisters since I don't have one to play with yet." Minnie's three year old voice was excited, the discernible words mixed with a few incoherent tries at the big words she was thinking.

"I'm so glad you have Maggie to play with. Now, sleep well, sweetheart," Charley kissed her cheek and turned to rise. A sudden loud thud from the kitchen brought him to his feet and across the room in seconds. The children jumped out of their beds and rushed in behind him, eyes wide with fear.

Salina lay on the floor, eyes closed, her hand still resting against a cast iron skillet. He knelt beside her and lifted her head. She groaned and looked up into his eyes.

"What happened?"

With concern in his voice, he said, "You fainted. Let me help you sit up."

His strong arms lifting her, she sat down on the bench and clasped her hands together. She spoke in a low voice. "I don't want to alarm you since you have plenty to worry about."

Three fearful faces gathered around their mother.

"I can get a wet towel for her head," Henry stammered.

"That's a good idea, then return to your beds. Mommy just needs some air."

He waited for the little ones to disappear then sat beside her, his arm around her shoulders., his hand on hers. "Now you better tell me what's going on."

She put a hand to her brow holding the cool cloth in place. "It's how I've been feeling. You know that monthly time women have. I had to stay in bed most of the days you were gone because I was too weak to get up. The doctor says it is because I loose so much blood."

He had never heard this before. Was it a recent sickness? He looked into her face and kissed her soft lips. "How long has this been going on? Can the doctor give you a potion or mixture to help?"

"It just started about the time you decided to become a posse man. I did not want to mention it because you had your first trip all planned. The doctor gave me an iron supplement that helps a little. If I rest and stay quiet, I recover faster than if I try to get up and tend to the children."

He thought for only a few seconds. "I'll speak to Mrs. Davis, tomorrow. Maybe she'll be willing to come over and help you with the housework on those days."

She laid her head against his shoulder and sighed. "I don't want to be a bother to Mrs. Davis. She has six kids of her own to manage."

"Just let me tend to this. Mrs. Davis has two half-grown boys and a right smart daughter who can help with her younger children when she's over here. If I am going to be gone with Deputy Ayers, I'd feel a lot better if you had someone to rely on. I want you to have the best help we can find in this part of the country."

She did not reply but stood and moved toward the bedroom. "The children are in bed now and you can have all the quiet you need for a good night's rest. I feel fine now and will finish the dishes."

He sat on the bed and loosened his belt while she moved the beautifully decorated privacy screen in place around their bed. It had been passed down to her from her mother on their wedding day and was covered with scenes of Japanese water gardens and Geisha girls in long kimonos.

He sighed as he settled under the quilt. It felt so good. His mind swirled to suppress the worry about Salina's illness. His semi-dreamy state was only interrupted by little Joey's harsh cough. *God, please bless and help Salina and this little boy. No one else can help them now. Protect me in this dangerous undertaking and let me live to see my children grown.*

Chapter 7

A Deadly Affair

Charley searched for his clothes and boots as he moved around the dark bed, glancing at his sleeping wife and Minnie on her little cot by the door. He exited the quiet bedroom and groped for the kerosene lantern on the kitchen table, the brightness of its flame as he lit it illuminating the clean dishes stacked by the cupboard, the basket of fresh vegetables ready to be peeled for dinner, his packed saddle bags on the table. His heart constricted at the thought of leaving. What if something happened and he was too far away to help? He would have to rely on the Lord and his loyal friends and neighbors to step in where needed.

Forcing aside his worry, with an expertise born of other early morning departures, he slipped on his pants, shirt and boots and grabbed his saddlebags. One pouch held the laudanum he now packed at all times since his first knife wound, carried not so much for himself as for others who may need it. Gunshot and knife wounds were common hazards.

It had been almost a year since he had started riding with the deputy, a time of adventure, surprise, danger, and boredom. He had tracked down criminals despite their cunning, desperate plots to elude capture, and boasting of their vile escapades to family and friends who shielded them from the law. When they had no one to turn to, they intimidated innocent folk. His mind raced toward the trip ahead. Would it be successful?

Pale yellow beams from the lantern swung with his steps, illuminating the path to the barn. Nothing seemed amiss this morning - no sounds except the quiet snorts of the boys' sleeping piglets and the gentle chorus of roosting chickens in the hen house. A cup of oats from the feed barrel shaken into a bucket caused Billie to toss his head. The horse started munching while his master went to the saddle rack. When the eager beast had eaten everything, he opened his jaws in obedience to the pressure of the bit. It took only seconds for Charley to cinch up the saddle and strap on the saddle bags.

He patted the big horse's shoulder and turned him toward the house. His mare watched, her soft whiny begging for her share of oats. Her colt stood nearby, the one he planned to break next summer, just in time for Henry and

Joey to have their own mount. At the back of the house he secured the reins to the hitching post and slipped in the door.

As the darkness of the night shifted to gray, he approached the sleeping form of his wife and gently brushed his lips against her cheek. She opened her eyes and smiled, watching him strap on his revolver.

"Did you get everything I packed?" she murmured in a sleepy tone.

"Yes, darlin'. If you need me, send a telegram to the Ft. Smith Marshal's office and I'll get it when we report in. Keep the cellar door unblocked in case of a cyclone." He was trying to delay saying good-by, stroking her soft hair where it molded her face.

"Don't worry. You know I will Be careful and God be with you, sweetheart ," she sighed as her eyes moistened and she turned her face into the pillow with a sob.

He gave her a final hug and kiss and stepped to his daughter's bedside, giving her a brush on the cheek with his lips. He surveyed the peaceful scene of his twins fast asleep in the next bedroom, their silent forms resting side by side under the patchwork coverlet. The last item to pick up was the Winchester on its rack above the fireplace. The stock felt smooth and warm under his grip.

He paused at the front door and surveyed the room he hated to leave, his wife's knitting in a basket by her rocker, the children's few toys in the corner. His life seemed to be moving too swiftly now; he tried to visualize what his children would look like as young adults, how he and Salina would age together. He was glad God withheld the future. Each day's events were enough for him to handle.

Billie responded to pressure on the stirrups and broke into a gentle trot as they cleared the front yard and joined the public road. The summer sun broke the tree line in the east intensifying the morning's warmth. This trip with Ayers promised to be brief - the last before roundup and corn harvest. Long journeys increased his concern for Salina and Joey. It was time to ask his older brother, Abel, to be his posse and ride on his own schedule with Tyne. Ayers did not need their company.

Dan Griffin's chuck wagon loaded to the sideboards with supplies stood in the yard of the deputy marshal's office, Zack Moody standing by his mount arranging saddle and gear. Ayers came down the steps toward him and extended his hand.

"This'll be a light trip, only six arrests and some subpoenas for witnesses. Tyne and Ben are gone and will meet us at Cherokee Town in a week."

Charley removed his hat and mopped at his forehead. "That leg will take a week, won't it, clear out to the west end of the Chickasaw Nation?"

Ayers stroked his moustache and smiled. "We should make thirty miles or more a day without prisoners."

Rolling hills covered with grass as high as a horse's ears soothed Charley's mind and helped him focus on the task before them. This could be the easiest trip he had made. At first light on the seventh day, the party neared Cherokee Town - a busy crossroads where the Texas cattle trail headed north just to the east of Fort Sill where the Comanches under Quanah Parker had surrendered five years ago.

Their leader selected a camp site well outside of town away from the large herds and their drovers. He pointed to his companions. "I'll take Zack with me into town to serve the subpoena and three arrest warrants. Tomorrow, we will stay here and allow Ben and Tyne to go hunting for their people.

In his concern, Charley blurted out, "Will, are you sure you don't need a little more company? This is a small town but, it can be pretty wild."

"The men I'm seeking are not hostile. I think a quiet approach will work best."

It was early evening when Will Ayers and Zack Moody road into Cherokee Town, busy with freight wagons, stage coaches and chuck wagons. They hitched their horses in front of the general store. The sign said "John Walner, Proprietor."

The lawman turned to his brother-in-law. "Stay here while I give this summons to Walner," As he walked into the store, his eyes adjusted to the interior light and he noticed a well-dressed man standing behind the counter. Several customers awaited attention of his assistant, a young woman dressed in the traditional Chickasaw dress, modified to the white man's fashion with a pretty silk scarf tied around her hips.

Her pleasant voice revealed a mild accent. "Hello. May I be of assistance, sir?"

"Yes, Ma'am. I'm Deputy Marshall Willard Ayers, looking for Mr. John Walner."

"That's him at the front counter. I will let him know you're waiting."

She answered his thank you with a bow of her head as she turned to speak to the man. He looked over at Will as she spoke, a flicker of anxiousness in his eyes.

"I'm John Walner."

"I've a subpoena for your appearance as a witness in the murder trial of Patrick McGowan."

Walner stared at the piece of paper as he unfolded it. "I hardly know McGowan."

"People like to jaw when they come into town. He may have passed around threats in your store."

Walner's brows knitted into a scowl. "When will I have to be in Ft.. Smith?

It's a long trip."

"This subpoena is for two weeks from now. That should be sufficient notice."

The store owner grumbled, "I'll go as soon as I can get someone to run the store."

Ayers looked at the young lady standing beside a barrel of brooms. "She seems to know the business."

Walner's face grew serious. "My daughter, yes. But this is a rough place. I won't allow her to be alone in the store."

Ayers read the folded warrant he pulled from his vest pocket. "Another request. Do you know where I can find Emmanual Patterson, William Fisher and Henry Alfred."

"Fisher and Alfred live just down the street, past the livery. Patterson has a small cabin about two miles down the trail to Shawnee. If you're lucky, you'll find him - if he's not out stealing horses."

"I'm mighty obliged, Mr. Walner," Will said, touching his hat brim. He was relieved that the three men were in town. This would be quick and easy.

He found his brother-in-law leaning against the hitching post, in close conversation with a man who appeared from his dress to be of some means, new boots and jeans, a blue cotton shirt, tie and hat.

Moody spoke as he drew near. "Will, this here is a rancher from outside of town, knows Patterson. Claims he is harmless unless caged."

The rancher mumbled his greetings and pointed down the street. "Patterson lives in an old cabin down there about two miles. He works for me during the roundup. He's a Freed Creek Negro, but not as wild as some. Just a little nervous."

The lawman watched the man move down the board walk then turned to his assistant. "Let's get a cup of coffee at the hotel and plan this out. The other two men we want are in town." They crossed the busy street dodging saddle horses and wagons.

At the restaurant over coffee, Ayers began the plan. "These horse thieves don't have a history of violence, but I don't know how they will react when they see my badge. We're two hundreds miles out from the court. Let's go find Fisher and Alfred, first and see how it goes."

They rode up to the house they had been directed to. At their knock, the door was opened by a young woman whose face paled at the sight of the badge on Ayer's vest. A young man about the same age as the woman moved toward a rifle propped against the fireplace. With rapid strides, Moody snatched it from its perch. Another man, his long hair pulled back in a rawhide tie, rose from the table and put his hands in the air.

His pistol levelled at the young man's chest, Ayers's voice cut through the silence. "Keep your hands where I can see them. I'm Deputy Willard Ayers and I have a warrant for your arrest on horse stealing."

"Billie, what have you done?" The young woman ran to her man and held him by the neck, tears welling in her eyes. "You promised me you would go straight if I married you!"

Ayers watched Moody shackle the men to the sound of sobs, which robbed even the toughest lawman of his composure. He bowed his head and chewed his lip a moment. Why couldn't these men see what they're doing to their loved ones? He addressed the young woman who was crumpled in a heap on the sofa. "Ma'am, you can come out to our camp and see him before we leave tomorrow, if you like."

He shoved his rifle into the saddle boot. "Take them back to camp. I'll pick up the last member of the gang, Patterson, and be right along."

If he hurried, he could catch the deputy still in town. Charley knew he was disregarding orders, but the nagging thought of two lawmen underpowered in a lawless town pushed him to kick Billie in the flanks. After meeting Moody with the two prisoners, he grew even more concerned. Ayers was attempting an arrest head-on without any back-up. Just on the edge of town he glimpsed the deputy's familiar figure in the distance. Not too late.

Ayers turned in his saddle at the sound of the approaching rider. "What the heck are you doing here?"

"I decided I'd just come and ride along in case you changed your mind when you got into town."

"I'm glad you're here though I don't expect any trouble. Patterson lives a couple miles down this road."

When they got closer, they dismounted and surveyed the area from the shelter of the scrub oaks that lined the road. Ayers pointed out a horse tied up at the back of the house and a few horses in the corral. "Cover me from the side of the porch, and I'll give him a chance to surrender."

A black man stepped outside at the deputy's command, his face without expression, his eyes trained on Ayer's pistol. "I'm Patterson. Just let me pack some clothes and I'll go with you peaceable like."

Before Charley could step to Ayers' side, the man slammed the door. When Ayers tried the latch, it was bolted from the inside. Heavy furniture hit the floor behind the door.

"Get around back, fast!" Ayers shouted.

Reaching the back door Charley spun around at the sound of three shots in rapid succession. Fighting for his balance, Peacemaker in hand, he ran to the front of the house. As he bent down to examine the fallen deputy, he heard the back door open. His sprint to the back of the house got him a glimpse of a shadowy horseman fleeing into the thick trees forty yards away. Firing several shots at the moving target, he was not sure if he had even come close to the man or horse as the figures disappeared into the blackness of the night.

His wild heart-beat filled his chest and his breath came in gasps, as he knelt at Ayers' side. Blood ran down the lawman's chest in a river of crimson that soon covered the porch boards. He tugged at the unconscious victim then bent his face to the fallen man. "I'm sorry, Will. I have to leave you to get help. I'll be back as soon as I can."

He covered the two miles into town in what seemed like seconds. The closed sign was just being put in the window by the pretty young woman when he flung open the door of the general store. Her startled look was answered by Charley's demand.

"Where's a doctor? Deputy Ayers has been shot."

"Second house past the hotel."

He bolted out the door, covering the distance in a long running stride. People on horseback and in freight wagons stared at him as he ran with all his might. Pounding on the doctor's door, Charley prayed that he would be in.

"Yes?" - a muffled question through the door.

"Open up. I need a doctor. I'm a posse man with Deputy Marshal Ayers who has been shot. "

The doctor asked the location of the downed deputy as he put on his hat and jacket. He grabbed a medical bag by the door.

"He's two miles out of town at Emmanuel Patterson's place."

"Alright, I'll follow you in my buckboard."

Walner came running up and jumped in the buckboard with the doctor. He carried a Winchester under his arm. "Sadie told me the news. Let's go."

They found the wounded lawman exactly where he had fallen. The bleeding had abated to an ooze. After a quick look at the chest wounds, three gaping holes in the vicinity of the right lower lung, the doctor looked at Charley and shook his head. "He probably won't regain consciousness or last the night."

As they lifted Ayers onto the stretcher, he moaned - his eyelids fluttering at the motion.

On arrival at the doctor's office after Ayers had been placed in the surgery, Charley turned to Walner. "Would you send a messenger to our camp, just east of town? His brother and brother-in-law are there."

"Of course."

Seated on the hard oak chair at the foot of the bed, Charley held his head in his hands. How had this happened? Will was such a cautious, experienced lawman. As the dying man's breathing became slower and more shallow, Charley tried to rest.

A knock at the door roused him. Ben Ayers and Zack Moody entered the room, their faces masks of sadness and grief.

Moody spoke first. "What happened? How's Will?"

"Patterson said he wanted to get some clothes and then slammed the door in our faces and bolted it. I was heading for the back door when he shot Will three times right through the door. The doctor says he won't make it to morning."

Ben ran his hand across his beard as he stared at his brother's pale, motionless form. "Damn. Where's Patterson now?"

"Got away while I was tending to Will."

They chose chairs on either side of the bed and settled down to wait for the inevitable. About midnight when his friend's last breaths were apparent, Charley turned his thoughts to God and prayed. *Dear God, why has this happened? What good can come of the death of this brave man? I vow to be as good a lawman as he was and honor him with my life.*

At first light Ben and Zack wrapped the body in a blanket and placed it in a simple pine coffin. His boots, hat, badge, gun belt and pistol had been set aside for his wife. The posse men and friends from Cherokee Town bore the casket to the little cemetery on the edge of town.

Ben stared into the grave then turned to Charley. "Being as how you are a Bible-believer, could you say a few words?"

He gripped his hat and spoke a few words to the crowd. "Ashes to ashes, dust to dust. Dear Lord, please accept the soul of our friend, Willard Ayers, one of the bravest men I have ever known. May his soul rest in peace. Amen."

After the burial, the men gathered at camp to make their plans. Moody laid out a proposal. "I know Will's heart in this matter. He had discussed with me on a few occasions what should be done if anything ever happened to him while on a trip. He wanted the arrests made as planned. Ben and I will head out looking for the other fugitives; there are only three more to pick up and they are on a line towards Fort Smith. Charley, you and Tyne, take Dan and the two prisoners and head to McAlester, the nearest telegraph line. Send the Marshal news of the shooting. We'll come in as soon as we can.

When they rode into McAlester four days later and sent the terrible message, Marshal Dell sent back a reply requesting they come into Ft. Smith as soon as possible and file their report. He would have further instructions for them when they arrived.

The Marshal, grim faced, shook their hands when they entered his office. "Well, boys, what happened out there?

In as clear words as possible, Charley described the event. When he was finished, Dell bowed his head.

"Another good man, that makes six this year. I will need one of you as a replacement for Deputy Ayers."

Charley hesitated. "I would, sir, but my wife and son are ailing."

Tyne paced around the office, stopping at the picture of President Hayes, hanging on the wall above the Marshal's desk. "I can do it. I've been working with Will for the past year and have a good feel of the country."

"Alright, Deputy Hughes. Come back in the morning after you rest up at the hotel. Deputy Barnhill, when you are available full-time, let me know."

Charley shook Tyne's hand at the hitching post. "I'm heading for home. Good luck."

As he rode southwest out of the city, he rubbed the bruise on his right knee. He had hit the front porch beside Will really hard, not even noticing the pain at the time. He dreaded giving the news to Salina. She would worry even more. *Please, God, help us all.*

Deputy Willard Ayers

Chapter 8

Indian Justice

Straining against the wind that tried to pull the reins out of his hands and his hat off his head, Charley struggled with the corral gate. He wondered why he had consented to watch an execution or go anywhere in this weather - 1881 had come in with severe storms covering the wild grass on the rolling hills with a layer of snow. Billie moved away, skittering as the gate swung towards his haunches. Tying off the knot around the corral gate with a tug, Charley turned to mount, pulling his long wool coat around his hips as he settled in the saddle. The big roan, eager to go after being cooped up for a couple of weeks, rabbit-hopped and shook his mane before breaking into a smooth gait.

He rode into Cameron three miles north of Kully-cha-ha. It was on the main road leading north to Fort Smith through the Choctaw Nation. The two horses tied at the general store belonged to his companions. Since Ayers' murder, he rode with two deputies most of the time, Tyner Hughes and James N. Cole. Cole was exactly one year younger than himself, an Illinois boy by birth, living in Arkansas for two years and now a new deputy. Cole took to being a deputy with his natural insight into tracking and catching men, taking no unnecessary chances. He liked that in a partner. He didn't want to carry anyone home sown up in a sheet.

He smiled as he saw the two men descend the steps of the general store. Judge Parker and his reputation attracted the best Arkansas men available, men of character, honor, courage and ability. The few charlatans eventually got weeded out for padding their expense accounts, being too quick to shoot or just generally being full of boasting and nothing else.

Tyne stopped at Charley's stirrup. "We're ready to go. There is a whipping and an execution to be carried out at 2 p.m. sharp."

"Why do you two think this is a good thing to see?" Charley asked his friends. To him it was reminiscent of the old executions English kings had held, to display the harsh reality of crime and its punishment to all. His Scotch-Irish heritage bristled at the thought of public punishment.

Cole spoke from behind Tyne. "If we can understand the severity of the Indian justice system, I think it'll help us deal with the people we live and work among. Honor is life to the Choctaws and the humiliation of a public whipping attacks their pride."

"What about the public execution?" Charley countered.

"The family and the family's clan bear the brunt of that shame," Cole explained. Charley knew Cole loved the Choctaw people and supported them every opportunity he got.

"Alright, maybe this'll be a learning experience for us," Charley agreed. He nudged Billie. What a day to be riding in the cold. It already penetrated his long johns.

The three friends arrived at the Scullyille Court House grounds by mid-afternoon. It was a two story building made of split logs. The white man's system of justice was administered here consisting of: judge; jury men; lawyers for the prosecution and defense; and court clerk. The county treasurer and county sheriff maintained offices on the second floor. White men, who must pay for permits to live and work in the nation, came here to do business with the tribal leaders. The system worked smoothly as long as everyone agreed but bloody shoot-outs had occurred on several occasions when inter-tribal factions clashed.

Charley shuddered as he noticed a pole in the center of the yard. It was about six feet tall and large enough that a man's arms could barely reach around it. Toward the top was a large iron ring.

Spectators from all over the county filled the front porch and yard. A prisoner could roam free until the day of punishment. They knew they could be hunted down and shot on sight by the Light Horse Indian Police if they did not appear. White men who married Indian women were subject to the same punishment since they were considered members of the tribe by adoption.

A murmur went through the crowd as a group of men exited the front door of the court house. Two carried between them a large basket filled with a tall bundle of willow branches.

"There are thirty-five switches as ordered," an attendant announced to the sheriff.

A young man came forth from the crowd and presented himself to the sheriff.

The sheriff spoke to the on-lookers. "The prisoner, Charley Hill, has been found guilty of horse theft and is to receive thirty-five lashes."

Two men took the youth to the whipping post, removed his shirt, and made him kneel. His hands were then secured around the pole in such a manner as to make him hug it, causing the muscles of his back to bulge under the strain.

Tyne explained to his two companions. "Each man that is to whip the lad will step forward and be given one willow switch. He applies the lash as hard as he wishes; however, any subsequent lashes must strike the back in a separate area. The cuts cannot overlap or converge."

In absolute silence the first blow was applied to the young man's back. He jerked under the force of the blow as blood flowed from the foot long cut that appeared instantly on his shoulders. He murmured not a sound and slumped down against the whipping pole. All he could do now was endure thirty-four more.

Charley watched as each man in line applied his lash, stepped back and handed it to an attendant who put it in a separate basket. When all the switches had been used out of the first basket, thirty-five lashes would have been applied. The men applying the blows were lined up several deep, some coming back into line for another lick. Would the whipping ever end? He watched in silence and revulsion as the young man's back and sides dripped red with blood. It pooled in the waist of his trousers and covered his legs.

After twenty-five or so lashes, the line of torturers had disappeared. No one could bare the sight of another stroke. The sheriff stepped forth and applied the last ten lashes, easing up as much as he could without losing his honor. It took fifteen minutes to complete the punishment. When it was over, the young man was untied and his shirt placed around his shoulders. He knew he must not utter a sound in order for his family honor to be upheld. Without assistance, he struggled to his feet and walked on unsteady legs out of the compound.

Wow, no white man could stand that kind of punishment without screaming or fainting.

"That's one tough kid," Charley said shaking his head in respect. Cole's face showed the same reaction, disbelief at the severity of what they had just witnessed. Charley hadn't witnessed a hanging at Fort Smith, yet. *Which was worse?*

The crowd, which had started to discuss the whipping in whispers and a few whoops, kept their eyes on the sheriff. After he had ascertained the whipping had been done properly and had verified so on the certificate for the judge, he turned to an attendant.

"Bring out the woman."

All eyes focused on a Choctaw woman as she walked out of the court house. She appeared to be middle-aged with graying hair that was tied in two braids down her back. She wore a traditional long cotton dress with tassels on the hem, sash at the waist, a blouse of home-spun cotton, a necklace of beads, moccasins on her feet.

The sheriff nodded to two attendants who escorted the prisoner to the middle of the compound. Cole bent his head and explained to his companions.

"Her family picks two members to attend her at the execution. They are most probably her husband and a son."

The sheriff read from a paper handed to him by the judge. "Mary Perkins has been found guilty of poisoning her husband's younger wife in a fit of rage and jealously. She is sentenced to death by bullet."

It was then that Charley noticed a pine coffin that had been placed close at hand. He was surprised to see Reverend Fulsom from Pocola Methodist Church at the end of the crowd. Reverend Fulsom was a mighty man of God and a preacher of some renown in the Choctaw Nation. He had visited his parents' home on several occasions.

Charley riveted his eyes on the prisoner who was made to kneel in front of the coffin. The older man attending her pinned a yellow star on her blouse right over her heart. For a moment he stood before her, his eyes searching her features.

The sheriff addressed the doomed woman. "Do you have anything to say before the sentence is carried out?"

The woman spoke in a voice so soft, Charley could barely hear her words, Reverend Fulsom translating for the whites. "No, sir. I'm ready to pay for my evil deed. Reverend Fulsom assures me I'll see Jesus face to face."

At the completion of her statement, the sheriff nodded to the two attendants. They knelt on either side of the woman, holding her arms in a tight out-stretched position.

After the sheriff made sure no one was standing behind the woman in the range of a stray bullet or a ricochet, he pulled out his six-gun, a heavy forty-four caliber Colt and aimed it at the yellow star. He was standing only six feet away. The blast of the gun made everyone jump. The woman fell on her side, unmoving. He walked up and stood over her for several seconds and then turned away, his face impassive.

The family members picked up the woman's body and placed it in the coffin leaving the lid open. With screams of grief, the women and children rushed forward to pat and kiss the dead woman's face. Her husband brought his wagon into the compound. The Scullyville Cemetery would be her last resting place. This man had lost both wives in a sad triangle of hate and jealousy.

Charley thought of the Bible story of Isaac and Rebecca. *Love and jealousy wreck havoc, no matter how much man thinks he has progressed since the ancient of times.*

The three friends rode away in silence. They all had thoughts about what they had just seen.

Cole, the compassionate one, broke the silence. " I would rather see a man hanged than whipped. And to see a woman executed, never again! It must have a life-long effect on the family and the tribe to go through what we just saw."

Charley, the analytical one of the bunch, tried to reason it out. "I think the Indian justice system works just fine when sentences are carried out. The problem seems to be getting people to stand up and testify truthfully just like in our courts."

Tyne finally commented. "If more people viewed what we just saw today, the white man's justice system would be more highly regarded than it is. Eastern newspapers label Judge Parker a hanging judge for sentencing men to death for murder, a sentence which is mandatory, whether in white man's court or Indian's court. "

Charley summed up their thoughts. "The next time I go after an Indian for murder, I know now he will be desperate and dangerous, preferring my bullet to a rope." Charley's thoughts dwelt on that last word, *dangerous. Well, I'll face that when the time came.*

Last Indian Court Execution in the Choctaw nation, Silon Lewis, Nov. 5, 1894

Chapter 9

New Blood

Heat devils flung fine grains of dirt against his face, filling his mouth and eyes. Charley spat and wiped the sweat out of his eyes with his handkerchief. The tornado season fast approaching, he wanted to get this project done before he left on his next trip. He descended into the root cellar through the outside access underneath the back window of the kitchen to inspect his morning's efforts - another door in the kitchen floor and a small ladder leading up. It would a safe and dry refuge against severe weather or unwanted intruders.

Popping up through the kitchen floor, he spoke to Salina who stood at the stove preparing dinner. Fresh loaves of breads covered with a clean flour sack cooled on the window ledge. "Umm. I sure am hungry. Where are the kids?"

"They're out back in the woods. Go ahead and ring the dinner bell," Salina said wiping her hands on her apron."

He pulled her into his arms and nuzzled her cheek. It smelled of flour. "How's Mrs. Davis been?"

"She's so helpful. I can't manage without her."

As he rang the bell, he spied the children running out of the woods, the older boys in front and little Minnie toddling behind, crying out for the others to wait for her. They tumbled into the wash room with giggles and pushes.

Charley gave the blessing on the meal as all the little heads were bowed and hands were folded in laps. The children ate ravenously and then peeked over their shoulders to see if there was dessert today. Yep. Blackberry cobbler. Blackberries grew wild in the fields and ditch banks and were plentiful this time of year.

Pushing back from his empty dessert plate, he stood and stretched his stiff muscles. "I think I'll ride into town and check the post office before I see Tyne."

The short ride gave him time to think about what was worrying him - the need for more deputies in the Choctaw Nation. The coal mine towns of Krebs and McAlester attracted immigrants, gamblers and illegal whiskey operations and the MK&T Railroad was a magnet for train robbers. It was time to leave his peaceful home to go full-time and bring Abe with him.

He stopped at the post office in Kully-cha-ha which had been established two years before. It saved him riding an additional eight miles for the mail. The postmaster handed him a letter. Glancing at the address, he opened the message from his brother, David Samuel, who lived in the Cherokee settlement of Briartown on the Canadian River.

Dear brother and Salina,

I hope this letter finds you well. As soon as the first growth is high, I will be cutting prairie grass and bundling it to sell to the travelers that come through this area on a daily basis. The flow of wagons and buggies seems to be constant.

There are some problems that have developed in this area recently as relates to the Starr family. They live a couple of miles from us on the Canadian River. Tom Starr's son, Sam, married a woman from Texas named Belle Reed. She is slightly older than him and very taken with wild men. She and her previous husband, Jim Reed, had a run-in with the law in Texas and he was killed for the reward. Since she has moved to Starr Bend, she has renamed it Younger's Bend, for her old friend, Cole Younger. Their ranch seems to attract desperate men. Several neighbors have had horses stolen and when confronting the Starrs, they are laughed at and threatened with their life if they go to the authorities. I would appreciate your input as to how to curtail these goings-on.

Belle's daughter, Pearl Reed, goes to school with my children in Briartown. She is well enough behaved. Her mother is very strict and does not allow her much freedom. I feel that the situation is only going to get worse, since the crimes committed by these people seem to involve their neighbors and people they have befriended. The social graces Mrs. Starr displays can quickly turn to rage and the pulling of twin pistols that she wears every where she goes.

Hope to see you soon, Sam

He slipped the envelope into his vest pocket and walked across the street to the deputy marshal's office. He could smell pipe smoke before he opened the door.

Tyne stood to greet him and then pointed his pipe at the warrants covering the desk. "Ever since the new President, Chester Arthur, appointed him in February, Marshal Boles has every deputy he can muster coming and going as fast as they can."

Charley knew this was the time to speak what was on his mind. "I'd like permission to speak to my older brother, Abel, about helping us. Most everything I know, he taught me. He is steady and level-headed and no one can beat him in a fight. He is married to a tribal girl and is looking for opportunities."

Hughes' eyes lit up at the prospect. "If he is anything like you, I suspect he will jump at the chance. You Barnhills must have grown up with a Bible in one hand and a six gun in the other."

Hughes began to search through the stack of papers. "We've twenty-two men to track down. We'll need Abel's help if he's available."

"Just call him Abe. I'll see him today. He lives just six miles west. Dan going along as cook?"

"He's as reliable as the rising sun. These trips give him time to recover from work his wife piles up for him. I've an extra wagon and driver. We'll hire guards as we need them."

Charley rose and picked up his hat. "I'll stop back by and let you know before I head home. By the way, what have you heard of Sam Starr and his new wife, Belle? "

"Ole Tom claims he has turned over his place to Sam and is retired now. Hope so. Sam is young and wild. I hear that's what the new Mrs. Starr likes in a man."

Abe Barnhill could make out the outline of a rider on the main road and recognized Charley on ole Billie. The same height and build as Charley, Abe was three years older. His thin cheeks hid a stoic personality, giving an observer no hint of pain or fear, yet his eyes revealed a compassion only suffering could have created. He had tried to be an example to Charley since childhood when cholera had taken four of their brothers and sisters in one week. He had struggled to raise his daughter after the loss of his young wife several years before. Now he had a young bride who had taken him and his daughter to love until death parted them.

His long legs carried him to the visitor's side in a few strides. "Howdy, brother. What brings you here this fine day?"

Charley placed his left hand on the saddle horn and shifted his weight to dismount. On the ground he patted Billie's shoulder and turned to face him. "I've been talking to Deputy Hughes. We're short-handed. I told him you were looking for an opportunity."

Abe rubbed his clean-shaven jaw in excitement. It's something he had been hoping for ever since Charley had begun working with the deputies. "I'd like that a lot but I should discuss it with Amanda."

"That'll be fine. If you're able, come into town by sun-up ready to go. Now, where is that new wife of yours? I haven't seen her since the family Christmas get-together."

They ascended the porch and took off their hats as they entered the home, a comfortable log building with a front and back porch. The door was flanked by a window on each side that was decorated with colorful curtains, a new wife's touch. It was cool inside and the aroma of fried meat reminded Abe it was near supper time.

"Honey, look who's here to visit."

Young Mrs. Barnhill's gray eyes glittered as she gave the newcomer a big hug. In her mid-twenties, her finally chiseled nose and chin indicated an Indian connection. Two long braids down her back were woven with colorful silk strips reminiscent of the ribbon dances so popular in the local tribe.

"How are you, Charley?" Her voice was polite and soft.

"Just fine. How's Mollie doing with school?"

"Very well when she gets to go. She's been sick most of the spring with a cold."

"I hope she is better now. Abe will fill you in on a proposition I was discussing with him. I need to head back to town."

"How about a tall glass of tea before you go. I just made some , but it is not cooled down yet."

"Thank you, that will do."

"Honey, would you care for some?" she asked her new husband, a gentle smile turning up the corners of her mouth.

"Yes, darling, then I'll get back to repairing that corral fence. Ole Bossie seems to find a way out of that corral just at milking time."

Abe lifted an eyebrow when Charley passed him a letter.

"Got this today. What do you think?"

Abe read through Sam's letter quickly then raised his eyes to his brother. "We need to see him as soon as possible. I've heard rumors of the Starr gang robbing local farmers and torturing an old Indian and his wife. They use cipher language to communicate and confuse the victims allowing time to escape."

"Cipher language? You mean hand talking? "

Abe paused. "More than that, code words and phrases too."

"We'll stop by this trip. Should take us three days to get there."

Abe watched his brother ride out. He knew the challenge he had been offered. Though older, he would be serving under Charley who had always looked to him for guidance. He vowed to be the best posse man any deputy would want.

Belle Starr as a young woman

Chapter 10

Briartown

The men hunkered down in the saddle, their hats pulled low against the gale force winds sweeping across the valley. Riding in trail behind Tyne, Abe hoped they could hold on to the trail in this late spring snowstorm. Behind him Dan's chuck wagon team strained against the slippery road bed. The additional wagon and driver (Zack Moody's younger brother, James) took up the rear with Charley. Sugarloaf Mountain, rising to 2500 feet and normally visible for a hundred miles, had long since disappeared from sight in the blinding weather.

Sugar Loaf Mountain

He maneuvered his horse as Tyne turned in the saddle and eased up so he could ride alongside.

"Heading into the storm like this we'll not make our schedule. We'll stop for the night while it's still light enough to make camp.

"Alright, I'll let the others know." He wheeled his horse's head to turn back.

Tyne caught Abe's arm as he started to circle in the saddle. "Glad you're with us."

Abe tightened his shoulders as he turned his back to the biting wind. He was glad he was there. Would he feel the same after the first gun battle? He shifted his feet in the stirrups to restore circulation to his cold toes, wishing he had not left his wool socks in his saddlebags. Several miles later, he followed Tyne off the road along a slight rise to a small clearing surrounded by a windbreak of thick trees.

"This should do us for tonight. Make camp," Tyne ordered.

Dan made the evening enjoyable by stoking up a great roaring fire on which he cooked up biscuits and heated up the supper he had already prepared before they had started out that morning. He poured coffee into Abe's cup. "Enjoy these fresh fixings. Next week it'll be dried meat, beans, biscuits and coffee."

Abe sipped his coffee and exchanged conversation. The men who had just met him had a lot of questions.

Tyne shifted his gaze from the fire to Abe's face. "So, who's the boss in this Barnhill group of brothers, you or Charley?"

"Neither. Our older brother, David Samuel, is. He's the one that moved to the Indian Territory first with his Cherokee wife."

Dan interjected with a look of genuine interest. "Charley has bragged of your marksmanship. How did you learn to handle a rifle so well?"

Abe scratched thoughtfully at his face as he continued "During the War, our father owned a farm east of Bentonville, Arkansas. After the Battle of Prairie Grove in December of 1862, both armies pulled out of the area which left us at the mercy of bushwhackers from both sides. Pa figured, for our own preservation, we should a have rifle and learn to use it well. Even though he is a man of God and does not believe in war, he bought an old Enfield rifle. We could soon shoot the head off of a bird or squirrel at 100 yards. My wife cooks the best squirrel stew you ever tasted."

Dan shook his head in agreement. "Sounds familiar. Glad those days are behind us. But these times are pretty tough too. No one should walk through this territory without a pistol."

Abe looked at his brother and frowned before he again spoke. "We had to hightail it into the woods one day when some bushwhackers surprised us out in the fields. The same patrol had come by the week before and killed one of our school mates as he stood on the front porch with his mother. He was only fourteen, but they figured if he did not consent to fight with them, he was better left dead then left to the other side."

Tyne took a drag on his pipe. "Those were terrible times. I'm glad we can offer our children a more peaceable life. Though the Indian Territory is full of outlaw gangs, I know we'll eventually get the best of them. Well, I am ready for some shut eye. See you all in the morning."

During the night the "Norther" blew through as they had hoped it would. Abe woke to a pile of snow on his tent. Blowing on fingers, he tugged on his boots then sought the warmth of Dan's fire and a mug of hot coffee. Figuring his lean frame did not need to be any leaner he grabbed a biscuit, pulled the top and bottom apart and filled it with several pieces of bacon. He felt his empty stomach welcome the energy-giving fat.

Wiping his hand on his jacket sleeve, he strode over to his mare on the picket line. He clucked his tongue and gave her a sugar cube. He had thought to stuff some in his saddle bags before he left. A daily treat like that would keep her agreeable the whole trip.

When all were ready, Tyne raised his hand in a signal to start the wagons. The horse teams were in a better mood this morning after a night's rest and a bucket of corn for breakfast.

The three men rode single file, crossing the Sans Bois Creek a few miles northwest as they moved into the Canadian river bottom. About noon they were on the outskirts of the little settlement of Whitefield and its ferry across the Canadian River.

Tyne asked, "You ever been this way before, Abe? This place isn't much. The Katy railroad coming through Indian Territory has caused the towns along the railroads to grow, but not these."

"No, I haven't. It doesn't seem to have much activity, " Abe answered as he surveyed the log structures with a careful eye.

A couple of ponies in front of the general store swished at the flies that hovered about their flanks. Two men came out and walked to their horses. They seemed surprised to see three horsemen and two wagons in this sleepy little settlement. Without a greeting they whirled their horses around as they kicked their flanks. Abe coughed at the dirt that was kicked up in his face.

The two brothers followed Tyne inside.

Abe examined the shelves behind the clerk noting boxes of cartridges and handguns. Rifles hung on the wall. Along one side of the wall behind him were bolts of cloth, scarves, and other colorful materials.

Tyne pulled back his vest to reveal his badge. "Howdy. We're from the Fort Smith. Heard there is horse stealing going on around here."

Spectacles perched on the clerk's thin-bridged nose moved up and down as he looked them over. A nervous twitch to his left eye made him appear to be winking. He extended his hand in greeting. "My name is John Turk. I trade with the Cherokees, most of whom have been here for years and have well-established farms and ranches. The number of riffraff moving in seems to have gone up since Sam Starr married that woman from Texas. I wouldn't go to Starr Bend without an armed escort. Belle, Mrs. Starr that is, bought herself a piano in Fort Smith and the poor fella who delivered it said he was lucky to get out of there with his money and his life."

Tyne squinted at him and asked in a more pointed tone, "Have there been any complaints of horse-stealing in the neighborhood?"

"Ole George Crane was in here last week complaining that his son had lost a horse."

"Where does Crane live? "

"Up north of Briartown."

"Much obliged to you for your assistance." Tyne shook the man's hand. "Oh, by the way. Who were those two that rode off as we came in?"

"The taller, dark one is Sam Starr. His side-kick is Jack Spaniard. They've probably headed out to Starr Bend to warn them of your presence. They're known for shooting at strangers to scare them off."

"Many thanks." The lawman tipped his hat and turned to leave.

Charley put his hand on Tyne's shoulder. "Let's visit my brother, Sam, who lives at Briartown. I received a letter from him complaining about the Starrs."

The Canadian River was in flood stage. For most of the year, it was a mile wide and a foot deep. As they moved off the ferry after some difficulty getting across in the swirling waters, they found the road to Briartown; the unfenced fields on either side of the road showed spring growth of wild grass, berry bushes, and trumpet vines; gnarled branches of timber oak twisted toward the sky. Abe estimated the height of the prairie grass to be four feet. As was the custom with the Indians, the houses were far apart. Their saying was 'If I can hear my neighbor's dog bark, he's too close.'

As the men moved into the yard, Mary Barnhill came out of the house, her hand shielding her eyes from the sun. She smiled as she recognized her two brother-in-laws, unmistakable figures with their drooping moustaches and wide-brimmed hats.

She wiped her hands on her apron and smoothed the hair at her neck before coming down to greet them.

Her movements were graceful and fluid as a young doe. "Well, I declare, Abe and Charley. You all look like you could use a cool drink and some supper."

Charley tipped his hat to her and dismounted. "Hello, Mary. This fella here is Deputy Marshal Tyner Hughes, my partner. Dan Griffin is on the chuck wagon and that's James Moody on the freight wagon. Is Sam around?"

"Yes, he's out in back of the barn shoeing a horse. Since it is almost supper time, I'll ring the dinner bell." Her hand went to the bell rope. "What brings you here today?" she asked, a shy smile crossing her beautiful Cherokee features as she turned to Abe.

"Charley and I are attached at the hip now. He needs me along to keep him out of trouble," Abe explained. His gladness to be part of this man-hunting expedition was evident to Mary as he spoke with an eagerness unlike his normal slow drawl.

By now all the children were gathered around, inspecting the horses, men and wagons, excited to see their uncles and the marshal force that was with them. They shouted excitedly to each other. Being the oldest brother, Sam's children were a mite older than Charley's or Abe's.

Abe dismounted to hitch up his horse and gave a couple of the kids a rubbing on the top of the head. Emily, 13, and Elizabeth, 12, the two oldest girls, had long dark hair and sparkling brown eyes like their mother. Bill, 10, the oldest boy, was tall and thin. The younger girls, Lena, 8, and Mary, 6, were cute little thing with bright eyes. Coming up at the end of this troop, were the two youngest boys, Earl and James. As was common with large families, they all were about two years apart in age.

"Uncle Abe, how old do I have to be to help you catch outlaws?" Bill asked.

"Come see me in about eight years. In the meantime, do your schooling and mind your folks. "

At the sound of the dinner bell, Sam appeared from the far corner of the barn, leading a horse that he turned into the corral. He was tall and dark, a cookie cutter form of his younger brothers. He walked over to them with long strides offering an out-stretched hand. After the introductions were made, the menfolk sat down on benches on the porch for a quiet conversation. Mary discretely headed back into the house to finish her supper preparations and instructed the children to wash up.

Tyne was the first to start the questioning. "Mr. Barnhill, your brothers tell me that there is some horse stealing in the area. Mr. Turk in Whitefield mentioned something about a Starr gang."

"Just call me Sam. There's a dispute going on right now between Sam Starr's wife, Belle, and John West. West is from a large prominent Cherokee family and is a member of the Cherokee Light Horse. He claims she took two horses even after he had pointed out to her that they belonged to his neighbors, Crane and Campbell. She says they are strays but in this open range, livestock graze all over. "

"Well, where can we find any of these parties?"

"Starr Bend is five miles west, but you can't get out there without them being alerted that you're coming. They have a spy network amongst the people who cooperate either out of fear or as accomplices. Crane and Campbell live a few miles north."

"After we enjoy the supper your wife has so kindly offered, do you mind if we bed down in your barn? We will head out first thing in the morning to find our witnesses."

Abe sat in the kitchen around a large table and enjoyed the meal and a pipe afterwards. He watched his nieces and nephews with pride. This was a good, strong family. Now that his hunger was satisfied, the warmth of the house soaked into his body. He was eager to turn in as soon as it was dark.

After leaving Briartown, the lawmen forged north looking for the homes in question. They approached a sizable dwelling for this part of the Nation, situated on a hill facing the road. Appearing quite spacious, the building was augmented by a large corral around to the side and a shed with a lean-to attached in the back. A scruffy-looking farm dog came growling around the side of the house as they approached.

A tall, handsome man stepped out on the porch and silenced the dog with a gruff command. His face was expressionless under his short patchy beard, but his eyes were piercing and alert. Abe noticed a Winchester propped up against the door frame on the outside of the wall, just in grabbing distance if needed.

Tyne dismounted and approached the man slowly.

"Hello, I'm Tyner Hughes, and this here's Charley Barnhill, Deputy Marshals from Fort Smith. I'm looking for John West.

"I'm John West. What can I do for you?" the man answered. His back was now turned to the Winchester.

"We've been told you know something about horse stealing going on around here."

"Well, I know that my neighbor, Andrew Crane, has lost a horse and so has Sam Campbell."

"What can you tell us about all this?"

"I saw both horses in the Starr's possession around the middle of April. I told Andrew about it. When he went looking for his horse, someone took a pot-shot at him near Starr Bend."

"Are you willing to swear out a writ of complaint concerning this matter?" Tyne asked with a stern look. It did no good to pursue horse thieves if they scared off the witnesses.

"Yes, if Crane and Campbell will too."

"Alright then. When we get to a telegraph office, I'll send a message to Fort Smith. In the meantime, I suggest you keep this to yourself." With a tip of his hat, he turned to his horse and mounted.

West stepped down and put his hand on Tyne's saddle. "Just be aware. Mrs. Starr is a friend of the James and Younger gangs. They have been spotted in the vicinity of Hi Early Mountain which is north of Starr Bend. They use it as a hide out."

A half an hour later they drew up at Andrew Crane's modest home, two rooms separated by a dog. A young man of about twenty-five, with a bad limp, walked out to greet them. He appeared quite intelligent in his speech and manner, but somewhat anxious as his eyes roved over the area around his home.

"My father and I rode over to visit the Starrs after John West had reported to me that he had seen them round up my horse with theirs. Mrs. Starr knows who took my horse away. She claims she did not ride it away, though. I just want either the money it is worth or the horse back. Then when someone took a shot at me along the road, I felt this was getting too dangerous. I'll come into Fort Smith to file a complaint."

As they rode out away from Briartown, Tyne briefed them on the plan for the rest of the day. "Since it's already early afternoon, we'll ride west along the Canadian River. It meets the Texas Road about twenty miles away, east of Eufaula where I can send a telegram to Chief Deputy Barnes. After that it'll take us a couple days to reach McAlester."

That night they camped along the river. It was too early in the year for mosquitoes, so Abe slept well. He gazed at the sky now overcast with low clouds and shifting winds. His thoughts were on the long trip and the problems they may face. Then he remembered Proverbs 10: 24 "What the wicked dreads will overtake him; what the righteous desire will be granted." With that comfort his thoughts turned to the mundane and safe.

UNITED STATES OF AMERICA,
WESTERN DISTRICT OF ARKANSAS.

Sam Starr and Belle Starr Arrest Warrant

Chapter 11

The Sweep

Black smoke billowed from the locomotive engine, streaming back over its cars as the engineer of the northbound Muskogee express applied steam and released his brakes. With the screeching of a dying bagpipe, the pressure brake valve opened. The squeal of steel wheels against iron rails rent the air until the wheels caught and the train began to inch forward. Charley fought to calm Billie as he backed away in fright, tossing head and tail and lunging at the bit. Tyne and Abe led he way through the maize of cattle pens and loading chutes. He could smell the cattle pens before he saw them, Texas longhorns rattling their horns against the wooden pens and calling for release with plaintive cries.

McAlester's general store and warehouse lay beside the railroad depot. Delivery wagons lined the loading docks piled high with sacks of flour and other provisions. The only fences in the whole area extended six miles in either direction from the railroad depot. These cattle fences kept the livestock off the tracks. A cow killed on the tracks was an inconvenience for the owner, but a train derailed from such an accident was costly.

Tyne pulled up in front of the store and signaled the others to dismount. They had been out five days already and replenishment would guarantee their supplies would last the full month. Deputies were responsible for the feeding of their prisoners receiving, at this time, sixty eight cents a day for each prisoner in custody.

"Take a few minutes to rest. I'm going to get some information from Mr. McAlester if he's in and pick up a few more supplies," Tyne directed the others.

Charley took the opportunity to look around. He thought this was a perfect location for the growth of commerce. The Missouri, Kansas and Texas railroad line through Indian Territory had been built in 1870 alongside the Shawnee Trail used by cattlemen from Texas to move their huge herds. This railroad stop was named 'McAlester' in 1872 for the owner of the local trading post, James Jackson McAlester, who in that same year had married a Chickasaw maiden, thereby becoming a member of the tribe through marriage. Italians and Irish flocked here to work in McAlester's coal mines. There were a few widely scattered ranches to the west and some Choctaw families over past Krebs to the east.

"Hello, how's business today?" he inquired of a passing worker who had just helped another man lift a fifty pound sack of flour onto his buckboard.

The young man wiped his hands on his kerchief and extended it to Charley.

"Morning, Deputy. My name's Fritz Sittel. Business is just fine. Who're you after this time?"

"We have warrants for twenty-five men, some in the Choctaw Nation and some in the Creek. We'll be looking in a lot of places."

"My father is over at our hotel, the Elk House right across the street there. He may have some leads for you."

"Much obliged. What's it like to try and ranch around here?"

"Mr. McAlester has the largest ranch in the area. Most of the full-bloods live in the woods and don't make much effort to ranch. A white man , of course, has to get a permit from the tribal council or marry into the tribe."

"Thanks for the information." Charley touched the brim of his hat and walked back to where the others were lounging on a bench outside the store. He spit into the dirt of the yard and stared at the assemblage of humanity moving to and fro in front of them. Small Indian women struggled beneath huge bundles of hides being traded at the general store, their husband or brother leading the way, many carrying rifles.

Before he could move toward the Elk House, Tyne came out with a bundle under his arm which he handed to Dan. "Got some matches, tobacco, coffee and sugar. McAlester reports a bunch of white men came through here yesterday headed southwest towards the Creek Nation. They were trailing several unbranded horses. "

With those words, the lawmen grabbed up their horses' reins as Dan and James ran to their wagon seats. They followed the Army Road for a few miles out of town and then broke off to the southwest through rolling prairie dotted with post oak, hickory and elm. Thick undergrowth of wild grapevines and green-briers, known as "roughs", filled the draws.

As he rode with the afternoon sun in his face, Charley squinted to make out anything unnatural in the local terrain. He had ridden this area before, but not in recent days. Most Indian homes were spread out ten to fifteen miles apart. A traveler could ride for days without seeing a single person. His head and eyes moved from side to side using his peripheral vision as much as possible. It caused less eye strain that way. The soil was soft, covered with thin tall grass, any impressions in the grass pattern, indicating wild game or horses.

Three hours down the trail, men and horses straining, Tyne called for a rest at a small creek. The men dismounted and took long drinks out of the water barrel then spread out on the soft grass. The horses buried their muzzles in the stream, snorting the cool water through noses and across tongues. A sudden far away sound penetrated the stillness, something they might not have heard over the sounds of the horses' hooves and the rattle of the wagons.

It was so faint that Charley was not sure if he had heard it or not. Total silence, like total darkness, makes the senses so acute that you can hear the sounds inside your head. But this was different, sporadic and muffled, seeming to come from over the rolling hills.

Tyne jumped to his feet and grabbed his reins. "Dan and James, secure the wagons and teams in the tree line out of sight. Get your saddle horses and let's go."

The five men started at a brisk gallop toward the disturbance. With his breath coming in gulps as his horse took the rolling terrain in long strides, Charley focused on trying to keep his mind clear and his saddle gun ready. He unbuckled the restraining strap and felt for the trigger of the Winchester. He noticed Tyne doing the same ahead of him. Abe was close behind Tyne, his horse eager to take the lead. Dan and James endeavored to catch up, as they kicked spurs into their horses flanks.

A few minutes later as they came over the rise of a hill where terrain fell off gradually to the southwest towards a densely covered gully, he could hear the shots more clearly and turned his horse in the direction of the bottom. Breaking through a thin spot in the brush, he could make out a man in the distance sheltered behind a small rock outcropping and firing toward a grove of trees.

Charley did not want to be shot by a stranger without figuring out the action. Tyne held his hand up for a dismount. Smoke and muzzle blasts coming from the trees indicated maybe four or five men with rifles.

The man behind the outcropping spotted their party and beckoned for help. They crawled up to him. The defender was on his belly in the soft dirt, his Choctaw features impassive.

Tyne surveyed the terrain between them and the shooters. "We're deputies from Fort Smith looking for a gang of horse thieves."

"You've found 'em. I'm Jonas Jackson from Boggy Creek. This morning these white men take my horses. I track them here, " he explained in broken English.

"Now that you have them cornered, what were you planning to do, keep them here until you run out of ammunition? Are you alone?"

"No, oldest son is on the other side blocking their escape. "

"Where are your stolen horses?"

"When I fired at them, they let them go. Now, I plan on finishing the job."

"It looks to me like you're out-numbered. Let me use my men to try and get them to surrender."

The distance to the grove was too far to call to the rustlers above the gun shots. Charley could make out their horses tethered to trees, but too far away and in too dense of woods to disable them. A good plan was needed to flush them out.

Tyne must have read his mind. "Charley, you and Abe cover the rear and Dan and James the front. I think I can crawl to within throwing distance and get a torch into that dry undergrowth."

The men spread out as ordered while Jonas kept up a busy fire His son, seeing the men coming to their aid, also stepped up his firing.

Charley looked up at the sun - they only had an hour or so of daylight. If they did not finish this now, the rustlers would slip away. Abe was off to his left, also eying the sun, backing him up as he had all his life. But it was different with his brother beside him now. He had to worry for his safety.

Minutes went by while he kept his head down. So far only Jonas and his son had been firing, the rustlers not aware that they were now outnumbered. Wisps of smoke coming from the underbrush in the grove darkened and turned into a roaring blaze. He and Abe now stood together in their first battle with outlaws. He didn't have time to think about whether they would get out alive. It was just something that had to be done.

Tyne had intentionally placed the torch on the upwind side of the grove so that the fire would burn downwind towards the stream to prevent it from spreading into the prairie. It did no good to start a fire to flush out rustlers and also jeopardize your own safety at the same time.

The thick smoke climbed skyward, compelling figures to scurry toward their horses which were crazy with fright, pulling at their reins and stomping the ground. One by one the four men managed to mount with difficulty and wheel for the escape. Each rider clung to the saddle horn, their faces covered with kerchiefs and heads held close to their horses' necks.

As the first rider burst from the grove, Charley opened up with his Winchester. The bandit went down, his horse dropped by a shot from Abe. Crawling and clawing to extract his feet from the stirrups of his thrashing horse, his wounded arm useless at his side, he attempted to raise his Winchester with his good arm. He lay back and grappled for his six-shooter which was trapped under his body.

A second rider flashed into view, and, seeing his wounded partner on the ground, pivoted toward the stream, as Jonas' son and Abe caught him in a crossfire. Jumping free of his falling horse, the rider landed on all fours and crawled to a defensive position behind a small tree some forty yards from Abe. Rapid fire from the Indian boy sent chips of rock everywhere as bullets hit the dirt around the tree. Charley was amazed at the scene. *That young man can sure shoot.* Momentarily, a wild gesturing hand threw out a six shooter and a Winchester. Abe motioned to the Indian boy to halt firing.

Two more escapees coming out the front of the grove met the same brutal assault and soon had their hands in the air. Charley peered over his protective cover at the first rider on the ground. His Winchester pointing at the rustler's belt buckle, the biggest target on a man, he moved toward the horse thief

The man fixed a face full of hate on Charley. "You'll never go me to Fort Smith, dead or alive. I'll kill you first chance I get," he snarled through clinched teeth.

Charley reached down to disarm the spitting fugitive; a burning blow to his back spun him around in the dirt as his head hit the ground. His consciousness returned through a gray tunnel-narrowed vision. He had no recollection of hitting the ground or of how long he had lain there. Abe's face pressed over him, his hands gripping him by his vest.

"Charley, talk to me. Are you alright?" Abe's desperate voice penetrated through the ringing in his head. He struggled to focus on Abe's eyes full of fear inches from his nose. He moaned and tried to move against the searing pain in his back.

"Wha ..wha.. happened?" His moan sounded like a crock.

Abe smiled when he heard his voice. "Thank God, Charley. I thought I'd lost you. What would I tell Salina?"

He did not care about telling Salina anything at the moment. He just wanted to be able to breath and move.

"There was a fifth rider we didn't see. He was hiding in the grove to see if his buddies could escape. He made the mistake of coming out to shoot as you approached the man pinned under the horse. "

Charley's gaze went to a crumbled figure laying about twenty yards from the grove. "What happened to him?"

"That youngster drilled him. He's a great shot, that kid. Saved your life. The bullet hit just as the rustler fired and knocked his aim off."

With help from Abe he raised up on his elbow to survey the young Indian standing over his fallen foe, a proud look of accomplishment, but not a word. Charley looked down at the crimson pool in the dirt around his fingers. He just wanted to rest. *Thank God for Abe and his young ally.*

After the round up of the rustlers, Dan got out the liniment to clean his wound after cutting away his shirt. He gently applied a clean soft bandage to stop the bleeding and handed Charley a shot of whiskey to kill the pain. The whiskey was for medicinal purposes only and was locked up in the box with the ammo.

"The bullet cut deep into the muscle of you shoulder blade. It'll need sewing to close. There's a doctor in McAlester. We'll get you to the wagon for a good night's rest and then take you there in the morning."

The next morning he rested on bedding in James' wagon trying to stay still, but the jostling of the wagon made him grit his teeth. Out the back of the wagon, he could see Abe riding close behind. The two rustlers that had horses were riding with the bridles secured to the side of the wagon. Their hands were chained to their saddles and the chains looped around the horses' bellies. The one that had lost his horse was chained directly to the wagon. The one that had threatened to kill Charley was riding, chained to the tailgate, his injured arm in a sling, his eyes still glaring.

Tyne stuck his head through the canvas opening. "Charley, how're you making out?" His eyes were full of joy.

"I'm grateful to be breathing," Charley answered with a quiet smile. "Who're these guys we rounded up? Did Mr. Jackson get his horses back?"

"This is a bunch of rowdies out of Texas. They make a run into Indian country every month or so and steal as many horses as they can. Then, they drive them down to McKinney. Mr. Jackson got his horses back and was mighty grateful for our help. I don't know how that standoff would have turned out if we hadn't showed up."

"What are you going to do with me? I'll be able to ride in a couple of days."

"I'm gong to leave you at McAlester for a few days. I'll send you a telegram when I get to Paul's Valley and let you know where to meet us."

He nodded his head and lay back on the bedding. His back and shoulder were stiff and he was unable to move his left arm. He took one more sip of whiskey. Though fire water would not cross his lips under normal circumstances, he knew his Pa would understand.

Chapter 12

The Storm

The doctor closed his bag with a swift click of the latch and helped Charley sit up on the edge of the bed. He felt dizzy from the pain medication.

"Well, young man. You're going to be fine. I've stitched up your shoulder and dressed it. Keep still for a couple of days. I don't know where Marshal Boles finds such fine specimens of manhood, but you're going to be back chasing outlaws again real soon."

"Thanks, Doctor. I appreciate your help." Charley shook his hand gently so as not to aggravate his left shoulder. "Why did I pass out after the bullet struck?"

"That's a fairly new discovery in medicine called shock. Even a minor injury can cause such a drop in blood pressure that a person looses consciousness or even dies, but you're young and healthy. So you just lost consciousness for a few seconds. If that shot had been direct on, it would have entered your lung and probably your heart."

After the doctor left, Charley lay back on the pillow. Mr. Sittel at the Elk House had insisted on giving him lodging without charge. He said it was the least he could do to help the lawmen who came to tame the Indian country. Charley thought about the shot that had nearly taken his life. Abe and the Indian lad had been there for him. *Thank you, God, for your protection.*

Tyne had sent a telegram to Fort Smith and also to Salina. She would worry until he got home, but at least she would know he was all right.

As he rested, he reflected on his life, grateful that he had made it this far in the marshal's service. Three years was the average length for a deputy due to either injury or over-work. Most resigned to go back to a peaceful, non-threatening existence. As he had promised when Will Ayers was murdered, he would be the best law enforcement officer he could be. He would use these couple of days to inquire of Mr. Sittel and Mr. McAlester about the region and its residents, getting to know the people he may have to work with in the future.

After a good night's rest, he struggled to dress - his inability to raise his left arm caused some difficulty, but he managed to wiggle into a blue denim shirt and get somewhat presentable before he went down for breakfast.

A young lady smiled at him as he approached the dining room. "Deputy Barnhill, how are you feeling? Better, I hope."

"Much better, thank you," he replied as his eyes roved over the room. Red checkered tablecloths on all the tables presented a bright and cheery atmosphere. Mr. Sittel's establishment reflected a homey German taste.

With a slight curtsy she motioned to the empty room. "Please be seated wherever you wish. May I get you some coffee?"

He seated himself at a table that offered a view of the rail yard and depot. "Yes, thank you. Is Mr. Sittel available?"

"My father is in his office. I'll let him know you would like to speak with him."

The menu was written on a chalk board above the counter. Steak, of course, was prominent as well as wild turkey, prairie chicken, and venison. Side dishes consisted of potatoes, squash, corn, cabbage and beans, even the Indian dish, Tom Fuller, (made of fermented corn).

The young lady returned for his order. " What would you like?"

"Steak and potatoes with biscuits will do for now."

"If you come down for dinner or supper later in the day, the Elk House kitchen, run by my mother, is known for its dried fruit cobblers and German dumplings," Miss Sittel offered.

Drinking his second cup of coffee after cleaning his plate, he watched his benefactor move across the dining room. Edward Sittel's medium stature covered by a dress shirt struggling to get out of its suspenders moved with a lightness of feet in low cut shoes. Charley rose to shake his hand feeling the strength of his own grip returning.

The owner had a thick German accent. "Deputy Barnhill. So glad to see you up and about." Charley gestured to him to have a seat which he did with a quick look around to make sure there was no one else waiting to talk to him. "I apologize for the delay in seeing you. When the northbound passenger train from Denison is expected, we are very busy while it's here."

"I've thought of moving closer to the rail lines, " Charley explained.

The German ran his hand through his thinning hair line - an irregular scar that moved into his temple disturbed the traces of gray. "What would you like to know?"

"How long have you lived here and what can you tell me about the future prospects of McAlester?"

"I came here after discharge from the Union Army. That's where I got this scar. I served in the Indian Territory and liked it very much. There are three groups of people living in these parts. The first are the full blood Choctaws who live mostly out in the woods to the east. They're peaceable and keep to themselves, living as most of the Choctaws do - growing just what they need and killing just what they can eat. They do lease some of their land for farming. The immigrant workers are a rowdy lot when they get their pay checks, but since Indian Country is supposedly dry, they have a hard time getting into too much trouble. They bring in their families and try to make a good life for themselves. The cowboys from the ranches to the west and south do not cause much trouble either. Gunfights happen, but no more than usual for this territory. "

Charley spoke after a few seconds. "I was thinking of McAlester as a location for a deputy marshal's office. It's halfway between Paul's Valley in the center of the Creek Nation and Ft. Smith."

"Until an east-west railway corridor is developed, you will have to make the two week trip from Paul's Valley in a wagon. We have a telegraph office which helps immensely."

"Well, thank you very much for the information."

Mr. Sittel rose and bowed slightly to him with a click of his heels. Must have been in the German Army too.

Charley leaned back from the table and groaned from the bounteous meal. He was not used to this amount of food. Deciding to look up McAlester before going to his room, he found him in his store entering figures into a day book.

McAlester rose and greeted him. "Hello, Deputy Barnhill, Glad to see you up and about. What can I do for you?"

"I want to thank you for taking care of my horse at the livery. I wasn't doing too well when I arrived yesterday."

"Certainly. The doc says you're a lucky young man."

"God's will, more likely. I talked to Mr. Sittel over at the Elk House. I'm thinking of using this area as a hub for my assigned territory. "

"It would be most beneficial to have a deputy marshal living in the area. Right now, if any trouble comes up, we have to telegraph to Fort Smith for assistance and it takes several days for an officer to arrive."

" Marshal Boles would like to see more of the officers living in the Indian country, rather than around Fort Smith for that same reason."

McAlester moved to a map of the Territory hanging on the wall behind him placing his finger on the rail depot and sweeping his hand around the area. "I know that if you chose to live here, it would help the whole area develop and become more attractive to settlers."

"Thanks for your help. Do you have any 44.40 cartridges? I shot up a good amount in the fight we had with the horse thieves. I need one box."

"That will be fifty cents. Come see me before you leave and we'll settle up your livery bill."

He went to his room, exhausted from all the activity, climbing the stairs with a measured step. He hoped to get his old bounce back. He hated laying around.

He slept though the night with the help of the sleeping potion the doctor had left him and felt well-rested the next morning. The doctor came by his room about three o'clock to check his wound and seemed satisfied with the results.

"I'll release you to get on a horse in two more days, but no lifting or swinging that arm for any reason. Do you need more laudanum to sleep tonight?"

"No, I think I can get through the night all right."

After the doctor closed the door, Charley listened to his steps slip down the stairs; he decided to write Salina a letter. He could post it and it would get on the northbound train and then on a mail stagecoach to Kully-cha-ha. It would take a week for her to get it, but he would still be gone for three more weeks if the posse stayed on schedule.

Dearest Darling Salina,

I know you have been quite concerned since you received the telegram from Tyne. I assure you I am well and mending fast. The doctor has released me to ride in two days. I am taking the time to rest and to make some decisions about our future. I will discuss all this with you when I get home. The posse will be out through the middle of next month. I will keep you informed if anything changes. I have met some very nice people here in McAlester. It is a little town I think you would like. Give my love to all of the children and pray for all of us, that we will continue to be safe and successful in our quest for the fugitives we seek. Abe is doing well and is such an asset to me and the other members of this posse. My thoughts are with you.

Fondly, your devoted husband, Charley

He took the letter down stairs, and posted it at the front desk to be put on the next train to Muskogee. The western sky, uncommonly dark and ominous, caught his attention as he walked to the livery to check on Billie. The big horse chewed grain and swished his tail at the afternoon fly population, but he displayed a curious agitation, moving to and fro inside his stall. Charley patted its thick neck and murmured soothing commands to settle the horse.

As he walked back to the hotel, he strained against the wind which swirled through the yard in a ferocious mix of dust and tumbleweeds. Hail started to fall from the rising black cauldron. He hoped this would not get worse; twisters were often present in these dark clouds, hidden from view by the reduced visibility.

"Miss, just in case this storm gets nasty, where's your storm cellar?" he asked the attendant at the front desk.

"The entrance is just behind the kitchen door in the back. If we need to go down, I'll come knock on your door." The girl turned to watch the falling hail with some concern. She ran to secure the window sashes and bolt the door closed so it would not blow open and rip off its hinges.

He went to his room to rest as the doctor had ordered and slept for a few hours before he was awakened by the sound of heavy hail. He glanced at his pocket watch which showed about seven p.m. The hail increased in volume and the wind began to howl with a force that shook him from his bed. He peeked out at the rail yard.

The cattle in the holding pens moved about, stomping and clicking horns together. Lightning bolts descending out of the clouds hit close to the railroad and on all sides of the little settlement. The deafening thunder split the sky with unending force. *This could be bad.* He slung his coat over his good shoulder, strapped on his Colt and grabbed his Winchester. As he descended the stairs, the young lady was covering her ears with her hands. He grabbed her by the arm.

"Are there other guests here?"

"No, sir. The evening train from Denison has not come in yet."

"Get in the cellar, NOW!"

He dragged the shaking girl toward the back door and poked his head in the kitchen, gesturing to Mrs. Sittel to follow. She had dropped her bread dough and was sobbing into her apron. At Charley's instruction, she grabbed her bonnet and a lantern.

As he thrust open the back door, he saw it - a twister about two miles to the southwest moving toward the rail road tracks with frightening speed. The sound was horrendous, like a freight train out of control.

"Get in, quick." Charley threw open the cellar door and pushed the women into the dark interior. The mother was shaking and crying.

"Oh, where is my Ed and my Fritz? Please, Gott, help us. "

He took the lantern from Mrs. Sittel and lit the wick. The light helped allay some of their fear. The sounds from overhead were terrorizing, the hotel groaning and creaking. Just then, the cellar door flung open and the proprietor and his son jumped in, both out of breath and ashen-faced.

His wife grabbed them and began to cry hysterically.

Ed Sittel shouted above the storm."It is OK Helga, it will be all right. I built this storm cellar very, very strong. The walls are reinforced with river stone and covered with two feet of gravel for drainage,"

They huddled together in the small interior, Charley wondering if the door would hold against the fierce force of the twister. It took several minutes for the center of the storm to pass near the hotel. He could hear the screams of cattle stampeding in terror and knocking down the holding pens. He bowed his head and prayed. Dear Lord, protect us from this storm. Keep everyone safe.

After minutes of breathless and fearful agony, he could tell the noise was gradually diminishing and the rain torrents had reached a peak. Water seeped in around the door frame. He found himself sitting with his boots in a foot of ice cold water.

The women sobbed into their aprons, their feet and skirts gathered up under them. The men sat grim-faced and silent, their eyes cast down with fear and doubt. He knew it was too soon to check outside. They needed to allow the storm to fully resolve to avoid getting hit by a secondary twister running in a line with the first.

After a half hour had passed, the rain turned into a silent drizzle and the winds decreased to a whistle.

He looked over at Mr. Sittel. "Is it safe to open the cellar door now?"

"Yes, go ahead," he replied in a husky, quiet voice.

Charley unlatched the cellar door. When he attempted to push it open, it would not budge. Something had fallen against it.

"I can't push on the door because of my shoulder wound. Can you and your son try to open it while I hold the bar up?"

Ed and Fritz were husky men, and they put their shoulders against the door. The first effort raised the it only a few inches, allowing him to see that it was held by loose material, nothing they could not displace. Two more grunts and pushes and the door opened, grating against a tree limb that had fallen onto it.

As he climbed out of the cellar, he sucked in his breath with shock and fear. The area around them seemed to have been crushed with a giant hand, trees uprooted and thrown in every direction. Bricks from the hotel lay scattered about in heaps. The hotel, store and depot had no roofs, though the walls were still standing amongst the litter and debris. The livery resembled a pile of kindling wood. The cow pens were empty and trampled down by the terror-stricken cattle. Dead cattle lay about the yard.

The warehouse seemed less damaged, though one of the walls leaned precariously on its side with the roof trusses bent down to the ground. The warehouse workers climbing out of their cellar stood frozen by the scene of devastation. The station agent was no where to be seen.

"Is everyone accounted for? "Charley asked.

"The railroad agent's still missing." John McAlester replied.

"Let's spread out and look for him. Where's his storm cellar?" Charley asked.

McAlester led Charley to the north side of the depot building. There was a piece of roof laying over the cellar door. Sittel and McAlester moved it with some effort. As they did, they heard banging on the door.

"Help! Someone help me. I'm trapped!" A muffled cry came from behind the door. When they opened it, a white-faced railroad agent with his hat still securely on his head, emerged from the cellar, like a long-necked crane, peering around with caution looking for the predator that had taken his depot roof.

"Wow, where is my train? It's supposed to be arriving any minute."

Mr. McAlester explained. "The tracks are covered with downed trees for miles. We need to get a wood-cutting party to clear the tracks. That will be our only means of help." Deputy Barnhill, could you take charge of the clean up around here? I'll take some of my men to start clearing the tracks. The telegraph wires are down. "

He organized two teams of four men each to clear the rubble from the buildings and organize the water and food supply into one central location in the strongest part of the warehouse. That was the only safe building for everyone to stay in for the meantime. Amazingly, one small cabin and lone pine tree south of the depot appeared unscathed.

After that was started, he went to look for Billie. There was no sign of his carcass near what remained of the livery. Hopefully, his animal instincts had taken over and he had made a run for it. All of the animals from the livery were missing.

The topsy-turvy debris revealed the violence of the storm. An oak tree stood upright in the field unharmed, and next to it a whole row of huge red cedars uprooted and tossed about like kindling. A harness with all rings and reins attached was wrapped around one of the cedars, as if a giant hand had tied it neatly into a bow.

About a mile to the north, he found the first of several horses that had been killed, picked up from the livery or rail yard and carried aloft in the giant funnel. They seemed to be teams that had been hitched to wagons.

Just as he was about to turn back, he heard a familiar whiny. Billie emerged from the debris of the cedars dragging a fence post and barbed wire that were entangled in his tail and left hoof. Billie had bolted out of the livery and busted his way through the railroad fence to escape. He had some deep cuts where the wire had caught his leg, but other than that he seemed intact.

"Oh, Billie, you ole son-of-a-gun. I knew you were too smart for that storm. Come on, let's get you some oats and a bucket of water." He led his horse across the debris-ridden fields toward what was left of McAlester. *What a day. I guess Salina won't get my letter after all.*

Old original cabin in McAlester

James Jackson McAlester, later lieutenant governor of Oklahoma

Chapter 13

Heaven's Calling

An orchestration of hammers ripped open Charley's eyes. Why was he still in bed? He forced his legs to the floor and remembered he was in a tent pitched outside the ruins of the Elk House. After splashing water on his stubble-covered cheeks, he revived enough to reach for his clothes, stumbling into them, his shoulder screaming at him to stop.

The telegram from Tyner Hughes protruded from his vest pocket.

Be at Muskogee on the 1st of June. Tyne

It had taken several days to repair the telegraph lines. He had spent the time helping with the huge task of clean up. The news had been grim, especially for Krebs; 21 dead, 42 injured and 40 houses destroyed.

To meet Tyne's request, it would take two days of steady riding north along the Old Army Road. He needed to leave right after breakfast.

"Good morning, Deputy Barnhill," a cheerful voice called from outside the tent. He pulled back the tent flap and stepped out. The young lady from the Elk House held out a breakfast tray.

"Thank you, miss. Do you know where my saddle gear is?"

"Pa retrieved it from the livery ruins late last night. It should be over by the corral."

He found his gear and saddled Billie, fighting a feeling he could not explain. *I need to get home as soon as possible. I'll tell Tyne I need to go straight home, if he doesn't need me to go to Ft. Smith with him.*

The trip was grueling. He could only gallop for a few minutes before his shoulder began to ache. The next day at the outskirts of Muskogee, he pulled into the camp of two wagons in a meadow of wild flowers. More than a dozen prisoners sat on the ground behind the wagons, their tin plates filled with beans and corn bread. Some looked like they needed a good meal and a couple had bandages on various body parts. All were secured with handcuffs.

The armed guards that Tyne had hired sat nearby. He recognized one of the guards from Skullyville near his home.

"Howdy, Mr. McCoy. I see you got roped into this detail again." He greeted his friend with a handshake.

"Good to see you, Charley. I heard you had a close one out there."

"The Lord and an Indian boy's expertise with a rifle saved me."

Taking care to step well around the prisoners, he found his friend seated on a rotting cedar.

A sparkle of joy lit up Tyne's face as he pumped Charley's hand making him wince. "Charley! Good to see you. Ready to do some tracking? We still have warrants for two toughs that disappeared into the Cherokee Nation. It may take a few more days to find them."

With those words, he knew that Tyne needed him. It was critical that the guards, Dan and James, stay with the twenty prisoners. He could not leave yet.

"Sure, I'm ready to go. Just need a bite to eat."

Dan handed him a plate heaped with hot food. As he took the first bite, Abe came around the log and sat down beside him.

"It looks like you're on the mend. Feel like a little more riding today? The two men we are seeking are holed up over by Fort Gibson. We have a couple of scouts willing to lead us."

"I'm up to it unless it requires handling a Winchester. I can't shoulder it just yet."

"I'll take care of that. Just back me up with your Colt."

It was noon of the following day when the three lawmen followed the scouts to a two room cabin nestled against a hillside. Charley surveyed the dwelling, a single window, a porch in front and a lean-to in back. The clearing in front of the cabin was fifty yards across, the back of the cabin surrounded by thick trees and brush.

Charley's attention shifted to a stocky Cherokee moving toward them, his hands above his head. One of the scouts interpreted the man's words for the lawmen. "This here is Black Crow. It's his cabin and his family is inside."

Tyne shifted his weight in the saddle and fixed his gaze on Black Crow. "We've been following the two men who just rode up and went into your cabin. Are they Black Ben and Osey Hansen?"

The scout spoke in a low guttural voice. "He says they're friends of his. He thinks they'll come out if he talks to them. He wants his wife and children out of the cabin before you make a move."

A face appeared in a crack of the door as it opened to hear the messenger. A woman and three small children pushed through the door under the man's arm, running until they were well clear of the area.

The door slammed shut as Black Crow turned back, hurrying along on quick bare feet. He pointed to the scouts as he delivered the message.

The interpreter explained. "They won't come out unless we, the scouts, are sent away since we are their enemies."

Tyne scowled at the humble dwelling. "Have Black Crow try once more to tell them to come out. You and your partner move back out of sight."

After a few minutes, Charley glanced at his pocket watch; fifteen minutes had passed since the man had returned and disappeared into the cabin.

Black Crow came out, hoping across the yard to the lawmen. He waved his arms and shook his head. "No come out," he said in broken English.

Charley and Abe moved to either side of the yard at Tyne's instructions. "Spread out. Don't shoot unless you have to."

Charley sought the cover of a white oak thick enough to stop a 45 caliber slug. This stand-off was the last choice. You had a fifty-fifty chance of coming out alive yourself, but letting a fugitive get away would require tracking him down again, likely with the same results.

Loud prolonged whoops came from inside the cabin. He figured that meant the Cherokees were going into their "warrior" attack mode. Something would happen soon. He checked his Colt and spun the cylinder, holding it with a loose grip alongside his knee.

A man jerked open the door, Winchester held at his side, and ran to the steps. His long braids flapped above his shoulders as he bolted toward the tree line behind the cabin. His partner appeared, running in the opposite direction. Charley's concern was that both would escape while their attention was divided. They had only seconds to stop them or loose them in the forest. But none of them would shot a man in the back.

In a loud voice Tyne called out. "Stop and throw down your rifles." Neither runner missed a step.

The lawmen opened fire, kicking up dirt ahead of each running figure in an effort to stop them. The man closest to the trees turned and sent a shot that knocked splinters out of the tree at the level of Abe's head. Another shot from the Indian was even closer. Abe and Tyne fired in unison and the man spun around onto his back.

Seeing his buddy down, the whiskey bootlegger took refuge in the forest. Charley sent several shots toward the hideout. He heard a yell of pain and the brush parted as the man fell out.

He approached his opponent as Tyne came up beside him, his Winchester at the ready. The man struggled to get to his knees, blood flowing from his left hip. His eyes, the desperate look of a trapped animal, let Charley know he was still dangerous as a rattlesnake.

It was nightfall when they reached camp, tired and hungry. Dan tended to the prisoner's wounds, cleaning and bandaging them as best he could.

"This fella with the hip wound will have to stay in the wagon. I think the bleeding has stopped but the bullet's still in there. The doc in Muskogee will have to dig it out. Oh, yeah, Charley, a messenger brought you a telegram from Muskogee," Dan handed him the yellow form

Charley's heart fluttered as he read the message.

Come home. Joey bad sick.

Salina

He passed the paper to Abe whose eyes went to the brief message. "It's too late for you to ride. You better get some sleep and start at first light. I'll help Tyne take the prisoners to Fort Smith tomorrow. "

Facing two full days of hard riding to cover the eighty miles to home, he was ready at daybreak. Abe was there to help him saddle up.

"I'll be praying for you, little brother. Send us a telegram as soon as you know anything," Abe said.

Urgency drove him to push Billie to his limit. His shoulder turned into a burning ache after hours in the saddle. He bit his lip and concentrated on getting there before it was too late. Now he knew what unceasing prayer meant, his mind never stopping the flow of pleas heavenward.

His anxiousness increased as he rode over the familiar terrain of home. The house appeared normal, but where were his fun-loving children? He bounded from Billie's back at a run, not bothering to hitch up.

The door slammed against the wall as he jerked it open and crossed the parlor to the boys' room in seconds. Salina sat beside a pale, sleeping figure holding his hand. He breathed a sigh of relief. *He's still alive, but for how long?* Salina rose with tears in her eyes and hugged him.

"The doctor says his lungs are full of fluid. We had to stay in the cellar during a severe storm and it was really wet."

He sat down and took his son's hand, another storm victim. *Please, Lord. Take me instead. I'll do anything to save him.*

Salina wrapped her arms around Charley's shoulders. "You look beat. Would you like something to drink or eat? How's your wound?"

"I'm all right, maybe in a bit. Why don't you go rest? You look pretty tired. I can take over for a while. Where are Henry and Minnie?"

"Your father came and got them three days ago. He brings them over daily. Little Minnie doesn't understand what's happening, but Henry does. They're very sad."

As dusk darkened the room, Charley lit the oil lamp and laid his hand on Joey's out-stretched hand. The youngster labored and gasped, a bad omen. His eyelids fluttered open and he saw his father.

"Hello, son." Charley whispered.

"Hi, Pa. Did you get the bad guy who shot you?"

"Yes, son. You rest. I'm here now."

"OK." His son's eyes closed in relief.

Why did I waste time going to Muskogee? My son, my son.

Salina brought him some supper and a little soup for the boy who was too weak to open his mouth and swallow. As his head lay on the pillow, the pallor of death crept over his youthful cheeks. Charley prayed and watched as his son slipped quietly into the arms of the angels a couple of hours later. His peaceful countenance was etched in Charley's memory as heaven's gate opened wide for this eight year-old boy. *He's too young to die, why, Lord?*

Unnoticed by him Mrs. Davis had appeared shortly before Joey died. He watched as she washed the empty shell that once was his son and placed him in his best church clothes. Salina was unable to touch the stiff little form without breaking into tears. Joey's head rested on a soft pillow, his favorite toy, a brass whistle Charley had brought him from Fort Smith, placed in his hands across his chest.

Mrs. Davis wiped the corners of her eyes with her apron and sniffed. "I'll be back first thing in the morning with some breakfast for you. Please try to rest."

In his grief Charley clung to Salina for several hours. The cares of the world were nothing now. How could the birds keep on singing and people keeping on living and loving when his son lay dead? Why had he not seen that each life is precious and every breath a blessing? Whether he lived a day, a year, a decade or several, this awful memory would never fade. Never.

The next day neighbors came with quiet words and gestures to comfort the grieving parents. Women carried bright bouquets of flowers that filled the front room, a simple reminder of the source of life, the men holding their hats by the brims and shuffling their feet as they offered condolences. Death was an everyday matter in this country, but love for the grieving family was offered in abundance. Charley's church family kept the long table outside covered with provisions to feed everyone that came by.

His parents and brother were indispensable. They took care of the necessary decisions, seeing that the chores were tended by friends and neighbors. Abe and Amanda arrived the following day for the funeral. He had left the posse as soon as he got the message. David Samuel and his family came from Briartown. Family was important and the Barnhills stuck together through all of life's trials.

The day of the burial, the Choctaws came and performed a 'cry'. They cried out to the spirits and asked for safe and swift passage for the departed spirit, dropping pieces of corn bread into the open coffin, so the traveler would have provisions for his journey in search of the Great Spirit. The Choctaws were devout Christians but still had old ways integrated into their practices.

Alford Barnhill conducted the funeral for his grandson, praying for his departed soul, looking at family and friends in supplication. It was hard to bury a young child at such a tender age. He had done so for five of his own children. At times like this, he could only cling to his Lord and pray that His Will be done.

"Heavenly Father, we beseech you to comfort those that grieve. You are the Great Comforter. You promise us that we all have a place at your banquet table,. The corn bread of our friends symbolizes the promise of that great supper. Joey brought immense joy and blessings to our family. Help us to remember that the things of this earth are temporary, but your promises are eternal. Dear Lord, accept this little one into thy fold. We know that at the Great Resurrection, you will raise this little one to a glorified body as you did for your son, Jesus. Wrap your arms around us and comfort us with your love. We look forward to the day we will join Joey in heaven. In your Son's name, Amen."

Charley bowed his head as he grasped his wife's hand. He wiped at the tears that covered his cheeks with the back of his other hand. *Lord, how can we go on? Please give me your strength for I have none.*

Chapter 14

The Gathering

Sorrow wrapped its icy fingers around Charley's everyday routine. His grief was a heavy, dark pool without depth or limits. He threw himself into his daily responsibilities in order to smother the memory of his lost son, calling on God to ease his pain with no relief.

He watched his children struggling with the loss in their own way - rambunctious and loud, trying to get his attention. Though three months had passed, they could not talk of Joey without tears or long moments of awkward silence. The end of the harvest and the beginning of the school year remind them even more of the one person who would not be walking to school. Salina's pale face shrouded in grief rarely broke a smile. Her female problems continued to weaker her disposition. What could he do to help his family love and live again?

As he worked in the tack room that warm September morn, he heard the gentle gait of a single horse. Peering out of the barn door, he saw his father slide out of the saddle.

"Pa, how are you doing? Come into the shade and set a spell. Salina just made up some peppermint tea." He greeted his father with a handshake and a forced smile. He didn't feel like smiling, but it was an inborn reaction to someone he loved and respected.

Alford Barnhill wore a white clerical collar under his vest which accented his tanned features. The trousers with blue and gray pin stripes offset the scarecrow appearance of his long arms protruding out of a well-used jacket.

"I'm doing well and your mother sends her greetings. She would've come but she's drying berries and apples. "

"You look like you 're on official church business today, all dressed up in your preaching togs."

Alford removed his hat and sat down on the bench alongside the front door. "I'm headed to Poteau to visit the Baptist missionary superintendent. They're planning the preaching program for the harvest gathering of the Choctaws. I have been asked to speak at a united meeting of Presbyterians, Methodists and Baptists."

Charlie felt his heart soften. He loved the Choctaws and was encouraged by their faithfulness. "The Choctaws grasp the meaning of Christianity much more than the other tribes. Do you need some help? I don't have a trip planned for couple of weeks."

"That's why I dropped by. I'd like you and Salina to come to Fulsom Chapel for the preaching. Abe, Amanda, and your mother will be there, as well as Jimmy. He's eighteen now and wants to follow in your footsteps."

"And face being bushwhacked at every curve in the road?"

"You can understand how he feels. He worships you and Abe for all you've accomplished. Besides, you and Salina need to get your lives on track again, for the sake of your remaining children. Mourning and grieving will be your lot for a while yet, but the children need a fun-filled diversion."

Just as Charley was about to answer, Salina appeared on the porch with two tall glasses of peppermint tea.

"Good morning, Father Barnhill. How are you today?" She passed him a glass. Charley took the other from her hand, his fingers lingering on hers momentarily. The look in her eyes still covered deep sadness.

"Pa is here to ask us to attend the Choctaw Gathering. He's going to be preaching."

Salina bowed her head and sighed. "I don't know if I feel up to being around people right yet."

"We have time to think about it. The Gathering isn't until the end of next week."

Alford looked up from his tea. "Salina, I feel it would do you and the children a world of good to get out and be amongst other people for a change. You live a pretty quiet life out here, miles from your nearest neighbors. "

"I'd like some time to think about it. Would that be alright?" Salina said, turning back toward the house.

"Certainly, my dear." Her father-in-law put his arm around her shoulder and gave her a gentle squeeze. "Well, thanks for the tea. I must be on my way in order to make Poteau before nightfall. God bless you, my children."

He watched his father ride out of sight then turned to Salina, but found she had slipped back into the house. He found her sitting in the rocking chair, her head resting against the back, her eyes closed.

"Let's think about the offer and then bring it up with the children at supper," he suggested.

"Alright. I think I'll go rest for a few minutes before I have to start cooking supper. The children are playing out in the pasture."

When he heard the bell ringing on the back porch, he thought about his wife. She spent most of her days cooking, washing and sewing. She never failed to have supper on the table promptly at six o'clock. In the summer, that gave plenty of time to enjoy the long hours of evening. In winter it meant getting the dishes done and then sending the children straight to bed.

At the silent table he cleared his throat and heard utensils clatter to the plates. There was no horse play at meal time like there used to be. His father was right. Henry and Minnie needed to be able to visit and play with other children.

"Your Grandfather Barnhill came by today. He's invited us to attend a Choctaw Gathering next week. "

"Yea. Oh, please Pa. Can we go?" The chorus of small voices joined in unison. *Well, I guess I have my answer.*

The week passed quickly. Arrangements had to be made. Charley asked Mr. Davis to send one of his boys over to milk the cow each day and feed the animals. They would keep the milk as payment, a benefit to their large family.

Salina did not welcome the trip as she went through the motions of preparation. She would not disappoint her children with a sullen, downcast mood. She felt the sin of selfishness lurking in her thoughts and words. Maybe Father Barnhill was right - it would do them all good to go visiting.

She worked on the food they would need. "Henry, go to the barn and fetch me a small milking pail. Fill it with clean straw. I'll need it to carry the eggs. Charley, I need a small pen to carry two or three chickens."

Charley brushed her cheek with his lips. "Yes, Ma'am."

"Minnie, you can help me fill this wooden box."

Flour, salt, sugar, coffee, molasses and lard lay on the table within the children's reach though Minnie still had to stand on tip toes to get the lighter packages. When they had finished, Salina went to the door of the storm cellar and raised it.

"Stand here and I'll hand up the garden things we'll need."

They helped her fill gunny sacks with corn, beans, squash and onion. They giggled and laughed as they drug the heavier items to the wooden box.

"Thank you , you're such big helpers." She kissed them on their heads and scooted them outside. "Now, run along and play while I do my baking."

She could feel her spirits lightening despite her reluctance. Maybe the trip would take her mind off the constant picture of Joey in his coffin which was ever before her, day and night.

Several pans of corn bread and wrapped sides of smoked bacon in paper and cheese cloth came next in the food box. Snacks would be dried pecans, chestnuts, and berries. As she worked on the pies made out of fresh apples from the orchard, she prayed. *Please lift these bonds of grief off my shoulders, Lord. I give them to you.* The food preparations completed, she looked at everything with satisfaction, certain that she had not forgotten anything important. All was well.

The night before they were to leave, everyone was too excited to sleep. At dawn, Charley hitched up the team and brought the wagon to the front of the house. Roads were terrible in the Nations and wagons were not the best means of travel. They were heading to Fulsom Chapel at Pocola which was eight miles as the crow flies, but fifteen miles going by the only passable trails. It would take them at least a full day or more to get there depending on the condition of the trails. He was glad he rode this country day after day.

He moved to the step up beside the wagon seat. "Alright children, where do you want your bed rolls, behind the wagon seat or where you can sit on them?"

Little Minnie responded in her sophisticated five year-old voice. "Okay, Pa, I want mine where I can lay on it."

Salina had already placed everything in the wagon, except her sour dough starter in a crock and her sun bonnet.

"I won't be comfortable without my bonnet. The sun can ruin a complexion in no time," she explained as he watched her tie the strings. She had beautiful cheeks and he was glad she worked to keep them that way. Most frontier women had prematurely dried out skin from the summer sun and the dry winds. She even had on light-weight gloves and long sleeves.

"Everyone ready to go?" he asked.

"Yes, Pa."

"Get up." Charley commanded the team, who also was anxious to go, having been in the harness for more than an hour.

They were able to get to a spot alongside the Poteau River by late afternoon to make camp for the night. The river flowed out of the larger Arkansas River just outside of Fort Smith and coursed southward past Poteau and then eastward into Arkansas. It's banks were shallow and the river bed narrow at this time of year. He chose a spot away from the river free of nocturnal bugs and forest critters.

He lay beside Salina on their pallet beneath the wagon clothed only in his long johns and thought of the future. Losing Joey had made him more aware of how unpredictable life is. The Lord is in control, but unexpected events are a part of life. What could he do to protect his family?

"Darlin'?" he whispered to see if she was still awake.

"Yes, what is it?" Salina's voice was sleepy but clear.

"I just want you to know how much I love you and the children. If anything should happen to me while I'm marshaling, my brothers will give you all the assistance you need."

"Oh, Charley. Don't think of such things happening. You'll be alright. You are an experienced deputy. I know I had my doubts about the dangers of your job, but I can see you are careful."

"Yes, I am but lawmen are killed or seriously injured by the unexpected. I just want you to be prepared if something should happen to me. Promise me that you'll turn to my brothers if I should die. We've all talked about these things and have agreed that if anything happens to one of us, the others will step in and take care of the family."

"I promise, honey. Now, how about getting some rest?" She snuggled up to him in the quiet of the night, the chorus of the crickets and tree frogs a soothing backdrop.

The trip from their camp to Fulsom Chapel took only a couple of hours. They were joined by the Choctaws who came from miles around seemingly bringing everything they possessed. The women sat up straight in rocking chairs or bent willow chairs in the back of the wagons. They held parasols high above their heads and laughed at the scenery as they passed by.

An endless pack of dogs of all shapes, sizes and colors followed each family unit. As they met, the dog packs would get into it, the dominant dogs taking the lead. Soon, the lead dogs had scores of followers yelping and barking their way along. Every once in a while, a couple from the pack would break out and shoot out across the fields chasing rabbits or squirrels. The squirrel nests were high in the tops of the trees where no dog could go if the squirrel made the tree unharmed.

Henry pointed at the teeming mass of dog flesh. "Why so many dogs, Father?"

"That's their mobile food supply. If the Indians cannot get enough squirrel, rabbit or turtle, they resort to dog stew."

"Yuk!" Henry covered his mouth and screwed up his face. "I'm glad we left Mollie at home." Mollie was a young coon hound Henry had adopted in the spring.

Fulsom Chapel stood on the edge of the small settlement of Pocola surrounded by open range and a large field of high grass for feeding all the livestock put out to graze on tethers or hobbles. The Choctaws had permanent camp houses made of split logs and cooked over big fires in the yards.

Long tables of rough planking sat in the clearing. The dogs foraged for themselves, so food had to be protected - hung up in trees or locked in wooden boxes. A couple of the older children guarded the food tables with horsetail switches swatting at flies which were fewer now that the temperature had fallen.

Charley negotiated his wagon through the campsites until he found his father's camp. His mother, Sarah, came out of the tent, a joyous greeting on her lips.

"Children, you-all are here finally. It's so good to see you. Come on in out of the sun." As was typical of most Georgia women, she squealed with delight as she hugged each grandchild and gave them a big kiss on the forehead or top of their head.

Alford appeared and greeted Henry with a gruff "How you, boy?" Turning to Minnie, he surveyed her from head to foot then reached down and picked her up, giving her a bear hug and kiss on the cheek.

"My, my, Minnie. You sure are growing up to look as pretty as your mama."

"Oh, Papaw, I love you," she replied in a shy voice.

Charley's younger brother, Jimmy, appeared from inside the tent. He was a tall and wiry young man, six feet four and two hundred pounds. He had to duck to get in and out of the tent. To stand up inside, he had to stand right at the tent pole in the center.

Before he could greet him, he heard a familiar voice behind him. "Well, it's about time you got here. You get stuck in the Poteau?" Brother Abe pounded him on the back.

He turned to grasp his hand and noticed Amanda standing behind her husband. Her eyes hit Charley about chin level.

"Amanda, dear." Salina came up and hugged her sister-in-law. "How are you?"

"I'm doing well. It's so good to see you all," Amanda said.

"Uncle Charley, Aunt Salina." It was Abe's daughter, Mollie. Now nine years-old, she was dressed in a pinafore and dress with ruffles and sashes. Side-laced shoes and cotton stockings finished the outfit. She had a large bow in her long hair.

He kissed her on the cheek and held her out at arm's length to measure her growth. Yup, at least two inches since Joey's funeral in July when he had last seen her.

The rest of the day was spent in preparing the campsite for the few days they would be there. Each child had a hammock swung between trees. The adults were in tents with a canvas porch.

The long food tables of the many Indian families were up. Each family would prepare food and bring it to the long table to share. This custom would be followed by Alford and his family also. That way a person could choose what he was comfortable with eating for each meal. There was always plenty and it was usually very good. Trenches were dug by the men for the hog roasting which would take all day and be the main fare for the final feast on Sunday after church services.

Charley rose at dawn and went to the stream to wash up. Others were already there. To give the women privacy, a large partition hung from the trees, giving them the necessary covering to disrobe and bathe. The women were very shy and moved quietly in and out of the secluded compound. The children, on the other hand, just jumped in the water, clothes and all, and then drip-dried in the sun. The men took off their shirts and washed everything from the waist up.

Choctaws with freshly washed faces appeared at the long tables to share breakfast which consisted of corn bread, game, hominy, prunes, butter, corn and oats. The men ate first, separate from the women and children.

Alford and his three sons were accorded seats of honor at the table with the church and tribal leaders.

"I would like to present to you my sons, Abe from Shady Point and Charles from Kully-cha-ha. You've already met James Alfred." Alford spoke in English to the man to his left, the church superintendent, who interpreted for the others.

Each man seated at the table rose and greeted them in Chahta, the Choctaw language.

"*Halito* (Hello) *Binili, (*Please, sit down)," the superintendent said in Choctaw.

"*Yakoke* (Thank you)", Charley replied in the little Chahta he knew.

The church superintendent, a bronzed specimen of the prairie with short hair and a cultured English vocabulary, lay his hand on the Bible before him as he spoke. "I understand, sirs, that you are part of the Federal law enforcement from Fort Smith."

"Yes, sir. We've been working in the Indian Territory for over four years."

"I'm sure that you will bring great honor to your family in your work. May God bless you and protect you in your travels."

"Thank you for your kindness, sir." Charley was over-whelmed by his kindness. Hope began to rise up in his chest again. How could some people be so kind and others so vicious?

"Pastor Barnhill, what is going to be the topic of your preaching tomorrow, if I may inquire?" the superintendent asked. He was a man of mature years, but a couple decades younger than the man he was addressing. His apparel mirrored that which Charley's father wore.

Alford put on his preacher voice so all could hear. "I feel that in these uncertain times, I would be remiss if I didn't preach on the last coming of our Lord. The Revelation of Jesus Christ should be an uplifting theme for everyone."

"Good choice. Pastor Fulsom, here, will be your interpreter. " The superintendent gestured to a man seated at his right, a dark-skinned visage with royal cheekbones and thin lips which curled into a welcoming smile. Charley was struck by his likeness to a painting he had seen in an old church in Fort Smith, a portrait portraying the suffering servant, Jesus.

Alford greeted the man. "Much obliged, sir. I understand I am following you in the preaching and you have the reputation of being mightily used of the Lord."

"My pleasure, Pastor Barnhill." His voice, when he spoke, was resonant and full. He turned his attention to Charley - his eyes seemed to peer into Charley's soul. What did he see? A broken heart that would never mend or a life fit for service that would never fade?

"Deputy Barnhill, I have heard of your efforts on behalf of my people. If I can help you in any small way, please call on me at any time."

Charley knew he had an ally in this gentle man of God. "Thank you sir. I will keep that in mind."

After the men had finished, the women prepared the tables for the women and children. Necessary dishes were replenished and more chairs added to accommodate the greater number of women. The children sat on the grass inside the compound in the shaded areas. They kicked and yelled when a dog came near sniffing at their plates.

Before the preaching, the men and women separated, each group adjourning to a quiet place for prayer. By the time they came back together at the church house, it was late afternoon.

A brush arbor in the front of the church had been built for the Gathering. A frame of poles supported tree branches laid across the top. Each corner of the speaking platform held a pile of rich pine knots and split pine. The pine knots would be laid on top of the poles and lit as dusk descended. Preaching of the Word went on all day and late into the night at these Gatherings.

Pastor Fulsom, a Methodist, spoke first and his message was welcomed by cheers and whoops from the assembled Choctaws. He moved through the prophecies of God's word with remarkable adroitness. As he wrapped up his three hour sermon, the audience showed as much attention to his word as when he had begun.

"And Moses was instructed by the Lord to lead the people out of Egypt into the land of milk and honey. In a similar manner, the United States government sent us away from our homes into a promised land, a land of milk and honey. Though it was an unsettled frontier, it proved to be a very fertile area. What seemed to be a catastrophe to our people, the Lord has turned into a blessing. Which one of us has any want in this bounteous land? If we want meat on our tables, we walk outside and shoot it. We don't have to ask for manna from heaven. God has provided for us in this land. Give praise to the Holy One of heaven for his glorious provisions and protection."

Charley listened to the men and women about him praying out loud and shouting as the spirit took them. A petite Choctaw woman prayed with her hands lifted up, tears streaming down her face. She approached the front and knelt at the "mourner's bench" where the repentant sinner came forward to mourn and grieve over his sins. The people already there cried out to God. One who came forward this time was Abe's daughter, Mollie, her young face abeam with the commitment she was making.

They sang the final hymn in Choctaw to the accompaniment of the pump organ. *"Blessed Assurance, Jesus is mine. Oh, what a foretaste of glory divine. Heir of salvation, purchase of God. Born of His Spirit. Washed in His blood. This is my story, this is my song; Praising my Savior all the day long This is my story, this is my song, Praising my Savior all the day long."*

He held Salina's hand as they sang. He felt the cold fingers of grief around his heart start to loosen. Maybe he could find hope and live a normal life again. He smiled down at his wife. Her eyes were misty. The children, sensing their parents mood, sat quietly without the normal wiggling and squirming.

As they walked back to their camp, he encircled Salina's arm in his. For the first time since Joey's funeral that simple gesture of intimacy overshadowed his terrible ache.

Reverend Willis Fulsom

Chapter 15

Deputy for Life

Charley leaned hard on the pliers cutting the nails on the left front shoe of his favorite horse. Riding for the court at Fort Smith wore out a lot of horse shoes.

"Pa," Henry stood in the door of the barn. "There's riders comin'."

"How many?"

"Looks like six or eight and they're in a hurry."

"I'll be right there." He rubbed the nail tips smooth with a file and dropped the hoof.

As he reached the front of the house, the first rider slid from his saddle. It was Deputy Columbus Ayers, younger brother of Willard Ayers,. "Charley, I'm getting up a posse to go after Deputy Beck's murderer. I'd like you to come along."

"Gimme me a minute." Charley said as he bounded up the stairs of the house and came out with his saddle bags. He kept them packed with all the things he needed on the trail so he was ready at a moments notice. A quick kiss and explanation was all he could give Salina. His mood was somber as the men pushed northwest on their march. Each murderer of an officer of the court had to be found and arrested as soon as possible, before they could disappear into the hinterlands of the Territory.

His thoughts turned to Addison Beck, one of the best deputies in the marshal's office. Beck had joined the deputy force the same year as Charley in 1879 and was always thinking about the best way to catch outlaws. He had worked the murder case of a Creek Indian, named Tu-al-is-to who had robbed and killed a man traveling through the Choctaw Nation in 1881. The murderer needed money to attend a dance and decided to follow his victim to a secluded spot where he shot him in the back of the head and stole $7.40.

The murdered man's brothers had offered a $200 reward for information leading to the killer who continued his life of crime until he was finally arrested by the Choctaw Indian Lighthorse Police on a charge of larceny and was sentenced to the whipping post in August of 1882. Marshal Beck knew this would be an ideal place to catch him. While Tu-al-is-to was on the whipping post he bragged how bad he was but the lashes compelled him to confess to all the killings he had committed. Four buttons sewn on his hat were in honor of the three Indians and one white man he had killed. The confessions given in front of a crowd of witnesses was enough for Beck to serve the warrant. The murderer was convicted and sent to the gallows in July of 1883.

Two weeks ago Beck and his guard, Lewis Merrit, had tried to capture two half-breed Indian-Negro thieves, John Bark and Johnson Jacks. The chase ended in the southern portion of the Cherokee Nation near Big Vienne, where they followed the fugitives into a cornfield. The officers were killed at point blank range. John Bark, critically wounded, was captured and died before he could stand trial. Johnson Jacks had escaped.

It was a long, dusty twelve hour ride to reach Big Vienne. The sun was about to fade from the horizon. Charley knew they had only a few minutes of day light left.

A lone rider appeared from the west. "Hello," said the stranger. "My name is Samuels. I am a neighbor. I was real sorry to hear what happened to your men here last month."

"I was told Jacks is hold up in this area," Ayers replied.

Samuels leaned forward in his saddle. "He's at Tom Bearpaw's house, about a half-mile up the lane there."

The lawman wheeled his horse. "Thank you! Come on, men."

In a short time the posse had the cabin surrounded. Charley stationed himself near the front door.

"Tom Bearpaw!" Ayers called out from behind a gate post. "This is Deputy Marshal C. C. Ayers. Your house is surrounded. We want Johnson Jacks."

The door opened a crack, and then swung wide. The old Cherokee came out, his arms stretched high.

Charley crouched low and sprang in the door, his pistol at the ready. Jacks was asleep on a pallet, a loaded and cocked Winchester at his side. He placed the barrel of his gun next to the murder's head and jerked the rifle away. Jacks awoke with a start and began to rise, feeling for where his rifle had been.

"Don't even think about it!"

The big Negro was wounded in the left breast and screamed as he was pulled up by two posse men. "That deputy shot me first and I passed out. I didn't know I had shot him. I didn't even know he was a law man. Shoot me now. Don't take me to that 'Hangin' Judge'!"

Ayers looked at Charley. "These Indians sure hate the thought of being hung. They figure it's okay for whites and other miscreants, but they would rather be shot."

Addison Beck
1845-1883

The two men descended the stairs at the front of the court house. Deputy Ayers turned to Charley.

"The Marshal will be swearing in a new batch of deputies on the first of February. I think you should start lawin' full time. We're really short-handed."

"I'll give it some serious thought," Charley said as he pocketed his pay and stepped up on his horse. "I need to talk to Salina about this. She's the one who will have to keep the place going without me. If she's willing, I'm ready".

The mid-January thaw came early to the Indian Territory in 1884. Although there was plenty of rain and occasional snow, the days were mostly bright and sunny. Charley felt the change as he rode the twenty miles from his home in Kully-cha-ha, Choctaw Territory to Fort Smith to be present for the 'swearing in' ceremony.

He surveyed the courtroom and found himself among the others that were taking the oath. Some, like him, already wore the Deputy Marshal badge; they were being sworn in for their second, third or perhaps fourth term. How many of these eager faces would take a bullet for the law? He knew half would and many would be killed in the process.

U.S. Marshal Valentine Dell stepped forward to administer the oath.

"Please rise, raise your right hand and repeat after me."

All hands went up with a scuffling of boots. Voices repeated in unison after Dell. "I do solemnly swear that I will faithfully execute all lawful precepts, directed to the Marshal of the Western District of Arkansas, under the authority of the United States, and true returns make, and in all thing well and truly, without malice or partiality, perform the duties of Deputy Marshal of the Western District of Arkansas during my continuance in said office, and take only my lawful fees, so help me God."

He sat down beside Tyne and Bass Reeves, the first Negro deputy in this former Confederate state. Federal laws over-ruled the state laws which kept segregation in the law enforcement community. Reeves could not read but he sure could track men.

Judge Parker, a black-robed figure of justice, entered the courtroom and took a seat behind his high paneled desk at the front of the courtroom. He took the opportunity to speak to the group of new deputies.

"Remember, in the performance of your assigned duties, the men for whom warrants are issued are not guilty of any crime until found so by a jury of their peers. It is your job to bring them in without injury. Mistreatment of prisoners will not be tolerated for any reason. However, your courage and bravery in the face of armed resistance will not be diminished if you use your wits instead of your guns to capture wanted men. May God watch over you and preserve you in your endeavors."

The Marshal moved through the group of new deputies handing out badges. "I've assignments for many of you right away. Stop by my office and see what we have."

Charley pinned the new style badge to his shirt as he walked across the hall to the Marshal's Office. A symbol of law, it could also be a bull's eye for those resisting arrest. Maybe he could make at least one peaceful arrest before noon.

"Barnhill." a smallish man behind the second desk in the office waved a folded sheet of paper. "We have a writ here for 'old Bill' Wilson. He was seen this morning going into the Bull's Head Saloon. He's wanted for selling whiskey.

Charley glanced at the writ and then put it into his coat pocket. Leaving the Marshal's Office, he walked down the boardwalk along Garrison Avenue. The reek of spilled beer, tobacco juice and smoke assaulted his nose as he entered the dark, dank hangout. A few cowboys lounged at the tables drinking and playing cards, a couple of men at the bar. All eyes turned in unison to the star on his vest. Charley noted the force of the symbol on their expressions though all returned to their past times.

He stood close to the bar, examining all the faces. The bartender, a large dark man with a handlebar mustache, came to where he stood. "What can I get you?"

"I'm looking for Bill Wilson."

The barkeep pointed to the back room. "He's been here since morning, bought several bottles of whiskey and then sat right down and tried to drink one. He's been doing a lot of bragging and paying for everything in cash."

"Where's he now?"

"He's sleeping it off. He always gets like this when he first comes back from the Nations."

"Anyone else back there?" Charley asked.

"Nope. I'm the only one working right now," replied the bartender.

Charley walked slowly down the bar, pushed the back door open and peered into the bleak room. On a cot lay a small man well past his prime. Dirty gray hair bristled under a ragged bowler hat, the brim of which were smashed flat on one side as he slept, sprawled face down. His right hand held tight to a pair of old dirty cloth saddle riders. Stepping closer, he could see the protruding tops of quart jars of whiskey inside the bags.

Without a sound he removed the handcuffs from his pocket and secured the man's hands behind him.

"Wha..." Bill stirred. "Hey! What's going on here?"

"You're under arrest for introducing whiskey into Indian Territory." He took the startled drunk by the underarm and stood him up. He slid the saddle riders over his shoulder and left the saloon with his prisoner stumbling along in front.

A group of young men gathered in a row of chairs in front of a general store eyed the deputy and his prisoner. One of them snickered and thrust out his foot, tripping the prisoner. Old Bill went down in a heap as a roar of laughter went up from the crowd. The startled owner of the errant foot found himself looking down the bore of a Colt .45 Peacemaker.

"You will not touch a prisoner in my custody," Barnhill said.

The sallow-faced young clerk screeched and squirmed under the aim of the pistol. "I'm sorry, deputy. It was an accident!" He rushed to the side of the prisoner and helped him to his feet. "I'm sorry," he said to the old bootlegger as he brushed him off.

Without another word, Charley took his prisoner under the arm and was on his way.

He left Fort Smith with high hopes. Giving up farming to take on marshaling as the sole support for his family was risky. Most deputies made less than $500 a year though he could make more if he picked up some rewards. Tyne and Bass Reeves were good at that. He would have to learn from them.

Abe put his back against the bureau and groaned with effort. It moved only a couple of feet. Making room for a new baby was tough work in the small room stuffed with a double bed, bureau, and night stand. The wool rug on the floor that had been a wedding gift from his parents was rolled to the side.

"Hello in the house." A familiar voice, Charley's voice, came through the bedroom window.

"Come on in." Abe shook hands with his brother. "How is the family doing?"

"Salina is wrapped up in canning and drying the garden surplus. Busy work keeps her mind off of Joey. Minnie has a little house for her doll and the kitten sleeps in it too. Henry's helping in the garden. They're pretty quiet. It'll take time."

Abe wiped his face and gestured at the disarranged furniture. "I could use your help. Amanda wants to be able to reach the baby during the night. The bed goes against the inside wall and the bureau against the opposite. Give me a lift on that end."

Straining under the weight of the bed frame, Charley grunted. "This maple bed is solid! "

Amanda appeared in the doorway with a tray. "I have a little reward for you fellas, a cup of sassafras tea and some biscuits and jam."

After they were seated on the porch, Charley took a bite out of his first biscuit. "Where's Mollie?"

"She went to the neighbors to visit. The baby kept fussing last night and we didn't get much rest. She's finding out babyhood is taxing."

As he sipped the tea, Abe watched a vulture circling in the afternoon heat, seeking it's provisions in the fruit of the ground below, and waited for Charley to speak.

" I'm heading to Pocola to visit with Tyne. Our writs will be ready tomorrow, if that's not too soon for you."

"That's OK."

Charley gave a farewell peek at the new baby. "Take care of little Jenette. Minnie will want to hold her as soon as she sees her."

Abe could sense his brother's broken heart on seeing a healthy newborn when he had buried his son less than a year ago. God had sustained him in *his* sorrow when their little girl of only a few months had died last year from croup. He bowed his head and prayed knowing that no power in the world could answer his prayers, only the Eternal Power above. A bright future for his children, one of peace and health, the ability to take each day's troubles and blessings as they came, allowing tomorrow to take care of itself - what more could he ask?

I Charles Barnhill , do solemnly swear that I will faithfully execute all lawful precepts directed to the Marshal of the Western District of Arkansas, under the authority of the United States, and true returns make, and in all things well and truly, and without malice or partiality, perform the duties of Deputy Marshal of the Western District of Arkansas during my continuance in said office, and take only my lawful fees, so help me God.

Charles Barnhill

Sworn to and subscribed before me this 1st day of February 1884

Stephen Wheeler Clerk

by [illegible]

Charles Barnhill's Swearing-in Papers
Febuary 1, 1884

I.T. Deputy Marshal Badge

Chapter 16

Ambush

The hay and dust of the livery stable floor swirled in Charley's face. He fought the urge to cough as he tried to get his hands around the reins - Billie was ready to go, tossing his head in eagerness. Beside him Abe struggled with his mare in the dim light. A lone milk wagon plodded through the section known as "The Row", brothels on each side of Front Street disguised in colorful houses which beckoned to the steamboat passengers. He was never tempted to explore the interiors because he had the most beautiful woman in the world waiting for him at home. The lantern still burned in the Marshal's office as he stepped inside.

"Good morning." Chief Deputy Barnes greeted him with a smile that stretched his mustache to the corners of his face. Barnes had a demanding job and he did it with great tact still working on the last day's entries. "These arrests may take you a while, because the men are spread all over the Creek, Cherokee and Choctaw Nations. Make sure you have provisions for at least a month."

The clinking of wagon and harness signaled the arrival of Jimmy driving the guard wagon and Dan on the chuck wagon. For Jimmy, who had finally persuaded them to take him along, it would be a learning trip. His newly acquired shirt and vest contrasted with Dan's worn, faded outfit.

His team converged around Charley who shuffled the paperwork. "We'll cross the river here at the ferry and head for Fort Gibson, a good central location for our searches. We're looking for a dozen horse thieves, a couple of murderers and assault."

"How about a spy this trip?" Dan asked. He could scare up a good informant amongst the people of Fort Gibson, having farmed there for many years. Spies were locals who knew the area and the people and did it for the opportunity to rid their community of undesirable elements, but some did it for revenge.

"When we get there, see who you can recruit." Charley explained a little more about their current assignment. "Chief McCurtain of the Choctaws recently sent a letter to Washington complaining about illegal settlers, a great many of who are engaged in nothing but stealing, drinking and carrying pistols in defiance of the law and setting bad examples. We're to be on the lookout for men *on the scout*."

Abe interrupted. "How long will we be out?"

"Maybe a month."

Choctaw Chiefs: Jefferson Gardner, Edmund McCurtain, Basil LaFlore, and Thomas McKinney

Even though the morning was early, the ferry was crowded with customers. The ferry operator tried to gave the deputies preference. Charley led their way through the line of customers, tipping his hat to the ladies and smiling at the children. The men acknowledged them, touching fingers to their brims. The ferry strained against the current, its steam engine chugging and coughing a rhythm. Steam engines always intrigued him. But they were dangerous, if not made of sufficiently strong steel. He had seen a riverboat come into Ft. Smith with half of its side missing from a boiler explosion.

They cleared the ferry landing on the other side of the Arkansas River, picked up the road and started at a good trot while the terrain was even. The flat bottom lands along the Arkansas River would soon give way to tree-shrouded ravines. The wagons bounced in their effort to keep up.

Trees obstructed the view at ground level. As they topped a ridge, Charley turned to check the area behind them. That's when he saw it. A bright but brief flash from a rocky cliff some distance behind them, a glint that could mean only one thing, a warning signal.

"It look's like the outlaw spy system is working today. Anyone ahead of us is going to be scattering," he explained to the men as he pointed out the mirror flashes. "When a deputy and posse leave Fort Smith, signals by mirror or gun shot tell others that lawmen are on the way."

The sun grew higher in the sky. He ordered a break at a stream just east of a fair-sized settlement. The horses buried their noses in the cool water.

"Let's rest here. If you aren't familiar with it, this settlement is Muldrow. Emigrants from Arkansas came in after the War to clear the land and farm it under contract with the Cherokee Nation," Charley explained.

Abe spit out his mouthful of water. "My neighbor was swindled by these folks. Let's get out of here.

Charley took the time to reach for his canteen before explaining. " A person who has a claim of Indian blood goes to the local clerk and reveals all they know about their ancestors. The magistrate looks at a "list" of claims which include these details and declares it legal for a certain fee. Then he pockets the money and the victim leaves thinking he has a valid allotment."

Abe's face showed a look of disbelief. "Can the Fort Smith court do something?"

"The victim is usually too embarrassed to press charges. The Indian Nation turns the disallowed claim over to the Indian Agent for investigation."

Now traveling northwest toward Fort Gibson on the Old Army Road, Charley eyed the terrain. An occasional clearing broke the pattern between houses that were miles apart. A fast-moving gang could avoid detection in the forested ravines and gullies.

This old road had several coach stops for changing horses. The party reached Childers Station late in the afternoon. It was run by Johnny Childers, an original Cherokee settler from an old and prominent family of chiefs. He and his wife, Lucy, were well-known and loved by everyone in the area. Typical of the Cherokee, he would do anything for you and did not require anything in return. He was as honest as any person Charley had ever known.

"Abe, go find us a camp site near Sallisaw Creek," Charley instructed as he dismounted. He entered the low log structure, two wings with a covered dog-run in between. The front room on the left was a store with a storage area behind. The room on the other side consisted of a post office in front and a sleeping area in back for the stage agent.

"Howdy." He greeted a young man whose pleasant face was covered with an attempt at a beard. He was so young that the hair on his chin did not cooperate. It formed a small goatee at best.

"Good morning, sir. What can I do for you?"

"Is Uncle Johnny around?"

"He's taking a nap in the back room."

"Could you ask him to come out? I'm Deputy Marshal Charles Barnhill from Fort Smith."

"Certainly, deputy. Make yourself comfortable while I fetch him."

Uncle Johnny came from the back room, rubbing his face and blinking his eyes. "What you need, Marshal Charley?" He spoke in broken English. Most full-bloods had not learned English even after so many years. They depended on their children who had gone to tribal schools to take care of that.

"You know of any bad white men in the area causing trouble? "

"A gang near Fort Gibson. Horse thieves and whiskey peddlers. They no bother me."

"Do you know anyone that could lead us to them?"

"My nephew, he take you."

"Have him meet me tomorrow morning at my camp on Sallisaw Creek."

Johnny gave a grunt in agreement. Without further words, he turned back into the storeroom to resume his nap.

Charley turned his attention to the clerk. "Any passers-by recently?"

"When the stagecoach came in yesterday, the driver reported a gang of men paralleling the stage route. He thought at first they were going to molest him, but then they moved off and seemed to be tracking a definite course."

"Many thanks."

He reached their camp in a few minutes. It was a sheltered location just off the stage road."Abe, We need to make plans for the night. A large body of men passed through here yesterday. "

Abe's thin cheeks tightened. "What do ya' mean?" By now both Dan and Jimmy were at his elbow.

"Gangs have been known to fall upon camps especially if they think they're the deputy's target. "

"What's the plan?" Abe said.

"Leave the chuck wagon here and move the guard wagon a hundred yards into the brush. Picket the teams out of sight. We'll eat our meal here with a roaring fire and then let it burn down. Each of you pick a location to bed down, keeping a sight on this wagon. If anyone wants to cause trouble, we'll catch 'em in a cross-fire."

Supper was prepared and served so everyone could get to their positions by dark. A full moon lit the area as bright as day.

Dan had the first two hour watch. Charley wanted to get some rest and be alert for the second watch. He felt he had slept a couple of hours when Dan crawled over and nudge him awake.

"It's your turn. Everything's been quiet so far."

"Check and make sure Abe is resting so he can relieve me in two hours."

Sheltered by the branches of a fallen red cedar, he watched and listened to the normal night sounds, frogs, crickets, hoot owls, and screechers of some kind. He held his Winchester across his lap, the fingers of his right hand resting lightly on the stock, his left around the barrel.

It was about time for Abe to relieve him when he heard the sound of fast moving horses on the road. He held his breath to see if they would pass, his heart beating in his throat.

A rider came into view in the bright moonlight and then a group. The leader slowed as he saw the chuck wagon, waving his arm toward it. Charley held his fire not knowing if they were friend or foe.

As they got closer, the horsemen pulled rifles and started pouring fire into the area, under the wagon, into the wagon, and anything in the vicinity of the still smoldering fire.

Charley took careful aim at the leader and fired. He heard the man cry out in pain and saw him fall across his saddle. By now the rest of the lawmen were awake and firing at the intruders.

The attackers attempted to whirl and fire at their muzzle blasts. Their cover held and they continued their withering shots. More of the outlaws fell. A man cried out to the others above the gunfire. "Let's get out of here!" kickeing his horse over a bush just yards ahead of Charley who aimed at the man's features, a heavily bearded face, a mouth yelling in rage. The shot reeled the man to his left, but he managed to cling to his horse which followed the others as they retreated the way they had come.

The smell of gun powder and blood filled the air. Charley stood up and surveyed the damage. The wagon had been shot up pretty good, but was still usable. The cargo could be reloaded in the morning. "We gave them an unexpected welcome party. Let's get some sleep."

The next morning the night's fight was evident. Two patches of blood indicated wounds of a serious nature. Horse tracks led to the main road and then disappeared into the brush about a mile west of the campsite.

Abe scratched his head. "I wonder who might have wanted to stop us?"

"I don't know, but now we have something to track. As soon as Uncle Johnny's nephew gets here, we'll see where these lead us."

They had survived a close call in this attack. Deputies and posses died because of such an ambush. His men were safe, thanks to the hard lessons learned from experienced deputies like Tyner Hughes and Will Ayers.

Chapter 17

Marshal or Executioner

After the late night visitors had been driven off, Charley slept little, the face of the man he had shot at point blank range invading his sleep. He never wanted to kill anyone, but self-protection was a necessary part of survival for him and his men.

He rolled up his bedroll to place in the chuck wagon when he heard an approaching horseman. It was a young Cherokee man, an erect and handsome figure in knee-high boots, rough homespun riding pants and a cotton shirt. The leather pouch around his neck indicated a chief's clan. His wide brimmed hat cinched under his chin covered long braids. He stopped his horse in front of Charley. "I'm looking for Deputy Barnhill."

"I'm Barnhill."

"My name is Joseph Childers. I've come to guide and track for you."

"We're about ready to go. Care for a cup of coffee while you wait?'

"Sure, I'm grateful."

"Dan, you and Jimmy proceed to Fort Gibson and camp there. We'll be going where wagons cannot. If you don't hear from us in a couple of weeks, send a telegram to the Marshal's office in Fort Smith."

As the two wagons veered off to the west along the Old Army Road, the three horsemen turned their mounts to follow the tracks from the previous night's attack. The young guide hesitated only once when he dismounted and touched the dirt.

"This is fresh, less than a couple of hours. Six sets of tracks, two horses limping. "

The thickly brushed ravines and high, steep ridges made the going slow. The horses skittered down the slopes, the riders clinging to their mounts and leaning back in the saddle to balance against the effects of gravity. When the horses lunged up the other side, the riders held on to the saddle horns to keep from sliding backwards off the saddles. It was very tiring for both horse and rider.

Charley called a halt at a stream. "Take a break and let the horses rest." His fingers fiddled with the cinch for five minutes, loosening and then tightening it repeatedly. He laid his forehead against Billie's flank and thought. Three of them against six were not good odds. Surprise was the only chance they had.

Abe followed Charley and pulled open one of his saddle riders. "Sure glad Dan gives us extra grub when we're ranging. I'm plenty hungry already." He offered a piece of the corn bread to Joseph who gulped it down.

"Alright. Let's get moving. Maybe we can overtake them before nightfall," Charley said in his normal slow drawl.

Abe was now tuned in on his brother. He needed to find out what was bothering him. The men they sought were desperate and hurt and would fight to the death if cornered.

After crossing the Arkansas River at Lynch's Ferry, they entered the small settlement of Webber Falls on the south side of the river. It had its share of notorious residents including the Griffin brothers who ran with Sam Starr. It would be a likely shelter for fugitives on the run.

Abe surveyed the settlement from the outskirts. "How about we go to the stage coach stop and inquire of the locals?"

Charley turned to their guide. "Do you have friends or relatives here, Joseph?"

"Yes, two cousins. They live just outside of town along the river."

"See if they know of any white men riding through this morning."

"If they will cooperate. They are from a group of Cherokees who oppose white man's settlement and distrust the deputy force."

The stage stop lay in the center of the sleepy village. Nothing indicated business except two wagons hitched in front of a general store and a saddle mount in front of the livery. A man standing in his garden hailed them with a wave. "Marshal, Marshal. Hold up."

Abe put his hand on his Colt as he surveyed the dusty street. Last night had made him jittery.

"Relax, Abe," Charley ordered as he watched the stranger. The man was of medium height, wearing work type brogans, overalls and a blue cotton shirt. He tipped his hat back off his forehead as he walked up.

"Name's Alan Johnson, have a farm here on the main road. Wondering if you were looking for a group of men?"

"What do you mean?" Charley asked in return.

"Well, early this morning before day break, I was getting ready to get up when I heard several riders coming down the road, riding real hard. I didn't have a light on in my place so I moved to the front window to see what was happening. They went by pretty quick and it was still fairly dark."

"What did you see?"

"Maybe five or six riders. A couple were leaning in the saddle and the horses seemed hurt too, limping like."

Abe relaxed the grip on his Colt and turned to follow Charley. "Let's verify that farmer's story. He could be a plant to throw us off."

"Alright. You go inside the stage stop while I talk to the store owner."

Abe walked into the log structure, letting his eyes adjust as he strolled to the counter. An attendant came out of the back room, rubbing his hands on his apron. "What can I do for you, sir?" He was a young man with a reddish blond beard and spectacles perched on his nose.

"I'm Abe Barnhill, posse for Deputy Marshal Charles Barnhill. Any riders come through here this morning?"

"I heard a number of horsemen ride by just as I was getting up to dispatch the stage to Fort Smith. It leaves here at 6:45 a.m."

"Did you see the direction they went?"

"No, I wondered who was out at that time of morning. Thought it might be the Cherokee Light Horse. They've been about recently looking for horse thieves."

"Much obliged." Abe turned to the door and that was when he noticed the saddlebag on the floor leaning against the wall. He had not seen it on coming in. It had a bullet hole in the middle of the pouch and blood stains on the top and back. "Who does that saddlebag belong to?"

The young man frowned and pursed his lips. "It was brought in by the stage coach driver. He says he found it in the middle of the road."

"Mind if I take it for evidence?"

"It's not mine."

Charley was just coming out of the general store as Abe moved toward his mount.

"What did you get?" Abe asked.

"The store owner is a Mr. Blackstone. He says he lives about half a mile off the main road so he didn't hear or see anything." Charley pointed to the saddlebag. "What've you got there?"

Abe handed over the soft leather pouch. "The stage clerk heard a group of riders come by early this morning. This was dropped in the road and picked up by one of his drivers."

He examined it inside and out and then handed it back. "Looks like we're on the right track. Let's find Joseph and get moving."

Following the directions the young Indian had given them to where his relatives lived, they rode up a narrow trail to a cabin hidden in the woods. The one room had only a front door and no windows. A woman in the front yard stirred a kettle full of something resembling a stew. It looked intriguing, but Indians had some quirky eating habits.

Joseph came out of the door with a man about the same age. He walked up to Charley. "This is my cousin. The Cherokee Light Horse came by yesterday asking questions about a gathering of horse thieves going on south of Fort Gibson. Several bands of strangers passed through the area this week. Some neighbors are missing horses. "

The anxious look on his brother's face at this information startled Abe. What was going on in his head to cause that reaction? What wasn't he telling him?

As they rode back to the main trail, Charley wondered if the tracks could be picked up again. "Joseph, which direction did the bands seem to be moving?"

"My cousin says they were headed north, but each group seems to take a different trail. "

Abe scratched his chin and looked at his brother. "Where do we go from here?"

"Checking all large groups of tracks that lead off the main trail is the only way. This will take some time."

They spent the rest of the day searching either side of the road where houses were scarce and no one seemed to have any information. Charley was beginning to think it futile when he heard a sound that was unmistakable. Gunfire - and close by - rattling off the hillsides and echoing up the hollows.

The trackers wheeled in the direction of the sound. About a mile down the main road, a group of men sheltered behind trees aimed their fire across a ravine. Charley recognized a tall man with a patchy gray beard, John West. He had heard he was now an Indian police officer, but had not seen him since West had been a witness at the trial of Belle and Sam Starr two years previously.

He dismounted at a safe distance and approached with caution.

John's scowl turned into a smile. "Deputy Barnhill, what brings you out to these parts?"

"I've been instructed to look for a horse thief ring in these parts."

"Well, look no further. We have some pinned down in that hollow."

Charley turned and gestured to Abe and Joseph to approach.

"What can we do to help?" Charley asked.

"I think we're about done with this. Go see for yourselves."

Charley descended into the ravine expecting to see a furious fight in progress. He was surprised to see a dozen Indian police sitting around two still forms lying face down in the brush. Shots still rang out from the hollow.

"Give up, now, or we'll kill all of you," John West shouted between the shots. "This is your last chance to give up, now." He turned to his deputy who motioned all the men to get back to their horses.

"We're going to use an old cavalry trick," John explained.

When all of his men had ascended the hill except a couple left behind to keep the outlaws pinned down, John had them tighten up their cinches before mounting. "Use your horse as a shield and fire from across the saddle."

Charley and Abe took this all in from the top of the ravine. A dozen Indian police moving at a gallop toward their opponents whirled their horses to the side and swung down as instructed. The fire power put into the thicket was tremendous and withering. Who could withstand it? A white cloth tied to the end of a rifle barrel appeared above the smoke.

Two outlaws came out with their hands above their heads, their wounded companions attempting to rise. A couple more would never rise again.

Charley walked forward with John to examine the scene of battle. The two dead men appeared to be the ones that he and his men had wounded, one with a bandaged left shoulder and another a bloody head wound. He recognized the bearded face he had seen in the moonlight. Well, at least he had not missed.

The two standing prisoners were young white men. "Please, don't kill us," the youngest one begged, his face now as flushed as his red hair. He appeared to be about twenty and was dressed in the attire of a Texas cowboy, pants stuffed into high-topped boots, a low-slung gun belt on his right hip, the belt stretching across his chaps. His companion who was a little older and similarly dressed stood mute, his head down expecting the worst.

The police force dragged the two wounded horse thieves to stand before them. One had a foot that oozed blood from his ankle. He was a youngster about the same age as Jimmy, his face pale, his eyes filled with terror. The Cherokee Light Horse were rightly feared by all intruders.

The second wounded prisoner was one of the meanest looking men Charley had ever seen, a crooked smile enhanced by a scar that extended from his chin to his ear, vacant eyes that stared defiantly into Charley's face, daring anyone who came near. Those eyes were familiar. Where had he seen him before? The felon held his right hand. It appeared he was missing a few fingers.

Charley was startled out of his contemplation by West's next words. "Well, Deputy Barnhill. What shall we do with these four? Horse thieves are *shoot to kill* in the Cherokee Nation."

Ranchers and cattlemen routinely killed rustlers when they were captured and no one said anything about it. If he let them be killed, no one would ever hold it against him.

Abe came to stand beside Charley and gave him a look that said "You know what is right. Don't mess up".

His heart beat in his ears as he struggled with the decision. Every man deserved a fair trail before a jury of his peers, that was the American way. He knew he could not live with himself or God if he took the easy way out.

"Thanks for capturing these horse thieves, West. We'll be glad to take them off your hands now. You and your men will have to swear out complaints as well as the owners of the stolen horses if they can be identified."

Abe slapped his brother on the back. "You're good, Charley Boy. Your ole

Pappy will be proud."

"I'm grateful the Light Horse caught up with this band before us. We could never have taken them, out-numbered as we were." He knew God had provided the way to protect them and capture the thieves.

Choctaw Light Horse

Chapter 18

New Clothes Catch a Killer

The long chain hanging between the trees secured fourteen prisoners. Twenty feet long, it was suitable for logging or towing a ferry across a river. Abe shook each link and tugged on the individual chains that ran to the prisoners' shackles. Three weeks into this trip, their camp was in the southern part of the Choctaw Nation only fifteen miles above the Red River which was the boundary with Texas.

The four rustlers turned over to them by the Cherokee Light Horse were their first prisoners. The two young cowboy-types adjusted to the routine, not causing undue concern. But those were the ones you really had to watch. Abe tugged on their leg irons.

The youngest one with the red hair protested, "Hey, not so hard, fella!"

"Quit your grumbling. You'll be out of these in a few days. Then you can take up living with a roomie in a five by eight cell."

They had taken the two wounded rustlers to a doctor in Muskogee. The one with the broken ankle wore a splint and shackles on his wrists and waist attached to a ring inside the wagon. The desperado with the injured hand burst out in harsh oaths, his eyes challenging Abe who stared back unblinking. This was one he would have to warn Charley about.

Dan handed Abe a cup of coffee in a tin cup. "Try this to clean out the dust."

"Thanks." He swished the hot liquid around to help loosen the dust caked to the roof of his mouth and watched Charley move across the camp site and sit down next to him with his coffee. Dan had a more elaborate facility than when they had started five years ago. His separate cook shack resembled a tent with hard sides.

"What do we have left this trip?" Abe asked.

"Tomorrow we'll head south to the Red River. There is a murderer lurking out there on a ranch. He shot down his neighbor in a dispute over livestock up above the Canadian River."

Abe took a deep breath and let it out in a sigh. "It's good we're almost done. It'll take at least a week to reach Fort Smith."

Charley handed his cup back to the cook. "Have all the prisoners been fed?"

Dan chuckled and gestured at the empty cook pot. "They ate plenty. They don't get a lot to eat when they're on the scout."

Charley turned away and thought about tomorrow's task. Flushing out a murderer was never easy. Cornered killers used desperate measures. Secrecy was his best ally.

When Abe rejoined him at their tent, he explained the plan. "We'll ride down to the ranch where the murderer is working. I'll go in disguised as a rancher heading down to Texas to buy livestock. The people at the ranch may be unaware of the man's identity."

Abe loosened his gun-belt and settled on the cot. "I want to be close enough to step in if anything goes wrong."

"You'll be right beside me as my foreman."

"What about clothes? We look like lawmen who've been on a long hunt."

"We'll buy different clothes."

"I need some new clothes anyway. Whose buying?"

"I brought extra money with me."

"When do you want to leave?"

"At first light. If we show up at the ranch in time for dinner, they'll not be suspicious."

In the dim light of morning Abe applied spurs to his mount to catch Charley who was already fifty feet down the trail to Eagletown, a nearby settlement that had a general store, livery, and blacksmith. As they rode into the town from the north, few people were about. Charley reined up in front of a small building with a false front, the sign above the porch announcing Smith Mercantile.

Abe dismounted and took time to look around. Anyone observing their arrival would know strangers were in town. Did this murderer have spies? They'd soon find out.

A short man with a bald head came to the counter. All Abe could see of him was his pin stripe shirt, string bow tie, and suspenders, all protected with a merchant's apron.

His smile and voice were cordial. "Good day, gentlemen. What can I do for you?"

"My name is Adams. I need a new suit before we get to Paris," Charley explained.

The store owner waved his hand at the shelves stacked with merchandise. "My store has the finest available in these parts. Every rancher headed for Texas comes here to get fixed up. Where did you say you're from?" He handed Charley a hat, shirt and jacket to try on.

"We have a ranch up north in the Creek Nation, leased from the tribe and run about three thousand head. We're going to Paris to buy stock horses and mules. The horse rustlers have about wiped us out. We had to string up a few to run them off."

The retailer swept a hand across his chin as he sized up the Colt 45's on their hips. "They're a menace everywhere. Livestock is the only thing of value in the Nations other than people's private stash of cash. At least in this area, the robbers have not resorted to holding up people in their homes. However, we just had a terrible incident right here in town."

"What happened?" Abe asked from his position behind Charley who was looking in a tall mirror at his profile.

"A tenderfoot from back East stopped at my store, He had his wife and two pretty daughters with him. He said he was going to Colorado. Unfortunately, he didn't know the Indian ways and started flashing around a wad of bills.

"Two no-account Indian boys hanging around the store followed him. The old man wasn't aware of the caution required in these parts, especially when traveling alone without other men or weapons. The boys followed them and killed them all with an axe. "

Abe's casual mood was replaced by visions of slaughter. "What happened to the murderers?" he asked, now interested in a possible manhunt.

"Pastor Travis Ely of the Methodist mission here witnessed the goings on at the store and was the one who discovered the bodies along the road. He sent word to Ft. Smith. His cousin, United States Deputy Marshal, Ely Miller and his partner were sent down to arrest the boys. They didn't have any trouble finding them. One was hiding under his bed and the other out in the brush. They left for Fort Smith yesterday."

"Well, at least they were caught quickly before they could go on the scout."

Charley finished trying on the hat and shirt. "I need pants and boots to go with these."

"Here, sir. These should do." The merchant had gone to a shelf and pulled down pants and boots without asking Charley's size.

"Hey, these look like they're a perfect fit. How did you figure that out so quickly?" Charley asked.

"I was a quartermaster under General Blunt during the war. I was with him when he ran the Confederates out of northern Arkansas after Pea Ridge. I had to figure out sizes and numbers for thousands of men. It just comes natural after a while."

"See what you can do for my brother here." They looked too much alike to not claim being closely related.

The merchant turned to Abe and waited. "Certainly, Mr. Adams, what can I get for you?"

"Give me the same thing, but I'd like a shirt with a string tie. I like to fancy up sometimes. "

"I may have only one selection with that type of collar configuration. Yes, here it is."

Abe held the shirt, enjoying the scent of the clean cloth. It was the first thing he had smelled recently that didn't reek of dirt or sweat.

"Alright, what do we owe you and where can we change?" Charley was ready to get into the disguise.

"That'll be ten dollars each. You can change in the room behind that curtain."

Charley paid the merchant with a twenty dollar gold piece and stepped behind the curtain. While he was changing, Abe took a moment to ask directions to the ranch they were intending to visit. "How do we get to the B-Bar-S ranch? We promised a friend of ours we'd visit his ole buddy."

"Just take the road south out of town, When you get about three miles, take the fork to the right to Mountain Fork River. Another mile or so and you'll find the ranch house along the river. You can't miss it. It's the only ranch between here and the Red River."

In a short time both men were dressed in their new apparel, looking and feeling the part. Abe wondered how they would identify the suspect. "Do we have a description of the man we're hunting?"

"The family of the murdered man saw him before he fired the fatal shot. He has blonde hair, is fairly tall and slender and walks with a slight limp. But the most distinguishing thing is he has the top half of his left ear missing as well as two front teeth."

"What's your plan if we discover him?"

"If we can positively identify him, we'll take him when he least suspects. I'll signal you. If I decide it is time to go after him, I'll take my hat and place it on my lap."

"Let's go. I'm anxious to get home to Amanda."

"Me, too. I mean home to Salina." Charley laughed.

The newly clad horsemen swung down the fork to the right as instructed. As they approached the river, Abe could see a low ranch house about a mile in the distance. He scanned the area looking for signs of activity. None were apparent except for some cattle near the river. "Well, looks quiet enough from here. I guess it's dinner time."

They rode to the gate over which a wooden sign read "B-Bar-S".

Charley called out in a loud voice. "Hallo the ranch." It was dangerous to approach a house without hailing the occupants. Otherwise, you might be eating lead.

As they slowed to a walk and entered the ranch yard, a man stepped out on the porch, his hand shielding his eyes from the sun, a Winchester gripped tightly in his left hand.

"Howdy, boys. What can I do for you?" He had deep crow's feet around his eyes and a tan that comes from days on the prairie.

Charley removed his hat. "I'm Bob Adams and this is my brother, Luke. We're headed to Paris to buy livestock. Thought we could get a meal from you, since you are the only ranch in the area. Your friend, Tulsa Jack, said you would be good for it."

"How's ole Tulsa doing now? How's his partner, Bill Doolin."

"Last time we saw them on the 101 Ranch, they were fat and happy." Charley failed to disclose that the last time they had seen those two was after arresting them in a bar fight at Fort Smith.

"Come on in. Cookie is about ready with dinner. You can wash up at the well behind the house."

"Well, so far so good," Abe whispered as they washed their hands and gave their horses a bucket of water in the trough.

"Take the horses back around front when they're finished. I'll go in and see who's around." Charley walked into the back door of the house through the kitchen. It gave him a chance to examine any escape route the suspect may use. The only person was a big man stirring beans in a large iron pot. He nodded to Charley and continued his task.

Abe brought the horses around front and slip tied the reins to the railing. As he ascended the porch, he saw a man near the barn. Abe watched him out of the corner of his eye. *Yup, that looks like the man in question. This might be too easy.*

"Thanks for your hospitality," Charley said to the rancher. The owner sat at the head of a large plank table with Charley to his right. He indicated for Abe to be seated at his left.

"Cookie, ring that dinner bell. I'm hungry."

As the bell finished its last vibration, two men entered the back door and came through the kitchen. The first one was a short, stout cowboy wearing spurs and carrying a riding quirt. His hat was pulled down over his ears so that they poked out some. His clean-shaved face had a deep tan and firm thin lips that parted into a greeting smile at the strangers

"Howdy."

"Bart, these are the Adams brothers from Tulsa, Indian Territory, heading down to Paris, Texas on business."

"Nice to meet you," he replied as he placed his hat on a sideboard and sat down on Charley's right, his gun hand side.

The blonde-haired man behind him slowed before he sat. On close inspection, Charley was positive they had the right man.

The second man only nodded his head and seated himself beside Abe.

As the meal progressed, Charley observed the location of weapons. The boss had a shotgun on the mantel and was wearing a hand gun. The two ranch hands both had handguns. Cookie probably had a scatter gun in the kitchen. It would be a shoot out, if he didn't do this exactly right. They would have to take the killer when he left the dining room alone.

He tried conversation to put the men at ease. "How is the range around here? We've had a drought up in Tulsa the past two summers. In the heat the flies get a lot of our cows."

The boss man stuffed a biscuit in his mouth and swallowed before answering. "We've had the same problem. All the watering holes are dried up. We have to depend on the creeks for water right now."

Charley rose as the boss man got up and extended his hand to him. "Well, thanks for the good meal. I think we need to get started on our journey so we can make the Red River before night fall."

As they rode away, Charley picked out a thick stand of oaks at a bend in the road. "Let's take cover," he suggested.

"My thoughts exactly, brother. I hope the killer doesn't get anxious and try to run."

"We'll see. Take the horses far enough away so they can't be heard. Then take cover in the oaks toward the rear of the house on the left side. I'll cover the front and right side."

After he had dozed in the sun for nearly an hour, Abe watched the stout cowboy move to the front of the house leading a saddle horse. The boss man came out of the house and mounted to ride leisurely toward the creek away from the ranch. At least he was not suspicious.

The cowboy entered the corral. Where were the other two? Abe crawled closer to the house around the right side. The back door swing open and he heard the sound of a dishpan being dumped. So Cookie was still inside. He crawled up to the window.

It was the killer speaking. "I don't trust those strangers. Something didn't make sense with their story." His voice was agitated, the words fast and full of emotion.

Cookie's voice showed no concern. "Well, I don't know. If they aren't who they claim, why are they snooping around here?"

"Hand me that shotgun. I'm going into town and see if anyone knows who these strangers really are. You coming?"

"I dunno'. I don't have a gripe with anyone. Do you?"

"No, of course not. I'm just curious about these two. They could be getting ready to rob the boss. He keeps a lot of cash around here, you know."

Abe scooted back to the brush as he heard the back door open. The killer moved across the barnyard, a Winchester in one hand and the shotgun in the other. *Take him in the barn or wait until he gets on the road?* In the barn the stout cowboy could come to his aid. On the road would be a better choice.

He moved around the perimeter of the ranch house and motioned to Charley to withdraw to the bend in the road. Abe explained. "He's heading out to try and track us down. I'll move a hundred feet out in the trees so that we can catch him between us."

A few minutes later, Abe watched from his position as two horsemen rode from the ranch, Cookie and the killer. They had Colts, Winchesters and shotguns, heavily armed for an afternoon ride. As they passed, he raised his Winchester and aimed his sights on Cookie - the big man would be an easy target.

When the men reached half way between the two brothers, Charley rose up from his cover. "Deputy U.S. Marshal - Put up your hands."

The killer raised his Winchester to fire. Abe shifted his aim and fired, knocking the rifle out of his hands. Another save for his brother. The next shot from Charley threw the rider into the road. Cookie was holding his hands straight up in the air. *Wise man.*

Abe walked toward the prostrate form, his Winchester pointed at the man's chest. He knelt and picked up the damaged rifle.

"You're under arrest," Charley pointed at the moaning man who gripped his arm. Then he turned to Cookie still on his horse with his hands up. "Get down and pick this fella' up and put him on his horse. We're going to take him to our camp north of here. You can pick up your horse there in the morning. If you don't, it'll go to Fort Smith with us."

"What's he done," Cookie asked.

"Murdered his neighbor up on the Canadian."

The open-mouthed gape on Cookie's face told Charley he knew nothing about the identity of this killer. This country was full of desperate characters who hid out amongst respectable people. They connived with a lie or manipulated with their smooth ways. This outfit had gotten off easy before the killer had the opportunity to turn on them.

Chapter 19

A Photograph for Sarah

The Cedar Mountains surrounded the party as it crawled through the rolling terrain. Spring rains had pushed creeks to their banks. Charley knew everyone was worn out: the horses pulling the wagons, the prisoners jostling around inside. It was time to stop. He called a halt and then unsaddled Billie. In no time the cook shack was set up and producing tonight's supper. Jimmy took the shackled prisoners to the creek to wash up while Abe dug a latrine.

Charley rustled through his paperwork then raised his eyes to the cook. "That rustler we got from the Cherokee, the mean one with the bandaged arm, looks familiar to me. Have you looked at him up close?"

Dan stopped stirring the beans. "Now that you mention it, he looks like someone I knew over in Fort Gibson, a fella wanted for a holdup. He and a buddy robbed a store of several hundred dollars up in Kansas and then went on the scout. I figured he'd gotten caught or killed."

"When we get to Fort Smith, I'll have the marshal wire Kansas about him."

Just as Charley was about to stuff his papers back in his saddlebag, he heard a voice from the brush behind him. Instinctively, his hand went to his Colt as he turned.

"Hullo, at the campfire. Can we come in? It's Deputy Marshal Ely Miller and partner."

Charley turned and relaxed the grip on his six shooter. "Come ahead, you're welcome." Two men stepped into the fire light leading well lathered horses with heaving chests and mud-caked hooves.

Miller extended his hand. "Hello, Charley. Didn't know you normally got this far down in the Choctaw Nation?"

"Where you heading?" Charley tried to keep his tone nonchalant. What were they doing here if they were on their way to Fort Smith, two days ahead of them?

"We were taking two Indian boys to Fort Smith. We feared an escape attempt by their friends so we moved directly into Arkansas."

Abe had just finished with his prisoners and walked up to join Charley.

Abe's hand on his shoulder was a warning to him to stay calm. Charley squinted his eyes, something he did when he was seeing through lies and summing up situations. "Where are your prisoners now?"

"They were real cunning and slipped their shackles. We had to kill them both to keep them from running. "

He sucked in his breath and tightened his grip on the gun belt. Abe stepped in front of Charley and extended his hand. "Let me congratulate you on a job well done. Too bad they didn't make it to trial."

Charley finally forced words from between clinched teeth, his mind reeling. "You can bed down with us wherever you can find room. Dan will have supper ready soon."

As the two men passed through the camp with their horses, Abe pulled his brother into the shadows of the camp fire. "Now, Charley, don't be too judgmental. Maybe it happened just like they said it did. You don't know, do you?"

"How could they slip their shackles unless they were intentionally left unlocked or loosened. It sounds like their escape attempt was planned as an excuse to kill them."

Abe took a deep breath and exhaled. "Well, maybe so, but those boys would have hung anyway. We stand by our oaths for the rule of law and order. But who played fair with that poor family that was slaughtered? "

"I know that won't ever happen to any of our prisoners."

"No, it won't. Now let's go eat."

The party continued north through Smithville and into the Kiamichi Mountains which took all of the next day and part of the following. Ahead was the Winding Stair Mountains, a place of wild and terrible deeds where deputies and posse went with great care. It was here that some of the most diabolical of crimes had been committed, the victims' bodies being lost forever in the wild ravines.

Charley and Abe rode ahead to make sure the trail was passable for the wagons and prisoners. The wagon wheels seemed to ride on the very edge of the precipices. Dan and Jimmy had their hands full keeping the horses under control. Brakes and the prisoners holding on to the wagons from behind prevented them from hurtling down the grades out of control. By the time they reached Hodgen at the end of the fourth day, everyone was grateful for safe passage. While camped, a prisoner took sick, developing a sudden high fever.

"Let's put him in the wagon for the night and see how he does," Charley instructed.

"He could have typhoid fever since we've used water from some local wells. It has been raining a lot and as the water table rises, the water becomes stagnant," Dan offered, concern heavy in his voice.

"What container has he been drinking from?"

"The water barrel I filled when we went through Smithville two days ago."

"Well, dump it out just in case. There is a fresh water spring here in the mountains that should be pure enough to use. Who else drank that water? "

"I just used it to cook with, but that should be alright since I bring everything to a boil."

The next morning the prisoner was still feverish, but coherent. After drinking some beef bone broth Dan had cooked during the night, he slept peacefully as the wagon jostled along.

The days crept by. Day five they reached Poteau. Day six they made it to Pocola just ten miles from Fort Smith. Everyone was ready to get off a wagon or horse and sleep in a bed.

They had been out for a month and had fifteen prisoners, including three with wounds, and the sick one. What a load for four men to handle. As the "tumbleweed" wagon pulled into Fort Smith from the southwest and headed toward the Old Jail, Charley looked around at the city and the changes since he had started lawin' five years before. Several hundred new homes had been built which had gas and electric. The street lights were gas. New businesses went up as people moved here from all over the United States.

As the wagons entered the gates to the jail, Charley noticed another wagon with Tyner Hughes in the lead.

"Partner! How was your trip?" Tyne asked in his normal self-assured tone.

"I could've used your help. Abe and I had our hands full. Jimmy is coming along fine as a guard."

"Let me know when you're available. I always learn something new when I go out with you." Tyne pushed his hat back. "How many times have you saved my skin?"

"Too many. I'll come visit on my way home sometime."

They ceased the cordial exchange to turn their attention to the task at hand. They mounted the steps of the jail together and entered Marshal Boles' office, taking off their hats and smoothing down their hair before presenting themselves to their boss.

"You two again. How many you got for me today?" The Marshal always greeted his deputies in a helpful and appreciative manner. As a former judge and experienced lawyer, he knew the hardships they undertook to bring in these prisoners.

Charley beat Tyne to the desk with his longer legs. "I have fifteen, but one needs to go to the hospital right away, some kind of fever. Three are wounded and need to be checked by the prison physician. Here's my paperwork."

Tyne winked at Charley. "I have seven, no wounded. Everything was pretty routine on this trip."

Charley pointed to the paperwork he had given to the Marshal. "Four prisoners don't have writs of arrest. They were turned over to me by John West and the Cherokee Light Horse. He said they would be in to swear out complaints on them. I think one of them is a man wanted in Kansas. Dan can point him out to you and give you the particulars. He was his neighbor out in Fort Gibson."

"Alright, deputies. Turn in your expense reports as soon as possible so I can get you paid. I'm sure you want to head home."

Charley and Tyne walked out to dismiss their men and gather up their gear. Another day in the life of a Fort Smith deputy.

Abe was waiting for Charley, an expectant look on his face. "I need to get home."

"No time for a bath before you leave?" Charley called after his fleeing brother. He turned to Jimmy who stood in front of the railing. "Let's get cleaned up and get something to eat."

After a bath, shave and haircut, Charley put on the new clothes he had purchased in Eagletown. He felt like dressing up for some reason. Jimmy wore a similar-styled jacket over a white shirt and bow tie. "How about we go to McIntire and Reed's Photography over in their tent and have our pictures made for Ma. She is always after us to have one made. "

The tent held a comfortable waiting area furnished with French Provincial sofas covered in silk and brocade and a Turkish carpet on the floor area. His mother, Sarah, always fawned over such items at the furniture stores in Fort Smith. A humble minister's wife could appreciate such fancy fixins' but never own any.

The proprietor came from behind a black curtain when Charlie's hand hit the bell on the counter. He made a slight but courteous bow. "Hello, may I help you, sir?" His slim frame with pork chop style whiskers, gold rim glasses and a pale complexion reminded Charley of the Eastern tourists who crowded the train platform each day.

"I'm Deputy Marshal Charley Barnhill and this is my brother, James. We want our pictures taken as a surprise for our mother."

"Yes, of course, a loving gesture. Please come this way."

They followed the young man into the tent area behind the black curtain. It was spacious with various types of back drop scenes. The young man pulled down several for them to examine.

"I can present you in different scenes if you like, formal parlor, out-of-doors, European, Italian, or Roman."

"How about something simple."

"Yes, sir. If you will be seated on this chair, I will pose you with this simple colored drape. Most deputies like to have their weapon in hand. Would you like that?"

"Sure, Jimmy, hand me my Peacemaker."

"How about your badge? Do you want it to show on your jacket?"

"Oh Yeah. How's that?" Charley moved his badge from his front pocket to his jacket. "You can tell I don't do this very often."

James Alfred Barnhill, Circa 1884
Courtesy Louis Lish family.

"That's alright, sir. I don't go out and chase down fugitives every day either. It's all what you're used to doing. Now, hold still. Once it is done I'll go in the dark room and make sure it turned out."

Charley tried not to look too stern or nervous. He felt strange and a little embarrassed holding his weapon up in a pose. He was used to handling it in action. His hand and arm started to cramp in the unnatural position. At last, it was over.

"You may stand up now, sir, and I'll take your brother's picture next."

Jimmy stepped forward. "Can I wear my hat, sir? I like it very much. It's the way I want my ma to see me."

"Yes, young sir. You may. Do you want to hold your pistol in the same type of pose as your brother or if you like, you can sit with your pistol showing in your holster."

"Let's try that. I use a cross-the-chest draw."

Charley smiled as he watched Jimmy trying to look tough. His right hand rested on the chair arm, the cross draw holster and .32 Navy Colt in prominent display. He just hoped he would not have to learn the hard way how to be tough. Bushwhacking was a favored method desperadoes used to get rid of guards, just shoot them out of the wagon seat from behind a tree.

"I'll have these pictures ready for you in two weeks. It's pretty busy right now and I'm short of help. How many of each would you like?"

" I would like four of each. How much do I owe you?"

"That will be $1.00 with the deputy marshal discount."

Charley paid the bill and then headed for the Marshal's office, Jimmy in tow close behind. He moved into the office and laid a paper on the desk. "Here's my expense report for this trip. I'm heading home for a week. I'll pick up the check when I come back ."

Marshal Boles handed them their pay for the month's work. "Have a good week off. I appreciate your dedication."

He pocketed the check after glancing at the sum. The Marshal's office got one-fourth to cover their handling of the prisoners and the Marshal's pay. The wages hardly compensated for the time, effort and risk it took to earn it, but there was more than money involved. He felt proud to do his duty and serve the citizens of the United States and Indian Territory. Men like Tyner Hughes and Bass Reeves were the big wage earners, but they spent every waking hour hunting down fugitives. He felt it was urgent he got home as quickly as possible. The longer he was gone the more anxious he always became for the safety and well-being of his family.

Chapter 20

A Cold Blooded Killer

The front door of the general store slammed against Charley's boot. Charles Wilson, the owner, pulled the door open and motioned him inside. "We're closing up since it's election day." Wilson put on his jacket and pocketed a pistol.

"I forgot you're running for county treasurer." Charley frowned and pointed at the bulge in Wilson's pocket. "Are you man-hunting for the Feds on the way to the election?"

"I think there may be trouble with my opponent, Bob Benton. His group of progressives want to Americanize our way of life. I support the old treaties and ways. I'm going to try to compromise with them if I can. But Jack Crow has a grudge against me for arresting him and taking him to the United States Court at Fort Smith in January, and I suspect he will be there, too."

The smile faded from Charley's face at these words - fighting words. Someone was going to die in this dispute. It was only a matter of when. "Are you going alone?"

"No, my nephew is riding down with me to the Sugar Loaf County Courthouse south of Poteau. On the way back I will spend the night in Poteau at Mrs. Goodnight's boarding house."

Charley shook the man's hand. "Watch your back. These elections can be dangerous."

As he watched them ride away, he wondered if they would return. Indian political disputes got real nasty at times, just like their ball games where heads were cracked and limbs broken in the tussle. There was nothing he could do about it since it was Indian on Indian.

The next day Charley made it to his office shortly after sunup to beat the heat of August that made his little office a steam room. As he stared at the expense report he needed to mail to Fort Smith, a shout from the street broke his concentration.

"Help, somebody help."

He shivered at the alarm in the voice - something bad had happened, but what?

A crowd had already gathered around a young Indian boy. "Help, somebody. They've killed Charles Wilson."

The county deputy sheriff reached the breathless youth at the same time as Charley. The sheriff spoke in a stern voice, trying to calm the young man enough to make sense of his shouts. "What happened?"

The messenger, shaking in fear, caught his breath. "He is in the middle of the road south of town. He's been shot five times and his head beaten in. He was still breathing, but just barely."

"Is he alone?" the sheriff asked.

"I left two of my friends to tend him and take him to the nearest house."

"What did you see?"

"We were on the road when we heard a group of men quarreling in the brush about ten yards from the road. I crept up behind some trees to look and saw a dozen men on horses. Bob Benton was dismounted and aiming a pistol at Wilson who was standing in front of his horse. When Benton cocked it, Wilson grabbed the gun barrel and jerked it towards him before it fired."

The young man paused for a breath and swallowed hard to clear the saliva running from his mouth. "I heard three shots before he fell face forward. Then Benton started beating him over the head with his pistol and Wilson grabbed it again and would not let go. A black man, I think it was Jack Crow, jumped off his horse and shot Wilson twice in the back with his rifle. Benton said 'Why did you do that?' Crow said, 'You wanted him dead didn't you.' They all rode off laughing."

The deputy looked at Charley. "This is big trouble. If I go after Benton, his friends will come after me. If I don't go after Benton, Wilson's friends will come after me."

He turned back to the boy. "Who else did you see?"

"There was Peter Conser, Corn McCurtain and Dixon Perry.

The lawman shook his head. "All these men are pillars of the community and no one will find testify against them."

Charley knew he had no authority in this matter but he could make a suggestion. "Bring them in and let your court system deal with them. At least you will have done your duty. In the meantime I will send a telegram to the Marshal and see if Jack Crow ever registered for Choctaw citizenship. If not, I can go after him."

The young man, who had quieted down, frowned. "Crow boasts about how many men he has killed and won't hesitate killing a deputy marshal."

Charley threw down the newspaper as he sat waiting in the front of the commissioner's office. Just as he had suspected, none of the men involved in Wilson's killing had been indicted due to the lack of evidence. The Indian Chieftain described the arrest and pretrial hearing.

The year 1885 was almost finished and it was over a year since the murder. Now, if the Federals will just go after Crow who is likely hiding deep inside Indian Territory.

Why did the commissioner want to see him? Normally, he dealt directly with the Marshal. Must be something important or I am about to be fired.

Stephen Wheeler, Commissioner of the U. S. District Court, Western District of Arkansas, came to the door of his office and beckoned him in. Charley tried not to stare at the bald head glistening in the afternoon heat. Wheeler's smile was amiable and his manner in keeping with the dignity of his office.

"Deputy Barnhill," Mr. Wheeler leaned back in his chair, "I have several writs for you today. Most of them are very routine, but one is an early Christmas present for you. The court has been trying to get its hands on Jackson Crow since August of last year for the killing of Charles Wilson."

Charley exhaled in relief. Not fired yet. "I remember it well. It happened just a few miles from my home. I've had an ear to the ground ever since, but I haven't heard a thing."

"Wilson was your friend." Commissioner Wheeler handed a handful of folded papers across the desk to the deputy. "I'm giving you the capias that's on top of this stack as a special order. I know you've established a strong relationship with the people of the Choctaw Nation and I think you can ferret out this Crow and run him to ground. Spare no effort and use whatever means you must, but bring him in, preferably alive."

He took the stack of arrest warrants in his left hand. "I'll give it my best shot. It might be that we can pick up this skunk's scent by using Choctaw trackers."

Wheeler smiled as he looked Charley in the eye. "You're developing quite a reputation among the general outlaw population. They're calling you the 'Bible believing deputy.' Prisoners have stated to me that if they had to be arrested, they'd rather have you do it than any other member of the Marshal Service."

Charley fingered his thick black mustache with his right hand, a casual habit when he was thinking. "It could be that some of my Pa's preachin' has rubbed off on me. I prefer to talk first and shoot later."

"There is one more thing of which you should be aware. Some of Jack Crow's cronies approached the Choctaw Tribal Council and applied for citizenship for Crow."

"So where does that leave us?" He looked at the writ for Crow's arrest.

"The court has ruled that since he wasn't a citizen at the time of the murder, he's still under the authority of this district court. The Tribal Council has not yet been informed of this decision. It will give you a chance to get close. Deputy Algie Hall has a bunch of Choctaw trackers. Get him to help you."

Later in the fall, Charley arrested John Slaughter, a neighbor of Jackson Crow's on a charge of larceny. He had been present when Charles Wilson was killed but had escaped indictment by the Indian courts. He was accused of stealing a horse belonging to one of his neighbors.

"Listen, Deputy, I didn't steal that horse," argued Slaughter as the handcuffs were snapped on securely. "I found it running loose and kept him in my corral for two weeks waiting for someone to claim him. When no one came, I sold him."

"This warrant doesn't say you're guilty, John." Charley smiled down at the smaller man. "If you can prove that it was an innocent mistake, I'm sure the commissioner will dismiss your case."

"There must be something I could tell you to make you believe I'm tellin' the truth."

"You could start by telling me the whereabouts of Jackson Crow."

The young Choctaw ducked his head so Charley could not see his eyes. "I can't tell you where he is. I saw him last week near the Poteau Post Office. He said he was on the scout. I didn't ask him where he was hidin'. I don't care. He's a mean man and I don't want to be around him."

Charley pushed the prisoner toward the door.

"Wait! Wait!" Slaughter motioned for him to come closer. "I don't know where Jack is, but I can tell you where he's going to be. He's going to his home for Christmas. You gotta listen to me, Deputy. I wasn't the only one there. Benton said, 'Today Wilson dies,' and we just helped round him up."

"I'll let the commissioner know you helped me. He may give you a break."

On December 19th, 1885, Charley and Abe joined up with Deputy Hall who had hired twenty full-blood Choctaws for tracking. Nine days of tracking the fugitive southwest into the Palean Mountains in the inclement weather was brutal on the party, though the full bloods hardly noticed. On December 28th, after riding fifteen miles through a light snow storm, they found Crow's family home half way between the court house at Summerfield where the elections that started the murder had been held and the home of Peter Conser, one of the original defendants. It was a convenient location near the prominent Choctaws that were his cronies.

Abe dismounted and stood in the knee-high snow looking at the cabin through binoculars. "How do you plan to handle this, Charley? Remember what happened to Willard Ayers when he went to arrest Emmanuel Patterson."

"I remember. Ayers made the mistake of knocking on the door."

The fugitive held the upper hand. The cabin had a single door, a window in front and another on the right side offering a clear view of the surrounding area. No one could get near it without exposing themselves. A wood pile leaned against the opposite side of the house. Crow's horse was in the corral.

Charley pointed to several large boulders within forty yards of the cabin. "Algie, Spread your men out in a line behind those rocks. This skunk is going nowhere."

In a standoff the most important thing was to block any escape route. Once he could see all of his men spread around in a semi-circle he called out. "Hello in the cabin. Can you hear me?"

A large cowhide covering the front window was pulled back an inch or two. A harsh voice spoke in Choctaw. Hall's lead tracker interpreted. "Who are you?"

"Deputy Marshal Charles Barnhill, you're under arrest for the murder of Charles Wilson. Come out with your hands in the air."

"You can't arrest me. Wilson was a Choctaw and I'm a registered Choctaw. Tell that hangin' judge that he don't get to hang me."

"I can't do that. My job is to bring you in and that's what I aim to do."

A rifle barrel poked through the cow hide and a bullet struck the rock near his head. Shaking his head to stop the ringing in his ears, he tried again. "You can come out peacefully or we can shoot it out. You wouldn't want a stray bullet coming in there and hitting an innocent, would you?"

"Listen! Bob Benton was killing Wilson anyway. Wilson was struggling and thrashing around. I just put him out of his misery. There were six or eight of us there that day, and nobody has been charged. Why have you come after me?"

"I have a warrant for your arrest and I'm not leaving without you. If you're innocent, you'll be released."

Charley beckoned Hall to the pack mules. "Grab some tarps. This may take awhile. Come night, have your men take turns guarding the cabin. Build a big bonfire for them to sleep around over behind those boulders."

The light faded into twilight. Only the occasional stirring of a horse broke the quiet of the soft steady snowfall that continued throughout the night.

Come morning, Charley smelled coffee and bacon as he crawled out from under his tarp. He gritted his teeth and sighed - still snowing. Abe had a cook fire blazing in the woods. In this cold, they needed the warmth of the coffee and the fat in the bacon to keep up their body warmth. Dusting the snow off his pants, he took a bacon sandwich and gobbled it down.

"That's good. How about another?"

"Sure thing. How long we going to keep Crow holed up?"

Before he could answer Deputy Hall came up for a cup of coffee, swishing it around in his mouth before speaking. "What's the plan, Cap'n?"

"We'll allow him some time to think and see what happens."

Hall, red nosed with icicles dripping off his mustache, swallowed the hot fluid and spoke. "A skunk doesn't like to be cornered, ya' know."

Charley swallowed the last bite of his sandwich. "I don't want to eat any lead just yet. We'll hold out as long as we can tolerate the cold."

Four long days they stayed in position, alternately keeping watch while the others cooked a meal or rested as best they could in the snow. Charley knew freezing to death was a likely outcome if they didn't lift this siege. The horses suffered too, and Abe tried to keep blankets on them at night. On New Year's Day, Charley wrapped up in a heavy woolen blanket and laid down under the protective tarp. *Tomorrow I will either storm the cabin or burn it down.*

As the sun rose on the 2nd of January of the new year the snow had stopped and the sky was clear. Charley stirred under his tarp and quickly pulled off his left boot and rubbed his stockinged foot. He could not feel anything and his toes were ice cold. "Abe. You okay?"

"I'm fine. Just a little cold."

"We're going to have to do something quick. I think I've frozen my foot. I must have fallen asleep with it outside my tarp."

Abe examined Charley's foot and felt the toes. "You've got frost bite, for sure. Use your hand to try and get the circulation going." He stared at the quiet cabin. "I think I can work my way 'round to the woodpile and set it on fire. If he comes out, we'll kick it away from the cabin. If he doesn't, we let her go."

"Pass the word to Hall to be ready, but I prefer to take him alive." He put his boot back on and struggled to walk. His foot felt like a dead rock attached to his leg. Even his Winchester would not lever in the cold until he had warmed it near the camp fire.

He hobbled closer to the cabin, eyed the smoke rising from the woodpile, then called out, "Crow, we've given you a chance to surrender, but we won't wait 'til spring."

Flames began to lap at the building and smoke swirled through chinks in the log structure. The roof would be next and then the cabin would be engulfed. Come out, you fool, and save your family.

Crow screamed as he kicked the door open and came out with his hands in the air. "Put out the fire. I quit!" His wife and children tumbled out of the cabin behind him to fight the blaze and save their home.

"Keep your hands where we can see them."

Abe secured the irons and pulled a pistol out of Crow's waistband. He handed it to Charley who turned it over, to reveal the initials C.W. carved in the handle.

"That look's like Wilson's pistol." Abe exclaimed.

"Well, that seals this skunk's fate."

As they rode back to Fort Smith with their notorious prisoner, the brothers talked about the law in the Indian courts. Abe shook his head. "Conser and Benton have served as Indian police officers. How can men, who have sworn to serve the law of the Indian Nation, get away with murder? There were eight other men too who were let go by the Indian court."

"They felt Charles Wilson was over-reaching his position by pitting his deputy marshal commission against their Light Horse when he arrested Jackson Crow last year. A witness said Crow claimed to have murdered Uriah Henderson, a white man, but there was insufficient evidence."

"It sounds like the question is who is in charge, the United States government or the Indian Tribe?"

Charley's hand patted the badge on his coat. "Deputy United States marshals, whether they are Indian or not, should be accorded proper recognition. But the Indians hate *white man's law.*

The journey back to Fort Smith was one of relief for Charley, another fugitive successfully taken into custody without a shot fired. It took cunning and persistence to track these killers, and, in this instance, they had been fortunate to trap him in his lair. He wanted to make sure they kept him in their custody. The first night of camp, he called Hall to the campfire.

He handed Algie Hall a set of leg irons. "One of us needs to sleep with Crow. Handcuffs are not coming off of him until he is released to the jailer."

"Well, I don't mind that duty as long as one of us is standing guard with a shotgun." Hall's words were cautious with doubt.

"Abe and I will take turns at four hour intervals standing watch. You'll be able to sleep like a baby."

"Alright. I don't get paid enough to complain about the conditions."

The night was cold and uncomfortable. Charley's foot ached and throbbed. Though he rubbed his toes and warmed them by the fire, he knew they were beyond saving. He didn't dare take his sock off fearful of what he would find.

The next day the party made slow progress through the winter storms and slick, snow-packed trails. The arrest had been fifteen miles southwest of Poteau Post Office, making it close to fifty miles back to Fort Smith and three days on the trail.

The second evening in the comfortable home of John McClure, he tried to take off his sock. What he saw was ugly, blackened toes.

"Abe, my toes won't last long. See if there is a doctor in Poteau."

Abe left promptly, returning about midnight with a doctor. Charley lay on the host's bed, his foot propped on a pillow. McClure had insisted that the deputy, who captured the murderer Crow, deserved the best bed, and besides wasn't he injured?

The doctor was young and appeared to be very concerned about the condition of the foot. A frown cut his forehead under a thick crop of black hair. "How long has your foot been like this?"

"Two days but I hadn't had my sock off until tonight."

"I'm going to have to use chloroform and put you out. Those toes have to come off now before gangrene sets in and you loose your whole foot."

The last thing Charley remembered was the smell of the chloroform and then a deep darkness. His consciousness returned with a gray light penetrating his closed eyelids. He could hear the faint crackle of the fireplace and soft snoring as his eyes fluttered open. His attempt to rise from the bed was cut short by a sudden pain coming from his left foot. *Oh yeah, that.*

Abe sat in a rocking chair in the corner, a rifle balanced across his lap. He looked at Charley and smiled. "Hey, you're awake. How do you feel?'

"I can't say yet. What time is it?"

"About 3 a.m. You've been out for a couple of hours. The doc finished up and rolled up in a blanket in front of the fire in the other room. He wants to see your foot come daylight."

The dizziness in his head took him down again. Out of the corner of his eyes, he could see Hall and his manacled prisoner, both sleeping on their backs in front of the fireplace.

Abe stepped to the door and beckoned to someone on the porch. "I'm going to have one of the full bloods come in to spell me now, so I can get some shut eye."

Charley lay back and drifted back into a restless sleep, his foot waking him regularly throughout the night.

Someone shook him by the shoulder. Then he heard Abe's voice. "Charley, wake up. The doc wants to check your foot."

The doctor raised the edges of the bandage. "Let's take a look at this bandage first and then I'll check what's underneath. That looks alright. Now, I'm going to unwrap your foot to see the incisions."

As he worked on his foot, Charley watched Abe nudge Deputy Hall awake. With Abe's rifle trained on Crow, the deputy rolled over and prodded the prisoner with his elbow. Crow grunted awake and sat up.

Hall hauled the prisoner to his feet. "Get up, Jackson. Time to eat breakfast and get you to your date with Judge Parker."

The doctor ran a hand through his uncombed hair. “Well, Deputy Barnhill. You’re fortunate. Your foot looks clean and healthy. Change the bandage every day and have a doctor remove the stitches in about seven to ten days. I am going to fit a small splint around your foot over the bandages to keep the wounds from harm. I’ll send my bill to the marshal’s office in Fort Smith. Anyone who can track down and bring in Jackson Crow deserves the government paying for his care.”

After his caregiver left, Charley struggled to his feet. He had to rip open his left pants leg to get it over the splint. Awkwardly, he hobbled to the kitchen and sat down to eat the sumptuous meal Mrs. McClure had prepared.

"This is sure some breakfast. Thank you very much for your hospitality, Ma'am," Charley commented as the first biscuit reached his mouth.

“My pleasure, deputy. I can’t say I’ve been very comfortable having Jackson Crow under my roof. I can’t fathom how a man so degraded as him can have a wife and children.”

“Everyone deserves a family to love. He just didn’t think about them when he took up his murdering ways, is all.”

Charley signed the warrant verifying his arrest of Jackson Crow on January 2, 1886 and handed it to Marshal John Carroll, who had taken over from Marshal Boles. Carroll handed him back a temporary custody order known as a mittimus for placing Crow in jail.

“You did it again. I hear the full bloods were instrumental in tracking Crow.”

“The Palean Mountains are his backyard and he tried every trick possible. Without the trackers’ help, we would have lost him in the bad weather. Getting Crow is the least we could do for a fellow deputy.”

Marshal Carroll’s concern showed in his eyes. “How is your foot? How much time off do you need?”

“A week, maybe two. I can ride again as soon as I get the splint removed.”

“I’ve several arrest writs coming up for Sam Starr’s wife, Belle. She’s stolen a couple of horses and dressed up like a man to avoid detection in a recent robbery. I’m giving them to Tyner Hughes who may want your help.” Marshal Carroll extended his hand to Charley. “By the way, Happy New Year and I’ll notify the Wilson family to send the reward to you.”

The Fort Smith Elevator, February 10, 1888, reported:

Jackson Crow is a Negro desperado who has sent more than one man to the "Happy Hunting Grounds" during his life in the wilds of the Indian Territory. He was convicted on the 26th of last month for complicity in the murder of a prominent Choctaw named Charles B. Wilson. The murder was committed on the 7th of August, 1884. All of his comrades in the crime, being Indians, this court had no jurisdiction of them, hence Jack must suffer the extreme penalty of the law while they go Scott free, as the Choctaw courts have long since disposed of their cases by acquitting them. The only regret was that he could not suffer for some of his former crimes, also ...that some of his companions in the Wilson murder were not made to suffer with him."

On April 27, 1888, Jackson Crow was "hanged by the neck until dead."

Chapter 21

Hunt for Belle Starr

His boot would not budge, no matter how much he tugged and pushed. His foot was too swollen. Ignoring the discomfort, Charley pushed with all his might - no luck. He hobbled around the bedroom, his boot half on. *OK - there is more than one way to put on this boot.* He jerked it off and hobbled into the kitchen. Salina stood at the wood stove stirring something that swelled mighty good.

"Sweetheart, where are your sharpest scissors?"

She turned and pointed toward the corner hutch. "By my Singer sewing machine in the corner there. Why do you need them?"

"I'm going to fix this boot to fit my foot."

"And ruin a good pair of boots?"

"I'll cut along the seam so it can be resown later."

After cutting a slit in the boot that extended from the top down the side seam to the mid-ankle, his foot slid in. He wiggled his remaining two toes on that foot to get it seated. He had difficulty walking long distances without limping and to run without stumbling was a challenge he had not overcome.

He had just finished punching holes in the boot and inserting rawhide strings to tie it shut when he heard riders. Tyne and James Cole were right on time. He had not ridden with James since they had gone to the Indian execution back before Joey had died.

As he stepped out onto the porch, his eyes roved over Cole's tall frame. His slight build disguised a lithe young man who could wrestle a man to the ground and cuff him in seconds. He was the same age as Charley, but had not suffered the wounds of combat that Charley was struggling with today. Days of riding in the sun had tanned Cole's face which accented his blue eyes and blonde lashes.

The boards of the porch creaked as Salina came through the door. "Bring those men in for dinner before you ride off."

Charley chewed on a hunk of beef he had extracted from the bowl of stew. He delighted in his wife's cooking. After he returned from a long trip, she worried over his under-fed appearance and stuffed him with three full meals a day. He pointed his spoon at Tyne. "What chance do we have of catching Sam and Belle Starr at Youngers Bend?"

Tyne took a swig of coffee. "We have two warrants for her, one for horse stealing and one for a recent robbery where, dressed up as a man, she helped rob an old couple of their gold. James and I went out in February on the same horse stealing warrant and never got near them. "

Charley knew his friend was shrewd and this woman had out-smarted him twice this year.

Tyne continued. "She keeps her fastest horse saddled at all times ready for escape. Use of a spy unknown to her people may give us a chance. It will take one brave man willing to crawl into Youngers Bend without being detected."

Charley snapped his fingers. "I know some people down at Whitefield that would be glad to see her and Sam gone. One of them, a man named John Vann, owes me. I helped him beat a horse stealing charge with my testimony."

Their companion, who had been listening between swallows, spoke up. "If the Starrs are there, how will we come in?"

Tyne rubbed his cheeks and stared into his coffee cup for a few seconds. "Quickly before they can bolt."

James pulled a silk scarf out of his vest. "We could use the disguise of a peddler's wagon to get fairly close, at least to the edge of their sentry post. I have one already out-fitted that I plan to use when the winter slows us down. I can drive the wagon up to the place with you two hiding in the back and then you can approach the door on foot."

"Where's this wagon?" Tyne looked skeptical.

"At the livery stable in Spiro, just down the Fort Smith road."

"Why didn't you suggest this before now?'

"I had time to think on the ride out from Fort Smith. I wasn't sure what would work since we came back empty-handed last time after just riding around letting her spies track us."

Charley lifted his cup in the air. "Here's to a successful arrest. We'll let James use his wagon and keep several miles ahead of us. That way the spies won't see us together until it's too late."

The Whitefield settlement was unchanged, sleepy, a few Indians wrapped in colorful blankets sitting in front of the trading post. Tyne dismounted and led his horse to the watering trough in the center of the square as Charley pulled up at the front of the store.

John Turk recognized him as he came through the door. "Deputy Barnhill, what brings you here?"

He looked around at the merchandise before answering. Turk had prospered as indicated by the well-stocked shelves. "We're looking for John Vann. You seen him in town today?"

"Yes, he's over at the livery getting a horse shod. What's he done?"

"Nothing. We just want to talk to him. By the way, see anyone come through here today?"

"Just a peddlers wagon heading west."

Good, James is on schedule and the disguise is working.

Back outside Tyne moved toward him and indicated to a silent figure sitting at the edge of the watering trough. "One of Starr's spies, I'll bet. He knows we're deputies. He'll probably leave as soon as we go into the livery."

As they entered the stable, Charley glanced behind him. Sure enough, the man moved to his horse and rode off in a hurry, headed west toward Youngers Bend, five miles away.

Our presence in the area will be revealed. Will the Starrs' run or wait to see what we are doing here?

Inside, John Vann held a tin cup of coffee and watched the blacksmith working at the fire. His face lit up in recognition. "Charley, how are you? Haven't seen you since Salina's funeral."

"I'm fine, John. I've come to make you a proposition. Let's step outside."

The three men huddled in the shade of the overhanging roof behind the livery. May was already a warm month.

Charley wiped his face with his sleeve and looked his friend in the eyes. "You know the Starrs?"

"Who doesn't?"

"We need your help. A deputy can't get near their place because of all their spies. We could use a man like you who feels comfortable moving around in this area, one who could get close to them for us.."

"I would have to go into hiding afterwards if I'm found out."

"I hope that doesn't happen. Will you do it?"

Vann examined the toe of his boot and signed. "What do you want me to do exactly?"

"Go out there and see if Belle Starr's horse, Venus, is saddled and ready to go. Wherever that horse is ready, so is she. Sam's whereabouts is another matter. If we can catch him too that would be great, but I heard he is on the scout in New Mexico."

"You know that will require me to crawl on my hands and knees for miles. Their sentries would detect a horseman."

Charley could feel his anxiety. "What do you say?"

"Alright, but I'll need my pay now."

He pulled a gold piece from his pocket and placed in Vann's palm. "If Sam is there and we get him, I'll double that."

"I'll go out there tonight and let you know in the morning."

The spy was back before daylight. Coming into the ring of the camp fire,

Charley could see Vann's pale face and shredded clothes.

"You look like a pack of wolves chased you," Charley said.

Vann took the cup of coffee Charley offered. "The access to that hideout is through briers and brambles and steep ravines unless you're on the only trail that they can cover for the distance of a rifle shot."

Tyne stood up and brushed off his pants. "Well, what did you find?"

"She's there alright. Venus is tied outside. I watched the place for several hours and saw no one come or go, just her daughter, Pearl, going to the out-house and barn."

"Thanks, John," Charley offered his hand.

Vann shook his hand and turned to go. "If I run into trouble because of this, I'll expect some help too."

"Whatever I can do I will."

The peddler's wagon stood at the bend in the road. One fork continued on north to the next settlement and the other west to Youngers Bend. Charley tied his horse to the wagon while Tyne scrambled in the back. He had left his horse in the cover of the brush.

James pulled his floppy hat down over his face. "I figure it is another mile from here to the opening in the clearing where the hideout is located."

Tyne pushed his head through the canvas cover behind James. "When we get to where you can see the house, we'll approach on foot. Vann said it's about a hundred yards between the road and the house, all of it is open area."

"What if they open fire?"

"Then, you move your wagon up and cover us."

It was just coming daylight when the wagon stopped. Charley felt his stomach turn to quicksand as he climbed out and reached for his Winchester.

Tyne paused with his hand on his arm. "I know we're taking a big risk approaching this house in broad daylight and on foot. But, the Starrs are not known for fighting with marshals head on if they can help it. Ambush is more their style."

The house backed up within fifty feet of heavy timber and the front of the house opened onto a wide meadow. Since access to the house could only be gained by coming up a rock-strewn narrow canyon trail, anyone approaching could easily be identified and sized-up by the occupants of the house.

Nothing stirred as he followed Tyne who carried his Winchester with ease in his right hand. He clinched his teeth expecting any moment to get a bullet in the chest while Tyne walked with confident strides as if he were on Garrison Avenue with his wife on his arm.

Within twenty feet of the porch, Charley figured they had it made when he saw a curtain in the front window move. He sucked in his breath and held it as he took his next step, his Winchester at the ready. The door popped open to reveal a teenage girl of slight build, maybe seventeen years of age. His head cleared its whirling as he heard Tyne speak.

"Good morning, Pearl. Is your mother in?"

"May I ask who is calling, sir?" The polite voice surprised Charley.

"United States Deputy Marshals Hughes and Barnhill, miss."

The girl turned to speak to someone behind her and then opened the door wide. "Please come in and Mama will receive you."

Is this a courteous formal call of a gentleman on a lady or an arrest of a notorious fugitive? Charley could not believe their luck to be standing inside Belle Starr's home instead of lying in the dirt in the yard dead and bleeding.

The woman who came out of the side room was short, about the size of his mother Sarah. Charley had seen her at a distance on several occasions in Fort Smith. She was a frequent visitor to the saloons and shops and was a splendid figure riding Venus down Garrison Avenue with two pistols strapped over her riding skirt.

She extended her hand to both men and invited them to sit down. "Would you care for something to drink?"

Charley took the opportunity to check her features up close. She was slender with a moderate bosom and small waist. Though her head was held high, he could see her skin had not weathered the years well. She looked older than thirty-two which was her reported age, according to the Fort Smith Elevator. She was probably untruthful about her age just like any other married woman who is approaching forty. Her eyes were not unkind but held a fire of challenge in them.

He heard Tyne talking. "No ma'am. I have a warrant for your arrest and you must come with me to Fort Smith."

"Do I have time to pack a few things?'

"Yes, ma'am. Just make it quick."

"Why, Deputy Hughes? As you can see my husband is not here."

"Mama, may I come with you?" Pearl had her hand on Belle's arm.

"You must ask the gentlemen, dear."

"May I?" Pearl's eyes held tears.

Tyne swallowed and smiled. "You may come for a few miles, but you cannot come all the way to Fort Smith. I do not know how long your mother will be held there."

Charley picked up Belle's bag and carried it to her horse. Venus did not like the nearness of a stranger and backed away from the hitching post. Belle came up and put her hand on the big horse's shoulder. "Shh! Venus. It is alright." She wore a full riding skirt over high boots.

With Pearl mounted on a pony and Belle in tow on Venus, the men walked back to the peddler's wagon. He got on Billie and picked up the reins to Belle's horse. He wanted to get away from there and back on the main road before the gang could be alerted.

James waited until Tyne had taken a seat alongside of him and then turned his team. When they reached the place Tyne had left his horse, he jumped down. "We'll head back through Whitefield. I'm sure you can stow your wagon there."

Around the campfire that evening, Charley eyed the woman already in her bedroll alongside the fire. She had given her word she would not attempt to escape. He didn't know why his partner was willing to trust her.

"Why don't we have her at least chained to a tree?"

Tyne rested his eyes on the still form. "She is a woman of her word. I've seen her take care of sick women like John West's wife whom she nursed back to health after having a baby. She has a tender side."

"But is she truthful? I heard her testimony in court at her trial in '83. It's no better than any other fugitive's word."

James Cole spoke up. "James White went to arrest her one time and she told him she would meet him at a certain place later if he would not require her to be dragged all over the Territory while he was searching for other fugitives. She was there when he came back by."

Charley's skepticism strangled in his throat. "Another deputy told me when he had her in custody, she made his life miserable, throwing things and cussing and chasing other prisoners around the camp with a butcher knife."

A chuckle escaped Tyne's lips. "Sounds a little crazy to me, but I think it depends on the deputy. If she likes you, she will come along quietly, if not she is a handful."

Charley's foot throbbed and he needed to get his boot off. "Alright, good night. Hope she's here in the morning."

Tyne checked his side arm. "James and I will take the first two watches. You can have the early morning duty."

The next morning Belle was still there and had risen early to make a pot of coffee. She handed the cup to Charley who sat in the darkness near the horses. "Thank you, ma'am. Any idea where your husband is?"

Belle looked at him in the dawning light. Her eyes now sparked with that fire he had seen the day before. "No idea. He comes and goes as he pleases."

The morning was almost over when the lawmen started across the San Bois Creek which was half way between Youngers Bend and Fort Smith. They had made good time covering 23 miles and getting away from Youngers Bend without a pursuing party. Tomorrow they would deliver the prisoner to the jail. Charley hoped they would not get ridiculed for taking three deputies to arrest one woman. The Starr gang was formidable though and three was nothing to them if they tried something.

He was shaken out of his thoughts by the sound of a rifle. He ducked and searched the area for the shooter - six men on Indian ponies and coming down the creek bed at a gallop, Belle's husband, Sam in the lead. They were outnumbered two to one and easy targets in the middle of this creek. The bullets sang near their heads, probably to save the horses.

He caught the reins of Venus' bridle that Tyne tossed at him. "Snub her horse in tight and we'll try to fight them off." Tyne raised his Winchester and began to pump out shells as fast as he could lever the action. James, behind Charley, let out an oath as a bullet struck the water between him and Charley.

With a start Belle threw her hands in the air and shouted at Tyne. "Let me stop them and you men quit shooting. If you don't, my boys will kill you fellows."

"All right, stop them." Tyne lowered his rifle and nodded to James.

Charley pulled Venus even closer. If Belle was wrong, they would soon be floating face down in the San Bois.

He was startled when she screamed out at the gang in an unrecognizable guttural, gesturing with her hands and shaking her head. Sam hollered back in the same coded language, his face growing stormy. Finally, Belle gave a last shout in English, "I said, get out of here. Now get going." She flung her arms toward the men who turned their ponies and fled down the creek bed as quickly as they had appeared.

Tyne turned to the petite woman. "What did you say to make them not kill us?"

Belle smiled her coquettish best. "I told Sam that he was stupid to shot three deputies just to free me. I would be out on bail as soon as we got to Fort Smith. And besides I wanted to go to Fort Smith to do some shopping. And if he killed my horse, I would kill him." With that she gave Venus a nudge and pulled away from Charley's side.

Tyne cursed beneath his breath as he tried to turn his horses' head. "What's the matter, boy?"

Charley saw that Tyne's rein had been severed by a bullet. Checking his own equipment, he found three bullet notches in his reins and a bullet embedded in his pommel. In amazement he stared around him at the sky which was bluer, the clouds whiter and the birds' songs sweeter. Death had come close again, but he was still breathing. What a story to tell his grandchildren one day.

The three deputies stood in the marshal's office, the paper work for Belle Starr in their hands. Carroll squinted at the writs of arrest. "It took three of you to find this woman?"

Charley gulped as Tyne tried to lighten the sarcasm in his voice. "When you go after Belle Starr, you're going after the whole Starr gang, you know that."

"Well, your pay will be mighty skimpy. But you can claim the reward offered by the old Indian Ferrell. He and his sons have a $300 reward out for her since she took thousands from them."

"We'll contact Ferrell then." Tyne turned to leave.

A female attendant from the women's jail on the fourth floor came to the door. "Are you the arresting officers for Mrs. Starr?"

"Yes, Ma'am," Tyne answered. The three men looked at each other. What was wrong?

"The matron of the women's jail would like to see you."

Charley followed Tyne up the stairs, his left foot awkward in the laced up boot. When they arrived before the desk of the good woman, she looked up from her paperwork. She was middle-aged, attractive, a former teacher at a girl's academy. Her reputation for fairness and care for her charges was known all over the state.

"Thank you for coming, deputies." She opened a drawer of her desk and brought out a big hog leg, a Colt .45. She picked up the pistol and opened the bale. It was loaded. "You over-looked something when you arrested Mrs. Starr. This was found concealed in the folds of her riding skirt."

Charley felt his stomach tighten. She could have killed them all as they slept, but she did not. Thank God.

Tyne tried to mask his surprise. "Ma'am. I've dealt with Mrs. Starr before and I've always found her to be a woman of her word, so I did not feel it necessary to search her person. She had plenty of occasion to use that but did not. She's no killer."

The three deputies left the jail to the sounds of laughter from the guards and marshals who met them in the hall. Word gets around fast.

The newspaper correspondent from the Dallas Morning Star held his notebook on his knees. Belle Starr sat in a chair talking of her recent capture. "I was never more dumbfounded in my life than when Deputy Hughes and Deputy Barnhill rode up boldly to my house. And then I found out Deputy Cole was in a peddler's wagon at the end of the trail too. Hughes was most polite and informed me that he had a writ of arrest to serve on me and Sam. Sam wasn't home and I told him so."

"What happened then, Mrs. Starr?" The correspondent sat on the edge of his seat in anticipation. Belle Starr, know in Texas as Reed, had lived in Fort Worth and had a reputation as a woman of crime. He wanted her life's story from beginning to end.

"Why, I'm not used to that manner of approach, as the marshals generally come into the Bend with a crowd of twenty-five to forty men and crawl upon their hands and knees in the darkness. Whenever I see a deputy marshal come in, with the knees of his pants worn out, you may be sure he has invaded Youngers Bend. Hughes is a brave man and acted the gentleman in every particular, but I hardly believe he realized his danger."

The reporter closed his notebook. "I would like a picture of you and Deputy Hughes for our readers."

"Why, certainly," Belle said. She smoothed her riding skirt as she rose.

Charley threw down the newspaper in disgust. Belle Starr's interview was full of half-truths and errors and the source of much nonsense. It made them look like incompetents, not withstanding the fact they had finally caught her completely unaware.

He picked up the paper again to read Tyne's comments. "I had a warrant for the arrest of both Belle and Sam Starr. I found no one at home at Youngers Bend except Belle and her daughter, Pearl. Mrs. Starr made neither resistance nor remonstrance but quickly mounted her horse and came with me, chatting away amiably."

Not a word about the ambush and gun fight. Tyne was reticent when talking to the press. The less Sam Starr knew of what they were up to the better. He read the newspapers too.

Belle Starr and Tyner Hughes, May 23, 1886
Courtesy Fort Smith National Historic Site

The photo of Belle sitting on her beautiful horse was splendid. She sat in the side-saddle sideways to the camera which showed her flowing riding skirt, trim waist and bosom, riding gloves, hat cinched under her chin, earring in her ears and a smirk on her race. Around her waist she wore two six-guns that she had bought while in Fort Smith. He guessed she needed to replace the one the jailer had taken from her.

In contrast Tyne sat on his hard-ridden horse face on to the camera in his worn riding clothes. He looked like an average deputy marshal, his comfortable hat covering a shrewd head that had out-witted many a criminal.

He laid the paper aside. The Fort Smith Elevator reporters did a good job of covering the news of arrests. This reporter from Texas was looking for sensationalism and had managed to make Belle Starr's name a common household word now. Yellow journalism had found the Indian Territory.

Reading the rest of the paper, an item down at the bottom of the second page caught his eye. "John Vann, recent of Whitefield, has departed the Territory to parts undisclosed after someone burned his house and ran off his stock. Vann claims parties are out to get him in revenge. Vann is the adopted brother of Chief Bill Vann of the Cherokee Light Horse."

This man had taken a great chance in helping them. Now he was homeless and on the run from the Starrs. The Cherokees had constant inter-family disputes and this one could spill over into something more deadly than a burned house.

Pearl Starr as a madam in Ft. Smith

Chapter 22

A Choctaw Wedding

The bald spot on top of Commissioner Stephen Wheeler's head glistened in the bright morning sun streaming through the windows.

"Here you go, Deputy Barnhill, your voucher for sixty dollars, your pay for posse with Deputy Hughes. I had to dock you both three days as excessive time."

Charley grumbled. "Mr. Wheeler, you come ride with us and see what it takes to find these prisoners. Three days is nothing when tracking someone in the Territory. We covered five hundred miles in twenty-three days. That averages out to more than twenty miles a day and all the time trying to track down fugitives."

"I sympathize with you, but the policy is strict on allowable days when tracking a fugitive. It's to keep the costs reasonable for operating this court."

Three twenty dollar gold pieces clinked together in Charley's hand after he turned in the voucher at the bank. He held them lightly, feeling their smooth surface as he walked along crowded Garrison Avenue. Riverboats laden with stacks of hides, cotton and casks of merchandise lined the docks on the Arkansas River. Fort Smith was growing, along with the whole Indian Territory.

He entered a long narrow building, its front on Garrison Avenue and its back opening on an alleyway. Pleasant smells of coffee, leather, and bolts of fresh cloth straight from New England factories mingled to make an unforgettable impression on his nose. Gleaming horse bridles with sparkling bits hung from the rafters. The shelves held saddle blankets of every design and color. These merchants supplied both the locals and the merchants in the Indian Territory.

"Howdy, Charley." The owner, Columbus Ayers, smiled and extended his hand. The brother of Will Ayers, he had been the deputy in charge of the posse Charley had ridden with that had captured his brother's murderer back in '83.

"Hi, Columbus. How you doing? I thought you were spending more time over at the jail?"

"I'm too busy with the store to go man-hunting. As soon as my partner gets back from St. Louis, I'll be on the trail again. It sure gets in your blood to see justice done. What do you need today?"

Charley fingered the hem of a little girl's dress that was on display. "I need to pick up a few things for my family. Do you have this little dress for an 8 year-old girl? And some boots?"

The merchant turned and pulled a similar dress down from the shelf. He shook it out and handed it to his customer. "How about that?" He turned to search through the girl's boots.

"Looks about right. I also need shirts, trousers, stockings and shoes for my boy. He's eleven."

His friend piled the articles high on the counter. "Anything else you need?"

"Let me have a bag of that stick candy, a pack of marbles and a pen knife. That should fix them up nicely. I need a pound each of sugar and coffee, and a pouch of tobacco. Give me some of that pretty material over there, the blue cotton, five yards and some new Singer sewing needles for Salina."

"I'll wrap this all up for you in two bundles that should fit in your saddle-riders."

He paid his bill and lifted a bundle under each arm intending to walk to the livery to pick up Billie. A crowd gathered around a man on the street. As he approached, he could see the tip of a dark hat pulled down over a familiar face. A chill went up his spine as he saw Bob Benton, the affluent Choctaw politician who had been named by witnesses as the killer of Charley Wilson. Sometimes guilty men got away because honest people would not step forward to testify. One day Benton would get his just reward - if not here on earth than in the place God reserves for unrepentant sinners.

Billie nickered as they drew near the school house at Kully-cha-ha, calling to the students' horses in a corral in back. It was a very nice building for the Indian Territory. It consisted of one room with finished plank sides, shingled roof, and glass in the windows, two on each side and in the front. It had stood since 1850 and was attended in the fall and winter by children, ranging in age from first grade through eighth grade.

Charley dismounted under one of the trees surrounding the school yard. He wanted his children to be properly educated. He had seen how the inability to read and write had hampered people who wanted to work at something other than ranching or farming. He had not seen his family in a month and his heart pounded in excitement. As the bell rang the children poured out the front.

Henry was among the first ones out. "Pa!" he exclaimed, surprise heightening his voice. He ran to his father and threw his arms around his neck. He was growing and was chest high to Billie.

"Hi, son. I thought I would surprise you." He winked at him and rumpled his hair. "Where's your sister?"

"Home with a sore throat. Let's go. Want to race?" Henry asked as he saddled his horse.

"You can't beat me and ole Billie. Let's see who gets to the half mile fence first."

A clatter of hooves and whoops signaled the start of the race. Billie jumped out and took a good lead, but the lighter boy and his fast pony began to gain at the quarter point. He looked back over his shoulder and smiled. *That boy, I'm so proud of him Let's give'um a little edge.* He allowed Billie to break his gallop to a trot just at he approached the fence. The horses came in nose and nose.

"You're too fast for us," he chuckled.

"Aw, Pa. You could've beat me." Henry slapped his horse on the neck in reward for his effort.

"Let's see what your ma has for supper." Charley nudged Billie back into a gentle trot.

The smoke wafting from the chimney was a welcome indication of home-cooked food. He hugged Salina, her clean scent tickling his nose as his mouth found hers. Would he ever grow weary of her kisses?

Little Minnie came running from the bedroom. "Pa, I missed you so much." She wrapped her arms around his chest and gave him a hug, unmindful of his cartridge belt that bit into her shoulder. Sarah had braided her long brown hair and tied it behind her head with a bright ribbon. Her pink cheeks added radiance to her joy.

He looked around the comfortable room, a fire in the fireplace against the evening's coolness, rows of drying herbs hanging from the kitchen ceiling, potatoes, corn and carrots in baskets for storage in the root cellar - it was a palace to him. With regret, he knew it was time to say good-bye to this home of many years. He was so busy now making trip after trip that he knew he could not continue the upkeep of this place. The lease was up soon and he needed to speak to Salina.

After supper, he brought out his gifts. While Salina sat by the fireplace with her knitting, he unwrapped the two large parcels, the brown paper falling away like the petals of a beautiful spring flower, revealing the surprises underneath.

Henry waved the trousers and shirts in the air. "Pa, thank you." He reached down and grabbed up the boots and socks. "Holy Smokes." He had grown so much that his present trousers and shirts hit him half way up his lanky arms and legs. He shouted in delight again when his father brought out the pen knife. "Wow, my own pocket knife. Thank you, Pa."

Minnie shifted expectantly from one foot to the other. "What did you bring me, Pa?"

He held the paper-wrapped bundle just above her head. She danced around on tip-toes, jumping for the package. He watched in pleasure as she ripped it open. Squealing in delight, she held up the beautiful dress for all to see and then discovered the boots.

"Oh, Pa. I love them. They're so beautiful." She squealed again as he handed her the bag of candy from his pocket. As he watched his children, the words of Jesus in Matthew 6:26 came to mind. *Look at the birds of the air; they do not sow or reap or store away in barns, and yet your heavenly Father feeds them.* He knew that the Lord loved and provided for him and his precious children.

Next, he handed packages to his beloved who had watched while her children discovered their gifts.

"Such lovely material, I can make a new Sunday dress. How did you know I needed sewing machine needles? " Salina pecked his cheek with a kiss. "The coffee and sugar are perfect. I'll make a cake for Sunday dinner and have the Davis family over for cake and coffee."

"How long can you stay this time, Pa?"Minnie's little brows lifted.

He turned to his wife and picked up her hand. It was warm and soft. He was amazed at how dainty the weaker sex really was. Even Belle Starr had been smaller in stature than he had imagined. "I figure about a week. Let's ask your mother what needs to be done while I am home."

"You need to bring in the rest of the corn into the crib for the hogs and cut down the stocks for silage. Saturday your father has to ride over to Pocola to perform a marriage. He has invited us to accompany him. A white man is marrying a local Indian girl. They want the traditional Indian wedding before the church ceremony."

"That might be interesting," Charley answered, his mind wandering to his own wedding day. When his father had united him and Salina seventeen years ago, they had been so young, only sixteen and eighteen.

As the children left the room to play with their items, he caught Salina's arm and pulled her close. "How would you like having me home for longer periods of time?"

"What do you mean, sweetheart?"

His eyes held her face. She squirmed around to look at him.

"I've been thinking about giving up the ranch. It's too much to maintain since I am making so many trips and will likely continue. I come home and have to work non-stop to get caught up. I want to surrender the lease."

"And go where?" He knew Salina yearned to live in more "civilized" surroundings. "How about nearer Fort Smith?"

"Oh Charley, I would love it. My sister lives just east of Fort Smith in the little town of Bloomer. Would that be close enough?"

He kissed her forehead. "It's only five miles closer to Fort Smith than Kul-ly-cha-ha, but it has better roads. So I could get home a half day quicker. Let's get this done before school starts."

The family rode the eight miles to Pocola early Saturday morning, the wedding scheduled in the afternoon at the Baptist Church. Minnie, wearing her new dress, rode in the wagon with her parents. Henry had on his new clothes; face, ears, neck and hands scrubbed and hair slicked down. Riding beside the wagon, he swatted at the dust to keep it off his new clothes. It was a losing process.

Charley tried to explain the event to him as they rode along.

"When a white man wants to marry an Indian girl, he has to get ten good citizens of the tribe to sign a petition and then pay a fee, or license permit. Once married, he is considered part of the tribe and is subject to all their laws and punishments including whipping. He can hold any office except chief or judge."

Henry seemed satisfied and turned back to enjoy the country side. Charley figured marriage ceremonies were something to be endured when you are eleven years old and would rather be fishing.

At the church the families and their friends collected, many coming from miles around to witness this special event in wagons loaded with women and children, men riding on their saddle horses along side. Those men of more humble means rode a horse, the rest of his family walking behind. The families of the bride and groom had drawn up camps on opposite sides of the church yard which had room for all. The women sat in chairs carried from home in the back of wagons, the children on the ground at their feet. The men stood behind them gathered in groups according to clan.

At the appointed time, the bride appeared from her tent, led by the married women of her clan. She wore a bright red skirt and white blouse, both trimmed with ribbons tied along the hem and shirt tail, and a beautiful woven sash encircling her hips. Her braided and adorned hair sprouted more ribbons. She kept her eyes averted to the ground as she was seated on a large blanket in the middle of the clearing.

The groom's brothers and uncles approached from the other end of the encampment to place bundles of all sizes and shapes on her blanket. Her attendants scooped up the gifts which were a token for her family, not her.

At this break in the ceremony, Charley pointed to the bridegroom and his attendants who walked slowly up to the seated bride.

"Now watch what happens," he whispered to his wife

Suddenly, the young woman jumped up and ran away. Startled, Salina asked, "Doesn't she want to marry him?"

"That's part of the ancient ritual of pursuing your bride. If she allows herself to be caught, then she is assenting to the marriage."

She smiled at him, the late afternoon sun glowing golden red on her hair. "That seems pretty dramatic. If she runs away, the man will be publicly shamed."

"Don't worry. All that has been worked out before-hand. The father of the bride was well-paid by the bridegroom, either in horses or other valuables."

After several fun-filled minutes of giggling and laughter, the girl allowed the bridegroom's men to catch her and escort her to a tent, discretely placed in a quiet part of the encampment, away from prying eyes and ears.

He turned to his children. Henry's eyes were wide with surprise. He figured he had never seen such romping about amongst white folks. "If she accepts the bridegroom when he is escorted to her tent, then they are legally married according to Choctaw Law. However, the marriage must be solemnized by a judge or minister to prevent common law marriages from corrupting the children's right to allotment payments."

"Why perform a Christian ceremony then?"

Boy, is he growing up? Such questions. "Most Choctaws come from Christian families who believe that marriage must be solemnized according to God's Law."

With all the questions answered for the moment, the Barnhill family gathered in the church for the final part of the ceremony. Salina put her hand in his and squeezed. Her eyes glistened.

As he watched the bride and groom walk down the aisle, his heart constricted. What would he do if he lost her? He could not imagine life without her. He pushed the thought from his mind. He had enough worries without worrying about the future. Let each day bring its blessings and sorrows.

Chapter 23

The Outlaw Bill Frazier

The heat swirled around Charley's face, sucking the breath out of his lungs. The summer humidity made Billie's coat slick. The horses tolerated the heat better than the men.

He contemplated his current excursion into Sugar Loaf County, Choctaw Nation. One of the men to be apprehended was William Frazier, charged with larceny in a one-sided horse swap. The owner of the horse had pressed charges. The matter seemed pretty cut and dried, but no chase could be considered closed until the charged man was in irons. This particular individual had a reputation of using intimidation and threats to cover his actions like many of the white men who lived in the Indian Territory.

Poteau Mountain

Riding with him were two deputy marshals, George E. Williams and James B. Lee. George had been a deputy for over nine years, but James was new. Charley examined the young man, maybe twenty-four at the most, well-worn jeans and comfortable shirt, boots that had seen many a mile. He chuckled and remembered when he had so little himself. Lee's erect posture in the saddle was that of a trooper. He was permanently ruddy from the out-of-doors.

One thing was for sure, a new deputy faced monumental challenges: the rigors of the man hunt, danger around every curve, even the possibility of an early grave. Many good men had not made it six months carrying a badge. He did not hold that against anyone. The never ending pursuits through hundreds of miles of underpopulated wilderness left good men frustrated and disappointed.

Charley shifted his gaze to the ridge ahead. Black Fork Mountain lay to the south of Poteau Mountain. Both Poteau Mountain and Sugar Loaf Mountain could be seen for a hundred miles and were used as a beacon in an area where there were few established roads. Rivers and creeks were the easiest to follow which was why he found himself on the banks of a slowly flowing river, the Poteau.

"George, James. Let's stop and take a break. The horses need water," he ordered.

He watched Billie swill the fresh water into his mouths, his pink tongues working under the bits, clamping down on the metal with each motion of his jaws. He took off his hat and went upstream a few yards to catch a drink away from the mud around the horses' hooves. Wiping his mouth with the back of his hand as he studied the terrain, he addressed the others. "Bill Frazier has some notorious neighbors: Bob Benton, Peter Conser, Nail Perry and Simon Carshell, all involved in the killing of Charles Wilson. With friends like these to back him up, it could be a fight. Frazier may be at his home about two miles up that draw."

George Williams raised his hat and smoothed his long black curls, his eyebrows cutting a deep furrow as he squinted toward the mountain. "I don't trust him. His friends are thick as ticks around here and we could be riding into an ambush." He wiped his hands on the thick fabric of his trousers and patted his six gun. The polished barrel gleamed in the sunlight. Charley thought he would look wonderful on the cover of a pulp fiction magazine.

"If we can find anyone home between here and there, we'll inquire."

"Alright, but I think we need to cover our backs," George mumbled.

Crossing the ridge, Charley picked out a house sitting in the valley below. A woman stood in the yard stirring something in a big black kettle. As the three men rode in, she glanced up, threw the stir stick down and dashed for the porch.

"Well, I guess we aren't expected. Keep a close look out," Charley ordered.

A man came out on the porch.

Charley displayed his badge. "I'm looking for Bill Frazier. Have you seen him?"

"He lives up the draw a few miles. Have no idea if he's home or not."

"What's your name, sir?"

The man hesitated, startled by the question. "Erwin Justice. I own the general store in Conser. "

"Mr. Justice, are you friendly with Frazier?"

"He's my neighbor and, out here, neighbors depend on each other."

"Alright, thanks for your information."

When he spoke, George did not seem to care that Justice and his wife were still within earshot standing in their yard. "Dammit, Charley, you trust that man? He could be one of Frazier's gang. I've heard he has the whole neighborhood terrorized and under his influence. If they even talk to a marshal, he threatens to kill them,"

Charley knew arguing with George did no good."I have to take it as I see it. If he has the people in this area under his influence, we'll soon find out."

The veteran deputy growled. "You're going to get us killed trusting these people."

"We'll approach the house with caution, give Frazier a hail and see what happens."

Not content with that answer, George grumbled as he groped for his Winchester and checked the chamber for a cartridge. He glanced at James and whispered, "Get your gun ready. We won't give Frazier a chance to escape."

"But it does no good to kill a man if he'll surrender first," James answered, his boyish features tightened with the thought of a shoot out. His pistol was not as shiny as George's, probably a hand-me-down. It took a deputy a few trips before he could afford a decent handgun. But they all rode out of Fort Smith with the newest Winchester.

"We'll see. I think Frazier'll fight."

"Mr. Justice, do you have a spare rifle?" George asked the startled merchant.

Fear and concern swept over the man's face. He clamped his jaws together and closed his eyes before answering. "I guess I can let you borrow my Winchester. I'll have to have a receipt for it."

"Sure thing." George whipped out a tablet from his front pocket and opened it to the first page. After writing out the requested document, he read it out loud: "Borrowed from Erwin Justice, one Winchester rifle. To be returned in undamaged condition to owner or payment for same if lost or damaged. George E. Williams, United States Deputy Marshal, July 20, 1886." He tore it out and handed it to Justice.

Charley, anxious to ride out, did not pay much attention to their comments. "Why do you need another rifle, Williams? Come on. It does no good to boast about what we're going to do. Let's do it. "

"I just want to make sure I've plenty of fire power. Never wrong to be prepared. I learned that in the late Indian troubles. I'll make you a bet on which of us gets the SOB first," Williams smirked.

Justice and his wife lowered their heads and exchanged glances.

"George, you need to learn to keep your mouth shut. "

Justice walked slowly into the house and came back with a well-used Winchester. He wiped the side of the stock with his shirt sleeve before handing it up to George. Sweat trickled down the sides of his contorted features.

"Thanks. You'll get this back in about an hour," George said.

"Don't tell anyone where you got that or I'm a dead man. I shouldn't even be talking to you all out here in the open," the store owner said.

"Why? Has someone threatened your life?" Charley asked, the concern for these innocent neighbors causing him to pull Billie up short.

"I can't say anymore," Justice answered. He pulled his wife toward the house as the marshals rode off.

Frazier's house sat in an open area. A buggy hitched to a single horse stood at the post.

"Dismount. I'm sure he's seen us by now if he's home."

As the lawmen watched, a couple came out on the porch. They looked around with caution and hurried to the buggy. The man switched the whip above the horse's ears as it pulled away with a leap that almost unseated the passengers. Allowing the buggy to pass into the cover of the trees, Charley stepped out and hailed them as they approached. The driver pulled hard on the reins as he saw the deputy marshal.

"Hold up, I'm United States Deputy Marshal Charles Barnhill. Is Bill Frazier in that house?"

The man looked at his wife, his face turning pale at the question. "I can't say for sure. We came to visit with Mrs. Frazier, but she's not there. " His gaze shifted back toward the house giving Charley the answer he needed.

"Well, if he's there, we'll get him. Thanks for your information." He motioned them to pass. The man whipped his horse mercilessly in his haste to get out of the area.

"What do you make of that?" James asked.

"Frazier's there, alright. Let's see if he'll come out." Charley moved out from the trees. Before he could hail the house, a man stepped out on the porch. Charley raised his hand to wave. The motion of his arm stopped abruptly when he was deafened by the muzzle blast of a Winchester from behind his back. The bullet struck the porch just above the man's head forcing him back into the house.

He turned on Williams, who was standing with the smoking rifle still at firing position. "What'd you do that for?"

"I don't trust him. Now he knows we mean business and we can take him dead or alive."

"I like to avoid gun fights; now, you've put us into a stand off situation. What good is a dead prisoner?"

"We'll see how this plays out," George smiled smugly.

Charley called to the man in the house. "We're deputy marshals and have a writ of arrest for Bill Frazier. If you're Frazier, come out and surrender. You'll not be harmed." The answer was a shot from the front window.

He turned to his companions. "Looks like we have a fight on our hands. James, you go around back and cover the cabin. George, you take a position on the left that allows you to cover the yard. I'll try to get close enough to talk him out."

An out building with a wood stack stood fifty feet out. He dashed for it, running a pattern of sharp turns. Shots kicked up the dirt as he dove behind the wood pile. Bullets struck the wood knocking the top pieces down on his head. Chips flew as the bullets continued to strike above his head.

Laying with his Winchester held across his chest, he called to the cabin. "Frazier, throw down your weapon. We'll hold our fire."

"You 'bout took my head off. "

Charley motioned George to cover him as he dashed for the side of the cabin. His left foot with the missing toes caused him to trip. He had almost reached the corner when he felt himself spinning around. His rifle went flying into the dirt as he fell, gripping the ankle that had been struck. The bullet had passed through his boot, ripping open the leather and exposing his bloodied left ankle. As he clawed for his rifle, he felt the bullets hitting around him. *God, don't let this be the end. Help me.*

The face of the new deputy appeared around the corner of the house, his hand pumping the lever action of his Winchester on his hip. The remarkable feat of gun play momentarily subdued the gunman inside allowing James to pull him out of the line of fire.

He clutched his rifle and reloaded as Lee did the same. A thud of feet hitting the ground in back pulled their attention to the rear of the cabin. Unable to move, he watched Lee run to the corner and fire.

Lee returned, exasperation showing on his tanned young features. "He got away. I'll check the house."

Pain shooting through his foot and ankle, he tried to stand up as Lee and Williams came around the side of the building.

James' normally smiling face showed agitation and disappointment. "It's empty. He got away through the kitchen window. I'm sorry, Charley."

"We'll track him down later. Let's find a doctor to look at my foot." Charley leaned on the younger man, who was strong enough to pick him up. "Thanks for saving my life. Where'd you learn to shoot a rifle like that?"

"Sixth Calvary."

With arms around the shoulders of the two deputies, he hobbled up the stairs to the doctor's office. The sign outside the simple frame house in Heavener, Choctaw Nation, stated " Dr. Kilgore, M.D." The Poteau Valley now had two doctors practicing in the area. The doctor who had patched up him in the winter was out delivering a baby.

He breathed easier as he settled on the examining table. The doctor's office was simple but adequate: an examining table in the middle of the room, a side table with various instruments laid out on a clean cloth, a jar of chloroform, a bandage chest. He knew what to expect, his eyes settling on the doctor's hands as he examined his boot and foot, caked in blood.

"Well, deputy. I need to clean this up." Dr. Kilgore left the room for a few minutes, returning with a basin of water and towels. He gently peeled up the pants leg to reveal the boot. "Your ankle is too swollen to remove the boot. I'll try to cut it along the seam line."

A few minutes with sharp shears brought the boot off in one piece that unrolled like a filleted fish. He closed his eyes as the doctor gently tugged at the leather.

"As I suspected, the bullet entered the boot from the rear, grazing your heel. You probably have a chipped ankle bone. It looks like you already had old damage to this foot."

"Yeah. I lost those toes to frost bite last winter when I was chasing Jackson Crow."

"I read about his capture. You and your trackers did a fine job. Everyone in the area breathed a sigh of relief when he was captured."

He watched as Dr. Kilgore put pressure on his foot causing him to clench his teeth. "Doc, I appreciate the assistance. How long will I be mending?"

"I'll clean this wound and bandage the ankle. You'll need to stay in a splint for a couple of weeks, and then you can start walking on it as you can tolerate," the doctor answered. "If you don't mind my asking, how did this happen?"

Before he could answer, George Williams spoke up. "We cornered that no-good desperado, Bill Frazier, at his place. The skunk resisted arrest and fired on us before getting away."

The doctor worked in silence but was attentive to their conversation. Charley decided not to say anymore in front of the man. Frazier may have influence over the good doctor. He sent a warning glance to Williams. "Enough said for now. We can put it all in our written report when we get back to Fort Smith."

Deputy Lee stood near listening with keen interest. "Is he alright to ride, Doctor?"

The doctor looked at his patient. "Yes, he'll just have to stay off his foot for two weeks. When you get to Fort Smith, get a pair of crutches and have a doctor check your wound in a few days."

"We'll take good care of him. What do we owe you?" Williams asked.

"One dollar."

He threw a silver dollar on the table. "Thanks for the help. How's your practice amongst the Choctaws?"

"I treat more whites than Indians. The Indians usually come to me only when they are seriously injured. They treat illnesses with home remedies and medicine man incantations."

Williams seemed to know what the doctor was talking about. "Some of that wild herb stuff really works. I've seen Choctaw women treat their fevered babies with willow bark tea. I had typhoid fever real bad one time and an old Indian woman brought me a cup of broth. It about killed me to drink it, but I started getting well the next day,"

Supported on the shoulders of his friends, Charley nodded to the doctor and hopped through the door onto the porch.

The sun settling over the western hills lengthened the shadows in the yard. The heat had begun to dissipate. He mounted Billie with a good push from Lee. Billie flickered his ears back and forth at the site of the foot bandage and splint sticking out above the stirrup.

"It's OK, boy. Hold'er still." He patted the big roan's neck in reassurance. The ride to camp was a time to reflect on the day.

He frowned at his partner. "Frazier will be on the scout now. He was wanted for larceny, but now it will be assault with intent to kill after that shoot out. All we've done is forced a fox deeper into its hole."

He had to report the shoot out to Marshal Carroll. He would be up front about the stand off and let the facts support the case. When Lee helped him out of the saddle, he clung to the saddle horn for balance.

The lantern-lit windows in the growing dusk indicated Marshal Carroll was still in his office. Charley spoke in a soft voice. "I'll do most of the talking but he may have questions for you." Lee's arms encircled his waist helping him struggle up the steps with a tight grip on the banister. I'm going to need those crutches right away if I'm going to get anywhere." He entered the room and sat on the nearest chair as Lee stepped up to the desk.

"Hello, Mr. Barnes. Is the marshal in?" James tried to be courteous.

Barnes glanced at the bandage on Charley's limb and smirked. "Yes, as a matter of act, he's already gotten word of your difficulty with Frazier. He's been waiting for you to report."

George rolled his eyes as he knocked on the door and swung it open at the brusque "Come in."

Marshal Carroll stroked his long white beard as he eyed the three men "Hello, Deputy Williams, Deputy Lee, Deputy Barnhill. I've been waiting for you. Charley, you better have a seat. You other two may stand. What happened out there? I've already had complaints from citizens in the area, worried that Frazier is now on the scout."

Charley shifted his gaze to Carroll's face and began. "Sir, we wanted to apprehend him without anyone getting hurt. His neighbors are divided between supporters and those that fear the trouble he can make for them. It's a fine line to walk. We found him home alone. As I approached the house to hail him, George detected what he thought was an imminent attack and fired first. Then it was a stand off. He got away after wounding me in the ankle. Lee saved my life out there. "

"Well, he is just one of hundreds that are on the scout. Swear out a complaint against him for assault with intent to kill. That will add some meat to a grand jury investigation. That bunch in the Poteau Valley may get the message that firing on my deputies will not be tolerated. Now go get some rest."

He struggled to his feet. "Sir, I appreciate your support. Frazier will have witnesses that will swear all kinds of ridiculous things under oath."

"Don't worry about it. The jury will be able to figure out who are reliable witnesses. He can bring in the whole county. District Attorney Sandels will sort it out."

"Thanks. Good night." Charley turned to go. *That's not the last of Frazier, I'm sure.*

***

On a rock-strewn promontory a solitary figure studied his supplies: rope, canvas tarp, ax, bedding, extra cartridge belt for rifle and pistol, a sack of canned goods, biscuits, and coffee, poncho and hat. That would keep him up here for a while. Frazier surveyed the view below him - a sheer cliff face down to a brush covered slope a few yards from a running stream. He smiled. What more does a man need? His years of hunting on Black Fork Mountain had revealed the hidden entrance to the cave that led to the tight crevice he had wiggled through. The cleft in the rock provided an easy climb to the top. On three sides his fort had a sheer rock drop of a hundred feet - behind him the steep gradient up the side of the mountain. He could stand off an army from up here until he was starved out. His wife would see to it that his gang took care of him until the deputies had abandoned the hunt. His spies would get the names of the individual deputies and set up an ambush for them if they came to close.

Come on, you Yankee deputies. The next time we meet it will be to the death.

Chapter 24

An Ax Murder

The thin edge of his hunting knife glittered in the sunlight thrown across the kitchen table - it had to be sharp as a razor for the man he was going to kill. Billie Morgan glanced across the kitchen at his brother, John. "I think that will do nicely. Before night fall, one of us will be dead."

The Reverend William (Billie) Henry Harrison Morgan of Skullyville Baptist Church was the picture of health and respectability, his forty-one years encased in a solid frame from years of farming and preaching. His first wife, Celina, had found his temper too much and had left him and the children four years ago. Anna, his current wife, knew when to submit and keep her mouth shut as any good wife should.

He was pleased to find his knife fit easily in the scabbard inside his right boot concealed by the trouser leg. His appearance for this final day of his life - a spotless shirt and trousers, washed and iron just the way he had instructed Anna to do it, a neat beard and hair - offset his rugged features. He was ready for a funeral, a fight or death. He did not care which.

His brother's brows froze in a frown. "Why do you want to kill Louis, Billie? Your own son-in-law?"

Billie drew on his black jacket and dress hat. "You've heard the rumors. As one of my elders he has incited my own daughter against me telling Janey she should join whichever church she wants. If he is left alone he will draw everyone over to the Methodists. I've warned Charley Say to keep out of it too if he doesn't want a hole dug for him beside Louis."

"Charley has been your ward ever since you to come here as a missionary pastor. He's just a boy like Louis. Why not just take an ax handle to Louis and break his legs or something? You want to hang?"

Billie Morgan knew his mind. This boy was a rebel and had to be dealt with. "I know the devil is in me, but I can't resist him anymore. I plan on doing it quick and leaving on a fast horse."

"What about your wife and your five children? What about your congregation?"

"The Lord will take care of them. You just ride over to Andy Holman's and tell him to meet us at Louis Burrow's place about dark."

John Morgan, his bearded face tanned and lined with the worry of this day, September 10, 1886, tried to concentrate on how to stop this feud. His hat band bit into his forehead as he worked it on his head after swatting at a blow fly, the itch between his shoulder blades growing as the sweat trickled out beneath his blue cotton work shirt.

If he warned Louis, Billie would likely come after him. If he didn't, then Louis' blood would be on his hands. Holman was married to his sister, Malissa, and sometimes worked as a United States deputy marshal. He was reluctant to draw him into this mess but he would discuss it with him. Maybe *he* could stop it.

At the barn, he found a tall man, his face covered with a handle-bar mustache. "Howdy, Andy. How's your day going?"

Holman looked up from the hoe he was sharpening. "Just preparing to chop some weeds. Come in the house for coffee if you have time."

John sat at another kitchen table. How to bring up the subject? He frowned and stared into his coffee cup. "Billie wants you to meet us at Burrows' house this evening about dark."

"What's going on?.

"He plans to provoke Louis Burrow into a fight so he can kill him."

Holman's eyes roved over John's face then to his wife who was standing at the kitchen sink. "Malissa, honey. You best step out of the kitchen for a few minutes."

Her face paled and she cried out. "What is Billie going to do?"

"Never mind, darling. We'll take care of it." Holman rose and took his wife by the arm, moving her toward the door.

John knew his sister well. She had always played the part of protector for her brothers. During the War in Georgia she had often hidden them from the bushwhackers under the house or in a brush-covered hog pen.

Holman resumed his seat. "This is madness. Billie will not get away with it. Why does he want us there?"

"In case the Burrows try to jump us. There are five of them counting Old Man Burrow's brother and sons and only two of us."

"I'll try but I don't take to such matters. I would hate to have to pull Billie in to Fort Smith for murder."

After Morgan left, Holman sat at his table for a long time, turning the possible outcomes over in his mind. He needed to be there to prevent a murder, but could he? Unpredictable things can happen fast in a fight.

Malissa entered from the front room, carrying a ball of wool chording. She sat it on the table and stared at him before she spoke. "You can't go. If the Burrows jump you, you may all be killed. Billie has made this mess and he needs to back off. Maybe he will if you're not there to help him."

"I think you're right. I'll leave it be. May the Lord protect them all."

**William Henry Morgan
Photo courtesy of
Deborah Hertie**

**Anderson Holman with
daughters Mary Ales
and Sara Josephine - Photo
courtesy of Jennie Hill Cobb
ca. 1887**

Pastor Morgan smiled. His plan was developing just as he had hoped. Louis Burrow was at his Uncle Henry's black smith shop. Morgan's nephew, Davis House, sat on the wagon seat beside him. In the back riding on the cotton bales was Charles Say.

"After we unload the cotton, you go over to Louis there and see if you can get him riled up a bit."

Davis stared at him. "What for?"

"Just do as I say, boy."

Davis finished his job and walked over to the smithy. Before he could open his mouth in greeting, Louis, his young face gleaming with sweat, pushed away from the ax grinder, dropped his ax and grabbed him by the lapels. They were the same size and weight, though Louis had the biceps of a smithy and a grip Davis could not break.

"You owe me money. When am I going to get it?"

Davis fell back toward the street trying to extract his shirt from Louis's grip. "I don't have it and besides I owe it to your brother, not you. I'll pay you as soon as I can get it. "

"I'll have the money by this evening or I'm going to whip you."

That was just the cue Morgan had been waiting for to climb down from his wagon seat. He stepped between the two young men and pushed them away with his long arms. "Do not strike him or I'll have to whip you, boy."

The attacker's eyes flared as he lunged toward Davis again, losing his control. Morgan clenched his fists in anticipation. "I'll pay the money myself if you'll leave the boy alone rather than have this row. Besides, Louis, you've been talking about me and been mad at me for some time and you have no grounds."

Louis spat out his words. "You want to separate me from Janey."

"Whoever told you that is a liar, and if you say so, you are a liar too."

Beyond all restraint now, Louis balled up his fists and raised them to his face. Before he could strike, his Uncle Henry came between the two men with a raised iron bar. "Both of you cool down, now or I'll split some heads."

Morgan stared Henry in the face and backed away. "What does Davis owe you?"

Louis shook with fury. "Seventy cents."

"That's nothing to start a row over. You'll have it before night fall." Morgan turned and walked away, a smile spreading across his face. The boy was good and mad now, just one more push and he would strike and Morgan could kill him in self-defense.

He had the change he had gotten from the store keeper. He was ready. He flexed his right arm, ready to strike the lethal blow with enough force to send that knife into Louis' heart.

He stepped out of the store when John came from the road. His voice sounded sure and strong in his ears. "It'll be dark in an hour. Let's get this over with. I don't want to sleep on this another day."

John led his pony as they walked the quarter mile towards the Burrows' house along the main Fort Smith road. Garrett Ainsworth, the store clerk, walked with them. A hundred yards from the house, two men stepped from the brush and doffed their hats.

"Good afternoon, gentlemen."

Morgan was dismayed- deputy marshals. "Good afternoon, Deputy Barnhill. What brings you here?"

"Abe and I are camped with our prisoners over by the creek. Deputy Phillips is there also. Care to come over and have a cup of coffee with us?" Deputy

Barnhill always extended the courtesy of his camp to the locals and under normal circumstances, Morgan would have accepted.

"Thanks, but we have to get home before dark."

"Alright then. Some other time." They walked away toward the creek where they were camped.

Morgan knew it would be harder to get away with three deputies breathing down his neck, but it did not matter. He turned to John. "Keep your pony close in case I need it."

Ainsworth looked at him at this remark. "Well, I must leave you here. My wife is peeking out the front curtain as usual." He turned into his front walk.

As they approached the Burrow's house, John stopped and placed his hand on Billie's arm. "I don't see Louis. Let's just go on home."

"I'll speak to my daughter," Billie said as he moved toward the front gate.

Janey came to the gate and greeted her father. Her face was solemn. She must have heard of the argument in town. "Dear Papa, why have you come? Louis is in the timber chopping fire wood."

"I'll leave this money with you then." If he delayed long enough his adversary might show up. A man cannot chop wood in the dark.

Before he could hand her the change, Janey's husband came striding from the forest with his two cousins, an ax balanced across his shoulder.

"What do you want here, Morgan?"

"I want to give you this money as I promised."

"I won't take it. Davis owes my brother. You'll have to find him."

"You treat me worse than a dog. I'm your father-in-law."

Louis placed his hand on Janey's shoulder.

"I've treated you no worse than you've treated me. I won't hurt you because of the love I have for this girl. Otherwise, it would have been settled long ago."

Out of the corner of his eye, Morgan saw Old Man Burrow striding over from the cotton wagon followed by two Indian boys. He had little time to complete his deed. The hand that extracted the knife from his boot did not tremble. He lunged at Louis and cut him across the chest, blood flowing freely down his front.

Lorenzo Burrow stepped between them and pushed them apart. "Go on home, Pastor Morgan."

Morgan took a step around the father's left side and lunged again. The young man was quick. Too late Morgan saw the ax raised over head with both hands. He stepped back, the blade missing his skull but hitting him in the middle of his chest. The shrieks of his daughter were the last sounds he heard as he hit the ground.

Throwing his reins over the wagon bed, John Morgan had stepped forward from behind the cotton wagon where he was standing when Billie made his first lunge. By the time he reached his brother's side, he was dead. In one sweeping motion he picked up the knife and stuck it in his belt and grabbed the ax, advancing toward the murderer. Louis paled and ran toward the fence line, jumping it in one hop, trying to make it to the timber line.

He was right behind even though the Burrow kid was younger and slimmer. Louis turned to look over his shoulder and fell into a tangle of undergrowth. John swung the weapon. Louis screamed in pain as it caught muscle and bone in his forearm. John swung again. He did not want to kill this boy but sure wanted to cut him a bit for what he had done to Billie. Suddenly, he was knocked flat by a massive hard fist to his temple.

Louis' father stood over him, kicking and slugging him with his fists. He crawled backwards away from his attacker. The man reached down for the ax and John ran for his pony. Clearing the fence again, he grabbed the reins and mounted in a flurry of dust.

He tried to clear his head as he rode up the road toward his house. He needed to get help to capture this murderer. But all he could see was Billie's face, the shock and surprise and then the eyes closing, his hands still holding on to the murder weapon he had jerked out of his chest. "Help. Help. Help."

Ainsworth Store, Skullyville, I.T.

Chapter 25

Louis Burrow, Killer

The sounds of the forest inhabitants settled around Charley like a comfortable cloak. It was time to rest and get the good meal that Dan still put out, the best grub of any cook out of Fort Smith. He looked across the camp at Abe who was checking the shackles on four prisoners. The abode for the night lay a quarter of a mile from Skullyville and a half day's ride from Fort Smith. It was a very nice area of the Choctaw Nation where the wealthy families of the tribe had settled and raised cotton on large plantations before the war. Afterward, everything had been destroyed and had to be rebuilt. With only ninety-four residents now it was the county seat for the district which registered seven hundred Choctaws and where the Indian agent lived and made out payments.

Skullyville Choctaw Agency and Stage Depot after it was remodeled by the Ainsworths

They would have made Fort Smith by night fall except for the delay in finding Sam Davis, the last fugitive. They had to track him for half a day after he had given them the slip.

Tyne had left camp for his home a few miles away in Spiro. Charley planned to go visit his parents and children later in the evening. Deputy John Phillips and his posse man were in camp, ready to depart on a month trip.

"What kind of writs do you have?" Charley asked as he took the saddle off of Billie and laid it over a nearby stump.

John tapped tobacco into his pipe and lit it. "Mostly larceny. Horse stealing gangs are rampant, filling farmers and ranchers for their stock. Most of the big ranches in the Creek Nation have doubled the number of cow punchers on the range."

Charley took a long pull from his coffee cup. A shrill howl like a stricken wolf filled the forest around them. He felt his heart race in preparation for whatever was coming at them. *What in the world was that terrible sound?* His hand moved to his Colt, his muscles tensing for the expected fight. As he grabbed his hat, he hollered at Abe and Dan. "Stay with the prisoners."

John threw down his pipe and grabbed his Winchester. "It's coming from the big road just outside of town."

Charley took off running, jumping over brush and logs, John behind him. As they approached, he could distinguish the awful sound - the shriek of women and children, a howl of fear and terror.

Breaking out of the trees, they made the main road and turned toward the sounds. They covered the distance to a crowd gathered in front of a home just a hundred yards away, arriving breathless from the cross country sprint.

He approached the group to find a man a few years older than himself lying on his back in the dirt. He recognized him as one of the locals he had just talked to on the road. *What is his name, Morgan?* Blood flowed out in rivers of crimson from a large wound in the chest.

Phillips knelt down and examined the man. "He's dead, but still warm."

An older man turned to Charley and spoke in an agitated voice. "I'm Lorenzo Burrow. My son, Louis, killed Morgan with an ax."

"Where's your son now?"

"He's inside my house. Went in there with his wife, who's this man's daughter, but it was self-defense. Morgan came at him with a knife."

"All right, everyone stay here so we can get Louis." Charley tried to count how many people there were: Lorenzo Burrow; Mr. Kimbrough whom he recognized from the store in town; a young Indian man, all standing close together. The old man put his arm around a woman of similar age, probably his wife. A teen-aged boy of about fourteen, a girl a little older and several younger children stood at the edge of the road in front of the house, all with wide eyes and tear-stained faces. The shrieks had lessened but were still plaintive and mournful.

"Papa, Papa, Oh, Papa!" The cries came from behind him now. As he turned toward the sound, a young woman came into view running with all her might down the middle of the road. Long curls flowed behind her in tidal billows, her shawl hanging down from her shoulders, skirts lifted high. She stopped at the sight of the body on the ground, gasps of air filling her lungs. Her hands to her face she started to crumple. Charley reached out and caught her as she slumped toward the dirt. She was light and lithe, a feathery form wrapped in woman's clothes. She breathed slowly but seemed otherwise unharmed. The old woman came over to him and knelt down beside her.

"Here, marshal. I'll tend to Irene. Go find my boy before the Morgans do."

"Who is this young lady?" Charley asked, trying to keep all the faces and names straight.

"This is the man's daughter, Irene. She must have run all the way from their house. Poor thing."

He stood up and looked at John Phillips. "Cover me from the gate. I'm going to see if I can get the boy to come out peacefully." Family murders were difficult to handle when so many of the parties were watching. He did not want this to turn into a lynch mob or a street fight between clans.

John rested his elbow on the gate post and steadied his Winchester as Charley crept toward the front porch. The group in the street stood still and watched the drama. Would the boy fight or give up?

"Louis, it's Deputy Marshal Barnhill. Open up. I need to talk to you." He rapped on the front door with the side of his left fist, his right hand gripping his Colt, his back to the side of the door frame Soft foot steps approached the door. It opened a few inches to reveal a face which was a twin to the young girl who had collapsed in the street.

"Come in, Deputy. He's waiting at the kitchen table. He'll not cause any fuss."

When John made the porch, they entered the door together, both still holding their weapons. A young man of about twenty sat on a bench at the kitchen table, his head in his hands which were still trembling. On the table in front of him lay a Colt revolver. He had a long cut across his chest and wounds on both forearms, which were oozing red. His chest wound appeared to be the more serious.

"Are you Louis Burrow?" He wanted to set up a conversation with the dazed young man. This type of reaction after violent acts was normal.

Louis took his head out of his hands and looked at the marshals, seemingly unconcerned with their presence. His wife came around the table and stood behind him, her arms reaching around his shoulders in an embrace.

"Louis, we have to take you into custody for questioning concerning the killing in the street. Witnesses say you did it. You must surrender your revolver."

The young killer made his first acknowledgment of their presence by gesturing at the pistol. "I was going to shoot John Morgan. He tried to kill me with my ax."

Charley reached out and took the six gun, placing it inside his waistband and then put away his own.

"Stand up and come around the table. Put your hands behind your back."

Louis complied and waited patiently while Charley secured his wrists with rawhide ties. Charley and John each took an arm as they escorted him out to face his family and friends.

No one said a word though Charley heard the children and women snuffling. Louis's mother and his wife both looked like they were going to collapse. The young girl, Irene, knelt beside her father's body. A younger girl and a woman clenched Morgan's lifeless hands.

He stepped forward and spoke to the woman in a soft voice. "Ma'am. May I ask your name?"

"Anna Morgan. Bill is my husband. This is his daughter, Ella."

"I'm so sorry, Mrs. Morgan. I'm Deputy Charles Barnhill. I have to call for a doctor to examine him before he can be moved."

"I understand," she said through her tears.

He turned to one of the men he knew and trusted, Crawford Kimbrough.

"Mr. Kimbrough, I'm putting you in charge to keep everyone here for questioning while we take the suspect to our camp. We'll return right away to hold an inquest so the body can be moved. "

"Certainly, Deputy Barnhill."

He instructed the willing assistant. "Mr. Kimbrough, would you be kind enough to search the body for any weapons? If there's a doctor in the vicinity, please send for him?"

Kimbrough ordered a young man standing nearby. "Go fetch Dr. Foyil!"

Kimbrough explained to Charley. "This is a small town. He should be back with the doctor within a few minutes."

Abe had grabbed his Winchester and stepped away from the wagon when Charley and Phillips had disappeared out of sight. Dan, who was busy feeding the prisoners, dropped the pan on the fire and went to his rifle.

He signaled with his rifle barrel for the men to move. "Get over to the wagon. Whatever this is, the marshals'll take care of it." He felt a churning inside his gut, but his hand was steady as he pointed the barrel.

Sam Davis who they had to track all day gestured toward the ruckus. "What if they need help?

"Get over there behind the wagon with the others."

Dan helped him shackle and secure them to the long chain at the back of the wagon. Desperate men would use desperate measures to evade even a minor sentence of the court and this was a perfect diversion.

The crying and shrieking continued as he moved toward the disturbance. In the lowering daylight, he could barely see a hundred yards. He listened, his eyes and ears groping for anything. *What is happening? Charley and John must be all right. I haven't heard gunfire*. After a few minutes, everything seemed to quiet down.

As he strode back to the camp, two figures on horseback moved into the campfire ring. He recognized John Morgan whom he had seen on the road earlier and Lige Fannin, a part-time United States deputy marshal. The men dismounted quickly, dropping hard to the ground without using the stirrups.

"Where are the marshals?" John asked through clenched teeth.

"They took off up to the main road to see what the disturbance was. What happened?"

"Louis Burrow killed my brother with an ax."

"How could this happen? We just saw the both of you less than half an hour ago?"

John exhaled to curb his agitation before he answered. "They got into it in front of Ole Man Burrow's house. There's been bad blood between them ever since Louis married Billie's daughter. They argued over some money and it got out of control. Louis lost his temper and killed Billie."

"Charley and John Phillips went up there about fifteen minutes ago. They aren't back yet," Abe said.

"Come on, Lige." John climbed on his horse and let out a loud whoop used by Confederate rebels and Indians preparing for a fight. A whoop meant you better get your gun because trouble was coming.

Lige put his hand on Morgan's bridle. "Don't try anything. The deputies, I'm sure, have everything under control."

"We'll see. Ole Man Burrow chased me off with the same ax all the while Louis was threatening to kill me too. I am going in prepared."

He turned his horse and headed toward the road, his friend following close behind. Both were armed and ready for anything.

Abe turned back to the campfire. He was amused to see the prisoners standing very still. With shackled feet, they were vulnerable to anything that might go wrong. The guard and the cook were their only protection.

It was now quite dark, dusk having given way to the blackness of night in Indian Country. A full moon provided enough light for them to reach camp.

"Put Louis in the wagon," Charley instructed his brother. "I'll have the doctor come look at his wounds after he checks Morgan's body."

"John Morgan was just here looking for you." Abe reached for the young man's wrists to loosen the rawhide ties.

Deputy Phillips put his Winchester back into the saddle boot. "Do you want me to question witnesses with you?"

"No. Go find Tyne and ask him to go to Fort Smith for a writ of arrest for Louis. I'll need that before I can take him to jail."

46–590

UNITED STATES

versus

Louis Burrow

SUBPOENA.

Issued April 2 189 7

Returnable July 17 Term 189 7

Fort Smith, Ark. 189

I certify that I served the within Writ of Subpoena on the 10 day of

189 , at the

by then and there reading the same in the presence and hearing of the within named

JOHN CARROLL,
U. S. Marshal.

By Deputy

MARSHAL'S FEES.

Services, $

miles at 6c per mile

Witness subpoena Louis Burrow trial served by Charles Barnhill

Dan handed him a quick cup of coffee. Sam Davis sat by the fire finishing his supper, his hands still shackled. The other three prisoners rested on a log behind the chuck wagon.

"What happened?" Davis asked in a casual way.

"William Morgan's been killed."

"Did you leave anyone to guard the body? "

He did not answer and turned away. Why was a thief so interested in this case? That answer, to his dismay, would come later in the court room.

As he returned to the murder scene, he could hear a right smart amount of hollering: men's voices raised in loud accusations, women's pleas, children's cries. John Morgan stood over his brother's lifeless body, grief and revenge on his face, a look that could cause more bloodshed if not stopped.

"He killed my brother for no reason. I want him dead for what he's done." John put his hand on his pistol and gestured to a group of grim-faced men standing near the body. "Get your guns. We'll take him from the deputies."

Lige Fannin stepped away from the group. "John, you're crazy. Let the law handle this."

Charley chose that moment to come into the light of the lantern. Deputies had been overpowered by mobs before. This would not happen under his authority. John Morgan, startled, removed his hand from his pistol butt.

"John, you need to help me. Go get a chain and lock from Ainsworth's store and take it to Abe." He had plenty of chains, but that would keep the trouble-maker busy.

A larger crowd had gathered in the few minutes he had been absent. A dozen women and children stood on the porch. What he presumed was the victim's family milled around by the fence, Anna, Ella and Irene Morgan among them.

"Which of you are Morgan's family?"

A tall man with bushy dark hair and handle bar mustache stepped forward. "I'm Anderson Holman and this here's Bill Cowart. We're brother-in-laws of the dead man. These are our wives, John's wife and Billie's parents." He pointed to the rest of the group. "I should've been here. Billie asked me to come. Maybe he wouldn't have been killed."

Two families on opposite sides of a tragedy, each one calling on their family to come together for revenge, justice or redemption. What would it be? These were Christian people - Morgan a missionary preacher. How could this happen to a man of the cloth?

"Has anyone bothered the body?" Charley asked the shopkeeper who stood where he had left him.

"No, sir. His women folk have been leaning over and kissing his poor dead face. It's a terrible thing to see someone you love killed in such a dreadful manner. I imagine they will never get over it."

"Who saw the killing?"

"I don't rightly know, since when I got here he was already dying. You can ask Old Man Burrow. I saw him chasing John Morgan with the ax when I came up."

He walked over to Lorenzo Burrow, who was still comforting his wife, his face hard against her tears, his farm-worn hands clenched into fists. Charley focused his gaze on the man, knowing that he had to get some answers and quick.

"Who was here when Morgan was killed?"

"Louis's wife, Janey, was behind him tugging at his arm, trying to pull him into the house. I kept between them. The three Indian boys helping me weigh cotton were within five or six feet of us. John Morgan was behind the wagon and my son, Reuben, was watching the argument from the fence."

"Who are these other people here?" Charley gestured to another group of people assembled near the front of the house.

"They's all my family. None of them were present until after the fuss. They all live close."

"What happened?"

"They commenced to arguing when Morgan came to the house to pay Louis some money, just pennies. Unexpectedly, Morgan pulled a hunting knife out of his boot and cut Louis across the chest. I went between them and pushed them back, but he came around me and lunged again. That's when Louis hit him with the ax." The man stopped and ran his hand across his gray beard.

"My boy's no killer. He was just defending himself. John Morgan ran up, picked up both the knife and the ax and chased my boy off down the fence line. I took off after them and hit John with my fists to make him stop. He had already struck Louis several times and I was afraid he would kill him. He dropped the ax and ran for his pony as I chased him with the ax."

Charley asked, "Who speaks Choctaw here?"

"I do." Charley recognized Uncle Spence Ainsworth, the shop owner, and one of the early Choctaw settlers.

"I need to talk to each of the Indian boys that were here. I was told there were three, but I see only one. Where are the other two?"

"They took off to their camp."

"Please, go fetch them."

John Morgan reappeared from the direction of the camp. Fidgety and anxious, he paced back and forth in the road. He had regained his composure but still had blazing eyes.

Kimbrough handed Charley a pocket knife. "Morgan had this folded up pocket knife inside his shirt pocket, but he also had a knife scabbard hidden inside his right boot. No knife was there though."

At that moment the doctor arrived, an older man with his waistcoat unbuttoned, having come in great haste with his doctor's bag. He ran over to the body, and motioned Kimbrough to help him turn it over. The blood had pooled along the spine. He probed the chest wound and made an examination of the deep wound through the collar bone.

"Well, I am sorry. That wound caused almost instant death," the doctor explained. "It cut though the aorta at the top of the heart. You can release the body to be prepared for burial."

"Thank you, Dr. Foyil. I need you to go to my camp yonder in the trees.

Louis Burrow is there and he's been cut up pretty good. All right, you men, help us get him into the wagon."

Ainsworth and Kimbrough helped Morgan's menfolk lift the body into Mr. Burrow's cotton wagon, now a hearse. The horses pulling the wagon shifted ears back and forth, snorting at the smell of the blood.

Charley gathered the women into the wagon. Irene leaned heavy on his arm as he assisted her into the back. She managed a wane smile before ducking her face into her hands. What a sad day for her. And so young. The menfolk who had arrived on horseback took to their saddles to ride to Morgan's house, a mile up the road.

Charley extended his hand. "Mr. Kimbrough, you may go with the party if you like. Thank you very much for your help."

John Morgan did not join his family in the sad procession, but lingered behind. "I need to talk to you, Marshal. I want to give my side of all this, " John said in a lowered voice while watching Old Man Burrow.

Charley turned to Mr. Burrow. "You should take your wife into the house now. She's been through enough. Where is Louis's wife?"

"She's inside."

"I would like to come in and talk to her after I get done out here."

Charley motioned John to sit down on the porch steps, then stood in front of him with his arms crossed. He could not go to his camp, too many people there to listen to what was said.

"What did you see?"

"I was standing behind the cotton wagon waiting for Billie to get done so we could walk on home. He talked with Louis for some time, then he started to swing at Louis and Old Man Burrow stepped in between them. When Billie stepped around him, Louis struck him with the ax and let go of it. When it fell on the ground, I took it and chased Louis."

"Did your brother have a knife during this argument?"

"No, sir. He did not."

He stared hard at Morgan who dropped his eyes under the scrutiny. "You sure you didn't pick it up before you grabbed the ax?"

"No, sir. I didn't do no such thing. I was too busy grabbing that ax to kill that murderer."

"Why would Louis strike an unarmed man with an ax? There must have been a weapon. All right, I need to talk to these Indians in private."

The three Indian boys stood out of hearing range of what he had just discussed with John Morgan. He pulled one boy aside a few yards and instructed Mr. Ainsworth to translate. "What's your name?"

"James Jones."

"What did you see?"

"The two white men argued in front of the house. The young one had an ax held between his legs and the older one had something in his hand. He tried to give it to the younger one. They began to shout. I know a few words in

English, but couldn't understand. The young one raised his ax and struck the other in the chest. I went to him right afterwards. He was already dead. John Morgan took the ax and ran after the man. Old Man Burrow followed them over the fence. John Morgan ran back and got on his horse and left."

"What happened then?" Charley asked.

"The killer came back and went into the house with his wife, said he was going to kill John Morgan. I understand some English. I could understand that much. Then I went off."

"Did you see a knife in Morgan's hands?"

The boy shook his head. "No, sir."

It became apparent that although all three had been very close to the fuss, none of them could say that they saw Morgan with a knife. It was natural for them to feel that they were caught in the middle of two families about to go to war with each other.

After they were dismissed to their camp, he turned back to John Morgan.

"I need to talk to Louis' wife for a few minutes. Go over to my camp and have a cup of coffee and I'll be along shortly."

Charley knocked at the door. As he entered, he took off his hat and said in as kind a voice as he could, "Mrs. Burrow, I need to talk to you about what is going to happen to your man."

The young lady, more composed now, motioned to him to sit on the parlor sofa. She dabbed a hankie at the sides of her eyes. "My poor Pa, my poor Pa. Why did this have to happen?" Her head high, her shoulders back, she fiddled with the hankie now held in her lap. Her long brown curls fastened at the back of her head with a bright ribbon had come untied, the ribbon now dangling from a single strand of hair. She was as pretty as her younger sister, he thought. He moved his pistol barrel out of the way so he could settle down without it punching into his thigh.

"I know you've had a frightful time tonight. I'm sorry for what happened. After I receive a warrant for Louis' arrest, I'll take him to Fort Smith. You may come visit him at the jail anytime you wish. This is a very grave matter and you'll have to come to Fort Smith when the commissioner schedules the hearing. If your husband is held awaiting trial, you will need to make arrangements for a defense attorney. The judge will help you select an attorney. Do you have any questions?"

"When can I see my husband?" Tears began to streak down her cheeks.

"You can come to my camp tomorrow morning and see him."

"Thank you, so much, Deputy Barnhill. I appreciate your information."

Charley rose and grabbed his hat from the sofa. "By the way, your family, how will they fare in all this? You're the oldest?"

"Yes, I'm sixteen. Irene is the next behind me in age. She's fourteen, almost fifteen. Then Ella, twelve, John Henry, ten and the baby, Laura. Today is her seventh birthday. Pa was one his way home to take her a gift."

He swallowed hard. This was a day this family would never forget.

When he got to his camp, he settled down by the fire. Abe sat near the campfire with Dan, the prisoners asleep under the wagon. Louis Burrow was inside the wagon secured with the chain John had brought from the store. Taking a cup of coffee from Dan, he turned to John Morgan.

"I've interviewed both sides in this matter and there are conflicting stories. The attorneys will handle any inconsistencies."

"What do you mean by that, Marshal?" John asked, his jaw clenching in anger.

"If Louis killed your brother, when in fact, he did not have a weapon, he deserves to hang. But if you're lying about a knife that you pocketed, then he could be freed on self-defense. The testimony of multiple witnesses will establish that fact to the satisfaction of the jury. As Judge Parker says, it is better a hundred guilty men go free, than one innocent one not."

"I am telling you the truth."

"You need to go home and get some rest, Mr. Morgan. It has been a bad day for everyone."

After John Morgan left, he noticed the prisoner, Sam Davis, was awake when he moved and Charley caught his eye. Had he been eaves-dropping? Prisoners were always looking for ways to twist things around to their advantage, including private conversations overheard. He felt a burning in his throat. He had a responsibility as an officer of the court to establish a clear chain of evidence and to interview witnesses. In many cases like this, it became a "He said" versus "He said" battle. But he also wanted to see justice done to this young man who had destroyed the peace of two families in such a tragic way. Innocent or guilty, which would it be? That was not his job, but the job of the jury.

David Spence Ainsworth

Chapter 26

Til Death Do Us Part

Charley and Abe parted ways at the hitching post in front of the jail, Abe west to Shady Point and Charley east to Bloomer, a small farm community 18 miles east of Fort Smith. He had moved his family here a few months ago after several grueling years living in the Indian Territory. Salina liked the amenities of Arkansas civilization and being near her sister and family even though it was almost the same distance to Kullychaha from Fort Smith. Two months of riding and arresting fugitives had worn them both down. Charley looked forward to the quiet pace of a winter schedule. By the time he rode into his yard, it was early evening, the shadows long and the birds ceasing their calls. Something seemed out of order. The yellow quarantine sign on the door made his heart pound. *My children? Salina?* When he opened the door and was greeted by Salina's sister, Mary, he realized that it was very serious.

"Charlie, I'm so happy to see you. Salina tried to send a message to Fort Smith but there was no one available to make the ride. She's in the bedroom resting."

"What's wrong?"

"She went to nurse a neighbor who had children sick with the meningitis. Now, the doctor says she has it. He has put a quarantine on the house. I'm the only one here."

His insides constricted. His pale wife reached for him as he approached the bed. She turned her head on the pillow and smiled at him. "Hello, sweetheart. I'm so glad you're here. I can't imagine what all the fuss is about."

The snakes building in his stomach caused his voice to quiver. "I got back as quick as I could." His words sounded inadequate but he was relieved to see that she appeared normal except for the dark shadows encircling her eyes, those eyes that he always found so comforting. Now he had to comfort her. As he took her hand he saw a splotchy red rash on her arms.

Her sister brushed Salina's hair back into its comb. "Your children are at my house. The doctor didn't want them exposed. I've been extra careful, washing every time I touch her and boiling everything she touches. I keep a big pot of boiling water on the stove night and day."

"I appreciate your help. Why don't you head on home to your family?"

"I'll send some supper over. My daughter should have it ready."

At the front door he helped her with her shawl and bonnet. "Thanks, Mary." As he watched her slip out the door and hurry down the path, he said a brief prayer for his wife. Why did he jump right in and talk directly to God when big problems came up, but everyday worries were brushed aside until tomorrow?

He pulled up the rocker to the bedside. "Mary is going to send over some supper. Do you want to sit up for a while?"

Her voice was faint and strained. "Yes, please."

When he fluffed the pillows behind her, he felt the heat of her skin through her night gown. "Let me get you a cool wash cloth for your head." His heart began to pound again as he reached for the bucket and started for the well pump. Pestilence and disease was ever present in the primitive areas of the Indian Territory, but he had never imagined it would strike his loved ones.

After supper, he walked over to visit with the children. They were glad to see him. Minnie muffled her squeals behind her hands. She seemed almost to be crying.

Henry grabbed his arm and hung on. "Is Ma going to be alright?"

"The doctor says she must have lots of rest and quiet. That is why you children must stay here until she is better. "

Henry became still and quiet then whispered, "Could she die, Pa?"

Charley swallowed and prayed quickly for the right words. "Your mother is a strong, young woman and there is no reason she will not get well. This disease only kills the weak, the infirm and the young, and your mother is none of those." His voice sounded firm and sure, but his feelings were in a turmoil. This sickness was a trial and he knew he would have to accept the outcome whichever way it went. It was in the Lord's hands now.

He slept on the parlor sofa - a hard horsehair affair with unforgiving cushions. In the morning he rose early to check on Salina. A touch of his hand on her wrist assured him she was resting and without discomfort. He prepared breakfast for her. A tray balanced in one hand, he grabbed a cup of coffee and entered the bedroom, settling in the rocking chair to watch her eat, his mind full of worry and doubt. When he felt like this, he knew it was time to turn to the Lord.

"Salina, honey. After you finish that tray, let's read from the Bible. "

"I would like that very much. When Sis comes over, sometimes she reads a few verses to me. It soothes me."

After he had cleaned up the tray, he lifted his Bible from the night stand. "What would you like to hear?"

"I love Luke. Read about Jesus healing the sick."

Turning the pages to the appropriate part, Luke 8:47-48 the healing of the bleeding woman, he began to read and could feel the comfort of the Holy Spirit.

> *"Then the woman, seeing that she could not go unnoticed, came trembling and fell at his feet. In the presence of all the people, she told why she had touched him and how she had been instantly healed. Then he said to her. "Daughter, your faith has healed you. Go in peace."*

Salina closed her eyes and sighed. "I really feel like that woman, but I don't know if God is going to heal me."

His lips brushed her cheek. "We can only pray for God's healing and then leave it in His hands. To unbelievers that sounds cold and cruel, but God knows His plan for us."

"Yes, you're right. I feel so weak. Can you stir me up some of my powder?"

It only took a few minutes to prepare her tonic. The mixture smelled pleasant. She gulped it down and gave his hand a pat. "If something should happen to me, sweetheart, I want you to find a new mother for the children."

His mind rebelled against such a thought; life without her would be impossible. "Let's not talk of such things. I could never find anyone to take your place. I wouldn't even want to try."

"Abe found himself a fine new wife after being a widower for almost four years."

"That's God's will for Abe, but I doubt if it would be for me. Besides, you're going to be feeling much better soon. Try and rest a while."

He took her hands as he prayed. "Dear Lord, heal Salina and bring her back to good health. You are the Great Healer. We give you her health and well-being to do with as you choose. Amen."

Many times he had prayed and felt that God was listening. Today his heart was telling his head something else. Would God heal her? He didn't know.

He watched the pale figure in the bed and waited for her to sleep. In a few minutes, he stepped out and closed the bedroom door. How would the children take it if Salina didn't improve?

An uneventful day passed and Salina rested. The doctor came by once and cautioned her to maintain the strict rest. He pulled Charley aside and led him out of the room.

"Your wife is very ill. If her fever does not come down, she may seizure. Keep the cold compresses on her head and arms as much as possible."

He sat down in the rocking chair to watch his sleeping wife. He must have dozed off, because he awoke suddenly when Salina let out a scream. It was dark. He groped for the lantern and lit it. Salina gasped for breath, her lips covered with a thick frothy substance.

"Darlin'. What is it?"

"I can't see, Charley. I'm blind. What is happening?" With another shriek, she began to convulse and shake the bed.

Now wide awake, he broke out in a run to get help. Mary came running with her skirts hiked up, her husband carrying a lantern down the path.

"Get going for the doctor, right now," she commanded to her breathless husband.

Her voice was sure and steady. "Help prop her up so she does not choke on her vomit."

Charley helped raise Salina up in bed. What was happening?

"Get some cool water. I'll try to bath her down and break the fever."

His hands shook as he slammed the wood handle down against the stops, water spraying into the bucket in gushes that ran down his pants legs. In the cold night air, he never even felt the shock of it and it seemed an eternity before the bucket was ready. He carried the pitcher and basin into the bedroom. Salina's weak moan told him she was in danger.

Mary took the pitcher, filled the basin and began to wash Salina's exposed body. Charley averted his eyes to the bed clothes which were yellow with vomit. His heart raced and he instinctively grabbed Salina's hand. Limp but still hot. *Please, Dear Lord, save my wife.*

Salina gasped, the deep heaving of her chest groping for the air it needed. After a few more efforts, her chest ceased heaving and her hand went limp in his grip.

Mary's resolve dissolved into a torrent of tears as she stared at Salina's face. Charlie moved to her side and pulled her down to the rocking chair. Then he rose and checked Salina's body. He lifted her eyelids, shocked at the unmistakable sign of death. He pulled the quilt that she had made so tenderly up over her still face, now at peace, a slight smile carved at the corners of her mouth. He continued to hold her hand until her body began to stiffen. Mary's sobs filled the silence of the death chamber. Even the creatures of the forest ceased to stir.

He stared at her, so peaceful and beautiful in her eternal rest. She would never grow old on this earth, but would be forever preserved in heaven. How could he go on living in this cruel world of evil men and tragic events? Then, he remembered his sweet children. He would go on for them. They had a right to a father that loved them and wanted to give them a future.

He closed his eyes and wept, tears of grief that only a loving Father in heaven could wipe away. He felt so tired, he just wanted to go to sleep and never wake. Mary rose and put her arms around him and then stepped out of the room. How many years before he could see his lovely Salina again? Only

God knew.

How quickly and easily life is taken away. Death had again robbed his life of value. Why must he go on living while his loved ones had been cut down in their prime? He forced himself to touch the face he had loved for so many years. It was cool and was losing its softness. As he bent down to kiss the cold lips, his hand brushed something under her pillow. He pulled it out and stared at the photo taken in Fort Smith two years ago - his likeness full of life and energy. Now the eagerness in those eyes was gone. Would he ever desire the normal things of life again? Numb inside, he reached for the rocker and moved it to the bed. He would dream and awake to find everything all right.

Chapter 27

A Time to Weep

There is a time for everything and a season for every activity under the sun, a time to be born and a time to die . . . a time to weep and a time to laugh. Charley's father stood over the grave and read the beautiful words of King Solomon, the wisest man that ever lived. What do those words mean? Charley groped for understanding as he stared at the coffin about to be lowered into the ground, his precious wife inside. The words were a promise he knew he must grasp if he was to survive this grief. As he watched the first particles of earth strike the coffin, a stabbing pain engulfed his heart. He wanted to cry out *Why God?* He wanted to wail and hit things. Instead, he buried his hands in his coat pockets and pressed his hard fists hard into his sides. To settle his emotions, he turned and walked to the perimeter of the beautiful pioneer cemetery.

There were a hundred old graves of families who had moved here since the 1830's. Tall shade trees and rolling stretches of grass surrounded the cemetery making it a place of beauty to comfort the mourners. Artifacts that the dead had needed in life adorned some headstones. He would come back later and lay such items on Salina's grave and see that the marker was properly fixed. The date of her demise, December 6, 1886 would never leave his memory, though he knew it was really a home-coming for her.

He had taken the train to Fort Smith earlier that morning to contact the funeral director. He was informed Salina must be buried immediately because of the threat of disease. They would ride the train back out with him and conduct the service at 4 p.m. after the proper handling of the body. He barely had time to send telegrams to his family members before catching the train back. He was surprised and comforted when his parents and Jimmy appeared on the afternoon train from Fort Smith. They had driven the buggy at top speed to get to Fort Smith in time. They all seemed breathless and a bit shaken.

Returning to the group of mourners, he grasped Minnie and Henry in his arms and held them close, feeling their life, their warmth, their tears. The black funeral drapes on the hearse hung limp in the still summer air.

Alford came to his side and spoke, his voice soft and low. "Son, we must rest today and let the Lord replenish our hearts. The church prepared a meal for us."

"Yes, I know. I just can't believe she's gone." Charley guided his crying children to the buggy for the short trip to the church. Silent thoughts of guilt washed over him. Why had he left her? She needed him. He could have helped her and maybe she would not have gone to nurse the neighbors and die with their children.

Shortly after arriving at the church, the pastor's wife came up and patted Charley's hand. "I know this is a terrible tragedy for you and your family. But our God will heal all pain and sorrow in His time. I would be glad to send some ladies over to help with the children until you have made arrangements for their care."

Charley could barely speak at this kindness. "Thank you very much. As usual, you're very kind. I'd appreciate the help."

Family and friends gathered at the church to eat the bounteous meal and partake of the Lord's blessings in remembrance of Salina. The hours crawled for Charley, who answered questions and smiled, but whose thoughts were far away - the last touch of his wife's hand, her winsome ways, her soft laugh-all gone.

He made his way to the front of the church away from the others to pray. As he sat on the backless bench, his head bowed, he felt tired and defeated. *How much more suffering will you ask of me, Lord? Suffering and death are a natural part of this life, but what can I do for my children, for these times that will surely come in their own lives?* He knew the answer before he asked the question - The One who knows and sees all who suffer and who suffered in the same way as a man would comfort them in their sorrows. He walked out of the church still feeling beaten, but not without hope.

He approached his parents. "I need to make arrangements for Henry and Minnie. I either have to give up marshaling or get help. I must talk this over with the children, who need to be in a family with other children, perhaps with Sam."

His father placed a hand on his shoulder and peered into his eyes. "Son, you know we'll help in any way possible. We would love to take them."

"Pa, it's been a decade since you had a yung'un in your house."

"We can handle it."

The children packed in silence, their normal giggles weighted down by the decisions of what to take. They would be going to their grandparents while he was gone, but when he was home between trips, they would stay with him. He kissed Minnie on the forehead. She was solemn and still, clutching her doll to her breast. Henry had his cardboard box packed, a slingshot sticking out of the top.

Gesturing at the bed where he had laid out all of Salina's personal items, he said "You may each take something of your mother's as a remembrance."

Henry clutched her favorite fan and his daughter a beautiful shawl that Charley had bought on a recent trip to Fort Smith. Her Bible, wedding photo, wedding ring and journal were in his trunk. In her trunk lay the simple baby clothes she had made for their newborns, two receiving blankets in a neutral color, three shirts, four gowns, several pairs of booties and diapers. He would keep the trunk and those precious hand-made items. Why? He didn't know; he just couldn't part with something she had made with her own hand. The rest of her belongings he would distribute to the needy families among their neighbors. His heart was too heavy to think of keeping anything else.

Minnie and Henry sat in the wagon, their bags in the back secured with a piece of rope. Charley tied the young horse that he had raised for the children to the back. Most youngsters walked, but he felt his son needed to have a decent mount, even if he was only twelve.

He gave the sniffling children a good-by hug. "Now, you mind your grandparents, hear? I'll come for you as often as I can. Be good and study hard in school. I love you and I'll write you often." Why did they have to face the abrupt harshness of life and death so soon.

Henry spoke for both of them. "We promise to mind and do our best for you." Minnie, her little fist stuffed into her mouth, waved at him with the other hand. Her kitten sat in a crate in the back. Charley stood in silence and waved as the wagon drove off.

When he had discussed the arrangements with them, the children had been mindful of the change in their lives and were grateful to be going with their beloved grandparents. He knew they would be safe and secure.

Charley sighed as he turned to the empty house his landlord would soon lease to someone else. He needed to go to Fort Smith and discuss a change in assignment with the Marshal. *What else do I need to do? Salina, I miss you so much. I can't think about going on without you. Lord, help me.* Tears of grief swept over him as he fingered Salina's bonnet, still hanging on the back of the rocker.

Two days later he rode into Fort Smith. It seemed like only last week he had been here and was looking forward to his time off. Salina's death had left him unaware of time. He moved through the motions of a life that had been ripped apart. Nothing seemed important anymore. Why hadn't he stopped and appreciated all the blessings he had been given?

He stepped up to the Marshal's office and knocked on the open door. Carroll was at his desk sorting through a stack of papers. He looked up at Charley and smiled.

"Come in. I received your telegram. I'm so sorry to hear of your loss. Are you sure you're ready to get back to work? It's so soon."

"I need something to take my mind off my worries right now. I would like an assignment in an area closer to my parents in Skullyville. They'll be tending my children."

"I need a deputy at Childers Station. Would that help? It isn't much closer to Skullyville, but is easier access from Fort Smith."

"I think that would be better for me. I'm going to talk to Abe and see if he wants to move there, too, since he and I almost always ride together."

"I'll consider that as your assignment, then. Who do you think would be good to send out to Kully-cha-ha?"

"One of the new guys, since it's pretty quiet around there most of the time."

"Thanks to you and Tyner Hughes' hard work over the past five years. I'll have your writs ready for you tomorrow. Is that too soon? There are nineteen alone for the witnesses called on the Louis Burrow murder case.

"How many men are on duty right now?"

"I've got forty. Hughes and Bass Reeves seem to be carrying the heaviest loads right now. "

"I'll see Abe today."

Carroll sighed and brushed his gray hair along his forehead. "Tell Abe I'm going to deputize him as soon as the holidays are over. He's too talented to waste on being just a posse man for you."

Morris Cemetery, Bloomer, Arkansas - final resting place of Sidney Salina Barnhill

Chapter 28

Thirty-One Outlaws

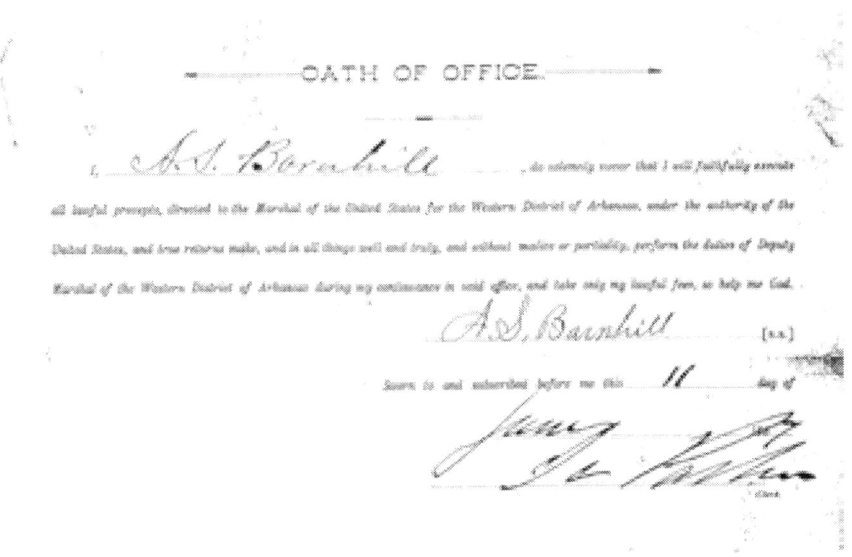

OATH OF OFFICE.

I, A. S. Barnhill, do solemnly swear that I will faithfully execute all lawful precepts, directed to the Marshal of the United States for the Western District of Arkansas, under the authority of the United States, and true returns make, and in all things well and truly, and without malice or partiality, perform the duties of Deputy Marshal of the Western District of Arkansas during my continuance in said office, and take only my lawful fees, so help me God.

A. S. Barnhill [L.S.]

Sworn to and subscribed before me this 11 day of

Abe's Swearing in Paper - January 11, 1887

A crowd filled the hall outside the famous courtroom. Lawyers sat on the benches nearest the entrance to the courtroom, portfolios in the arms of young trainees, all eager to see Judge Parker in action. Witnesses milled around, conversing with each other in excited voices. Some had been compelled to stay for weeks. It was a costly, lengthy affair to go to court. The backlog made even the most important murder case wait for a year or more.

Abe felt conspicuous as they nudged their way through the crowd and headed for a bearded man in a business suit. Marshal Carroll held his head at an angle as he listened to the complaints of a defense lawyer. Abe watched in silence as Charley approached him.

"Marshal Carroll, may I have a word with you?" Charley asked in a polite, but insistent tone.

"What's the problem, Deputy Barnhill?" Carroll's thin lips under his beard spread into a curved oval as if he wanted to grind his teeth at the interruption. Even the most even-tempered marshal could lose his Christian temperament under a querulous defense lawyer.

"Sir, we've been given thirty-one arrest writs and we don't have enough provisions or wagons for that many prisoners. I need another guard and wagon now."

"Sorry, Charley. I don't have any more wagons or guards available. You'll need to round up your own." The Marshal turned and walked down the stairs toward his office. Carroll's abruptness was uncharacteristic of him and it caught both men off guard. Charley turned to Abe, a scowl covering his normally pleasant features, and spat out, "What do they expect from us when we're not given adequate help?"

Maybe this trip was too soon after burying his Salina, Abe thought as he cleared his throat. He noticed curious glances from the nearest by-standers who had heard the exchange. "Let's go see what we can round up ourselves."

He placed his hand on Charley's arm, the tension of the muscles apparent under his shirt. As he followed Charley, he sucked in his breath and doffed his hat to acquaintances - merchants who were here to file complaints against the government for claims incurred in the past term. Their sympathetic eyes met his own.

Since he had been sworn in as a deputy marshal in January he had spent most of his time with Charley, dragging in wagon-loads of prisoners as fast as they could find them. This trip they had James White, a trusted and admired deputy. This gave the group three deputies, one posse man, a guard, a cook and two wagons. They needed at least one more wagon and guard before leaving and more needed to be picked up on the way. It would be a challenge to keep that many prisoners fed and shackled. Glad Jimmy was along this trip.

In the front of the jail, Charley tightened up the cinches on Billie. He did it with quick jerks of his wrist. Billie squirmed under the pressure, switching his tail to show his displeasure. Charley patted the steed's neck. "Okay, boy. Ready to go?"

Abe talked to his horse too. His mare was a devoted companion, that could sense a good rider's intentions before the command was given by knee or rein. His brother's abruptness with Billie was the frustration they both felt. They had to work at the pace of the arrest warrants coming out of the grand juries which never seemed to catch up with the charges being made.

Charley turned toward Garrison Avenue. "I'm going to the saloons to see who's around for hire and to get some breakfast. See that everyone is fed before we leave. I don't plan on stopping before nightfall."

The nearby hotel restaurant had a good early morning breakfast, all you could eat off of a buffet. Their Chinese cooks could make shoe leather digestible. Abe heaped his plate and watched with satisfaction as the others followed his example. Dan, the cook, relished eating someone else's food. Jimmy, a youngster with an insatiable appetite, dug into a heaping pile of potatoes. Ben Ayers, James White's posse man, nursed a cup of coffee and stuffed his mouth with bacon in between sips. It was cold and the beginning of a month-long trip. A full stomach would help.

Garrison Avenue, Fort Smith, Arkansas 1867

Two women in black dresses and veils entered the restaurant after them. When they raised the veils, Abe recognized Mary and Anna Morgan, sister-in-laws married to two brothers. Anna was the widow of William Morgan, whose murder he and Charley had investigated last September. Mary was John Morgan's wife; John was the government's chief witness. They were two of the nineteen witnesses that he and Charley had notified for the court in January.

On his way out he approached their table with his hat in his hands. "Mrs. Morgan, do you remember me?"

The pale face beneath dark curls bore a quizzical look then a smile of recognition. "Of course, Mr. Barnhill. You were there at the arrest of my husband's killer. Oh, I see a new badge, *Deputy* Barnhill. Congratulations."

"Thank you, ma'am. I hope everything goes well for you."

"You are most welcome," Mrs. Morgan smiled. "Mary, you remember the Barnhill brothers, don't you."

The younger woman eyed him from under her bonnet. "Yes, how are you, Deputy Barnhill?"

"Well, thank you. Good day to you both." He walked away from their table and paid his bill. The rest of his party was outside waiting on the board walk. He pulled his slicker collar close. It had started to rain.

Charley was at the livery with one of their neighbors from Sallisaw, Bill Thomas, who had worked as guard for them on many occasions.

Abe extended his hand in greeting "Howdy, Bill. You going along."

"Yup, I just brought in a load of hogs and pelts. I have an empty wagon and plenty of time on my hands until planting starts next month."

Bill was a slightly built man, who slouched under a heavy overcoat. His calloused hands gripped the butt of a Winchester. "I'll just keep this in my wagon until you start picking up prisoners." His boots sloshed in the mud as he walked to the wagon. On his return Charley introduced him to the other members of the group.

Abe moved up close and ducked his head to Charley. "I saw the Morgan women in the restaurant. I guess they're here to testify."

"We served enough witness subpoenas last month. That's going to be a long, hard-fought trial since the families were so close before the murder. You know we'll be called too, as well as John Phillips."

"What about the Morgan daughter, Irene? Surely, she will be called."

"She hasn't been yet. We'll see."

Charley turned back to the documents he had been discussing with James White in the shelter of the livery door. "We're tracking a band of rustlers. If we can locate their camp, we might get the whole group in one swoop."

Abe tipped the water off his hat and sucked on a toothpick. "A scout could do that before our departure gets leaked out. They won't suspect a single man riding alone."

"What do you think, James?" Charley turned his eyes on his recruit.

"It might work. Who do you have in mind?"

"I have a friend who lives in the area. I will send him a telegram to meet us at Briartown in three days. Rustlers like to hole up in the Robber's Cave area north of Wilburton," Charley explained. "Wait up while I head over to the telegraph office."

A few minutes later Abe signaled to the drivers to start their teams as Charley rejoined the group. The three wagons pulled out of the livery yard, the two mules on Thomas' wagon braying a call to the horses. Their necks arched as their mouths opened with a surprisingly loud greeting. The teams strained at the wagons, rain dripping off their ears and backs.

The men wore slickers over long wool coats. Abe was glad he had rolled every item in oil cloth before placing them inside his saddlebags. The temperature fell as the day progressed. If the weather continued like this, it would be a slow crawl to Briartown.

Near Skullyville the wagons circled into the clearing where they had held Louis Burrow last fall. The bare tree branches of the forest disappeared in the drizzle. The men spent the next hour putting up tents. Dan had his cook tent going long before their sleeping quarters were ready.

Abe knocked the rain off before entering the tent and pitching down his bedroll. He hoped to stay dry and avoid coming down sick. He remembered the manhunt for Jackson Crow only a year ago when Charley had lost his toes to frostbite. Rolling up his gun belt, he stuffed it under his bedroll to keep it dry. His thoughts turned to Amanda and the girls. He hoped the roof on the old place they were renting did not leak. He would check it when he got home. Ah! The romantic life of a deputy. If only people knew what hardships they faced everyday, but he did it for the satisfaction of bringing in the dregs of society. What about the innocent ones in the families like the Morgan women and children? Who would sustain them?

On the third day the caravan drove into Briartown. Charley wanted to take the evening off to go visit his children at Sam's home. He hadn't seen them since Christmas. His parents had taken a missionary trip into the Comanche lands.

"Jimmy, you want to go visit Sam with me tonight?"

Jimmy's face reflected his answer. A nod of his head sealed it.

Charley gave instructions to the others before he left as they huddled around the cook stove. "I want our presence kept quiet, so no visiting town or big campfire."

As he knocked and then opened the door to Sam's comfortable cabin, a room full of faces swung around, eyes open in surprise. "Papa, papa!" Minnie squealed.

Henry jumped up from the dinner table and threw his arms around his father.

"Hold on there, you're squeezing the breath out of me." He looked into Henry's face, and rumpled his hair with his left hand while hugging Minnie with his right.

When they noticed Jimmy standing behind him, his six feet four inch frame filling the doorway, the squealing started all over again. The rest of the family gathered around and added to the hugs. One thing about the Barnhills, they weren't afraid to hug anyone who came in the door. Charley put his hat on the rack beside the door and took off his slicker and long coat.

Charley smiled at his brother, Sam, and took the chair that was offered. Just in time for dinner, how did he manage that? "This sure looks good, Mary. We need a hot meal after the wet ride we took today. Abe is here with me but I wanted him to stay at the camp tonight and keep the other deputy company. We have a young fellow, named James White, with us on this trip. He's a good, dependable deputy. "

"Where's Tyne?" Sam asked.

"He's off on a trip and won't be back for another week. I couldn't wait for him. I have thirty-one arrest warrants to haul in this time."

"Wow, Pa. How're you and Uncle Abe going to do that?" Henry asked, his puzzled look almost making Charley laugh.

"Well, son. We do it one man at a time. If you keep plodding along, soon enough you have a whole wagon-load of prisoners."

Minnie sat on his lap while he ate dinner. He didn't mind. She was getting big and looked so much like Salina. He held her tight and tickled her whenever she tried to steal a morsel off his plate. Finally, his belly full and his head drowsy, he put her down.

"Minnie, darlin'. Help Aunt Mary with the dishes like a good girl," he instructed her, his hand gesturing toward the table.

That night both brothers curled up in front of the fire and slept soundly, the sleep of contentment in a house of peace. God's blessing was apparent on his family.

Charley met the neighbor, John Culberson, the next morning at the general store. He had news about the rustlers.

"They passed through here two days ago, eight of 'em, each one leading two horses with mixed brands. They were headed south toward Kinta. It could be some of the Starr bunch or invaders from Kansas. I didn't recognize any of them. Is that who you're looking for?" Culberson asked, spreading his hands in uncertainty.

Charley offered what information he had obtained before leaving Fort Smith. "The leader, Wilson, is described as tall, over six foot six, with long brown hair, beard and scar across the left cheek. Most of the time he rides a horse with four stocking feet."

"Yeah, that seems to be one of them. What do you want me to do?"

"I suspect they're at Robber's Cave. Before we get too close, I want to know if they're there so we can take them all together. We'll wait for you at Kinta until tomorrow afternoon."

"I should be able to get down there by late tonight. I'll watch the place and see what the day brings."

"If we don't hear from you, we'll head to Robber's Cave."

The hours waiting for the scout's return were a drag. The cook tent was warm and toasty from the fire of Dan's stove that he hauled around in bad weather. The cook and guards played cards and told yarns, the deputies listening while tending to their pistols and shotguns. Wet weather could rust a gun barrel overnight.

Charley's eyes drooped in the warmth. He should do something to prepare for the next day, but what? He cleared his throat and the men turned their heads. As he began to speak, the plan unfolded. "If there are eight men as Culberson saw at Briartown, I'll need you all."

There was only silence as the men looked down at their hands. Jimmy and Bill Thomas had never been asked to do something like this, but he did not want to be out-gunned.

"With Culberson, that will give us seven against their eight, but we've the element of surprise." *Would Ma be mad at me for putting young Jimmy in harm's way?* It had to be done for the survival of them all.

Bill Thomas expressed the feelings of the whole group. "We're with you in this, Charley."

He was humbled by these devoted men who forsook family and hearth to make a better life for their children. Who would tell their tale?

Two of the cave entrances to the Robber's Cave area

The lawmen got into position late in the evening on the day Culberson reported back. Each man spent the night trying to stay dry and warm on the rock-covered hills. The spy had reported the rustlers were inside and had been there for two days, according to a local farmer who had seen them arrive. There was only one way in and out of this canyon and there was no guard at the entrance. Their secrecy had paid off. The dawn opened with the smell of a campfire and cooking bacon, the smoke wafting out from the cave entrance.

Abe rested the barrel of his Winchester on the rock outcropping in front of him, fixing his sights on the entrance to the cave, a narrow opening just large enough for a horseman to pass. Granite and igneous boulders lay about the entrance as if a giant hand had thrown a few pebbles down from on high. He had been inside before. A wall of boulders in the front of the cave made a natural corral that could easily hold a hundred horses. So far, so good. They did not suspect anything.

Charley crawled over to Abe. "I've got White and Ayers on top. The others are spread out on either side. I'll wave when it's time to start shooting. They will wait for the first shots. I don't want to scare them back inside by firing prematurely."

By mid-morning Charley had crawled into the cave's entrance. He came back out shortly and showed eight fingers up. Eight men inside.

The beat of horses' hooves shook the ground under Abe's boots. Someone was coming out pretty quick. Shouts and whistles filled the air as a line of riders burst forth from the cave entrance, each man leading a double string.

He saw Charley stand up and wave his hat as the eighth rider cleared the entrance. Taking aim on the lead horse with a shoulder shot, Abe watched the rider disappear in a cloud of dust only to reappear crawling on all fours for the boulders. White's Winchester barked out from above as Ben's carbine added to the deadly fire.

The riders still in the saddle whirled around firing wildly in all directions, the dust thickening as riderless horses bolted. Two more riders went down. They had the gang hemmed in on all sides. A tall man with long hair and a beard finally raised his arms high above his head. The others followed suit.

Abe stepped from behind the outcropping and approached, the muzzle of his Winchester aimed at the big man's chest. "Get down and put your hands behind your back." He secured the braids on his wrist and turned him around. "I guess I don't need to tell you, you're under arrest." Eight men in one swoop. Not bad, Abe thought as he surveyed the area.

The stolen horses were put into a corral offered by the farmer. He was happy to oblige, getting paid a half-dollar per day to feed and care for the stock. Abe wrote down the brands and descriptions. The commissioner would try to find the lawful owners.

Charley thought about the day's work as hot coffee warmed his insides. He could hear the prisoners shackled inside two wagons coughing and grumbling, trying to get comfortable enough to sleep. He had evaluated the prisoners as they had moved into camp - who might cooperate with the lawmen over the next twenty plus days, a long haul for both groups in the winter weather. He would keep an extra guard on the toughest ones.

He took out the writs of arrest and noted the names of the prisoners. They were all there as the witnesses had stipulated. Fortunately, the commissioner had gotten correct information this time. He sipped his coffee and cleared his throat.

"We'll camp in the most central part of the area and spread out from there, in order to cover most of the Choctaw Nation. Abe, you and I will head to Atoka and James and Ben to Ardmore."

" I should have packed more socks," Jimmy complained, in a teasing tone. "Ma gets mad at me for wearing my socks more than three days."

"That'll be the least of your worries while riding herd on all these prisoners, boy," Charley reminded him with a smile and a wink. "I figure you'll earn every dollar you're paid on this trip, plus some."

"What happens if we can't locate the fugitives we're seeking?" White asked, his hand tracing a path on the map Charley had spread out on the ground. "The closer we get to the Texas border, the more likely they are to bolt across the line."

Charley tapped the map with his forefinger. "That's a chance we'll have to take. If any succeed in getting away in that direction, I'll send a telegram to the authorities across the line to watch for them." He knew his plan was sound, but men on the run scattered like rats at the approach of a lawman.

The next three days netted six more arrests. Next stop McAlester then Hartshorne. They used the same tactics, camping near Krebs while both parties of deputies spread out to tighten the noose around the fugitives in the area. By the time they were finished, they had twenty prisoners in camp. The guards had their hands full.

Charley rubbed his hands together for warmth before the cook stove. "I'm heading into McAlester to hire another guard and wagon. Mr. Sittel should have someone in mind." He had another purpose for going into McAlester, Mrs. Celia Morgan, Pastor Morgan's first wife.

Dan looked up from the boiling kettle of beans. "Bring back some flour. I'm running low. These fellas eat like they've never had a decent meal in months."

As he approached the small town, Charley remembered the storm of '82 that had wiped out Krebs and most of McAlester. The settlements had been rebuilt, though the mines had shut down and some houses were boarded up.

After procuring a guard and wagon, he made his way to the boarding house where he knew Celia Morgan was staying with her younger children. He had a witness subpoena for her. Billie Morgan's' temper had gotten him killed and the defense wanted to hear her description of his moods. His hand hesitated over the door knocker - would he remember what Irene looked like? It had been several months since he had seen her. At his knock, a woman, slightly older than himself with fine brown hair and a pretty face, answered the door. Now he knew where the Morgan girls got their beauty.

"May I help you?" Her voice was polite and low, her smile welcoming.

"I'm Deputy Marshal Charles Barnhill. Are you Mrs. Morgan?" Charley hoped his voice was reassuring.

"Yes, won't you please come in? "

He hesitated as he removed his hat "I've a subpoena for you to appear in Fort Smith next month. It has to do with the murder of your former husband."

Mrs. Morgan dropped her gaze to the folded paper. "Oh, dear. That terrible case. I knew Billie would get himself kilt one day. He was that kind of man." She softened her voice and said, "Let me call Irene. I'm sure she will be pleased to see you. She has told me how kind you were to her when you arrested Louis."

She turned and walked down the hall. He fidgeted with his hat as he waited for the woman's return. Would Irene be embarrassed by his unannounced visit?

The girl came down the hall, a shy grin on her face. Her gray eyes widened as she recognized him. "Deputy Barnhill, how nice to see you."

He spied Mrs. Morgan shooing three inquisitive faces back into the room behind the girl who wore a dark dress with a tight bodice and rows of buttons hooking down the front. He was glad he did not have to mess with something like that to get dressed.

"I had to deliver a subpoena to your mother. She will have to appear in court. How are your doing?"

"I'm very busy helping my mother take care of my sisters and brother. I help with the boarding house where I get to meet some mighty nice people."

"My brother saw your step-mother, Anna, and John's wife, Mary, recently in Fort Smith. I was surprised your name wasn't on the list of witness subpoenas I took out there in January.

"I'm in no hurry to face the courtroom trial with all this mess. My family has disowned Janey for standing by her man. But what can you expect a wife to do? She can't desert her husband in the face of a gallows. I dread the whole affair. I appreciate your concern for me and my family, Deputy."

Irene's smile made him feel like a school boy. Would Salina approve of her as a step-mother for her children? Why was he thinking that?

Abe followed the line of wagons into Fort Smith. They had crossed on the ferry with the three wagons and Dan's chuck wagon. Thirty-one prisoners in all, three guards, three deputies, a posse and a Choctaw cook. Though the citizens of Fort Smith were sated by the constant coming and going of the deputy's wagons, even they stopped their work to watch the long procession of prisoners. This was a record for the largest number of prisoners brought in at one time. Abe knew he didn't want to repeat this. It was a once in a lifetime event, you could look back on with pride, but say "Never again."

As he dismounted and walked up the stairs to the Marshal's office with Charley and White, he noticed the jailer inspecting the prisoners, a look of disbelief on his face. The jail was already over-crowded and he had to stuff thirty-one more in, at least until the ones who could give bail were released.

In the month they had been out, spring had started to show its head in Fort Smith. Small buds peeked out on the branches of the large oak trees on the grounds of the jail. Bright sprigs of little yellow blooms spread through the clover grass. A lone bird called to its mate high in the trees.

It reminded him of the change of seasons in life. His was in the summer. What would the fall years bring?

Chapter 29

Courtship

The sun rising in the eastern sky hit Charley's back. He gave Billie a slap on the withers with a rein tip to encourage him onto the ferry. The big horse hated riding on the little wooden ferry which crossed the Poteau River west of Fort Smith. His ears twitched as his master coached him with low soothing tones.

"Go ahead, boy. That's a good Billie." It might be better to swim across and risk drowning than fight with this horse, Charley thought. Abe was right behind him, trying to get his mare and the pack mule onto the ferry behind Billie.

"We're ready, Mr. Johnson." Charley gestured to the boatman who pushed off from the shore with his long pole.

Poteau River Ferry

His son, on the opposite side of the ferry, strained his back against the swift-moving current which threatened to tear the poles loose and send them downstream with the other floating debris. These rickety ferries across smaller tributaries during the high water season provided extra income for the local Indian families. The ones across the larger rivers worked year round and were steam-driven. It took several minutes of groaning and tugging to make the landing a hundred yards across the small river.

Billie kicked loose from the ferry and gained his footing on the well-packed shore. Charley held the reins as the horse ascended the slope. Mounting quickly, he motioned Abe to fall in. It was just the two of them this time, no guard and no cook. He had only one arrest warrant, but ten witnesses to find in Skullyville for the up-coming Burrow's hearing. What gave him the most anticipation was the subpoena for Irene Morgan in McAlester.

"We'll take the Old Military Road over to Skullyville. I gave Deputy Phillips his subpoena for the hearing before I left Fort Smith. We've been subpoenaed but your name hasn't come up yet."

"That's fine with me." Abe replied. "Amanda is in the motherly way again, and I'd rather be free to help her."

They rode through the countryside, the creaking saddles, the horses' hooves, a distant bird, the only sounds. Riding trail was tedious and wearisome. Charley could see the old Indian mounds off to their right, the location of a large city hundreds of years old. Local people dug into those mounds looking for the lost treasure of the Incas or something foolish like that.

He wrinkled his brow as he thought about the first name on his list, John Morgan, Irene's uncle who had witnessed William Morgan's murder. John was an aggressive kind of guy, like Billie Morgan, and he hoped he could locate him without trouble.

The Burrow house, the scene of the murder, passed off their left as they rode through Skullyville. A silent prayer for both families crossed his lips.

Charley knocked on the door at Morgan's home north of town. His wife, Mary, opened the door and greeted him.

"Deputy Barnhill, what brings you here today?" She glanced behind him at Abe still mounted on his horse.

"I've a subpoena for you and John to appear at Fort Smith."

"Again?" Her voice was soft, resigned.

"Yes, ma'am. This trial's going to be long and drawn out."

"John's down in the garden. I'll ring the bell for him. Please come in."

Abe dismounted and joined Charley in the house. It was cooler inside, the open windows allowing the breeze to flow through the wide hall that separated the frame home into two parts.

A few minutes after the clang of the bell, John Morgan appeared through the back door. He dropped the vegetables he was carrying on the porch and wiped his hands on his trousers.

"Hello, Barnhill. What can I do for you?"

"I have a subpoena for you and Mrs. Morgan to appear in Fort Smith on July seventeenth," Charley explained.

"I hope this is settled soon. Louis needs to face the gallows for what he did."

"Well, it may be a while. He has an excellent defense team."

Charley noticed hogs penned up away from the house as he stepped off the porch. There were only a couple, but they sure stank. Was John turning into a hog farmer? He'd take a smelly cow any day.

It took most of the afternoon to locate the other witnesses spread out around Skullyville. Charley lifted his hat and rubbed his eyes, raw from the afternoon sun. "I think we're done here. Let's head to Pa's for the night. He always has a bed for us."

Early the next morning they trailed south toward McAlester getting closer to Miss Irene. He had written her a few letters since February in which he had described his loss of Salina to meningitis and the emptiness he felt. She had answered politely and the relationship seemed to be mutually desirable. What was he thinking, a girl twenty years his junior?

"Abe, when you lost you first wife, did you plan on marrying again?"

"Not really. But then when I saw Mollie needed a woman's care, I decided I would if the Lord brought a suitable woman into my life."

"What about the age difference?"

"When I married Amanda I was thirty-three and she was twenty-three, but that doesn't seem to matter. Maybe it will when I get old and she's still feisty. Besides, Pa is sixteen years older than Mother. What you got in mind?'

"I've been keeping in touch with Miss Irene Morgan. Her father was only five years older than me. I hope she doesn't look at me as a father figure "

"I can't say what a woman thinks about age difference. You'll have to ask her."

Charley thought on the subject for a few minutes. His ultimate goal on this trip was to find out if Miss Irene was interested enough to start a courtship.

McAlester had grown since his first visit six years ago; more buildings at the edge of town flowed south from the train depot. He dismounted in front of the Elk House and attempted to clean off some of the road dust. He shook his hat, striking it against his knee. The particles that loosened soon mixed with the dirt suspended in the air by the stout wind from the prairie.

He spoke through the dust cloud. "Let's get a bath and shave. It'll be some time before we get back to Fort Smith." He took his saddlebags and Winchester off Billie.

"Sounds good to me." Abe said as he took Billie's reins to lead both horses and the mule across the street to the livery.

McAlester, Choctaw Nation, Indian Territory

He hadn't been by the Elk House in a couple of years. A young man flashed him a polite smile. "May I help you, Deputy?" eying the layers of dust that covered the guest from head to foot, concerned that some of it might be deposited on his counter.

Charley stepped up cautiously so as not to share the dirt with the clerk's immaculate shirt, vest and string tie. "Yes, I need two rooms for the night with a bath and shave."

"Of course, please sign the register. Your companion?" The clerk watched as he signed his neat signature, Chas. Barnhill.

"He's coming over from the livery, names Abe Barnhill."

"I've heard of the Barnhill brothers who are deputies. I'm very glad to meet you."

"Thanks. Now, how about that bath?"

"It'll be ready shortly."

Two hours later, he felt like a new man, the barber's tonic making him smell like a prairie flower. His weather-darkened face stared back at him from the bureau mirror contrasting with the white shirt collar. He settled his brushed hat on shorn hair. He felt he looked good enough to go courting.

The subpoena in the breast pocket of his jacket, he walked the few blocks to the boarding house amazed at the number of wagons of all sizes that lined the street in front of the feed store and McAlester's warehouse. The boarding house curtains flapped gently in the wind as he opened the door and entered the hall, the dining room to his right and a parlor to his left. He climbed the stairs to the second floor, his head racing at what he had to find out. He wasn't leaving here without an answer.

Tap, tap. The door knocker sounded loud in the still hall. He heard light footsteps behind the door. It opened. Miss Irene stood facing him, a startled but happy expression on her young face.

"Deputy Barnhill, what a pleasant surprise. Do come in."

"How are you, Miss Morgan?" Charley asked, his voice polite.

"I'm just fine, thank you. Please sit down, and I'll get Mother."

He waited for their return, his head down staring at his boots. He tried to concentrate on what to say. But what was the right thing? "Ma'am, I want to marry your daughter?" or "Can I have Irene's hand in marriage?" Maybe he had better talk to Irene first.

He rose from the chair as Irene's mother extended her hand to him which he took with a slight bow. "Mrs. Morgan."

"Would you like some coffee? I've just made some downstairs in the kitchen," she said.

"Thank you." This woman was shrewd - giving him private time with Irene. As soon as she left, he turned his eyes to the girl. Her slim waist invited an embrace, but he forced his arms down, gripping the chair arms instead.

"Did you get my letters?"

"Yes, it's very kind of you to take the time from your busy schedule." She blushed as she spoke.

"The hearing, have you thought much about it? Testimony in the court room can tear a family apart. I just want to make sure you're prepared."

"I've spent many hours in prayer; this burden is weighing us all down. My father was a stern man and could see no way but his. That's one of the causes for my parents' divorce. When is the hearing scheduled?"

"That's why I'm here. Deputy Phillips and I have to appear at the same time." He handed her the subpoena. "Do you want me to explain it to you?"

"Yes, please." She unfolded the document in her lap.

"I have to read this to you and certify to the court that I have served the subpoena. *You must appear on the said date under penalty of law. The court will reimburse you for your travel at six cents a mile and provide vouchers for lodging and meals.*"

"Oh , dear. I don't feel up to traveling alone all that way."

"I would be most honored if you would allow me to escort you and your mother. . She may want to observe the proceedings. I would be glad to pay for her trip." He had a little money sat aside and felt this would be a good cause.

"Let's discuss it with her when she returns." Her smile was inviting, drawing him to her soft pink lips. He averted his eyes and tried to focus on what to say next.

Mrs. Morgan returned with a walnut tray loaded with coffee and cookies. After everyone had been served, Irene turned to her mother. "Deputy Barnhill brought a subpoena for me to appear in court on July seventeenth. He has offered to escort both of us to Fort Smith."

"I appreciate that. I don't really want to hear about the whole unpleasant scene, but I need to support my children." Mrs. Morgan's sad glance down at her folded hands made him regret this family's loss.

He sighed in relief, not realizing he had been holding his breath. "Then it is settled. You can ride the train to Checotah where I'll meet you. We'll ride the stage from there."

The older woman looked at a calendar hanging on the wall beneath a picture of the Morgan family which was at least five years old judging from Irene's size. "When would we have to leave?"

"No later than July thirteenth. It'll take two days to get to Fort Smith and get settled in a hotel. I'll go down to the depot and purchase the tickets before I leave."

"Thank you so much, Deputy," Mrs. Morgan's eyes glistened with tears. "You've been so kind to my family." She gathered up the cups and saucers and went through the door to the downstairs.

Irene turned to him, a look of concern on her face. "She's only thirty-nine and spent eleven of the thirteen years she was married as a missionary's wife in this harsh land. It's scandalous for a preacher to divorce. But she had no choice after enduring my father and his abusive language toward people who disagreed with him."

"Ministers are just men and some can't handle the extra burden it places on them and their families. My father's been a minister for over sixty years."

While Mrs. Morgan was downstairs, he realized this was his last chance to speak what was really on his mind. He reached over and took her hand. She did not pull it away. "Miss Morgan, I've found myself drawn to you ever since I met you. I know there's a huge difference in age between us, but you're a thoughtful young woman who understands life. I'd consider it an honor if you'd allow me to court you. I'd be glad to speak to your mother."

Irene's startled look changed to a smile. He held his breath as he waited for her reply.

"Deputy Barnhill, you show me great honor with such a request. I'd not even considered the possibility that you cared for me so. There are many mature women who'd jump at the chance to be married to a handsome, brave deputy marshal."

"Yes' ma'am. I haven't given it any thought except in regards to you. I feel you could love my children and be a mother to them."

"I think I'd like that very much."

He heard the words he had dreamed about. This young woman had just made his life whole again. "Then, when your mother returns, I'll speak to her."

Charley had a song on his lips as he stepped off the porch of the boarding house. He could face the future and he thanked God for this young woman who was willing to share it.

Abe stared at his brother. There was something different about him as he walked back from the boarding house, his gait and actions energized. As he placed his foot on the first step of the hotel porch, Abe called out. "What'd she say?"

"She honored me by saying yes. I can't believe what a fortunate man I am."

"Congratulations." Abe smacked Charley on the back with a resounding clap. "Let's go celebrate with a big meal."

Chapter 30

Commissioner's Court

The up-coming Burrow murder hearing had opened a flood gate of witness subpoenas. On July 10th Charley found himself headed back to Skullyville to serve subpoenas to Garrett Ainsworth and another for John Morgan. He remembered a recent conversation he had with a local old settler.

> *"It's kind a rough these days in Skullyville. Fellows who get in trouble in other parts of the country hit out for Indian Territory since the Territory Law has no power over them. They are too smart, though, to go in too far. Mostly, they just stay all around Skullyville, just far enough to stay clear of Judge Parker's much feared court."*

How many more murderers and rustlers would he have to dig out of this area?

Ainsworth's store was a narrow frame building about twenty-five feet by seventy, a wide entry with double doors framed on either side by glass windows. Benches lined the porch on either side, a good place to meet and talk about important community issues or mundane gossip. This morning a couple of old Indians sat wrapped in blankets despite the hot morning. Double back doors stood open to let the summer breezes flow through.

Garrett was a handsome man with dark hair slicked back off his forehead and a handle-bar mustache. Deep furrows ran down either side of his handsome nose and granite lips. His father, Uncle Spence as everyone called him, had come to Skullyville as a young Choctaw with the first resettlement. The storekeeper, who had lived his whole life in this small community, knew everyone and everything.

Garrett mopped at his face with a handkerchief. "Hello, Deputy Barnhill. It's right smart hot out there."

"Sure is, but it feels much better in here. How's Uncle Spence doing?"

"Just fine. He hopes to have a big crop of cotton this year. He keeps pretty busy for a man of his age."

"My father's the same way, seventy-seven years old and still going strong. He'll never give up his preaching."

"What brings you by?"

John Garrett Ainsworth

"A subpoena for you to appear at a hearing on July seventeenth. I know that's only a week away. I came by in June and you were gone to Kansas City."

"No problem, I'll be there. I hope this mess gets settled soon. Those two families are still at each others throats every day. One of them is going to have to move out of here to let the dust settle. I also think John Morgan is up to something."

"Whatta' you mean?" Charley asked, remembering his last visit to John Morgan's place.

"Let's just say, some of his neighbors are complaining about missing hogs and John's place seems to be the center of the disappearances."

"Do the people here notch their hogs' ears?"

The store owner shrugged his shoulders. "Most do, but some of the ole timers think it isn't necessary."

"I'm headed over to John's place now. I'll take a look."

"Thanks, Charley." Garrett extended his hand and turned back to his ledgers.

As he approached John Morgan's house, it seemed quiet. His knock brought out a mangy farm dog, growling at him from the corner of the house. He waved the dog off and walked around back, heading toward the hog pen. It contained two hogs with notched ears. He didn't know John's mark. It would be hard to prove stolen pork if the owner didn't notch his hog.

"Hello." A voice called from behind the barn.

He turned to face Morgan. "Howdy, I was looking for you. No one answered at the house."

John's face was suspicious. "What do you want, Barnhill?"

"I've another subpoena to match the one I gave you last month. It seems the court wants to make sure you're there on the seventeenth."

"Fine. This whole process is taking too long. Louis is over there in jail making a name for himself as a good guy, playing the pious church elder. He even holds Bible studies with the other inmates."

"Maybe the Lord has gotten his attention with all this. He may turn out to be a better person for it all."

John snorted, "At the cost of Billie's life."

Charley took a breath and looked at his future relation. "On another subject, I've started courting Billie's daughter, Irene."

"What? We don't need a lawman in the family. You're old enough to be her father. You should be courting her mother, Celia."

"I knew you wouldn't approve, but Irene and I feel that it is what we both want."

John snorted again, and stuffed his hands in his pockets. The conversation was over.

"See you in Fort Smith. I am escorting Irene and her mother to the hearing. I've also been called as a witness."

"Great!!" John rolled his eyes and stalked away.

Morgan seemed too upset about having a lawman in the family. Maybe he was up to something after all. Pigs? What kind of money could a thief make from those critters that the Indians let run wild in the forest? He would have to ask.

The sound of a train whistle sent Charley scurrying to the train platform at the little depot at Checotah. Though the railroad had a published schedule, it was often delayed by broken parts, weather or loading. Today wasn't too bad. He had waited two hours. The locomotive hauled into view about three miles away around the curve along the river. The engineer applied the brakes and by the time it reached the depot, the train had slowed to a smooth stop.

Anxious, he hurried to the first passenger car. It was used by business men and politicians and had plush chairs placed around tables. Though the fare was a little more, the ladies had warranted the best, since this was such an important trip for them.

A smile crossed his face as he spotted the lithe figure who led her mother down the train steps. The conductor offered his hand up to them as they descended. Irene held her long flowing skirts discretely above her ankles. He noticed her booted foot underneath the lace of her petticoat. He reddened as he realized his wandering eyes. As he stepped forward, the conductor moved aside.

"Deputy Barnhill, here are your charges, safe and sound. I had strict instructions from my boss to see that these ladies were delivered safely into your hands," he said with a broad, knowing smile. Tipping his hat, he walked down the station platform to the other coach.

Charley took Irene's arm as she turned to face him.. She felt so light and airy. He was used to holding onto muscular male forearms with a death grip. He forced himself to relax his grip.

She placed her hand in his leather-hardened fingers which dwarfed her fragile hand. Her eyes searched his face as if she were trying to memorize every inch.

As he raised her hand to his lips, the brush of his lips across her fingertips was electrifying. "Miss Irene, how've you been?" He tried to keep his voice even and unexcited.

"I'm very well." Irene's voice was breathy and soft. "And how have you been?"

"Waiting for this moment with great impatience."

She blushed and changed the subject. "We packed a basket to eat on the train but it didn't last the day."

He turned to Mrs. Morgan. "The stage doesn't leave until the afternoon. We've time for a meal at the inn. Let me get your bags. It's just across the street."

They walked down the platform, Irene's arm resting lightly on his. The soothing gesture was so intimate that he felt redness creeping up his face and ears. Only engaged or married couples walked in such a manner in public. Well, it was official. They were a couple now.

The harrowing stage coach ride to Fort Smith began, the road so rough in spots that he thought the passengers would loose teeth. The driver whipped his six horse team into a frenzy to pull the steep hills. The wear on the team required stopping every twenty miles for fresh horses.

They stopped first at Webber Falls where they crossed the Arkansas River on the Lynch ferry. The passengers stepped out to stretch. Then, "Hee-haw, giddy-up!" as the driver put the whip to the team.

He attempted to inquire as to the condition of his important cargo. The ladies smiled in response, the jarring ride making speech difficult. Irene soon slept with her head in her mother's lap. After she had rested, she sat up and cradled her mother's head in her lap. By this method the weary trio passed the long hours. He would be so glad when the rail line from Fort Smith was extended west across the Nations.

At nightfall the bruised and sore assembly reached the second team swap at Childers Station, where he now lived and where they would spend the night, the stage departure set for 6 a.m. He assisted the ladies down from the coach and placed their bags inside the station. They each took a small satchel for the night, personal items to tidy up and change.

He rented a small two room home on the edge of the settlement so his children could stay with him when he was home and not impose on Abe whose family was growing. He was relieved to see that Mrs. White had freshened up the home. Deputy James White's mother was a sweetheart who thought he needed tending, coming over once a week to clean.

After a good night's rest, the travelers returned to the stage, refreshed and ready to continue. He was eager to get the ladies settled. He looked at the telegram he had received at Checotah instructing him to report to the marshal's office on his arrival. He wondered at the message. He always stopped by the marshal's office when in town. Why the request?

The stage rumbled into the growing city late in the afternoon, a cloud of dust swirling through the open windows. The driver pulled their satchels from the top of the coach and opened the door. "Ladies." The shotgun rider hauled the heavier cases from the boot in the back, the whole lot piled up on the boardwalk.

Charley whistled at a hack driver, resting with his rig near the stage depot. "Please take these ladies to the Anderson Hotel." He handed the driver a generous tip

He placed his hand on the rig. "Miss Irene, Mrs. Morgan, I have to report to the marshal's office. I will pick you up at six for supper."

After he watched the hack move down Garrison Avenue, he walked to the Old Jail office. Chief Deputy Marshal Barnes sat at his desk.

"Has Deputy Phillips checked in?"

"He's waiting for you at the district attorney's office."

Why did the district attorney need them? He found John Phillips waiting outside D. A. Sandels' office.

Sandels, a stickler for the law, wanted everything in order before a hearing. He came out and greeted them. "Come inside. I have a few things to discuss on the Burrow hearing."

Phillips, his lanky form minus six shooters and badge, looked like a county parson, black string bow tie, white shirt under a well-cut jacket, cotton trousers tucked into neat boots. His features were that of a man content with the world and himself with a self-assured smile of greeting. "We're happy to help out in any way we can, sir." Charley looked at him for a clue. He shrugged and moved into the cool interior of the office.

Charley sat down in the smooth oak chair, his nose tickled by the pleasant scent of cigar, paper, ink and furniture oil. It reminded him of the school room where he had sat learning his letters under the stern tutelage of a master from St. Louis. That was before the War had taken him out of the school and into the fields. He had finished eighth grade but not until the War had ended and schools had resumed.

The D.A. picked up a sheath of papers and thumbed through them. "I've gone over your reports this morning. I want to freshen the details in your minds before your testimony."

"What'd you need to know?" Charley said. He knew this man to be fair in every way, but also knew that defense lawyers would try all kinds of tricks to undermine their testimony.

"Deputy Barnhill, you and Deputy Phillips discovered the murder?"

"That's right. We were camped together and heard the ruckus near by."

"Who questioned the witnesses?"

"Phillips and I both spoke to Ole Man Burrow whom we found standing nearby. We then went in the house and disarmed the suspect."

"When did you separate?"

"After that John left to find Tyner Hughes so they could get an arrest warrant from the Marshal."

"Who did you talk to then?"

"Everyone who had seen the fight: Ole Man Burrow, John Morgan, the three Indian boys, family members who had been present. It's all in my report."

"Two men in camp nearby claim they overheard you instructing John Morgan on what to say and urging him to bring the Indian boys to you for the same reason. A prisoner at your camp by the name of Sam Davis gave the same testimony."

"That snake-in-the-grass Davis. I wondered why he seemed so interested in what was happening."

"I need an explanation for what they thought they heard."

"When I talked to John Morgan and the Indians, I encouraged them to be truthful."

Sandels turned to Phillips and eyed him. "When you got back to camp and was discussing this case with Deputy Barnhill, did you hear him say anything derogatory or biased against the accused?"

"No, sir. Not a word. He was professional in all he said and did that night."

"Deputy Barnhill, I've been told you have a personal interest in the Morgan family."

"Yes, sir. I'm engaged to Miss Irene Morgan, the deceased William Morgan's daughter."

"If I can, I will keep you off the stand. The defense will tear you up if this connection is brought out in court. That's all I need for now. Keep all of this to yourself."

Mr. Sandels rose and extended his hand.

"I'm glad to get off that hot seat." Phillips grinned.

"Me too. See you in court." Charley said. It seemed no matter what deputies did, they were under a looking glass. He should have been more suspicious of Sam Davis. Now he may have to defend himself to the commissioner.

Charley's eyes swept the hearing room as he escorted Irene and her mother toward the front. The defendant, Louis Burrow, and his attorneys sat to the left of the commissioner. Louis wore a new suit that highlighted his youthful appearance, pale and skeletal from ten months in the hell hole. His little wife sat behind him, her head bowed and face obscured by her bonnet. Irene tried to catch her eye. But Janey paid no mind to them as they passed.

Deputy Phillips sat behind the district attorney and Mr. Forrester, his assistant. He shook hands with Charley as he sat down.

The summer afternoon made the room uncomfortable even though the large open windows allowed a breeze off the river to sweep across the enclosure. The women used their large fans, even getting some of the air movement over to him. The men braved it out with frequent moping at the face.

As testimony commenced, everyone strained to hear the witness. One of the Indian boys, Jimmy Jones, sat near the commissioner's desk. He spoke through an interpreter. "I saw the men standing close together talking about something. I went to him (the deceased) right afterwards. He was dead. This man (the defendant) run off and John Morgan took the ax and run after him over the fence. Old Man Burrow followed them. John Morgan come back then, got on his horse and went home. When this man come back he went into the house, he said, to get his gun. I understood that, I know a few words of English. I was there when the deputy marshal come there with his pistol in his hand. That is the deputy." The witness pointed at Charley.

Next John Morgan came forward, dressed in his Sunday best, a deacon in the Skullyville Baptist Church. Charley cringed at the thought of church-going folks killing each other over such an insignificant cause. What kind of people were his future in-laws? His thoughts calmed as he glanced at the young woman sitting beside him, her hand tucked in his, eyes fixed on her uncle as he gave testimony. All families have outlaws and trouble-makers. A marriage brought two families together until parted by death.

"I was William Morgan's brother and was present when he was killed. We were coming home from Skullyville. William had 70 cents in his hand that he was going to pay Louis Burrow for Davis House."

William called for him from the big road in front of his house and the man come walking in from the woods. Morgan paid him. He says 'I am not collecting my brother's debts.' Morgan said, 'You have treated me worse that I would treat a dog.' That man Burrow got mad then . . . . They were about to come together and the old man came in between them. Billie walked around him. As he turned his face to the defendant, Burrow raised the ax and struck him, cut his collar bone in two down here into his breast."

When he struck him he let loose the ax and jumped off a few jumps. My brother took hold of the ax handle and said, 'Lord, have mercy upon me.' When the axe hit the ground I picked it up and run Louis off and hit him a couple or three licks. I thought when I picked up the ax I would do my best to kill him, but when he fell, he said 'Oh, John.' His father caught up and started to hit me with his fists. I ran to where my pony was. He got up and went into the house threatening to kill me. I went home. Then I went back over to where the marshals was to report, but they already had him arrested."

Mr. Forrester approached the chair. "When you started from Skullyville that night towards home before the murder, did you meet or talk to any parties?"

"Deputies Charles Barnhill, Abe Barnhill and John Phillips. That was about a quarter mile from Skullyville."

"You hadn't been away from the killing scene?"

"Yes, sir. I went and found Lige Fannin, another deputy, at home other side of Skullyville. We come back to the marshals and then went up to where he was dead and it was after that I saw Kimbrough get the knife."

"What became of the knife?"

"Charles Barnhill kept it."

" You took no knife out of your brother's hand when he fell? How close did you pass to your brother as you went to get the ax?"

"No, Billie had no knife out." John Morgan reached out and pointed to his path on the diagram that the district attorney had set up. The route extended from where John had stood behind the wagon to Morgan's body, opposite of where Louis Burrow had stood.

"Where was your knife when the killing took place?"

"In my pocket."

"Thank you. I have no more questions at this time." Mr. Forrester nodded his head toward Commissioner Brizzolara.

The commissioner rapped his gavel on the table. "I find sufficient facts to continue this case to trial. This hearing is dismissed."

Charley leaned toward the D.A. "What is the date for this trial?"

"Sometime next year. "

"How can another year in jail be of benefit?" Charley shook his head.

"If he had a trial now and was found guilty, he would have to hang. Time is in his favor. It encourages witnesses to come forward who may not have felt comfortable at first. His case can be played up in the newspapers and with the local church people who are the voice of leniency. It may sway public opinion to his side."

Charley turned to his charges. "Ladies, I'll escort you to your hotel so you can rest before supper."

On their way out Mrs. Morgan paused beside Janey. She gazed into her daughter's eyes and spoke. "I love you now and always."

These words of love melted the young woman's resolve and she collapsed in tears in her mother arms. Sobs racked her shoulders as she dabbed at the corners of her eyes. Finally able to speak, she glanced at Irene and smiled. "I love you both too. Please pray for me and Louis."

As they walked across the street, Mrs. Morgan turned to Charley. "I think I'd like to return to my children as soon as possible, but Irene may wish to stay. The Morgans don't want me around them, even if it's in the courtroom."

At the rooms, he rested his hand on the door knob. "Do you want me to take you home to McAlester?"

"Darlin', I'd like to stay close to you for now. I'll ask Anna Morgan if she'd like for me to stay with her for a few months. I'm sure she could use the help."

He smiled and mouthed a "thank you" to his future mother-in-law who stood in the lobby of the hotel. He fingered his chin as he turned away. *Yup! The sooner I fix up a wedding date, the better.*

The President of the United States of America,

To Abe Barnhill

Greeting:

We Command You, That, all and singular business and excuses being laid aside, you and each of you appear and attend before the Judge of the District Court of the United States of America for the Western District of Arkansas, at a District Court to be held at the United States Court-Room in Fort Smith, in and for said Western District of Arkansas, instanter, to testify and give evidence before said Court, touching such matters as may be inquired of you on the part of the United States, and not depart said Court without leave thereof, or of the District Attorney.

And this you, or any of you, are not to omit, under the penalty upon you, and every one of you, of two hundred and fifty dollars.

Witness, the HONORABLE ISAAC C. PARKER, Judge of said District Court, and the Seal thereof, at Fort Smith, Arkansas, in the said District, this 27 day of July A. D. 1887.

Clerk.

Abe Barnhill subpoena for Burrow case

Chapter 31

Black Fork Mountain

Lounging on the bench in front of the Marshal's office, Abe Barnhill looked at the sun rising above the banks of the Arkansas River. Charley had been busy all summer with the Burrow case so he had attached himself to Deputy George Williams, another of their invaluable friends. October promised temperate fall weather that would send deputies all over the Indian country. It was his favorite time of year: cool breezes, falling leaves, rare thunderstorms and the busy harvest.

Summer had filled his life with the relentless pursuit of outlaws, long days in the saddle, restless nights on hard ground, serving the citizens of this great country he loved, in the company of good, stout-hearted men. His mind focused on the task awaiting him, get through this trip and then home to his wife and two daughters waiting in Sallisaw, Cherokee Nation. Another baby was due soon to join 3 year-old Jenette

He gazed at his two companions, Lon Lovelace and J.C. Henderson. They were dressed commonly enough, trousers tucked into high-top riding boots branded by stirrup rubs against toes and arches, loose fitting shirts tucked in waists ringed with cartridge belts, rumpled jackets and the indispensable broad brim hats. Each man had a Winchester at his side. The deputies were not identical in uniform like a line of infantry but they knew what they needed and wore it. Some preferred comfortable, loose-fitting attire. Others, like Heck Thomas, dressed as if they were going to church, all shiny and clean and new. Abe tried to find the middle ground, not sloppy but well-fitting outfits that could be packed easily in a saddle bag. This trip Amanda had sent along three extra shirts, two trousers and a half dozen changes of undergarments. When he came home from a trip, she had to wash for three days to catch up his wardrobe.

The door opened and Williams stepped out, securing his hat over ample hair untouched by a barber's scissors. His gaze settled on his men. The toothpick between his lips gyrated as he spoke. "We've an ultimatum from the Marshal," he explained to his waiting men. "Don't come back without Bill Frazier. Two writs for assault with intent to kill have gone untended. He was last seen by hunters on Black Fork Mountain. They retreated when he fired warning shots. He comes to his home at the foot of the mountain regularly for provisions."

The three posse members examined their boots in unison, as if the leather were a sorcerer's ball that would reveal the outlaw's hideout. Abe shuffled his feet under the bench and then rose. "We'll get him this time if we have to stay out a month. He has to come home some time."

George chuckled. "I hope you're right. It don't pay much to sit around and wait. We'll head out and ask about his whereabouts as we get closer."

Mollie Frazier lifted a skirt from a wash tub straddling a fire pit placed fifty feet from her back porch. She hated wash day as did most country women. It took all day to wash one outfit for each person plus all the bedding and towels. The handle of the wooden agitator slipped in her wet hands, raising blisters over callouses. The red skin would heal only by application of liniment made of bark and bear grease, something she had learned from her Indian neighbors. As she brushed the hair out of her eyes, she caught the faint glint of light in the distance.

Dropping the skirt back into the rinsing tub, she moved out of the cover of the trees into the sunlight, shading her eyes to fix on the spot. Nothing in this forest reflected light unless it was man-made. She held still and watched. *There, a flash*. Her vision strained to make out the details. It was then she saw it - horse's ears above the low lying scrub brush along the creek.

She hiked her skirt up to her knees as she ran to the house. By the time she cleared the back door, she could make out a lone horseman riding toward the place at a casual gait. Her heart pounded as she gasped for breath, one arm supporting her body against the kitchen table.

"Bill. Bill. Rider coming," she shouted once her voice returned. She moved to the bedroom to find her husband looking out the window. An unannounced stranger meant trouble in this country.

"Get back, Mollie. Stay down until we see who it is," Frazier commanded, his voice coarse and low. "Where are the children?"

"Playing in the apple tree, I suspect. I best get them in."

"Go ahead, but stay out of sight."

Her voice quivered. "Children, come in quickly. Hurry!" Glancing out the window, she saw a tall man dismount at the edge of the clearing, keeping his horse between him and the house. She could make out a rifle on the saddle and a shotgun on the opposite side. It had to be a deputy marshal.

The figure cupped his mouth and called. "Hello, Bill Frazier. It's Deputy George Williams. I have a writ of arrest. Come out and you will not be harmed."

"Damn, Williams. I'll not surrender to him. Go out and tell him that."

Her heart sank as she heard those words. *Another fight, just like the one last year.* Her husband trusted no Yankee lawmen. He would die before he surrendered. She moved to the door and opened it. The lawmen stood still as she came out.

"He says he won't come out and you-all have to come in and get him."

"Mrs. Frazier, you best not stay," Williams said. "There may be trouble. I'll let you leave if you want to."

Mollie turned and went into the house. She hugged her husband, feeling his fury.

"Bill, please give up. I don't want to see you killed."

"Mollie, I've never surrendered to a Yankee in my life and I'm not starting now. You take the kids and get out. Go over to Erwin Justice's place and stay until I send for you."

She hung her head on her chest, eyes blurred with tears as she gathered up provisions for herself and her children. Would she see him again? She opened the door, urging the children through. They cried, unable to understand what was happening. She turned back and gave him one last desperate look. "Please, Bill, stop fighting. The War's been over for twenty years."

"Not for me, it ain't." Frazier pushed her out the door and closed it, throwing the latch in place.

She walked to the deputy who was waiting, still hidden behind his horse. "He's not coming out."

Abe watched from his vantage point as the woman and children left the house. He checked the cylinder of his revolver and knew his Winchester was full, 15 shots.

The other two posse men knelt beside him in the dust, squinting through the trees toward the house. A standoff could last for days. Frazier had sworn death to anyone who tried to bring him in.

George came through the brush and stopped in front of them. About Abe's age, his eyes were those of the Indian fighter he had been before joining the deputy force. Small lines creased his cheeks above his mustache. "He's in there but won't budge. Sent his family away. We'll see who can out wait the other. I'll give him some time before I try a parley. Abe, you go cover the back. Lon and J.C., move to the sides. I'll stay right here. I don't think he knows how many of us there are."

Abe reached the trees of his assigned spot, cautious to conceal his movements. He felt the prick of thorns going into his thigh and jerked his pants leg loose from a bramble. They had done well to find Frazier home, but a stand-off could be costly..

An hour later by the sun, his eyes burned and he reached for his canteen laying in the grass beside him, struggling to stay focused on the back door.

Any movement could mean danger. He took off his neckerchief and rubbed it across his face. A swig of water from the canteen cooled his dry throat. What was Frazier thinking? His throat was probably tight too.

He heard George at the front of the house. In the afternoon stillness, his words carried to Abe's position. "Frazier, come out. This is the last chance. Come out now - you won't be harmed."

Frazier shouted back. "That's what all you Yankees promise, but I know how you work; when I step out, you'll kill me and claim I tried to escape."

Abe heard the sharp discharge of the deputy's Winchester. The posse men on either side commenced firing, adding to the battle. That was more to scare Frazier than to force him out. He was safe behind a layer of heavy wood logs, probably with plenty of ammunition. The only way they would get him would be a lucky shot.

The firing ceased after a few minutes. George called again. "Frazier, come on out. Don't make it hard on yourself. You're surrounded." His answer was a blast from the front window.

Abe rose from behind his shelter, when the back door of the house opened and Frazier burst out, shotgun at his shoulder. He wanted to give the outlaw a chance to surrender even yet.

"Hold it right there, Frazier," he said.

The blast of the shotgun made him dive for cover. He fired as he hit the ground. Undaunted, Frazier fired the second barrel. Abe felt a hot jab in his right ankle as he scrambled toward the log. He rolled over on his back firing at Frazier who had thrown the shotgun aside and drawn twin pistols. The bullet caught the man in the right arm, knocking the pistol free.

To his dismay, the outlaw still advanced, his left hand clutching the other pistol. One of them was going to die in this face to face fight. The smoke from the barrel of his attacker's six-shooter filled his nose as his left leg went numb. Falling onto his back, the Winchester clutched in his hands, he still faced Frazier. Thank God, most gunslingers cannot shot with their off hand. But one more shot was all either man needed.

As Abe raised his rifle sighting through blurred vision at the figure only feet away, a shout came out of Frazier's mouth just as he heard the thunk of a bullet. The outlaw grabbed at his pistol which had dropped, blood spreading across his fingers. His eyes met Abe's as he turned and disappeared into the thick undergrowth. The challenge was still there.

Abe could not get up. Both legs were numb and he felt shock envelope his body, the numbness spreading from his legs to his arms causing him to drop his Winchester, then blackness.

Birds chirped in the trees above him, flitting from branch to branch. He watched the small creatures while his brain dragged him back from what? He remembered fear, pain, and helplessness, then falling down a hole of darkness. He groaned and made an effort to turn his head, taking in the umbrella of a great white oak above him, a blanket over his chest, a sensation of numbness where his legs should be. J.C. sat beside him, drinking a cup of coffee.

"What's wrong with my legs?" His inability to move panicked him. Did he still have legs?

"You were hit just above the left knee and your right ankle is full of buckshot. Lon's gone to Peter Conser's to get a wagon. His is the closest home to here. We've cleaned your wounds, but you need a doctor, and soon."

"What kind of gun play was it?"

"Pretty hot. We managed to hit Frazier just as he was getting ready to finish you off. He disappeared in the thick underbrush. George is tracking him."

J.C. leaned across to him, a tin cup in his hand. "Here, take a couple of gulps of whiskey to relieve the pain."

After as much of the whiskey as he could tolerate, a gentle tingling of his limbs set in followed by a feeling of weightlessness. So that was what firewater does to a man. He had never taken more than a sip in his entire life.

He roused from his fitful slumber when George came into camp with Frazier tied to his horse. The man was in poor shape, unable to move or dismount. George and J.C. pulled him down and laid him a few yards from Abe. He was semi-conscious, groaning and thrashing about, his shirt covered in blood. No challenge now.

"How'd you find him?" J.C. asked.

"Trailed him through the brush for a quarter mile and came to where he lay, bleeding like a gut-shot deer."

"He looks pretty bad off."

"He may not make it. Ride over to Justice's place and fetch Frazier's wife. I'd hate for her to miss seeing him if he doesn't."

George knelt beside Abe. He looked down and ran his forefinger in the dirt. "It's strange. He was out of his head most of the ride back, kept mumbling about how he's going to get even with Justice for turning him over to us."

"Justice is his nearest neighbor and he sent his family there. That doesn't make sense." Abe said.

"I guess it was just the fever."

Lon returned from Conser's the next morning, covering the twelve miles each way in record time. The ride to Poteau was unpleasant, but Abe knew the sooner he got to a doctor the better. He had taken a couple more shots of whiskey before they started and his head swirled from it. He wanted to scream at every bump that sent sharp pains up his left leg into his thigh. Suspended between consciousness and fading, he spent the hours in fitful dreams of smoking revolvers in the hands of a devil and Frazier's grinning face. In that instant Abe had known he would die unless he got in the next shot.

Smelling salts penetrated his nostrils, rousing him from his gray dream. It was the same doctor who had patched up Charley's frozen foot in January the year before.

The surgeon chuckled as he saw Abe. "Seems you Barnhills can't keep healthy." His face was expressionless as he checked Abe's injuries, but his eyes could not mask his concern.

"Deputy Barnhill, your left femur is broken just above the knee and ligaments have been damaged. I'll clean up the wound and put you in a splint so you can be taken immediately to the hospital in Fort Smith. Once I pick out the buckshot from your right ankle and apply a bandage, it should heal without problems."

"I just want to keep my leg, doc. Please. "

The doctor placed a soft cloth under his nose. "Take a whiff of this."

When he woke up, he was dressed up like a Thanksgiving turkey, a wooden splint going the full length of his left leg from his waist to his ankle, his right ankle wrapped in a bulky dressing. He did feel some better. Modern medicine sure had come a long way since the ole bite the bullet routine. He moved his head to see George step back in the office

"I sent a telegram to the marshal's office and to your wife. She'll be waiting for you in Fort Smith," he said.

"Thanks. I hope she can be. Our baby is due in a few months." Worry for her took his mind off the pain.

The doctor finished washing his hands and turned from the sink. "You're patched up enough to travel. I need to ride out and check on Bill Frazier."

Abe closed his eyes as the doctor gathered his black bag. Thoughts sneaked into his brain, things he did not want to remember - the barrel of Frazier's pistol pointed at his head, the knowledge that he would be dead in an instant if he did not react fast enough, the heaviness of his Winchester as he struggled to raise it and fire. He blinked and tried to push the memory behind the black curtain of his sleep.

He awoke when George and the doctor returned early the next morning with Frazier on a stretcher, his wife, grim-faced and pale following close behind. After an hour, the two men stepped out from the back room.

"You shouldn't move him until I know he is not going to die on you," the doctor explained.

"You're right. I don't get paid for dead men. I'll leave Lon, my posse man, here as a guard. Just send me a telegram when he can be moved. I'll take Abe on into the hospital."

Abe moaned as strong hands lifted his stretcher into the wagon, thanking God, for the laudanum. He prayed as his whole body shook on the ruts, his eyes fixed on the face of J.C., cradling his head in his lap.

As the wagon pulled into Fort Smith late in the evening, the street lights were already on. In the lengthening shadows, people turned to stare, some of them people that he knew.

C.C. Ayers, store owner and part-time deputy, called out as he ran to the wagon. "What happen to you, Abe?"

He fought to swallow as his mouth formed the words. "Gunfight with Bill Frazier."

"Who won?"

"No one."

The hospital staff was waiting for them; as the wagon pulled up to the side entrance, two burly orderlies hurried out and lifted him onto the wheeled stretcher. He felt it tilt as he was carried up the stairs and into an exam room. The bright electric lamps made him blink. All the larger buildings in Fort Smith had electricity. He watched a white-clad nurse ready instruments on a nearby table while someone tugged at his clothes. *Oh boy!*

In a deep dream he moved toward a bright light through a dark tunnel. It was pleasant. He did not want to wake up. His eyelids struggled but stayed closed. Nothing. One more try. He felt one eyelid quiver and open, then the other, a blurry face appearing out of the corner of his eyes. The slow focus, as his brain and eye began to work together, revealed a familiar countenance, Amanda.

"Darlin', I'm so glad you're awake." Abe could hear the fear in her voice.

He reached out to hold her, but his hand fell back on the blanket. "Hullo, there. I didn't mean to give you such a scare, honey."

"I just want you to get well. I'm not leaving your side." Amanda's face was solemn and ashen.

"What did the doctor have to say after the operation?"

"He set the bone and reattached the severed ligaments. He has to wait and see if you get any infection in the wound; that's the main concern."

"How's the baby doing?" Abe tried to pat her tummy with the same result, his hand flopping to the blanket.

"Well, it has been kicking around a lot, didn't like the fast ride over on the stage."

"Why don't you let George get you a room over at the hotel?"

"Only if I need it. I want to stay here. The doctor says I can sleep on a pallet by your bed."

He closed his eyes and realized how tired he was. He would think about these things later.

The hospital ward was quiet - the men in an eight bed ward on one side of the hospital and the women on the opposite side. There was also a laying in suite of rooms, but most women still had their babies at home. Only those with complications were brought in for care.

Abe was napping when he heard someone speak. Charley.

"Hello, Silvy." Charley used Abe's nickname, an emotional hangover from their childhood. He unfolded the newspaper from his hand as he approached the bed. "George sent me a telegram and I came right away. How are you doing?"

"I'm alive. Tell me what's happening with the Frazier gang."

"Well, you made the newspapers. Here it is in black and white in the <u>Vinita Indian Chieftain.</u> Abe took the paper and read the short paragraph. It certainly did not reveal the terror of five men fighting for their lives.

Edmondson, at Muskogee, says they were married on the train and continued their journey south.

One day last week a deputy marshal and his posse had a round with Bill Frazier in Arkansas, near the Choctaw line, in which Abe Barnhill was severely wounded. The outlaw was seriously wounded and his death was expected at any moment.

The supreme court convened last week, tried three contest cases, all between sheriffs, (for Delaware, Table-

"Is he dead?"

"Not yet. He's in the jail hospital. He'll probably lose his left arm from your Winchester blast. Two fingers on his right hand were already amputated."

Abe stared hard at his brother before swallowing and spilling out the thoughts that had been hiding inside his head ever since the shoot out. "I thought I was a goner when he kept coming after me. I've never seen anyone so set on blowing my head off."

Charley folded the newspaper and stuck it in his breast pocket before answering. Abe saw the concern in his eyes. "Frazier's like so many outlaws who'd rather die than face a jail cell. You're fortunate to have slowed him down enough for the others to drive him off. How long do you have to stay here?"

"I'm grateful to be in one piece. I get to go home as soon as the swelling is down and the doctor knows I don't have an infection. He says my ability to walk may not come back the way the muscles were torn."

Charley frowned, the furrows between his eyes ruining his pleasant face. "That's tough."

"Don't worry. I'll be on my feet by Christmas. I can't sit out the winter in a bed."

"Well, I'm taking a few days off to go over and visit Irene in Skullyville. We have some plans to discuss."

Abe felt a grin spread across his face, the first since his injury. "A wedding date?"

"Yup. I hope to be married by Christmas. Pa will perform the ceremony. But I want to wait until I know you'll be there to stand up with me."

"I'll be honored."

Abe looked out the window of the hospital at the falling rain. Christmas would be very special this year. A new baby, a new sister-in-law, a healed leg. He had faced death and won this time.

A few blocks away the rain fell against the windows of the another hospital room on the third floor of the Old Jail. Mollie Frazier sat beside her sick husband. She wiped his face as he tossed and turned with the fever that racked his body.

He groaned and flung his eyes open, fixing them on the ceiling above his bed. "I'll get him one of these days. Just you wait and see. Nothin's going to stop me." He spat out the words which seemed to rob him of his strength. He closed his eyes, once again incoherent in his suffering.

She wept beside his bed all night long. The pallet that the female warden had made on the floor was untouched. Why did he have to fight the marshals? Why?

The next morning the doctor came to the room before breakfast was served to the inmates. His eyes were grave and compassionate as he addressed her in the kindest of tones. "Mrs. Frazier, the only way to save your husband's life is to amputate his left arm. It has to come off. The amputation of the two fingers on his right was all that saved that hand."

"I understand, doctor. If you must, then do it. But I'll not leave his side until he is out of this jail."

The doctor motioned to the male attendants to get Frazier ready for surgery.

"Mrs. Frazier, you may wait out in the hall while they undress him and clean him up. We'll give you his clothes."

From the bench outside the operating room, she watched them move him through the white double doors. What would happen to her children while she stayed here with Bill? She needed help, Lord, so much help.

Later that morning, she stared at the bulky bandage on Billie's left arm. The amputation had taken the bottom half of his arm between the elbow and the wrist. He was asleep now, and not as fretful as before. Maybe this would save his life. She knew he needed more than physical healing. He needed God's healing. She slept and dozed in the chair, awaking only to wipe his face and offer him water from the white enamel pitcher.

Jailer Pettigrew came mid-afternoon to check on her accommodations. He held his hat in his hands and looked around the room "Mrs. Frazier, is there anything I can get you? Not a very good place for a respectable woman."

"As long as I'm beside my husband, I'm fine. I need to send a telegram to my sister letting her know she must keep my children until Bill gets well. I don't know how long that will be."

"If you'll write out the message, I'll see that it gets sent."

After he had left, her thoughts returned. The fear that had swept over her the past few days was now replaced with remorse and regret. All she wanted was peace and a home. Why could not God give her that?

Chapter 32

A NEW FAMILY

Two weeks later Charley stopped his rented rig in front of Irene's house. Finally!

He had just finished serving subpoenas to witnesses for another Burrow hearing scheduled on November 28. It had been over a year since the murder and the case was no closer to trial then last summer. In jail without bail, Louis languished his young life away. Was that to protect him or to prevent flight? He suspected the former. He had located Dr. Foyil west of Skullyville. The busy man had been unhappy at the summons, but grumbled he would be there. Respectable citizens did not want to face the charge of failure to appear and its consequent penalty of fine and/or jail time.

The lengthy courtship stymied his duties. He was accustomed to working without regard to personal needs, but now he found himself dwelling on the young woman who awaited him behind the white plank door.

As Irene appeared at his knock, he removed his hat and stepped into the parlor. "Good morning, sweetheart."

"Charley, is this the day we get to go to Fort Smith?"

"Yes. Is Mrs. Morgan coming along?"

"She needs to shop for some items, if you don't mind."

"How would it look if I took you all the way to Fort Smith unchaperoned? She will be more than welcome in the mother-in-law seat." He wished he could get his intended alone. Not yet, be patient.

The fifteen mile drive was pleasant, and the air cool. Here, at the end of November, the leaves had completely dropped. The women rode in the buggy with a lap robe over their dresses to protect them from the dust. After a good night's rest in the hotel, the shopping commenced, taking up most of the afternoon beginning at Mr. Ayers' store and progressing along Garrison Avenue.

"Anna, look at this lovely soft fabric. It's perfect." Irene thrust the bolt at her step-mother who ran her hand across the white cotton, fingering the texture and thickness.

"Lovely, it'll be easy to sew. You need a pattern, buttons for the bodice and lace for trim and for a veil.

"Here, how about these buttons?" Irene had selected what Charley thought were the tiniest pearl buttons he had ever seen. *Wow. I would hate to unbutton those on our wedding night.*

Patience and then amusement filled his head as he watched the two women enjoy the time together, forgetting the sorrows of the past year. He was happy to see them smiling.

Mrs. Morgan fingered red and green ribbon, satin and velvet. "Since it is a Christmas wedding, we can use Christmas colors for the bouquet."

Pulling the ribbon across her hands, Irene bunched it into a bow. "I like the ribbon that has both red and green. It'll be so pretty."

The clerk rang up the purchases. "That'll be 5 cents per yard for 10 yards of cotton and 2 cents per yard for the 5 yards of ribbon and 10 yards of lace. The buttons are 25 cents. The total is $1.05. Will there be anything else, Miss?"

Fixing her eyes on Charley's smiling countenance, Irene pulled Mrs. Morgan's ear down and whispered. A blush crept up her neck above the white ribbon of her collar.

Her mother patted Irene's hand and turned to the clerk. "Yes, sir. We need to look at some personal items for the bride." She took Irene's arm and they walked to the back of the store where such items lay folded in drawers, not for the public's eye.

Charley felt the heat creeping up in his face. "Call me when they have made their final selections." He found himself addressing the clerk's back which was discretely turned away from the women.

He took the time to step out on the board sidewalk and enjoy the cool autumn air. He spent so much of his time in the saddle in all kinds of weather, it was nice not to have the rain, snow or heat attacking him. After this trip, he was headed to Sallisaw to check on Abe and visit his children. They were very excited for the up-coming wedding.

The clerk poked his head out the door of the store. "They're finished, Deputy Barnhill."

Irene, still flushed and breathless, held a stack of unmentionables. "Darling, this is a six piece set for only $2.00. Is that too much to spend?"

"Whatever you need, sweetheart. How about shoes? You can't wear ordinary work shoes to your wedding."

"Oh, yes. I almost forgot. I will be just a couple more minutes." She brought back a tiny pair of white satin boots. What small feet women had. Irene was petite all over. His hands, when placed together, would encircle her tiny waist allowing his fingertips to touch. She should not be much to carry over a threshold.

Their purchases selected, he put a five dollar gold piece on the counter. Mrs. Morgan grabbed the paper-wrapped bundles refusing his help. "Your arm, Mr. Barnhill."

He escorted them, one on each side. Mrs. Morgan clutched the packages with an iron grip. *OK, you win. That lady is strong.*

Storm front winds howled around the jail compound as Charley rode into the yard, a few days before his wedding. He and James White had made a sweep into the Cherokee Nation to pick up fugitives at Muskogee. Like most of the other deputies, he only went out for the most desperate characters when the weather worsened. It slowed them down and prevented proper care of the prisoners who had to live in the outdoors while in their custody.

Dismounting in front of the steps that led up to the marshal's office, he gestured to James to take the prisoners to the jailer. The construction on the new jail wing was coming along fine. It would be as large as the whole building presently used for the old jail and the court offices.

Chief Deputy Barnes grinned at him as he felt the cold air from the door. His desk sat in the corner near the wood stove and the office was comfortable.

"Hi, Chief Barnes. Is the marshal in?" Charley asked as he slipped off his wool long coat. It was too warm in the office to keep that heavy thing on.

"Yes, he is meeting with someone else right now, but should be done shortly. Have a seat."

He took a few minutes to review the next few days. He had been living his life so consumed with man-hunting, it felt strange thinking about ordinary problems. He knew one of these days he would slow down as the progress of civilization took over this beautiful country. For now, he had a few more years he wanted to dedicate to bringing law and order to the Indian Territory. Where could he best serve now? That was the question he was going to ask the marshal.

"Deputy Barnhill, please come in," Marshal Carroll called to him across the office. "Have a seat. What do you need?"

He seated himself in the comfortable wooden chair in front of the spacious desk. The face of the President of the United States, Grover Cleveland, peered down at him from the wall. "I've come to discuss a new geographic assignment. I'm getting married in a few days and my new wife's family lives in McAlester. I've always thought that would be a good place to settle down. Do you need a deputy down there?"

"Where is your assigned base now?"

"It's Sallisaw, but my brother, Abe, is still living out there though he is recuperating from his wound."

"That was a close call he had with Bill Frazier. When will Abe be able to resume full duty?"

"He thinks by the end of the year. He is out of the splint now and getting around on crutches."

"As soon as he is able to take over at Sallisaw, I'll let you go to McAlester. Be sure to let Chief Deputy Barnes know of this change so he can send you the writs for that area. And congratulations on your marriage."

"Thank you, sir." Charley rose to leave then turned back. "What've you heard of Belle Starr. It's been pretty quiet out there lately since Sam was killed last Christmas."

"I've had reports that she is wandering around doing all kinds of strange things, but nothing we can arrest her for. It's hard to get credible witnesses for anything that happens in that area."

"My brother lives just down the road from Youngers Bend and he sees people coming and going out there almost daily. The neighbors have stories, but it's hard to tell what's happening."

Carroll squinted at the pile of warrants on his desk. "If I get something on her, I'll let you and Tyner Hughes know. You seem to have the best luck in tracking her down."

"Thanks. Merry Christmas to you and your family. I'll be back after Christmas."

Parson Alford Barnhill stood at the front of the church on the raised platform waiting for the music to begin. The little Baptist church at Skullyville was packed. Since William Morgan had been killed, things had settled down in the feuding congregation of fifty or sixty worshipers. Today it was standing room only. Family, friends and neighbors from all over the Choctaw Nation were here to celebrate the wedding. A guitar, a fiddle and an Indian drum would play the wedding march. Music was such an important part of this Choctaw culture. When they sang in church or at camp meetings, their harmony was as sweet as the angels.

He adjusted his vest lapels as he noticed his four sons, Sam, Abe, Charley and Jimmy come into the front foyer, Abe still on crutches. All were dressed in suits. He was proud of his sons and the men they had become. He thought about the happy event before him. He and Sarah had known blessings and grief. How recent was the funeral of his own grandson, James, only 9 years of age, killed in a fall from a mule. The Lord gives and the Lord takes away. Blessed be the Name of the Lord.

Charley's muscles tensed as he joined Abe in front of their father. He saw so many friends and neighbors, he could hardly believe it. Someone had gotten the word out. His attention turned to his bride as she was led to stand in the aisle. Her sister, Luticia, a very mature thirteen year-old, stood a few feet from him as her maid of honor. Irene's Uncle Henry Morgan would give her away. He tried to calm his breathing and concentrate.

The musical performers struck up a lively wedding march, the Indian drummer beating the tight skin of the drum with a soft mallet. The aisle of the church was only sixty feet long, but time seemed suspended as he watched Irene reach his side. She smiled up at him as he took her hand and they turned to face his father.

He hardly heard his father begin to speak. "Dearly beloved, we are gathered here today to join this man, Charles Fletcher Barnhill, in holy matrimony to Aramanthea Morgan."

Before he realized it, his father asked, "Do you, Charles Fletcher Barnhill, take this woman to be your lawfully wedded wife, to honor and cherish, until death do you part?"

He had to swallow and catch his breath. He'd rather face a gang of rustlers than to stand up here with everyone watching. "I do." His words came out in a husky emotional tone, somewhat louder than he had intended. He heard Abe chuckle behind him.

Irene peered into his face only inches away as she repeated her part of the vows. Her eyes were deep green and sparkled against the white of her veil. He could smell lilac soap and perfume.

As he placed the ring on her finger, he felt her hand tremble. At the words, "I now pronounce you husband and wife" he lifted the veil back from her face and kissed her on the lips. It was so much better than kissing fingertips. This was a great day.

"Ladies and gentlemen, I give you Mr. and Mrs. Charles Barnhill." A cheer went up from the entire congregation. Tyne and Mattie Hughes stood in the corner with James White and James Cole, Dan Griffin and his wife close by. They had as big a smile on their faces as he did.

His children waited at the back to greet their new step-mother. Henry held his hat in his hand. Minnie giggled, trying not to squirm. He reached out and engulfed them in a circle of love, a new little family coming together. God was so good. What more could he ask?

Chapter 33

Return to Duty

An involuntary shiver ran through Charley's body as his feet touched the braided rug, the cold January morning robbing him of the warmth of his marital bed. Irene lay dozing, her long brown hair swirled on the pillow. He stirred up the coals and added more fuel to the pot-belly stove in the corner. The dwelling in Krebs, just five miles from McAlester, was affordable on his deputy's pay. John McAlester's coal mine and others in the area were fighting a recession that had left many empty homes and store buildings. He sat back on the bed to pull on a corduroy shirt over his long-johns and felt Irene's arms encircle his chest. Her head lay against his back, the light touch of her lips on his left shoulder.

"Oh, sweetheart. This terrible scar on your back, how did you get it?" Irene's voice was full of concern and worry.

He tried to keep his voice reassuring and soft. "It's an old gunshot wound, nothing to worry about, darlin'."

"You're too young to have a body covered with scars. What if you wind up like Abe?"

"Most of those scars are from gun fights with cornered fugitives. Ambush is the more deadly."

Her eyes grew wide. "How do you avoid ambushes?"

"I try to out-maneuver the man I'm after, but never fear . . . I have the answer." He reached for his Bible on the bedside table.

Turning to the verse, he read Deuteronomy 20:4 "For the Lord your God is the one who goes with you to fight for you against your enemies to give you victory." He took her hands and kissed her open palms. "Remember that verse anytime you're worried about me."

Twas comforting to pull on wool socks and gabardine pants for warmth. The 75 mile ride to Skullyville to pick up Jimmy would take three days and then on to Sallisaw to visit Abe. He finished his attire with a wool scarf laid beside his coat.

After a breakfast of coffee and eggs, he kissed his bride on the cheek and walked outside, throwing on the coat and scarf. She drew a shawl over her shoulders and stepped out on the porch beside him. The winter sun peeked faint behind the gray clouds overhead, the wind gusted, its force sending brittle leaves across the yard. His beloved's ranging fingers stopped at each coat button making sure it was properly secured. "While you get Billie, I'll pack your clothes and food."

He pulled up his collar and stepped off the porch. "Thanks, put in some extra socks and shirts in case I don't get back as planned." It was nice to have a helpmate. He had forgotten how much he had missed Salina's tender care.

Later, standing beside the big roan, he encircled his bride in an embrace and kissed her upturned lips, his delight to taste and remember on his long trip.

"Tell the children I'll be back in a few days. They'll need the time to get used to this new home. It's a good place to start a new family."

Crimson spread over her young face. "Oh, darlin'. I'll miss you terribly."

Irene watched him ride out of the yard, her face pressed to the window until he was no longer visible. Her throat was dry and her heart cried. He was her life now. May the Lord protect him and bring him home safe.

As she returned to the bedroom, she noticed the six shooter on the gun rack above the dresser. She took it down and felt the weight - the smooth steel of the barrel and the warm wood on the grip. Like most young women of the Indian Nation, she was familiar with fire arms. Her father had taught all his children to shoot a rifle by the time they could handle the weight. A handgun was another matter.

If she ever had to use it, she would have to steady it with both hands. She shuddered to think of anything else she would need it for other than a threatening wolf or coyote.

Placing the Smith and Wesson .38 back on the gun rack, she checked the cartridge belt. It was full and an extra box of cartridges in the dresser drawer. She sighed as she sat at the dresser and reached for her brush. *Hurry home, darlin.*

The arms of the rocker swayed under Abe's grip as he attempted to rise, his jaws clenching to fight the soreness. He had thrown out his crutches after Charley's wedding. Would Charley and Jimmy see the progress he had made? Would it be enough?

He watched Amanda with their newborn son wrapped in a soft wool blanket. The babe would not live a month according to the doctor, but what did he know? How could his son who looked normal in every way be dying? His wife's face showed the care of a mother for a sick child, but also an acceptance of the inevitable. She kissed the tiny face and laid the little bundle in the cradle

Three year-old Jeanette called from the bedroom. "Mama, where's my dolly?"

"It's on the dresser, dear."

"Honey, let me help you," she said as she moved toward him. She bent down and put her arms under his shoulders and lifted.

Trying to walk without a limp almost pitched him to the floor. The limp would have to stay. "I'm going to the barn to feed the stock and mend the harnesses. Ring the dinner bell and I'll come in." He really was going to work on the exercises the doctor had suggested - climb up and down the hay loft ladder as many times a day as he could stand. At first he could not reach the top of the ladder, but now he could complete several ascents before the burning in his leg stopped him. Feeding the animals first limbered him up. Thirty minutes later he was sweating and gritting his teeth to complete the last climb of the morning.

The sound of hooves on gravel brought him to the barn door. He hurried out to his brothers, trying not to slip in the muck of the barnyard and greeted them with a pat on the shoulder. "Come on in. Amanda has hot coffee."

They gathered around the kitchen table. "How's your leg?" Charley asked, sipping at the hot liquid.

Abe watched their faces as he answered He knew he could not stay on a horse yet. "I sent Carroll a telegram last week that I'll be in Fort Smith by March." Sitting around doing nothing while watching his baby die was taking its tole. He had to have something to strive for after that tragedy.

Jimmy looked at Amanda, who was rocking her infant. "How's the baby doing?"

Amanda, her voice soft and sad, caressed the sleeping face of the child before she replied. " He's sleeping and eating, but can't hold down enough to live. The doctor says it's his stomach. We're praying for a miracle." Tears gleamed in her light blue eyes.

Charley mumbled, his head down. "We'll be on our way so as not to burden you with a meal." He gave Abe a handshake then a hug.

He watched them ride away, two sorrows weighing on his heart - a leg that needed healing and a baby who needed life. A prayer formed as he turned back to comfort his wife.

"I've a serious matter to discuss with you, Barnhill." The chief deputy looked at Charley, a frown creasing the lines around his eyes and erasing the good nature of his face. He was a great organizer and kept an efficient office so that inspectors never grumbled. He could account for every warrant that went out and came in.

When Barnes talked like that, it was serious. What had he done? He tried to keep his eyes from roving across Barnes' face. "What is it?'

"John Morgan and several accomplices have been charged with running a hog stealing ring. I want you out of the picture since it's family. I'm asking Tyner Hughes to pick them up. "

"I've suspected something of the sort for the past few months."

Barnes stared at him. "Why didn't you say something?"

"I didn't have any evidence, just suspicions and rumors."

"It'll hamper the Burrow trial with the government's chief witness in jail. The defense will try to discredit his testimony. "

Charley gritted his teeth against his frustration. "I feel sorry for his wife, Mary. The whole Morgan family is caught in a web of murder and larceny that they'll never live down."

"Desperate men ruin lives all around them," Deputy Barnes added as he placed the arrest writ for John Morgan aside. "I have witnesses for other cases that need to be found and two liquor arrests. Stop and visit Tyner Hughes if he's home. He can help you with this liquor peddler who lives at Skullyville." He thrust the paperwork across the desk.

"Thanks, see you in a couple of weeks." Charley pocketed the papers and stepped to the door.

The Morgan clan he had married into had put him in a dilemma - he had to do his duty as sworn by oath but keep his wife's feelings in mind. Marriages were destroyed by lesser problems.

Chapter 34

An Old Freedman

Tyne looked at the name on the warrant Charley had pulled from his vest. "This fella hangs around when it's pay time for the Indians. They can't get home without loosing a fiver to his whiskey wagon. You're best bet is to wait until Saturday night. He's always at the livery selling off his wares."

Charley tucked the paper back into his vest.

Tyne took a sip of coffee before continuing. "There's been a murder here that the Choctaw Nation judge says is not their jurisdiction."

Spreading his hands for warmth from the fireplace, Charley probed for details. "What happened?"

"In late November Jesse Lewis, a freedman, shot another negro named McKinney who suffered terribly until dying on December fourth."

"What caused the ruckus?"

"The dead man had been abusing the older Lewis for years, coming to his house uninvited, threatening to steal his wife and calling him names in front of his wife and children. The ole fella is a peaceable person but couldn't stand it any longer. He even told Deputy Sheriff Henry Shoate that he was going to kill McKinney three weeks prior." Hughes pointed to his vest pouch laying on the side table. "I've got to take a prisoner into Fort Smith tomorrow or else I 'd take care of it. Go visit Shoate and see what he wants us to do."

Charley had one more question before he left. He dreaded the answer, one way or another. "What happened with John Morgan and his gang?"

"I brought them in without a fuss. One has made bond, but John is still in jail trying to arrange his bond."

Charley murmured, "Irene is upset enough over the murder trial. She'll not take this well."

"Every family has black sheep. You just happened to marry into a family that has several. The younger generation may prove more responsible."

"Yeah, you're right." Which Morgan would go bad next?

Tyne frowned and brushed at his pants leg, a sign Charley knew to mean something serious was coming. "I need to tell you about my last trip. After I arrested John Morgan, Sam Wingo and I went to Stonewall last week for two liquor peddlers, Long George and Black Tiger. We took Tandy Walker, the Creek chief who is also a United States deputy marshal, and some of his scouts. The whiskey peddlers fired at us when we cornered them in a cabin."

Charley sucked in his breath as he listened.

"It all happened too fast. We killed Long George, but Black Tiger escaped. That's not the end of it. This was on Sunday, and Black Tiger and his Creeks have already killed the two scouts, John Leader and Barney Maliha. They may get Tandy next." He took a sip of his coffee. "I wish I'd not involved them. It cost them their lives."

"The Indians factions are always warring. You can't stop that," Charley said. "I'll go see Henry Shoate, the deputy sheriff before I head to Fort Smith."

Charley held the pen in his hand, steadying the paper on the lap desk in front of the camp fire.

Oak Lodge, C.N., I.T.
Feb. the 9th, 1888

Hon. John Carroll, U.S. Marshal,

Please send a writ for Jesse Lewis for murder for killing one McKinney on or about the 24 of November, 1887. Names of witnesses Henry Shoate, William Kiser. The Choctaws claim no jurisdiction.

Yours Respectfully
Charles Barnhill
U.S. Deputy Marshal

The next morning he posted the letter to Fort Smith on the morning stage. He and Jimmy headed out to round up the liquor fugitive but local informants swore the man had skipped the area. If he returned, they would be waiting.

He turned to Jimmy. "Let's go get the paperwork on Lewis. We'll hunt for the liquor smuggler when we come back."

"You just want to finish and scoot home to your new bride," his brother teased.

"Well, wouldn't you? I haven't seen her for two weeks."

This simple trip was taking way too long. One arrest would not even cover his expenses. Charley dismounted at the Fort Smith jail and bound up the stairs two at a time. "Howdy, Barnes. Did you get my letter about Jesse Lewis?"

"It just came over from the clerk's office. I also have writs for the witnesses."

He shook off his rain-covered slicker and hung it on a peg by the front door. "It should be pretty straightforward. Lewis has confessed and is waiting at home for us to pick him up."

When he turned to face Barnes, the chief deputy's face had blackened and he hesitated before handing over the documents. "I've another set of writs for you to serve on your way over to Oak Lodge. I'm sorry. It involves your partner, Tyner Hughes."

Charley glanced at the writ on top.

> *"I DO SOLEMNLY SWEAR and believe, from reliable information in my possession that Sam Wingo and Tyner Hughes, white men, did in the Indian Country, Western District of Arkansas, on or about the 4th of February, 1888 feloniously, willfully and premeditatedly and of true malice aforethought kill and murder one Long George and Black Tiger with guns and pistols against the peace and dignity of the United States, and I pray a writ. W.M. HARRIS*
> *Subscribed and sworn to before me on this 11th day of February, 1888.*
> *James Brizzolara, U.S. Commissioner*

He felt crimson creep into his face as he read the outlandish charges. Flipping through the rest of the warrants, he found the names of Tandy Walker and J.C. Hesbaugh, the posse who had accompanied the deputies and the Indians at whose house the shooting had occurred.

He struggled to keep the bitterness out of his voice. "I see that the law works both ways. This Harris is probably a partner in the liquor peddling business that was so rudely interrupted. How inconvenient."

The top of Barnes' white scalp pinked up. "It's terrible. I've seen so many murderers walk out of here after killing their witnesses. Now Hughes and Wingo are facing a gang of Creeks who will do anything to cause them harm."

"Did you know the Creeks have already killed the two Indian scouts Hughes and Wingo used?"

"Yes, but that is Indian on Indian. We can't poke our nose in that affair."

He felt the top of his head pulsing from his anger. "Why do we put our lives on the line and then have to defend ourselves? I've been wounded three times because I try not to kill a man and Abe's still laid up from a bullet. Carroll has lost seventeen deputies killed since '84."

Barnes ran his hand across his cheeks. "We can only do our best. History will be the judge. Hughes and Wingo will be allowed to continue in their duties pending the commissioner's hearing."

Outside, he shoved the documents in his saddle bags with such force that Billie side-stepped away from him. His heart sank thinking of the threat Tyne and Sam Wingo would be under until this was settled.

Locating the Lewis cabin just outside of Skullyville, Charley saw smoke coming from the chimney. He beckoned to Jimmy who sat on his wagon seat, hunkered against the sheets of rain that fell from a gray overcast. If they got home without pneumonia, it would be a miracle.

Ascending the porch Charley briefed his brother. "This ole fella is supposed to be peaceable. Cover the door just in case." A hand pulled back the leather covering over the window as he knocked on the door. It opened a crack revealing a dark face, the head covered with a red scarf.

"Is you the mawshal?" The woman drawled out her words.

"Yes, ma'am. I'm looking for Jesse Lewis. Is he here?"

"Yas suh, come in out of the rain, please, suh." She was middle-aged, wearing a simple house dress and apron, graying curls tucked in the red bandanna.

As he removed it, his hat splashed water on the tied rug he stood on, the dirt floor underneath packed hard from years of use. A bear skin covered most of the front room's floor. Indians felt only heathens left their floors bare. "Do you mind if I call in my guard?"

"Please, suh."

He motioned to Jimmy. An older black man sat in a rocker by the fire. He wore an old coat, the elbows missing and the front without buttons. He did not speak. Two teenage children, a boy and a girl, stood to one side beside the window.

"I'm United States Deputy Marshal Charles Barnhill. Are you Jesse Lewis?"

"I been waiting on you-all. I'm ready to take my punishment." He stood up and held out his hands. Charley pulled hand cuffs from his inside vest pocket and placed them gently but firmly over the old man's gnarled hands.

"I'm taking you to Fort Smith for arraignment. It may be quite a while before your case is heard. Have you made provisions for your family?"

"Yes, suh. My son can tend the place."

His wife began to cry into her apron.

His daughter in the corner wrung her hands in her apron. "Papa, please. Let us go with you."

"No, my child. Your place is here taking care of your mama."

The boy came forward and held the old man's hand-cuffed hands in his own. "Pa, please let me go with you. The white men over in Fort Smith don't know how to take care of you. I can bring you the food you like to eat and see that you're well-tended."

"No, my son. Your place is here now. I may never return."

The young man bowed his head and bit his lip. His shoulders heaved with sobs. "That no-good nigguh deserved killin', Pa. You just did what others wanted to do but didn't have the courage to. The Lord Almighty will deliver you from the prison cell like he did Saint Paul."

The deputy watched in silence. How many times had he seen this sad scene played out?

"Mrs. Lewis, you may come to Fort Smith any time to see your husband. His lawyer will keep you informed." He tipped his hat to the two women as he turned to go. Jimmy already had the prisoner secured inside the wagon, his meager bundle of clothes and food from his wife stuffed in beside him.

To his dismay, it took another nine days to find the liquor seller hiding out with friends in Oak Lodge and get back to Fort Smith.

Barnes accepted the writs of arrest for the two men without comment, his usual jovial appearance solemn and business-like.

Charley tried to make light conversation. "What's happened since I've been gone? Are Tyne and Sam still wearing badges?"

"The commissioner interviewed James Hesbaugh and Tandy Walker. Their testimony supports Tyner's report that he didn't even draw his gun during the whole episode, but he's the one cited since he was in charge. The commissioner ducked the issue and passed the case on to the grand jury which is backed up until at least May. In the meantime, they're still working."

His spirits revived as he rode. Jimmy would go home to Skullyville to prepare their parents for moving to Krebs when the roads dried out. It would be good having them close to him though his father refused to give up his ministry. The Free Will Baptist Church Association spread through the Territory and his father was it's senior pastor. The Barnhill family carrying Bibles to the lost and guns of justice to the fugitive.

Chapter 35

Loss and Renewal

Dead before nightfall? Was that what the doctor had said? Abe glanced over his shoulder at his wife, wrapped in a shawl, the baby clutched to her breast, as if the angels of heaven could not break her hold. Another baby to bury. How could they go on?

In the barn his lips moved in silent prayer as he cared for the animals, his thoughts on the dire event ahead. The doctor had promised to notify the parson from the Free Will Baptist Church on his way home. Within the hour, he heard a buggy, the clopping of hooves in chorus with the rattle of the wheels.

Parson Taylor, a long-time friend of his father sat on the seat, his wife beside him, her face kind and grave. "Mr. Barnhill, I came as quickly as I got the news."

"Amanda's inside with the baby." He pointed to the house as he shut the barn door and followed them inside never noticing the beautiful call of the whippoorwill in the distance.

After the visitors declined an offer of coffee, he sat and held the dying child and his tearful wife. The slow ticking of the mantel clock seemed to synchronize with the babe's efforts to claim one last breath. Abe stared at the angelic face before him watching for the miracle of life's departure. *Take me, God. Spare my son, Please take me.*

The parson cleared his throat and began to pray. "Dear Lord, you have chosen this little one for your heavenly home. Help those who have to stay behind. Give Mr. and Mrs. Barnhill the strength to accept your will. We praise you for your mercy and grace in forgiving us of our sins and preparing for us a place with you in heaven. Amen."

The light dinner Mrs. Taylor prepared grew cold. He could not eat. Amanda sang a quiet hymn, tears pouring across her lips unbidden. She pushed the little baby fuzz back from the child's forehead and caressed the still hand. Only the slight movement of the chest showed life.

Daylight moved into twilight before the parson's wife took Amanda and the baby into the bedroom. A sudden shriek pierced the dusk. He hurried to the door to find Amanda kneeling beside the still form, her distraught face against the baby's cheek.

Mrs. Taylor hugged Amanda. "I'll come back when you're ready." She stepped out and closed the door.

He placed his hand around the lifeless fingers of little Abel Silvanus Barnhill Junior and knelt in silence as the room darkened. His knees, his legs, his heart - they had all deserted him. An urge to weep and curse death held him in place beside the bed. He put his face down. It seemed an eternity before he felt he could rise and light a lamp. Looking once more at the two figures he loved, he opened the door. "Mrs. Taylor, we are ready for you."

"It would be best to take your wife into the front room to rest while I tend to the baby," she said.

Amanda lifted herself from the bed and walked to the chest of drawers. She pulled out a light blue gown and handed it to Mrs. Taylor. "This was his christening gown. Put that on him."

That simple gesture shredded his composure. He clenched his teeth and held his breath until he felt the wave of despair pass. Alright God, he's yours forever.

March winds blew across the prairie slamming the side of the "tumbleweed" wagon as it pulled into Ardmore, a little town almost to the Texas border in prime cattle land. The dusty square held only farmer's wagons.

It was difficult for Charley to watch Abe struggle with his weakened endurance and with his grief. At night he watched him sleep, his leg propped over his saddle. At the campfire, his brother's story-telling faded into staring at the embers. The silence was uncomfortable for Charley knew Abe's grief all too well.

In his saddlebags, he carried warrants for six men. The wagon behind them held two; John Berry, a wife killer from McAlester, was the second murderer Charley had arrested in three weeks. Berry had poisoned his wife with opium in order to have a younger lover.

Throwing his reins over the hitching post at the general store, he faced Dan and Jimmy in the wagons. "Caddo Creek coming off the Washita River runs near by. Head there and get supper going. We'll join you as soon as we pick up the men we're looking for."

He motioned to Abe to stay outside. Sometimes fugitives bolted when they saw a deputy.

"Howdy to you, sir." Charley tipped his hat to the proprietor. "I'm U.S. Deputy Marshal Charles Barnhill. I'm looking for Charles Cotlage and Andrew Colbert."

A small man with a gray beard and twinkling eyes looked up from his ledger books, peering at him over spectacles perched on the end of his nose. "Yeah, they stay over at the hotel when they're in town. If not there, then they're probably on the scout."

"Much obliged."

He walked outside and beckoned to Abe who was watering his horse at the trough. "Go to the hotel and inquire about Cotlage and Colbert. The store owner says they sometimes stay there. I'll check with the livery man."

Back at the hitching post, he listened to Abe's report. "They have room number four at the top of the stairs on the left. Spent the night gambling and carousing. They're probably up there sleeping."

He drew his Colt, checking the location of the shells in the chambers. "Let's go wake them up."

He beckoned to the clerk to follow. The stairs groaned under their weight, Abe swinging his crippled leg to reach each step. Charley waved the clerk to the side.

"Tell them you have a telegram for them when I give you the signal." He rapped on the door with the tip of his pistol, the sound echoing down the deserted hall.

"Go'way, I'm sleeping," a hoarse voice shouted.

He rapped again, this time a bit harder.

"Yeah. Whatta' you want?"

The clerk's voice was casual as he followed Charley's signal. "Sir, I've a telegram for you. Just came in."

"Alright." Bed springs squeaked. The door swung open, revealing a mop of hair under low cut brows, bare chest, drawers and bare feet.

Charley stuck his pistol under the man's chin. "You're under arrest," he ordered, shoving the startled whiskey peddler towards Abe in the hall.

A shadowy form in the room shifted towards the window. Covering the distance to the fleeing culprit, Charley grabbed him by the scuff of the neck. He parried a fist and stuck his gun barrel in the man's ribs. That settled the disagreement.

"Get dressed." He swept aside their pistols and rifles as he grabbed both gun belts and slung them over his shoulder. "Take the prisoners downstairs and I'll come back for the rifles."

Abe smiled as he secured the rot gut sellers with a long rope. A walk to camp would take the fight out of them.

Tyner Hughes rode into the jail yard, prisoner in tow as Charley walked down the steps.

"Howdy, Tyne. I see you're still out there. When's your hearing?"

"Sometime in the summer. I get to work while the mess is settled. My lawyers says it's because there is no case against us and the marshal knows it."

Charley shifted his hat on his head. "I hear Wingo is in trouble."

"He shot a man last week who tried to resist arrest with a knife. The county court in Van Buren which does not like Indian deputies working in their jurisdiction charged him with assault with intent to kill. I think it's the rift between federal and state again."

Trying to keep the bitterness out of his voice, Charley grumbled. "What's wrong with people? Even Frazier is gaining community sympathy because of his amputated arm. You ever thought of trying something besides lawing?"

Tyne's smooth face and neatly trimmed hair disguised the tough lawman that he was. "Nope. What else can a beaten down lawman do?"

"You're right. I guess when the time comes, we'll figure that out."

Charley admired the new jail wing as he walked away. It was modern and increased the old jail to double it's original size and added a second story to the old portion. Now the prisoners did not suffer in a stuffy, cold-in the-winter, hot-in-the summer basement confinement. He was glad. No man should be incarcerated in crowded uncomfortable conditions.

The red brick addition contained three levels for separating prisoners according to the seriousness of their offense, murderers on the basement floor nearest the guards, other felonies on the main floor, and misdemeanor offenses on the top floor. The women's prison stayed on the top floor of the old wing along with the dispensary. Builders of the new jail described it as able to hold everyone they brought in but was it escape proof? Only time would tell.

The roof of the house in Krebs leaked like it was made of brush instead of wood shingles. Irene had several buckets situated throughout the five rooms to catch the drips. A trip to the general store for nails and tar paper was in order. He also wanted to visit Jimmy who had settled on a farm near by. He was leasing the place and putting in cotton and corn in between his duties as guard. Oh, to be young again!

He poked his head in the kitchen were Irene was mixing up bread in a big wooden bowl. "Darlin', I need to visit the general store. Do you need anything?"

She dusted off her hands and came over to him. Wrapping her arms around his neck, standing on her tip toes, she kissed his cheek and whispered. "I need some soft baby flannel material, preferably yellow or green."

"Alright," he said quickly and turned to go. Baby flannel. He whirled around. "What did you say?"

"I need some baby flannel, preferably in yellow or green."

"Darlin' does that mean what I think?"

His young wife laughed and kissed him again. "Yes, it does. We're going to have a baby in the fall."

He picked her up and swung her around the kitchen. She giggled as her apron and skirt swirled in billows. "We'll tell the children as soon as they get home from school. Can I tell Jimmy?"

"Of course, sweetheart."

His spirits soared with the news. Another baby. Minnie was almost ten. What did it mean to have a baby around. Oh, yeah. Sleepless nights, worrying at the least little fever, bouncing the little one on his knees. Henry and Minnie would be excited.

Clucking to Billie, he set out with a song in his heart and a prayer on his lips. April had turned into a beautiful month, rain, leaky roofs and all. He had to leave on a trip next week, but the few days before then would be ones to cherish. Peace, wonderful peace. This country would one day be a wonderful place for his children and grandchildren. What would it look like in a hundred years when his body had turned to dust?

Mud blocked the stretches of Garrison Avenue that had not been paved with brick. He tried to avoid the holes but there was a large one right in front of the hitching rail where a jail wagon had gotten stuck. Charley stomped his boots on the porch as he swung open the door.

"Hello, Marshal Carroll." Charley extended his hand to the older man, sitting at the desk piled high with paperwork. "Where's Barnes?"

"Out sick. I'm trying to sift through these writs. He has them all categorized as to the deputy to whom he assigned them. Here's yours." The marshal handed him a stack of writs, all neatly folded in the triple-folded manner of legal documents. It allowed legal-sized paper to be inserted in the file cabinets.

"Anything unusual?"

His boss handed him three writs bound together, more subpoenas for the Burrow murder case. "The hearing on these is May fifteenth, eleven days away."

Charley glanced at the names - Captain Minehart, a well-known figure in Skullyville, Lem Thornton, Irene's uncle, Frank Tibbetts, a merchant - men who knew both Louis Burrow and Billie Morgan.

"I'll have these back in a couple of weeks. I've heard rumors of the court being shut down for lack of funds."

The marshal sighed and shrugged his shoulders. "We're waiting for the deficiency bill to pass in Congress that will provide for the court expenses."

"What happens in the meantime?"

"The court will close since we can't pay witnesses or jurors. The deputies will still be busy since I have a back-log of warrants."

Charley's thoughts turned to witnesses who had already been called. "The criminals will take advantage of this to threaten their accusers or even eliminate them."

"I know. By the way, Heck Thomas and Henry Moody tied your record for prisoners. They brought in thirty-one on the twenty-seventh." Marshal Carroll turned his eyes back to the heaped desk.

Wow. Ole Heck was a real work horse. One of these days he would have to take a trip with him. The most experienced deputies were best for catching the worst offenders.

This is the only known photograph of the three Barnhill brothers together who worked for Judge Parkers' court. The photo was taken at the Phillips-Bowers General Store in Ashland, Choctaw Nation, Indian Territory before 1898. On the left is James Barnhill (Federal Marshal's Service guard), his wife Alice Bowers Barnhill holding unidentified baby. Sitting on the step is Abe Barnhill (U.S. deputy marshal 1886--1889). On the right is William Bowers (Alice's father), Jonas Bowers (his son), Charles Barnhill (U.S. deputy marshal 1879-1905), Fred Bowers (son of William Bowers) and sitting on the step on the right, Ray Bowers, (son of William Bowers). Willliam Bowers was married to a Choctaw woman, Dorcas Melvina Tinker Bowers. Original photo courtesy of Jimmie Edwin Barnhill, great-grandson of James Barnhill.

Chapter 36

The Bloody Summer of '88

Charley checked Abe's front yard at Childers Station as he tied Billie to the corral post. Jenette sat under an oak playing with her dolly. She was four and the image of her mother. Seeing her father and uncle, she became excited.

"Papa." She ran to the men, arms out-stretched. Abe bent down and lifted her in his arms, covering her face with kisses.

They had searched all day for Moses Taylor, wanted for the attempted rape of his thirteen-year-old step-daughter. Old sins never changed. Rape was a hanging offense under federal law and this man was in big trouble if found guilty.

Abe slipped his giggling daughter to the ground. "Let's see what Amanda has for dinner."

Charley's stomach rolled at the thought of Amanda's home-cooking which was a treat he never passed up. He was still getting adjusted to his new bride's efforts, crisp biscuits, rock solid eggs, incinerated bacon. But he could eat anything she sat before him.

Amanda stepped out of the house with a note in her hand. "Parson William Randall came by just before noon. He was very upset - says to give you this note."

Abe read it, his joyous greeting turning to a warning as he passed the missive over to Charley. *There goes the home-cooking.*

> *"Deputy Barnhill, we need your help. Two of my parishioners, Joseph White and my son-in-law, Shannon Foster, have been threatened at gun point by two men who shot up our prayer meeting on Sunday evening."*

"Whadda ya make of that?" Charley asked.

"No telling." Abe was already strapping on his gun belt. He hefted the buckle to center the weight of the 7 pound Colt along his right hip.

Amanda's hands roved over his vest, smoothing his shirt. "Be careful, honey."

Charley turned away, hating the look in her eyes. Irene had not yet learned to fear like that.

Outside of the little hamlet, they turned toward Randall's farm. A rider came at a gallop. Mitchell Ellis, the Indian Policeman, fought to catch his breath. "I was just coming to fetch you. There's been a killing."

The brothers kicked their horses into a gallop and followed the policeman into the river bottom where the land lay flat and lush. A crowd outside a comfortable farm house surrounded a crumpled form. Charley recognized most of the men, Charley Fry and Thomas Perry, Cherokee leaders and merchants, Doctor Samuel Moore and others. His year of residence here before his marriage had produced many friends among these gentle Cherokees who would sell anything for a bottle of whiskey. It was a dilemma to Charley that such honest people would resort to violence over a tiny insult. Honor and pride ruled their world, not white man's law.

Mitch explained as they pulled their horses to a halt. "The dead man is the desperado, Jim Wells, who threatened just last week to tear off my police uniform and put two cartridges in my heart. A bad Indian named Holmes was wounded in the shoot out." He pointed to men standing near the body. "The older one is Joseph White, a preacher, the other's Shannon Foster. They're adopted citizens who mind their own business and never cause any trouble - perfect targets for bullies."

Charley felt he was spending a lot of time with preachers and murders. Spiritual warfare knew no bounds. He pointed the two suspects to the porch. "Have a seat while we look things over."

He bent over the messy scene - the outlaw was on his back, hands by his head, buckshot wounds to the left side of his head and shoulder. Claw marks in the dirt showed his attempts to get to a gun belt rolled around an empty scabbard.

Turning the dead man on his right side, he examined his back, no wound, no powder burns. "He wasn't back shot. Where's his pistol?" He looked around at the crowd - faces unmasked by the violence. Dismay, shock, horror, even relief.

Joseph White spoke. "I picked it up and gave it to Charley Fry." He was a slim man in his forties, sun-baked face, hands and arms, a farmer by all appearances.

Abe took the .45 Colt from Fry, checked the cylinder which was full and tucked it in his belt.

Charley stood and wiped his hands on his pants. "Where was it?"

"By his hand at his left shoulder. Parson Randall, his son, Lewis, and Dr. Moore all saw me pick it up."

Charley tried to sort out the scene in his mind. Wells was shot from the side while reaching for his pistol. Why had he taken it off? "Where is the shotgun?"

The deputy sheriff gestured to two double-barrel shotguns and a pistol and cartridge belt laying on the porch. "I rounded these up when I arrived."

"Any witnesses?"

Ellis pointed to the doctor. "Dr. Moore is the only witness besides the two shooters."

The man was so unnerved he was unable to respond except to move his head. Charley nodded to Abe who approached the witness. "Interview him while Ellis and I grill the prisoners."

He ushered the prisoners into the family dwelling, a one story framed house of the sort seen frequently in Arkansas, front porch and wrap around veranda with a front parlor. Silent and grim, the killers sat down and stared at the floor as if the boards could provide an explanation of what had just happened. A young woman came from the bedroom and put her hand on Foster's shoulder. Wailing from inside pulled Charley to the door. A wee child lay in a crib, her tiny eyes peering at him in alarm. She looked so much like his Minnie. A young boy lay on the bed, both fists stuck into his mouth.

He knew he must freeze his emotions and concentrate on the unfortunate task at hand. Family scenes were never easy. He remembered Louis Burrow's sweet wife, Janey, now his sister-in-law and how Irene had cried at the sight of her father. Pain and grief, that was his duty.

"Shannon Foster?" He pointed to the young man. "Whatever you tell me, I can testify in a court about your statements.

"I know. " He replied in a soft, shaken voice.

"You may wait in the bedroom with your wife until I'm finished talking with Pastor White." Foster stood up, guiding his distraught wife to the bedroom door.

"Alright, Pastor White. Tell me your side of this sad tale."

White exhaled and shook his head. "Wells, and his companion, Holmes who was drunk and brandishing a pistol, forced their way into our Sunday afternoon prayer meeting. Holmes was upset because he heard tell I had accused him of cutting the tail off my mare. When I tried to deny the accusation, he started shooting around the room. Pastor Randall deflected his gun hand several times as he tried to shoot. The bullet passed through the wall where I had been standing."

"What did Wells do?"

"He reloaded several times for Holmes who was too drunk to handle his bullets. Then, he too would shoot his pistol off and laugh. Holmes aimed at Shannon Foster and Pastor Randall's son, Lewis. One of the other church members grabbed him but could not wrestle the gun away."

He could predict the outcome of this story. It was one he had heard too often - local toughs terrorizing peace-loving folk just to see their fear.

White raised his hands in a position of prayer and bowed his head. Seconds passed before he raised his eyes and resumed his tale. "Holmes started shooting at women and children in the yard. He hollered and yelled, 'Run, kids, run!' Then he stumbled down the road and claimed he would be back to kill me and Shannon."

"And today?" Charley's heart grew heavier with each detail.

"After breakfast they came walking up accompanied by Dr. Moore who had just left our house. They had asked him to come back to act as messenger. They wanted to settle the fuss peaceably, but both were armed. I had Moore tell them to put down their guns before approaching any closer."

When we came out on the porch with our shotguns, Wells started to run for Holmes' pistol which was closest. We told him to hold up, but he wouldn't stop. I knew if he got to that pistol he would fire on us, so we both shot when he reached out for it."

"Where was his partner during all of this?"

"He took off running and Foster reloaded and got off two shots at him."

"Is there anything else you want to tell me?"

"We're peace-loving Christians. These men were bullies and determined to kill us. I had to protect myself and my family."

In cases like this, he could not understand the violence of this Territory. Would people ever be able to live here without fear of assault? "Alright. Have your wife gather up personal items to take with you."

He stepped into the bedroom and motioned to the other shooter. "Send your children outside. You don't want them to hear this."

From a rocking chair beside the bed he addressed the young farmer. "Mr. Foster, I need your version of the killing."

Foster, appearing to be in his mid-twenties, long blonde hair and a neatly trimmed goatee, wore a blue cotton shirt and overalls - neat, clean, conservative. His shaking hands twisted the loops along the leg of his trousers as he spoke.

"They sent word to us last night that they intended to come here in the morning and kill us. I spent all night worrying about what to do if they came for us. We decided to face them and try to disarm them."

"Why didn't you send for Mitch Ellis?"

"If we charged them with assault in the church shooting, they would for sure kill us. We sent Parson Randall to look for you in hopes of your assistance."

When they appeared this morning, we agreed to go with them to Parson Randall's house if they would disarm. When we stepped out on the porch still holding our shotguns, Wells made a run for Holmes' gun, begging us not to shoot him. He turned and said to me, 'No damned man can make me lay down my gun.' He was in the act of catching up his pistol when I fired."

Charley felt the tension of the interview ease as old habits kicked in. He would do his duty and arrest these men. The commissioner could sort out the details. "Have your wife pack your gear. You'll be kept under guard in camp until a writ of arrest comes from Fort Smith."

He watched the tearful good-byes, the wives clinging to their husband's necks, struggling not to break down. The younger woman buried her head in her husband's shoulder and wet his shirt with her tears, sobbing out muffled words of pain and fear. The children stood close clinging to skirts and hands. *Why, dear Lord?*

Prodding the prisoners, he stepped down from the porch. Dr. Moore was less shaken but still pale. Abe stood beside him, the shotguns under each arm.

"Did you get Dr. Moore's statement?"

"Yes and the names of the other people here."

"Set up camp while I look for Holmes. I'll hire a guard and wagon when I get back to town."

The desperado's body would need tending. He addressed Pastor Randall. "Can you arrange for the burial? In this heat he won't last long. By the way, are you and White associated with Pastor Barnhill's convention?"

"Yes, we are. Pastor Barnhill is a great man of God in this dark land. Is he kin?"

"Abe and I's father."

"God bless you in your endeavors. I know Pastor White and Elder Foster will be given a fair trial." The humble man of peace turned toward home, head high and back unbent from his toils for the Lord.

It took less than an hour to find Holmes nursing his wounds at a friend's house. Mitch Ellis could hold him for shooting up the church and keep him locked up until a witness subpoena was issued from Fort Smith.

Abe hobbled over to his horse. Riding still took a toll on his stamina, but at least he could mount up and hold on.

Charley tightened his gun belt as he glanced at him. "Taylor may make a fight of it. Check your ammunition."

Moving through fields of cotton in the bottoms, Abe thought the farm house with its empty corral was deserted, a few chickens in the yard scurrying out of the way. He stayed in the saddle, his hand on his Winchester, as Charley climbed the porch. "Hello, the house. It's Deputy Marshal Charles Barnhill."

The door opened a crack to reveal a gaunt face with sunken eyes and a toothless mouth. Life in Indian Territory was hard on women. This woman in her mid-thirties, hair pulled back in a single braid, needed some fattening up. "I'm Liza Taylor. I suppose you're looking for Moses."

"Yes ma'am. Can you tell us where he is?"

"He left yesterday to stay with relatives. I sent my daughter back to Arkansas after he threatened to kill her if she talked to anyone. That man deserves the rope for his actions. I'm only here to get my personal effects. "

"Give us directions to these relatives and we'll be on our way."

The woman's eyes fell to their six guns and gun belts. "It's the first house on the north side of the road heading west towards Vann, but he won't fight. He is a coward except around women and children."

Abe kicked his horse in the flanks and then held up. On impulse, he turned back to the woman who still had the door open. "Is anyone else around?" He was startled by her reply.

"Just Davis House out picking cotton. We hired him for the season. He's a good worker."

Davis House who had gotten into a fight with Louis Burrow the day of the Morgan murder. What was he doing here?

He dismounted and followed Charley out into the field to look for Davis. The young man had a half full cotton sack in trail, the strap straining at his shoulder.

"Davis, how've you been?" he said as he extended his hand to Billie Morgan's nephew. The Morgans seemed to be everywhere in this part of the Territory.

"How long you been here?" Charley said.

"Since the first part of June. I couldn't take waiting around for the trial any longer."

Toying the soil with his boot, Abe asked, "Were you about when the rape occurred?"

"I was working in the field and didn't know anything about it until evening when the girl started crying and telling her mother what had happened."

Abe glanced at the young man."You'll have to appear for this trial too."

"Hope it's after cotton season. Take care. Taylor is crafty."

Finding the house in question was not hard. As they rode up, Charley motioned to him. "Go around back. He may make a run for it."

Sure enough, as he rode to the back door, a desperate figure came charging out, his face turned toward the front yard. Taylor swung around into the muzzle of Abe's Winchester. "Hold up there, Moses. Put your hands above your head now."

The man put his hands high, a look of frustration and hate covering his ragged features. A greasy beard masked the snarl. "You've no right to arrest me. No complaint has been made out."

"We can hold you on suspicion while waiting for the arrest order. Now, get going."

The next day a telegram arrived instructing Charley to bring in Taylor. They arrived at the jail in the midst of a violent storm that drenched them as they unloaded the prisoners, unaware that the storm was not the only trouble awaiting them.

Charley walked into the office, dripping rain from his slicker onto the wooden floor. The chief deputy did not greet him with his normal cheer or grumble about the water on his office floor. Charley felt a tremble go through his body. Something was wrong. He handed him the writs of arrest. "What've you got for us? We're going to rest tonight and head out tomorrow as soon as we get supplies."

Barnes threw the writs on his desk without a glance and cleared his throat. "We got bad news while you were out. Deputy Marshal Trammel was killed a couple weeks ago over in Montgomery County."

"What happened?"

"Posse of twenty was fired on from ambush. He didn't have a chance."

"Trammel was a good man. I feel sorry for his family left without anyone to support them."

"That's not the end of it, I'm sorry to say." Barnes' hesitation sent another chill up his spine. "Charley, your friend, John Phillips and his posse were killed four days later." Barnes handed him the telegrams that conveyed the terrible news.

The first was dated Monday, July 2nd, 1888, at Eufaula.

"John Phillips and posse killed. Will Bury. Make provisions for expenses. What shall be done with the prisoners?" Crowder Nix, Deputy Marshal.

Another one read *"Phillips and McLaughlin were both killed last night. I just got here tonight. What shall I do, if anything, with his outfit? It is close here." A.J. Mattox, Deputy Marshal.*

Shifting his eyes from the ominous yellow forms, he fought for words. "I can't believe it. We're going to be wiped out, all of us, if something isn't done to reinforce the deputy service. Who's out looking for these scalawags?"

"I sent Deputies Salmon and Rusk to hunt them down. We suspect the Wesley Barnett gang. The bodies were brought into Fort Smith and the coroner examined them. They were buried with full honors in the Oak Cemetery."

"John Phillips was my friend. I worked with him on many cases. I can hardly comprehend the effect this will have on his family."

Barnes took a deep breath and blurted one more sentence. "To top it all off, Heck Thomas was badly wounded in a shoot out with outlaws last week."

"He's one of our best man-hunters. I hate to see him down."

The chief deputy shifted his eyes toward the windows to watch Abe walking across the compound. "Speaking of wounds, how is Abe getting along?"

"He is able to do most things, but I don't think he should go out alone. When does that outlaw, Frazier, go to trial?

"Like all the other cases, it's been delayed because of the summer shut down. Without funds we can't hire more deputies which is turning Indian Territory into a blood-bath. I need all deputies working around the clock. Take this arrest warrant for a local man, James Evans. He's reported to be in town. See if you can find him before you head for home."

Abe appeared at the porch and stopped at the sight of Charley's face. "What is it now?"

Charley was suddenly very tired and just wanted a clean, soft bed.

The arrest of James Evans for larceny was one of his most unusual encounters. Charley had stopped by the stable in the evening to check on Billie. As he walked across the courthouse yard, a man stepped away from the gas lamp at the front of the jail lawn. Charley's hand went reflexively to his Peacemaker. The shadowy figure appeared to be unarmed. Charley stopped and watched with caution as he approached.

"I hear you been looking for me, deputy." The man's grim face did not seem threatening.

"Who are you?"

"James Evans. You have a reputation for fairness, so here I am. I'd rather you take me in than some of the others who like to rough up a fella."

"Alright. I'll have to take you straight to the jailer."

"I'm ready." Evans held out his hands for the restraints. He was a young man in his twenties, calm blue eyes, a sadness around the mouth.

"Let's go. I will put in a word for you with the district attorney because of your willingness to surrender." Charley put the cuffs around his wrists and guided him toward the jail door. He reached in his vest pocket and took out the arrest writ. *That was easy. Thank you, Lord. I didn't feel like chasing any more today. You always know when I need rest. Be with the families of my dead friends in the hour of their great need.*

The killing of two deputy marshals and a posse man in a week raised a cry and hue across the nation and the Western District of Arkansas. The bloodshed had to stop.

Charley unfolded The Cherokee Advocate, for July 11, 1888. The headline read:

> *"Another Deputy Marshal Killed."*
>
> *"This is the seventeenth officer attached to this court killed since November 1885, and the second one during the past week. Phillips had been on the force about two years, and made the reputation of a brave man and a skillful officer. On this same spot in January 1887, his posse, guard and cook were all murdered in cold blood by an Indian named Seaborn Green, who was subsequently hanged in this city. Phillips leaves a wife and family living in this city. Deputy Marshals Cabel and Barlin left last night for Eufaula to bring in the remains."*

Charley bowed his head and closed his eyes, the memory of his friend Phillips pressing against his eyelids.

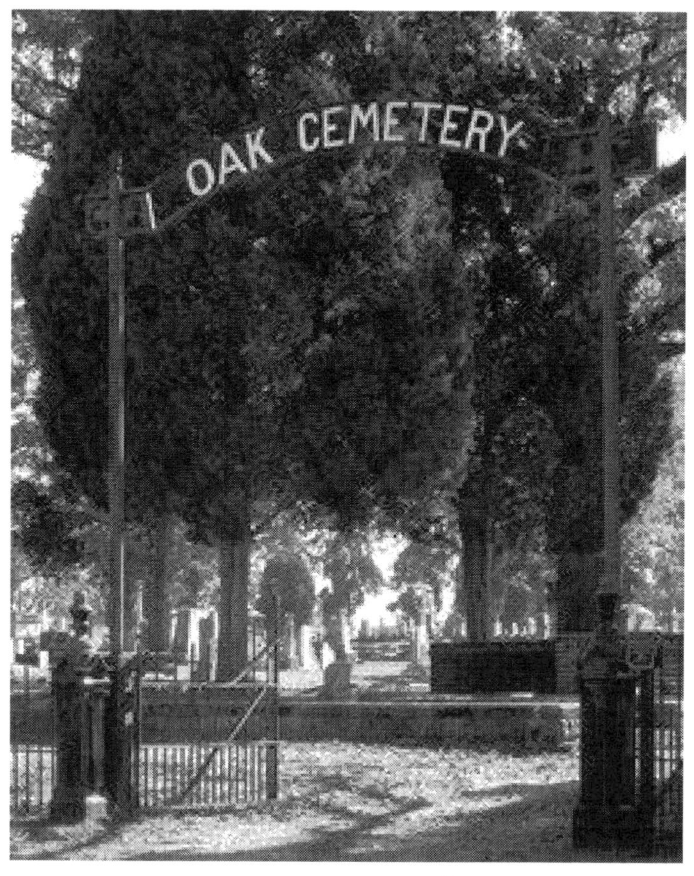

Oak Cemetery, Fort Smith, Arkansas, final resting place of Deputy Marshal John Phillips and posse man Billy Whitson

Chapter 37

Frenchy

Irene sighed as she lay the telegram from Charley on the kitchen table. *"July 23, 1888, Done in Fort Smith, leaving today. Fondly, Charley."* He had been gone most of the summer, despite a court shut down. She lifted the oil lamp and checked the bars on the window shutters and the front door as Charley had taught her. The top of the shutters were divided from the bottom, allowing them to be left open for ventilation.

Her husband was her whole world now though her mother and siblings lived just down the road in McAlester. Tomorrow would be a day of cooking and cleaning and primping in anticipation of his home-coming. She anticipated a restful night in preparation for the busy day ahead.

Then she heard it - horses in the yard. Was it Charley coming home early? That was not possible. Who was it?

Heavy boots on the porch made her reach for the Smith and Wesson hanging over the dresser. She heard the door handle being jerked and the door banging against the bar. *Oh, Lord, who is it?* A resounding kick on the door rattled the window panes. *Would it hold?*

"Barnhill, you in there? Come out, so's I can drill you, you son of a bitch."

She blew out the lamp and crept into Henry's bedroom, trying not to cry out as her knee jammed against the dresser. She could see his sleeping form by the moonlight that drifted through the top of the shutters. She shook him by the shoulder. "Henry, get up. There's someone banging on the front door. Get you rifle and come with me."

He rose groggy, pushing hair back from his forehead and rubbing his eyes. He fished for the shotgun under his bed, clicked open the chamber to check the cartridges and cocked both barrels.

"Don't make any noise. Maybe who ever it is will think no one is home."

He nodded and placed himself at the edge of the front room with a direct line of sight to the front door. The door handle jerked and the door creaked against the bar. One more push and it could collapse.

A fist pounded on the door. A voice slurred. "Open up, you cur dog, Barnhill. I'm going to kill you for arresting my brother." A heavy foot kicked at the bottom of the door which held firm.

Her lips moved in prayer and her hands shook as she held the heavy pistol with both hands. She glanced at Henry, his features pale in the moonlight. *Would the boy have the courage to fire if he had to? Would she?* She pulled the hammer back on the pistol and held her breath.

Another voice came through the door. "Come on, Frenchy. He's not home. He would've put a bullet through you by now."

"Alright, you coward. I'll be watching for you, Barnhill. Your blood is mine."

The steps receded. The horses galloped away with a thunder of hooves, their riders shouting insults and curses into the night.

She peered through the shutter at the empty yard, the moon outlining only the trees and grass. "They've gone. Go back to bed. Thanks for waking up so quickly."

Henry rose up from behind the sofa and smiled. "We would've been ready for them, for sure. You're alright, Irene."

"Just call me Mom."

She returned the pistol to its belt and resumed preparation for bed. She worried all night in fitful sleep, the sounds of the voices and curses echoing in her dreams.

Charley swung down from the saddle and led Billie into the barn. The big horse stuck his head in the trough as he dumped in a scoop of oats.

His nose announced the feast - fresh bread, venison, boiled potatoes, carrots, corn, pie. What a banquet! He paused at the kitchen door to watch his wife distracted by a pan of boiling gravy. Her slim form framed by sunlight reminded him of a painting of the Madonna. All she lacked was a halo. He walked to the cook stove and kissed her on the back of the neck. She turned in surprise.

"Sweetheart, you're home early. I wanted to get this all done before you got here." He kissed her again and then noticed the rounding of her belly. *Have I been gone that long?* Three weeks ago he had not been able to detect a change in her form.

"I'm just glad to be home but I can stay only for a week. Billie and I both need a good rest."

"We'll have dinner in just a few minutes. You've just enough time to wash up and relax for a few minutes."

After the children had consumed their second piece of pie, Irene indicated to Minnie it was time to clear the table. She turned to her task with a proper "Yes, ma'am" and a smile for her father.

Charley looked at Henry sitting across from him - almost as tall as he was, soon to be a man.

Irene removed her apron and moved into the front room without a word. He could tell by her expression something was bothering her. He followed, concern growing as he sat down beside her. He reached over and took her hand.

"What is it, sweetheart? You've got something you want to tell me?"

"Honey, when you're gone, I can hardly wait until I see your face, then everything seems fine. So maybe it's nothing, and I don't want to worry you."

His grip tightened on her hand. "Is it the baby?"

She shook her head, invoking a face that alarmed him even more. "No. I am fine. But last night as I was getting ready for bed, two men tried to break in the front door. They called for you to come out so they could kill you. I was so scared but I had the pistol and Henry his shotgun."

His eyes flared with anger. "Who were they? Did they get the door open?"

"No. One was called Frenchy and said that you'd arrested his brother."

He thought for a moment. "Oh, yeah, the two French brothers, always getting into trouble. Don't worry about it, honey. I'll tend to it when I go out tomorrow." He wrapped his arms round her and held her close. He'd find Frenchy tomorrow.

Krebs lay quiet in the afternoon sun, every living thing yearning for the cool weather of fall. Charley walked into the dark interior of the gambling parlor, his Peacemaker already in hand. Here, deep in Indian Territory, liquor was sold out the back door of almost every business establishment. Heads turned and hands dumped the contents of glasses into spittoons. He located his target sitting in the corner dealing black jack. The man's eyes flickered as his hands dropped the cards and reached under the table.

Charley raised the Colt, cocked to the firing position. "Don't got for it, Frenchy."

The cornered gambler ducked his eyes and relaxed. The men sitting at the table moved out of the line of fire. No one seemed eager to get involved.

"Raise your hands and get up slowly. Now, outside." Charley waved the muzzle of the big .45 toward the door. Moving through the door, the sunlight hit him in the face. Frenchy stumbled forward groping for a horse at the front of the building. His bullet kicked up dirt near the prisoner's boot. "Stop. The next one will be in your leg."

The sheriff burst out the door of his office, surprised to see Charley poking the man in the back with his pistol. "What's up, Barnhill?"

"Lock up this mangy critter for a day. He came by my house last night while I was gone. My wife says he threatened to kill me. If I find him slinking around my place anymore, I'll press charges."

The sheriff unlocked the cell door. "Well, you've been called out, Frenchy. You better get over your fuss with this deputy before you wind up in Fort Smith with your brother."

"Aw, I was just drunk and didn't mean no harm by it."

"Drunken Indians get in a lot of trouble. You can stay here until you think you can keep your mouth shut."

Charley shook the sheriff's hand and walked away. That should put a sufficient scare into the man. But he'd keep a close eye out when riding alone. When they were friends, Indians would do anything for you, including kill your enemies. If they did not like you, they would do anything they could to you, including kill you. He hoped this one realized his error.

Chapter 38

Bad Women

Will this summer never end? Charley'd had only a week off before being summoned back to arrest fourteen fugitives. The top four caught his eye. Jack Smith and three women accomplices: Annie McCann (Martin) , Louisa McCann, and Julia McCann (Martin) charged with murder of One Suggs from Pope County. The Fort Smith Elevator had said the man's charred remains had been found near Skullyville in May. The victim, reportedly carrying a wallet with several hundred dollars, had been seen last with two men and two lewd women.

Charley stared at Chief Deputy Barnes. "How am I supposed to bring in three women?"

"You arrested Belle Starr," Barnes replied.

"She was our only prisoner. All we had to worry about was preventing her escape."

"Don't turn your back. They're charged with a very unpleasant murder."

He saw the twinkle in Barnes' eye at his discomfort.

Barnes added a parting comment. "By the way, Tyner Hughes brought in your old adversary from the Charles Wilson murder. You remember Bob Benton?"

"I'll never forget that sly fox."

"Witnesses finally got up enough courage to file a complaint for introducing and selling whiskey in the Nation. Of course, he will post bond and disappear until trial."

"Wish it were murder charges he was facing."

Outside he growled at Abe. "We've got to arrest three women and Barnes was no help. What do you do if a woman comes at you with a gun or knife?"

"Search them from head to foot. Remember when you brought in Belle Starr and she had a big .45 hidden down in the pocket of her skirt? She also had a derringer stuck in her blouse when she was arrested the first time in '82."

"That's what I mean. You can't trust 'em but you can't shoot'em, either." Charley pulled his hat down over his eyes and faced the sun in the west. "Might as well get this over with. But we won't get careless. Three dead deputies is enough for this year."

Abe scanned the familiar grove of trees, dirt packed hard from horses and wagons, the same camp site in Skullyville they had used when Morgan had been murdered almost two years before. He hooked up the chains securing the ten prisoners between two trees and began to unlock half of them.

"Jimmy, let's take these men out to wash up." His brother had just finished unhooking his wagon team.

They ushered them to the stream to clean up and use the outhouse that had been erected by the town. Villages were doing what they could to keep down the seasonal typhoid fever that hit when the rains washed human and animal waste into wells.

His Winchester on his lap, he watched the prisoners. They were a rough-looking lot, scraggly beards, uncombed hair, eyes that shifted and searched like trapped animals.

He rose to escort them back to the camp. Jimmy was walking slightly to the side. Without warning the last man in line turned and grabbed at Abe's Winchester, kicking him in the legs as he pushed him backwards. The weight of the man pushing on the weapon toppled him to the ground.

"Hold up there!" Jimmy shouted as he poked his rifle in the man's back. Abe grunted as he strained to rise, using the rifle as a crutch.

Back at camp, Jimmy turned to him. "That was close. Are you hurt?"

"Just my pride." Tingling pain ran up his lame leg. Trying to ignore it, he secured the prisoners to the chain, double checking their shackles. Even the best deputies lost a prisoner now and then, but not on his watch.

Charley entered camp, his face cut with a grin. After a sip of coffee from the cup Dan had handed him, he spoke. "The three women and Smith are camped west of here."

"How come the Indian police hasn't run them off?"

"Each time they go out and tell them to move on, they just find another location. They ply on the travelers coming through this area: liquor, pick pocket stuff, prostitution, even a little black mail if a prominent citizen comes too close."

Abe knew the scheme. "Some local official must be getting part of their take."

"We'll ride in at first light."

"Should be a cake walk," Abe said, his mind running through the logistics of four more prisoners.

"Don't count on it. That's what got Frank Dalton killed when he and Deputy Cole tried to take in a whiskey peddler at his camp. When we ride into any camp the odds are against us."

Darkness enveloped the deputies riding west on the Old Military Road out of Skullyville. Just as the first rays of sun poked through the trees, they located the camp near the main road. Charley counted three tents and three horses in a make-shift brush corral.

He beckoned to Abe. "You and Jimmy take the middle tent and I'll head for the one on the left. The other seems to be a cook and supply tent. When you get to the front, hold up so we'll enter at the same time."

From his position he watched the others cover the middle tent.. With a nod of his head he flung open the tent flap, holding his breath as the musty smell of whiskey, vomit and unwashed bodies hit him in the face.

"Rise and shine, ladies, you're under arrest."

Two women reclined on a pallet, a pile of petticoats, corsets and boots nearby. They raised up with a start, hair falling down into their eyes, bare torsos barely concealed under the covers. They appeared to be sisters in their mid-twenties. The older one's face was streaked with dirt, her hair tangled in a long braid. Her sister was little better, a slack mouth with missing teeth, a scar across her chin.

The older woman frowned. "Whatta you want?"

"I have a writ of arrest for the McCann sisters. People in town say that's you. Get up and dress or else I'll take you to Fort Smith as you are."

The woman rose to her knees, her covers falling to reveal what only a husband should see from a woman. She encircled his leg with both hands, one of which strayed up the inside of his thigh. "My name's Julia, why don't you just come on down here on this bed for a few minutes?"

The heat rising in his face, he jumped back quicker than if he had seen a copperhead. "Don't get any ideas about leaving out the back. I have posse covering it. I'll wait outside."

He ducked out in time to see Abe and Jimmy ushering a couple out of the other tent. The man was tall, in a long sleeved shirt, each arm festooned with a garter, pants held up with suspenders, and bare feet. He held his boots in his left hand. The woman wore a dress with a tight bodice, the low cut neck line displaying ample bosom. Hair, piled on her head, trailed a ribbon.

"These two were in there snoozing, real cozy, fully dressed," Abe explained. He threw down a gallon jug of whiskey. "Guess you don't care how you sleep with a jug like this to keep you company." Abe paused and searched Charley's face. "Why are you so red?"

"Something I just saw and was not expecting."

"Brother, you're dealing with prostitutes. They wouldn't think twice about riding into Fort Smith dressed like Lady Godiva."

The male prisoner ran his hands through his hair. "I don't know who you think you've caught, but you've got the wrong camp. We're travelers heading down to Texas. "

Charley narrowed his gaze. "Jack Smith and Ann Martin are the names on this arrest writ. I figure that's you two. The shopkeepers in town say you keep them busy with your weekly purchases using a big wad of bills. We'll stop by Captain Minehart's store and see what he thinks about who you are."

"What about my camp and horses?" Smith growled.

"You can ride your horses to our camp. Then your friends can tend them. They're probably some one else's anyway. We'll check the brands."

He turned to his older brother. "Check the other tent."

Back at the scene of his embarrassment, he found the women attired in a mismatched assembly: blouses flung with abandon across shoulders, skirt hems uneven; faces flushed from the early morning heat inside the tent. "Get your personal items together," he ordered.

From a pile of items on the dirt floor, he sorted out a man's pocket watch, belt, and wallet. He picked them up. The initials RS were engraved on the belt and wallet.

He shoved the loot at the women. "Where'd you get these?"

The toothless younger sister answered. "Some men like a little company at night and pay with what they have." Her smile told Charley all he needed to know.

He stored the items in his vest pockets and kicked at the remaining clothing. Whoever he was, Suggs gotten more than he paid for. He grabbed a carpet bag lying in the corner and stuffed it to the top.

The older sister stopped her packing. "What you doing with our things?"

"Evidence."

Abe met him outside. He carried a bulging canvas bag. "These women seem to be pack rats. Let's check'em over for weapons before we go any further."

Amidst curses and oaths, Charley ran his hands over the two women's curves. He could not tell for sure what was under the petticoats without lifting them for a visual inspection. When he tried that on Julia, she just smiled and stared into his face while his eyes roved over her pantaloons. "You sure you don't want some entertaining, Marshal?"

"Get mounted or I'll tie you across the saddle."

"You go first, Louisa. I'll sit behind where it's more comfortable."

The toothless woman thrust out her ample bottom. "Well, Marshal. Y'all going to give little ole me a boost?"

"You want to walk to Fort Smith?"

Screwing her face up, she lifted her hem almost to her waist thrusting out a booted foot beneath her knee-high bloomers. "You're no gentleman," she snorted.

After much giggling and squirming, the women settled on the horse, whose ears moved with each gyration of its double load. Abe took Smith's horse in tow and Jimmy hauled on Ann Martin's horse.

That wasn't too bad. Now he had to get them to Fort Smith. Charley's mind returned to the scene in the tent. Such impressions were hard to blot out. That woman's breasts would have been a Renaissance painter's dream.

Dan turned his head at the sound of the horses along the road. He had anticipated the quick return of the others, preparing his wagon and team for the twenty mile trip to Fort Smith. Three horses in tow with three women and a man. They appeared ready to spring loose from their bonds at any moment. *I hope those braids are real tight.* He walked over to Abe and took the bags strapped across his saddle.

He peered into them. "What's these clothes?"

"Evidence. The camp was strewn with all kinds of loot. Charley and I picked up what we thought might be stolen like that money pouch and those wallets."

"I thought they were wanted for murder."

"It's usually robbery until things get out of hand." Abe dismounted and hobbled to the wagon. "Get that fella down and secure him with the other men at your wagon. Jimmy's going to take the women."

Jimmy pulled his wagon to a halt as Charley helped Abe loosen the women's restraints. On the ground, they began to hop around and hold their crotches.

"Oh, deputy. We need to go in the bushes, please!" Ann Martin begged, her hand pressing suggestively to her pelvis.

Charley sighed. These women took twice the work of a male prisoner. "There's an outhouse over yonder. The guard will escort you one at a time."

Jimmy blanched at the order. *I guess that means me.* As he walked behind the woman he tried not to focus on her round figure. He hadn't seen a female in custody other than Belle Starr. What type of woman got herself in this kind of trouble? He'd seen prostitutes in Fort Smith, but they were usually demure and polite, smiling and suggestive.

Ann Martin smiled as she entered the small wooden building, leaving the door ajar. "Guard, would you please stand by the door for me? I wouldn't want anyone to intrude on my privacy."

He turned his back and moved away a few feet.

Minutes later she came out with her blouse pulled off her white shoulder. He tried not to stare."

Why don't you come over here, handsome, and let me feel those muscles under that shirt?" Ann reached toward him.

He felt himself flush. "No, Ma'am. I can't do that," he stuttered, catching his breath. "Let's get going. The others need a turn."

"Oh, you're such a spoil sport. If you change your mind between here and Fort Smith . . . " Ann grinned as if she knew something special about him.

The women rode, chained in the back of Jimmy's wagon, their bedrolls and personal bags in between. They had some mobility of their hands, enough to take care of their comforts.

The morning was agony with them chattering away behind him. They began to laugh and call out suggestions to the male prisoners walking along side the wagon ahead. Some of the men hooted back, though most were too tired to be interested.

Ann Martin called to him again. "Hey, handsome, remember my offer. It's just between you and me." She laughed and pursed her lips as he glanced back at her.

Charley rode up along side the women. "Tone down your hollering, ladies."

"What ya gonna do if we don't? Spank us?" the older McCann sister challenged.

"Jimmy, Abe, give me your neckerchiefs, please." Without another word, he hitched Billie to the tailgate of the wagon and climbed in. Taking each woman by the back of the head, he tied a gag tightly around the mouth of each struggling, cursing female. "How's that?"

Jimmy sighed. *Blissful silence. Thank you, God.* He could not believe his gentlemanly brother had done that. *Woman or not, you can only put up with so much from a prisoner.*

> **Fort Smith Elevator**, August, 24, 1888: *Barnhill's Trip. Deputy Marshal Charles Barnhill came in Monday with fourteen prisoners as follows: Bud Casey, alias, G.W. Dodson, charged with killing Deputy Marshal Joe Henderson, at Lockwood, South Carolina 18 years ago; Jack Smith, Annie Martin, alias McCann, Louisa McCann, Julia McCann, alias, Martin, charged jointly with the murder of one Suggs, six miles above Skullyville, in March last; S.W. Hyatt, Pete Stewart, Riley Madewell, James Sheridan, Jim Walker, assault with intent to kill; T.W. Frye, John Murphy, H.C. Werner, Burrell Rushing, larceny. Walker gave bond for his appearance and the others were committed to jail. Jack Smith, the man charged with murder, is said to be wanted also on two charges of larceny and on assault with intent to kill.*

Pearl Starr - madam of a brothel in Fort Smith, Arkansas

Chapter 39

Guilty as Charged

The keys clanked in the bailiff's hands as he unlocked the double doors leading into the court room. Spectators and court officers shuffled into the dark interior as he threw open the shutters. September 1888 was an extraordinarily busy month because the court had reopened the first part of August. Cases delayed during the summer closure were being tried as rapidly as possible requiring judge, jurors, and attorneys to work day and night, the gas lights in the court burning late into the evening.

"Is the Morgan case still in trial?" Charley asked the man as he exited the room.

"Yes. Both sides have been going at it since Monday, over fifty witnesses to date. Never seen such a case over a bunch of hogs."

Charley removed his hat as he entered the chambers. The front row of chairs just outside the barrier which divided the lawyers' tables and Judge Parker's desk from the general public were reserved for court officers and lawmen. He took a seat at the end directly in line with John Morgan and his co-conspirators, Thomas Cheatham, Lafayette Hudson, James Napier, and Jeff Wilson. He had promised Irene he would attend the trial if he was in Fort Smith at the time. John Morgan's wife, Mary, and Hudson's wife were seated in the row behind him.

"Mrs. Morgan, how are you, today?" Charley bowed his head to the two women. They appeared tired and drawn. Waiting was hard on families of defendants, no matter what the charge. Hudson and Thomas Cheatham had been fortunate enough to afford bail. The rest had languished in jail for eight months. Though the new jail had modern amenities , it was still jail.

Mary Morgan spoke first. "I'm hoping for the best possible outcome, Deputy Barnhill. How is Irene? I understand she is with child."

"She hoped to be here, but she could not travel. She is doing very well, otherwise."

The deliberations had lasted all week in a hard-fought battle between the defense team of Madsen and Frederick and District Attorney Sandels. Nine men had lost ninety-four hogs. Eighteen indictments told a story of missing hogs and tracks that led to fields where large numbers had been slaughtered.

James Adams, a neighbor of Morgan's, had testified he had been hired by the defendants to help slaughter hogs and transport them to Fort Smith for quick sale. He did not know they were stolen.

Today the first witness was Charley's best friend, Tyner Hughes. The defense attorney indicated to the bailiff to call him forward. His long frame dressed up in his best Sunday-go-to-meeting clothes, Tyne turned and faced the bailiff.

After placing his hand on the Bible, he swore his oath.

The defense attorney, Madsen, jumped right in. "Now, Deputy Marshal Hughes, are you acquainted with the defendant, Lafayette Hudson?"

"Yes, I've been his neighbor for some years."

"On January 28th of this year, did you arrest the defendant, Hudson?"

"I picked him up west of Oak Lodge (that's Skullyville you know) along with the other defendants who live with John Morgan."

"How far does Morgan live from Hudson?"

"About a mile, I reckon."

"Did you see the three hogs Hudson brought to Fort Smith shortly before you arrested him?"

"I did."

Madsen seemed to be fishing for information. "Were they marked?"

"They had his mark, two under half notches and two full notches."

"Were the marks fresh, showing signs of scabbing or bleeding?"

"No, sir."

"Thank you, Deputy Hughes."

The district attorney rose and addressed Tyner, his voice firm and confident. "Deputy Hughes, do you recall hearing the testimony of John Ritter concerning his two hogs having their marks changed to that of Hudson's?"

"Yes, sir. I do."

"Could the hogs you saw with Hudson have such altered marks?"

"I have no way of telling that."

"Thank you, that will be all."

The lawyer for the defense stood. "Your honor, we have no further witnesses."

After each attorney made his summation to the jury, the bailiff led the twelve men to the deliberation room placing himself in front of the door.

Charley knew the jury could take a few minutes or all day. He rose and invited the two ladies to have dinner with him at the hotel across the street. The meal was delicious, but his guests were distracted. He tried to comfort them. "Rest assured the jury will be fair in it's decision. Judge Parker will see to that."

After finishing the meal, they crossed the street back to the court room. Groups of interested parties lounged outside, the doors secured until the jury was ready to offer its verdict.

By the middle of the afternoon, he had given up trying to keep his eyes open. His head rested on his chest, his hat placed lightly across his brow. He was startled awake when the bailiff opened the door.

"You may enter. The jury has returned."

The jury filed into the room, moping at their faces with hand kerchiefs in the afternoon heat. The bailiff instructed all to rise as Judge Parker came into the chamber from his adjoining office. Parker, always an imposing figure, looked as fresh as he had several hours before. His elegant beard showed the first streaks of gray, though his piercing eyes sparkled with anticipation of the verdict.

Parker turned to the jury foreman, W. H. Kersh. "Gentleman of the jury, have you reached a verdict?"

"Yes, we have, your honor."

The paper that would seal the fate of Morgan and his accomplices was passed to the bailiff who handed it to Judge Parker. The kindly man in the black robe opened the paper and studied the message that determined five men's fate. His gentle eyes registered the results, but his face mirrored no other change.

Charley held his breath as did most in the courtroom. He was awed each time he saw the great American justice system in action, a seal of finality on his work as a lawman. He glanced at the defense attorneys and the prosecutor. They showed concern - who would win?

"The defendants will rise."

Five men with hardened faces shuffled to their feet, ready for the verdict. "We the jury find the defendants, James Napier, John Morgan, and Thomas Cheatham guilty of larceny as charged in the second and third counts of the indictment. We the jury find the defendants Jeff Wilson and Lafayette Hudson not guilty as charged in the indictments."

Parker banged his gavel. "The defendants, John Morgan and James Napier, who have resided in jail since arrest will be taken back to their cells. Thomas Cheatham will be taken into custody and turned over to the jailer. Sentencing is scheduled for next Saturday, September 14th at 8:30 a.m."

John Morgan, thirty-two years old, would spend part of his life in the Little Rock penitentiary. He had a wife and family and had sacrificed it all for a few hundred dollars worth of hogs.

Charley turned to Morgan's wife. "I'm sorry, Mrs. Morgan. If there is anything Irene and I can do for you, please ask. I'll be in town all week attending the trial of Louis Burrow. We'll pray for you all."

"Thank you, Deputy Barnhill." She covered her mouth with her handkerchief, stifling the sobs racking her shoulders.

Mrs. Hudson disguised her relief with a hand over her mouth, her eyes flitting to her neighbor and then to her husband who turned and smiled at her. The two neighbors clung to each other, one in joy, the other in sorrow.

Chapter 40

The Hangman's Noose

District Attorney Sandels stood in front of the witness, his hand pointing to the diagram propped on the evidence table. "Where were you when William Morgan and Louis Burrow got into the fuss in Skullyville in the afternoon before the murder?"

C.M. Kimbrough pointed to the diagram. "On the porch of my store about 50 feet from the blacksmith shop. Louis had been there some time. Bill Morgan came there, I suppose, about 3 o'clock with a load of cotton, a couple of boys with him. Davis House, his nephew, was one. I came out on the porch when I saw Morgan go by in his wagon."

"What happened then?"

"After he unloaded the cotton, he started to leave. I suppose it was an hour before sun down. He called to Davis who had been stopped by Louis Burrow in front of the blacksmith shop."

"Could you hear the conversation between the two young men?"

"Yes, it was quite loud. Louis told Davis he owed him and he was going to get his money that evening or he would whip him."

"How did the deceased get involved in this argument?"

"Mr. Morgan stopped the wagon and came over to where they were and told Louis not to strike the boy. If he did, he would whip him."

The district attorney moved toward the jury enclosure to place a foot on the bottom railing of the banister. "Go on." This was the third murder case they had heard this month and he did not want to go too fast. As the story unfolded the twelve men sat on the edges of their chairs, eyes fixated on the witness. The spectators sat in silence, straining for every word.

"Morgan pushed Louis back and the boy back the other way and told Louis, as well as I recollect, that he would pay the money himself if he would let the boy alone. They were both mad."

Turning away from the jury, he faced the witness. "Was that the end of the fuss?"

"Yes. Morgan then came into the store and asked me to change some money for him to pay what the boy owed. I told him I thought it was best for him to drop the matter for the present and wait until they both cooled off. He said he had a large family to support in addition to his old father and mother and he wasn't going to have trouble if he could avoid it. I suppose a half hour from the conversation with him, he was killed, at sundown or a little after."

Both hands on the railing in front of the witness chair, the D.A. waited for the witness to take a drink of water. "After you gave the deceased the change, what did he do?" Every detail was important to this case. He would make sure the jury heard it all.

"John Morgan, Bill's brother, had been in town to tend a little field he had. They started off together just before sun down, John riding his pony and Bill walking. The two boys left with the wagon. After closing the store, I started for home. When I got in front of Ainsworth's house, I heard hollering in the direction of Burrow's house. Half way there, I saw John Morgan come around the fence bare-headed, and Old Man Burrow with an ax in his hand. John jumped on his pony and rode off toward town."

Attorney Sandels pointed to the young man, Louis Burrow. "Did you see the defendant?"

"Yes, he was right behind his father. I then saw Morgan laying there. I raised his head to see if he was breathing. He had some pulse, but very weak."

Sandels walked across to his table and picked up a document. "Mr. Lorenzo Burrow has testified that he stepped between them when the deceased gave the defendant the lie with his knife in his hand, that Morgan jumped around him and cut at his son twice. That's when his son raised the ax and struck. Does this agree with what you were told by the father?"

The store clerk shifted in his chair. " Yes. I asked him where the knife was that Morgan had and he said John picked it up and run off with it."

The attorney gazed back at the jury. "Was there a knife in John Morgan's hand as he came running to get on his horse?"

"No. He was running for his life."

The government prosecutor glanced at the clock on the wall behind the venerable judge. "Judge Parker, I see it's almost dinner time. I have only a few more questions for this witness." He knew a hungry jury was a distracted one.

"Proceed then, Mr. Sandels."

Light streaming through the windows fell across the floor in front of the prosecutor as he paused with his fingertips resting on his table. It outlined the trim polished boot he placed forward in a bold stance. "When did the deputies get there?"

"Deputy Barnhill with Deputy Phillips came up with their pistols out just as I finished speaking to Old Man Burrow and asked what was the matter. Morgan was already dead by that time. Deputy Barnhill asked where the young man was, and when Old Man Burrow told him, they went up to the house and presently brought him out. There were several people gathered there and Barnhill asked us to stay until he carried this man off to his camp."

After the marshal came back he sent for a doctor and asked me if I would search the deceased's body to see what he had on him. I found a closed knife in his right hand pocket."

Sandels smiled to himself. This witness had proved a goldmine for the prosecution "That is all I have for this witness." He sat down and clasped his hands before him on the table. He was satisfied this case would result in a guilty verdict unless the papers played up sympathy for the defendant to such a degree the jury would hesitate to convict on grounds of premeditated murder. He felt in his heart that this young man had been defending himself, but the defense would not be able to prove that without a knife to show the jury.

Defense Attorney DuVal stood before the jury, summing up his case at the end of a long week. As the oldest and most experienced barrister practicing before Judge Parker, his easy oratory style impressed the jury and spectators alike. He took his time and covered every detail, anything to cast doubt on a deliberate plan of murder. If the young man had not been so swift with his defensive blow, it would have been Morgan sitting here charged with the deliberate slaying of Burrow. "Many witnesses, including the deceased's own wife, Anna Morgan, testified to the angry and insulting manner in which the deceased treated his son-in-law. The deceased threatened him and others who were trying to get his daughter to join the Methodist Church and the deceased even had his nephew, Davis House, instigate the argument in Skullyville, in order to kill the defendant."

You've heard witnesses testify that the defendant was not looking for a fight: that he left Skullyville in order to avoid trouble with the deceased; that the defendant a few minutes before the killing expressed himself as sorry that there had been any trouble and that there was no danger as nothing scarcely could induce him to strike the deceased."

You've heard how the deceased came to the house and began to talk to the defendant in an angry and insulting way and struck at the defendant with a knife before defendant made any effort to defend himself. Several people testified to seeing a knife in the possession of John Morgan the night after the killing, and John Morgan identified it to them as the knife that his brother had pulled on the defendant, that the deceased had sharpened it on the morning he was killed and said he would kill the defendant before night and that he would have done so by cutting his guts out if it had not been for defendant's brothers."

The prominent defense attorney drew himself to his full height and gestured toward Louis who sat unmoving before his peers who would decide his fate. He knew sympathy for the defendant and mistrust of the deceased's motives would be the saving issue in this verdict. "You've also heard Doctor

Foyil testify that the defendant suffered severe slashes to his chest, probably made by a knife, in addition to the ax wounds to his forearms." He paused to look at his client and gestured to the jury.

"Here's a young man, only twenty-one years old, who has already spent two years in jail. You've heard testimony that the deceased, William Morgan, was a bad and dangerous man. In spite of his high calling as a Baptist preacher, he had a violent temper. This young man held the position of deacon in the same little church. Louis Burrow had the courage to woo and win William Morgan's older daughter, Elizabeth (Janey), a fair maiden of sixteen years."

The attorney shifted his eyes to the jury, stern men of the plow, the ox and wagon, men who knew what it meant to build a country out of a wilderness. They understood the necessity of self-protection. "Only a father can understand the normal suspicion toward a young suitor. But in this instance the young man stood his ground against a father-in-law who was, in all accounts, a man used to getting his own way in everything. The prosecution has tried to paint a picture of a young man overcome with passion who struck out in a fit of anger. Nothing is further from the truth. His desperate act was one of self-preservation in the face of a man who had vowed to kill him before nightfall."

Gentlemen of the jury, as you can see from the testimony, the deceased was the aggressor in this conflict and the defendant had every right to feel his life was being threatened. It is your duty to consider whether there is reasonable doubt as to the motive of the defendant in striking down William Morgan. Self-defense is a natural alternative to being murdered. This young man is at your mercy." Attorney DuVal sat down, satisfied with his summation. Louis' life was in the hands of twelve men and God.

His opponent wrapped up the government's arguments by pointing out the obvious. "William Morgan is dead, killed by the defendant, with an ax. No knife has been recovered and several witnesses for the government who were present at the time of the killing testified they saw no knife. It is your duty to return the verdict of guilty of murder, as charged in the indictment."

Charley took a deep breath and exhaled in relief as he tied Billie to the railing in front of the Fort Smith jail. His single prisoner was still on his horse. "Alright, Hulsey, let's go." Charley reached up and tugged at the prisoner's tied hands.

The man grumbled under his breath, "Take it easy, deputy. I'm not going to cause any problems."

He escorted the prisoner through the doors at the end of the new jail wing and turned him over to the jailer. "Is the Burrow case still in progress?"

"Judge Parker has turned it over to the jury. They left about two hours ago after a lunch recess."

"What about John Morgan and his buddies?"

"They were sentenced yesterday promptly at 8:30 - a year on each count, so a total of two years at Little Rock. Left on the train this morning."

Charley dusted himself off and walked down the hall to the court room. Finding it empty he crossed Garrison Avenue to the restaurant. As he sat at his table, across the street he saw the Burrow family walking across the grass which was green and lush, the long clover grabbing at Janey Morgan's skirt; Lorenzo Burrow had a Bible under his arm. As he sipped his coffee, he watched them sit on the stone wall in front of the jail. Old Man Burrow opened the Bible. At a time like this, prayer and meditation were the only things left. God's grace and mercy would be demonstrated in the verdict, whatever it might be.

He finished his meal and moved across the grassy area, approaching the couple. He waited for their greeting. Since he had been a government witness, though not a hostile one, he was not sure of their response. He had testified in the earlier part of the trial but had left on Thursday to pick up Hulsey. Burrow was reading aloud from Psalm 56, one of Charley's favorite verses: "Be merciful to me, O God, for men hotly pursue me; all day long they press their attack. My slanderers pursue me all day long; many are attacking me in their pride. When I am afraid, I will trust in you. In God, whose word I praise, in God I trust; I will not be afraid. What can mortal man do to me?"

The reader looked up and smiled. "Deputy Barnhill, how good to see you. Come sit with us, please."

Drawing an envelope from his breast pocket, Charley sat down and handed it to his sister-in-law. "Janey, Irene sends you this letter."

"How's my dear sister? I miss her so much. How's the coming baby?"

"She's well and hopes you will answer her letter."

"I will. The rest of my family has disowned me; only my mother and my dear sisters and brother stand with me. They are too young to be full of guile as the older people are."

He watched her face as she read the single page. The two sisters looked so much alike. They were only two years apart in age. How different Janey's life would be if her husband was hung. He prayed that this would not be the outcome for which they were waiting.

A figure appeared on the porch. "Those waiting for the Burrow case, the jury has asked for clarification of a point. If you wish to hear Judge Parker's explanation, he will be in court shortly."

He turned to the woman. "This is a favorable sign. If the jury has a question, they must not be set on a unanimous verdict."

The three of them moved into the court room and sat down on the side behind the defense attorney's table. The jury filed in and the foreman handed a written question to the bailiff who passed it to the esteemed jurist.

"The jury has asked for clarification of when self-defense can be properly claimed." Judge Parker began his explanation. "It is claimed by the defendant in this case, that what he did he had a right to do, that he acted in the defensive and not in the aggressive, that he had a right to kill William Morgan. If he had that right, of course, he must get it under the law, for none of us have any rights outside the law."

You are to see whether at the time of the killing the deceased had the means to execute a deadly purpose . . . and whether or not, under the circumstances, the defendant could not have avoided that condition or whether he could have avoided it by the exercise of less violence than he exercised. If it was danger that the defendant could avoid by running away or by apology, he must do so. This is called the law of necessity."

The men nodded their heads in understanding and retired back to the deliberation room. Another jury was in the commissioner's hearing room undertaking deliberation and filed in as the Burrow jury moved out.

Judge Parker's courtroom

It was eight o'clock in the evening when the bailiff stood on the porch. "The Burrow jury is in."

Charley squeezed his sister-in-law's hand and helped her up the stairs. Her face was pale and her lips drawn. He prayed as he led her to the bench. *Lord, please have mercy on this family.*

In silence the bailiff handed the paper to Judge Parker. Charley watched

DuVal nod to his client in assurance. Louis sat with bent head, his young face masked by the hair across his forehead. Sandels' rigid face was unreadable. Parker appeared as professional and neatly attired as when he had come from his home at 7 a.m. that morning. He glanced at the fateful slip of paper and handed it back to the bailiff who placed it in the hands of the foreman.

Every person present held their breath as the foreman read the verdict with dignity and solemn pronunciation. "We the jury find the defendant, Louis Burrow, guilty of murder as charged in the indictment. G.W.R. Smith, Foreman."

Charley put his hand out to steady Janey as she slumped down on the bench, her face buried in her hands, only eighteen years old and soon to be a widow. A murder sentence was a mandatory hanging unless the President of the United States intervened.

"The sentencing for this defendant will be announced at a later date. Court is adjourned." The sound of the gavel filled the court room as the spectators murmured amongst themselves. Some cast glances of pity at the defendant and his young bride.

Charley's mind raced, his tired body yearning for a soft bed. Two families so close and precious to his beloved wife devastated by two guilty verdicts in one week. He hoped the Lord would intervene. Louis was too young to face a gallows.

Recreated Gallows at Fort Smith National Historic Site

Chapter 41

Justice Denied

Abe Barnhill moved up the stairs of the jail building, his left knee rigid, clinging to the rail with both hands. He and Charley had spent most of September in Fort Smith with the Burrow and Morgan cases. It was his turn to face the questioning of a prosecutor. The United States vs. William Frazier was starting today, September 27, almost a year since the shoot out in which Abe had nearly lost his life. The trauma of that day in October 1887 came back in a flood of memories: the smell of gun smoke, the shrill call of frightened horses, the force of the bullet that had torn through his left leg just above his knee, the buckshot that had shredded his right ankle, constant pain to remind him of the affair. He smoothed down his hair after he removed his hat and stepped into the court room, Charley close behind. The eyes of the spectators followed him as he found a seat. Their faces showed curiosity and sympathy. Some of his friends from the Marshal's force were there, their hand shakes and greetings expressing a hope that justice would be served.

He grimaced as he located his adversary at the defense lawyer's table. It was the first time he had seen him since the shoot out. His stomach tightened as his eyes went to the emptiness of Bill Frazier's left sleeve. Frazier stared back at him with hard, hate-filled eyes. Was he himself also full of hate for the man who had crippled him for life? He had thought long on the teachings of the Bible to forgive an enemy since this incident. Frazier was his enemy. Could he forgive him?

The bailiff called the court to order as Judge Parker climbed to the great mahogany desk. Here was a man who had the best interest of the prisoners that appeared before him always on his mind, weighing their interests against those of society. He stated that the men whom he saw were "young men or boys, whose character was not yet formed, whose moral traits had not yet become sufficiently strong to dominate the mind, largely criminals from surrounding circumstances."

In Abe's mind, there was a no more fair-minded jurist than Judge Parker. His reputation as a "hanging judge" came from eastern newspapers who used yellow journalism to advocate other political appointees over the esteemed judge who was there for life.

D.A. Sandels began his case by calling Abe to the stand. After being duly sworn, Abe sat with his hands resting on the well-worn arms of the chair. His eyes ranged through the crowded court room before resting on the great barristers face. He had spent many minutes in this chair but now it was personal. He tried to focus on the prosecutor's voice ias he began to speak nstead of Frazier's face. "Deputy Barnhill, what are the circumstances that transpired in October of last year leading to your life-threatening wound?"

"George Williams and I and two posse men were looking for Bill Frazier. A warrant had been out for his arrest for over a year without any result. We were determined not to come back to Fort Smith without him."

"What happened then?"

"We located him at his home on Black Fork Mountain."

"Can you summarize the events for us?"

Abe's thoughts rushed into his head, the sensations and memory of the fight threatening his ability to speak. He had replayed what he would say many times. "Williams spent several hours parleying with Frazier from the front of the house in between rifle shots coming out of and going into the house. I was covering the back when Frazier burst out limping with a leg wound. He caught me in the ankle with his shotgun then came at me with both six guns blazing. I managed to hit him and knock one pistol out of his hand. He wouldn't stop. He charged at me and fired again catching me in the opposite leg. I fell back unable to move waiting for him to finish me when one of the others hit him in the arm. He was pretty well shot up when he stumbled off into the brush."

"Did your men offer him a chance to surrender before the gun fight began?"

"Of course. His answer was two rifle shots that almost took my head off before Williams sent me around behind the cabin."

"Thank you, Deputy Barnhill." Mr. Sandels returned to his desk, walking with a relaxed gait.

The defense attorney, his prim and proper stance in sharp contrast to his opponent's casual demeanor, started with a question. "What was William Frazier's charge on the arrest writ?"

"He was wanted on two counts of assault with intent to kill and the original count of larceny from two years prior."

"Who is he charged with attempting to kill?"

"Deputy George Williams, Deputy Charles Barnhill and Deputy John Lee."

"Would it surprise you if I told you the defendant feared for his life at your hands? He felt he would be shot and killed before reaching Fort Smith because the charges of assault with intent to kill were against three deputies."

"He would have been given safe conduct if he had surrendered - we're not executors."

The defense attorney switched to play on the sympathy of the jury. "The defendant was shot several time during this fight. Is that normal? One wound should have stopped him."

"Some men will give up after the first near miss, but others will fight to the death. The defendant showed no sign of putting his weapons down."

"The defendant also received a very serious wound in the left arm. This seems like over kill when disarming a fugitive."

Abe pointed at Frazier. "That wound is what saved my life."

"Thank you, that is all I have."

Abe stepped down and attempted to walk away with dignity, all eyes on his impediment. His jaw tightened as he walked passed Frazier, who smirked.

The next witness called was George Williams. The young man with the freshly tanned face smiled at Abe as he walked forward. The bailiff offered the Bible for his hand and the oath was taken.

"Deputy Williams, you were a participant in the arrest of William Frazier in October, 1887?" Sandels began.

"Yes, I was."

"Did you see the defendant fire at the posse members?"

"Yes, we caught him inside his cabin where he commenced firing at us from the front window."

"Who was the one that disabled him?"

Williams' firm voice did not waver. "Many shots were fired. When I'm in a gun fight, I try to keep my head down so it stays on my shoulders."

"Did you or any member of the posse call out to the defendant to surrender?"

"The answer was bullets flying over our heads. I parleyed with him for most of the afternoon hoping he would surrender. "

Sandels turned and walked across the room to stand in front of the jury as if a spectator. "Tell us what happened after Deputy Abe Barnhill was wounded."

"I left Barnhill in the care of the two posse men and went after Frazier. I hoped to get him before dark. Found him unconscious lying under a tree about a quarter mile from his place. He was bleeding severely and I administered care to stop the bleeding."

"Did you seek medical care for the prisoner?"

"I sent for a buckboard to transport Deputy Barnhill to the doctor in Poteau and then sent the doctor out to tend to Frazier. I was afraid he would die if I moved him very far."

"Did the defendant have a chance of survival?"

"I didn't think so and neither did the doctor, but once he got here to the jail he was operated on and pulled through eventually due to the good nursing of his wife."

"Thank you, Deputy Williams."

Sandels was replaced by the defense counsel. Abe watched the man as he flicked his coat back and inserted both hands in his pockets. He stepped forward and stood about a foot from Williams.

"Are you positively sure the defendant is the man you saw at the front window?"

"Yes."

"How far away were you at the time?"

"Maybe twenty-five yards." George answered, his eyes never leaving the defense attorney's face.

"Was there smoke in the air?"

"Yes, there usually is in a gun fight."

"Then, how can you be certain the man you saw firing was the defendant?" The defense attorney was questioning the credibility of one of the shrewdest, bravest lawmen in the Territory.

Deputy Williams began to rise in anger. Abe watched with admiration as the young man controlled his strong emotions and answered in a calm, polite voice. "It is the same man."

"Could you have taken this man into custody without shooting him to pieces?"

"No. He was unwilling to put down his weapon until it was shot it out of his hand."

The defense counsel was reluctant to leave the subject. "I thought it was the policy of this marshal's office to try to capture outlaws without injury. That's all I have for this witness."

He showed his true power of oratory when he approached the jury for his summation. "Yes, William Frazier participated in a gun battle with officers. But he was not sure who they were when they approached the cabin. It could have been another band of desperadoes that he feared. Inter-gang rivalry is common in the Choctaw Nation, each bandit pitting his wits against his competitor. There are two groups of men out there in this unholy struggle, the bandits in gangs and the lawmen in their posses. Each group goes to sleep at night dreading the possibility of the next deadly encounter. How could the defendant know these were lawmen even though they claimed they called for his surrender above the den of the battle? I think you will agree with me that the penalty the defendant paid in his wounds is sufficient enough."

District Attorney Sandels rose and approached the jury of twelve men, a mix of white, black and one Chinese. "You men are to judge the defendant on the basis of what happened according to the witnesses, on the established facts of this case, not on the basis of what the motive was when the defendant fired on the lawmen. His firing was an assault and the severity of the gun battle shows that it was with one intent, to kill the lawmen who faced him. Should he get away just as the Wesley Barnett gang did after murdering Deputy John Phillips and posse, Billy Whitson, and the Hodgen gang after murdering Deputy Trammel? You have no other choice but to find him guilty as charged."

Within the hour the jury was back in the box. "We find the defendant, William Frazier, guilty as charged of assault with intent to kill of Abe Barnhill."

Parker looked at the defense table. "Do you have anything to say regarding this verdict?"

The defense counsel rose. "Your honor, because of the nature of the defendant's wounds, many in this community feel he has paid his debt to society. I am, therefore, filing an appeal to the President for clemency."

Judge Parker addressed the court. "I will withhold sentence pending the appeal. Court is adjourned."

Abe's head rang with the word, "clemency." What had happened? Frazier was guilty as charged. Why did he deserve clemency? This man had tried to kill him. Maybe the Lord could forgive him, but could he?

> Fort Smith Elevator, October 5, 1888 "Wm. Frazier, assault with intent to kill was also convicted. His offense was resisting arrest, which resulted in his shooting a posse named Barnhill in the leg, inflicting wounds which will render him a cripple for life, but at the same time Frazier was shot several times. He was brought here and placed in the jail hospital, where his left arm was amputated and also two fingers of his right hand. He finally recovered and gave bond. He was charged with larceny when he resisted the officers, and after being convicted of assault, was tried on this charge, the jury acquitting him. He will likely be pardoned, as a strong effort will be made in his behalf. His devoted wife, who stayed at the jail and nursed him all through his long suffering from the wounds received, has been here with him all through the trial, and when committed to jail last Friday was permitted to share his quarters with him. She says she will not go home until she takes him with her. Such devotion is deserving of some reward, and will likely secure her husband's liberty in the near future."

The afternoon session of the court the following Friday, October 5th convened at 2:00 p.m. The bailiff made an announcement at the door of the court room. "The afternoon session is in order. The case is the United States versus Moses Taylor, the charge rape. Because of the nature of the testimony to be given, no one will be allowed in the courtroom except those called to testify at this time. Once the victim, a minor girl, has testified, only men will be allowed back in the court room. Thank you."

The crowd murmured as the bailiff checked identities off the witnesses list before allowing them to pass. Charley and Abe greeted Davis House and Irene's uncle, Anderson Holman, as they were let through the door.

Holman placed his hand on Charley's sleeve. "How's Irene doing? My wife wanted me to ask after her niece."

"She's fine, the baby should be coming along in about six weeks. I've moved the family here until she has the baby. I want her near a good doctor and hospital."

The rest of the spectators sat down in the hall to await admittance after the testimony of the victim. A few women, visibly disappointed, were taken outside by the men in their company.

A young girl came to the front, escorted by her mother who sat down in the front row after her daughter was sworn in.

Charley's eyes dwelt on the slim figure, the promise of womanhood evident in her form, young breasts firm under her dress. He judged her to be slightly older than his own daughter. He could understand the anger of the mother toward her husband at this vile act. The court had already hanged two rapists, but rape was hard to prove unless the victim showed signs of gross physical assault.

She identified herself in a soft voice, glancing sideways at the defendant who sat sullen and unmoving.

With a fleeting glance at his witness, the D.A. turned to the spectators and motioned with his hand. "Miss, these people are all here to help you and see that justice is done. Take your time and tell us what happened on the day in question."

The victim's face flushed with fear but her voice was steady. "Moses had started for his work in the cotton field when he sent my brother on and returned to the house. I was washing dishes. He caught holt of my arms and threw me on the bed and he pulled up my clothes around my waist. He tried to hold my legs apart with one hand and hold me down until his full weight was on me. My kicking him prevented him from hurting me. He told me to hold still. When he got up, he told me to hush crying and he hit me one lick across the face with his hand."

Sandels placed his hand on the rail in front of the witness. "Where was your mother during all this?"

"She was over at my aunt's about half a mile off milking. In two or three minutes after Moses left, my mother came in. I said nothing about it that morning."

"Why didn't you tell your mother about this attack as soon as she came home? And what about you face where he struck you?"

"I was embarrassed that a man would treat me so and was afraid she would blame me. I had put a wet cloth on the welt on my cheek and it had subsided somewhat. I kept my face turned away so she would not see it."

That evening, I was crying and my mother asked me what I was crying about and I told her the way he had treated me. She commenced shaming the defendant and asked him what made him do it and he said 'Nothing but god-damned meanness.' After I told my mother, I went out to get some milk and defendant caught up to me beside the chimney and told me if I did not keep my damned mouth shut, he would spread my damned brains on them rocks."

Sandels interrupted. "Has the defendant every tried anything like this before?"

"No, but I've noticed him eying me when I have had occasion to be alone with him"

After Sandels sat down, the defense attorney moved toward the witness. He reminded Charley of a hungry coyote who had just found his meal, his narrow slits for eyes resting on his helpless prey. "How old are you?"

The girl shifted her eyes to her mother than back to the man before her. 95
"Cannot tell you when I was fourteen, I am fourteen though, have been since the winter."

Charley knew where the attorney was going, trying to prove the girl was of the age of consent. His stomach tightened as he listened to the testimony. This guy might get off.

"Why did you not scream for help?"

"There was no one to hear if I did."

"Did the defendant do anything to hurt you physically?"

"He was holding my hands behind my back and trying to get my legs apart. When he threw me down on the bed, I told him to quit. I was not used to being treated that way."

The attorney turned his back to the witness. "That is all."

The D.A. pulled a jumble of documents across the table and shuffled through them. "I call Robert Higgins."

Higgins held his hand up for the Bible then sat down with a nervous nod of his head toward Charley and Abe. " All I know is just what defendant told me. He started to his work and came back to the house, that he took holt of her and shoved her back on the bed and tried to do what he intended but gave up in hopes of another opportunity. He was afraid his wife would come in. He told me this after he was arrested. I had just come up to where the deputies were camped."

The district attorney had only one question. "How long have you know the defendant and what is the reputation of the victim?

"I have known the defendant about 18 months. Have never heard anything against the girl."

Mr. Sandels turned to Judge Parker. "I have no further questions for this witness. The court rests its case, Your Honor."

"In that case, the defense may call their first defense witness," Judge Parker replied, his kind features now very stern from the testimony he had heard.

Charley put his mouth to Abe's ear. "This guy is going to be let go."

Abe's face darkened as he stared at Taylor a few feet away. "I wish the girl had more witnesses to back her up. Her bravery in testifying after his threat should not be ignored."

The questioning of Owen Fuller was brief. "Do you have personal knowledge of the victim's character?"

"On one occasion prior to this incident, I was in a corn crib with her. She proposed to me to have illicit sexual intercourse with her and I took her up on her offer."

Sandels stepped forth to get in his lick. "Mr. Fuller, by so admitting sex with this girl, you have testified to committing statutory rape with a minor."

"I . . . I guess I must have been mistaken. Maybe I just wanted to take her up on her offer."

After Sandels' treatment of the last defense witness, the next witness, George Schuck, looked around at the court room with wide eyes and gaping mouth. The defense attorney approached and reassured him with a smile.

The defense attorney turned to look at the girl. "Mr. Schuck, what can you tell us of the character of this prosecuting witness, the victim?"

"She proposed to live with me as man and wife without benefit of marriage."

"What about the mother of the victim?" The attorney was on a vicious attack now.

"I saw the mother of this girl break up some glass. She put it in some butter and sat it on the table for the defendant to eat. I think she is trying to kill him and get his tribal allotment."

Charley knew this trial was hopelessly confused now. No guilty verdict could be rendered with such accusations unchallenged. He spoke to Abe in a low whisper. "I hope the D.A. has this covered."

Sandels cleared his throat as he stepped forward and stared into Schuck's eyes. The man wavered and looked down. "Did you tell the defendant about this?"

"Yes, he laughed and said I must be drunk."

"And the offer of living with you?"

"I told her she was too young and needed to stay home."

Sandels turned to Parker. "I wish to recall the victim for cross-rebuttal of the defense's testimony."

When the girl was seated the illustrious prosecutor made a sweeping motion into the air above his head, as if swatting at an invisible opponent.

"Now, miss. You have heard the testimony of these witnesses. Have you any explanation to offer?"

"Mr. Fuller did not get it right. He asked me to lay with him in that corn crib and I refused. As for living with Mr. Schuck, I'll do anything to get away from that man." She pointed at the defendant.

The defense attorney, his smug disposition less assured, called his next witness. "I call Anderson Holman." Anderson sat down, glancing at Charley and Abe. The Burrow trial had familiarized him and Davis House on the protocols of the court room. He appeared to be relaxed and cooperative.

" Do you know the prosecuting witness, the victim?"

"Yes, I live near Childers Station, I.T. In that community, her virtue and morality are judged as bad."

"How can you prove that accusation?"

"She works in my cotton fields and the men tell me of her loose ways."

The defense attorney smirked as he sat down. The D.A. jumped up and motioned toward the defendant. "Has the defendant every spoken to you about his step-daughter or his wife?"

Holman hesitated, his face reddening. "Moses stated he wished he could get in on some of those offers his step-daughter makes since his wife never fulfills her wifely duties in bed."

The defense attorney had another question after Sandels sat down. "Did the defendant say anything about his marriage situation?"

"He was thinking of divorcing his wife and marrying the girl."

The defense was finished, having shown another side of the case to the jury. It was now up to them to decide who to believe.

Charley and Abe left for supper and then sat in the shade of a great oak tree, napping. Charley sighed. "The sun sure feels good. This is the most rest we've had in months."

When eight o'clock came and no verdict had been established, Judge Parker called the jury together. "Have you the ability to reach a verdict in this case?"

The foreman stood to answer. "We stand at eleven for acquittal and feel that we can make that unanimous. We have a question. If the defendant did attempt the act, but was unable to complete it, does that mean rape did not occur?"

"Yes, rape requires completion of the intended sexual act to the degree of the man's anatomy entering the woman's body. Otherwise, it is known as sexual assault with attempted rape. It is similar to murder versus assault with intent to kill. The act must be completed. Otherwise, the capital sentence of death that goes with rape is not warranted. Currently, the federal court has no jurisdiction in charges of attempted rape."

"Thank you. We should have a verdict first thing tomorrow morning."

"Very well. You are dismissed for the night until 8:30 a.m. for a final verdict."

The next morning as the first order of business, Judge Parker looked at Moses Taylor. "Please rise for the verdict" he instructed the defendant, as he passed the paper back to the foreman.

"We the jury find the defendant, Moses Taylor, not guilty of rape as charged in the within indictment."

The girl collapsed into her mother's arms, whimpering and crying. The mother fixed her eyes on the jury foreman and spat in his direction.

October was turning out to be as busy in the court as September. Charley rode up to the jail house the next week, his second trip of the month. In a show of Federal authority he had been sent after three prominent Choctaws, Peter Conser aka Coinson, Nail Perry and Henry Huntubbee. They could have presented themselves to the court when the indictment for an eleven year old murder of a white man named Williams was known, but they had chosen to make the court come after them. Charley had been asked for by the Choctaw Tribe since he was known and trusted by its leaders. All three had surrendered to him without interference.

Peter Conser, half-Choctaw, who lived in LeFlore County, was the most prominent of the three, an Indian deputy sheriff at the age of twenty-five, later assigned to the Choctaw Light Horse under Chief Jack McCurtain. He had been part of the "arresting posse" that had murdered Charles Wilson. The particulars of the present incident was that a man named Williams had been killed in a robbery and then buried, his horse killed, disemboweled and then sunk in a deep hole in the Poteau River.

Peter Conser (AKA Coinson)

He flung the warrants on the Chief Deputy's desk, on top of a large diagram of the new jail that was spread out from corner to corner. "Here they are, the three Choctaw leaders you wanted me to bring in. Abe's taking them to the jailer as we speak. Being men of means, I'm sure they will be out and home before I am."

Barnes frowned. "To keep them in jail for very long would be an insult to the tribe. That's just the way it is."

Charley tapped the warrants. "They get freed without delay but Louis Burrow who was finally granted bail of six thousand dollars in July was too poor and sat it out for two years."

Barnes stroked his chin in an absent-minded gesture. "This may cheer you. Tyner Hughes is out right now looking for Bob Benton and Simon Carshall, charged with accessory to murder in the same case. Those murderers of Deputy Wilson can't seem to keep out of trouble." He pointed to the cell layout. "We have one hundred seventy men in jail, the most we have ever had in a jail designed to hold only hundred and forty-four with two to a cell."He reached for the warrants laying in the middle of the diagram and put them in his box. "How's Abe doing after the face to face with Frazier?"

"He's not vindictive but when someone shoots you, punishment is important. His injury is a daily reminder of what happened. He wants to see the man sentenced. But that's not our job, is it?"

"No, I'm glad too. Judge Parker is a fair-minded man with a gentle heart. He punishes to the degree the law requires and no more."

Charley knew he was right. "Vengeance is mine, sayeth the Lord. How many times have I heard my father preach on that verse? Leave the punishment to the great Judge in heaven. Well, I'm worn plumb out. I'm heading home. "

The Chief Deputy waved him out the door. "Try to be back for Burrow's sentencing in a couple of weeks."

Chapter 42

The Sentence

Nothing was clear to her husband. Irene could see the tension playing along his jaw. He sat across the kitchen table from her sipping a cup of coffee. "The deputies are fighting an uphill battle, like trying to dig out a sand dune with a tablespoon. The pace of arrests and the murders of three deputies has made us all jumpy."

She rose and laid her hand on Charley's cheek and kissed him with tenderness. "You're just tired. It'll clear up after a few days rest." Her full belly now extended past her breasts and she had to stand on her toes to reach his lips. "I know how you feel. I still can't believe my sister is facing widowhood and my Aunt Mary two years alone while Uncle John's in Little Rock."

He looked at her intently before replying. "I brought in fourteen murderers this year just to see five of them released. The most disgusting case is Peter Conser and five others charged in an eleven year-old case and just released for lack of evidence. A man who poisoned his wife was let go when the witnesses refused to appear and testify, out of fear of what he might do to them. The old negro, Jesse Lewis, was released for lack of jurisdiction. The Choctaws have him in custody now."

"You've done your duty. That's all you can do," Irene said.

"You're right, of course. Feel like a drive or are you too uncomfortable?"

"I'll be fine. I'll call the children to get ready."

Enjoying the pleasant elixir of cool air and sunshine on her face, Irene smiled up at her handsome husband beside her on the wagon seat. The children giggled in the back, throwing pebbles at the ducks squawking along the road near a pond. She tried to imagine what it would be like living with him when they were both old and gray. When her beauty had faded, would he remember the past with regret? She knew her anxiety was caused by feeling fat and ugly just before childbirth. Her mother had warned her of such feelings.

"Darlin', what would happen if I got old and ugly?" she teased. It was a trap, of course. No husband could safely answer and keep his good standing.

"The Lord says beauty is in the eye of the beholder. I behold you as beautiful no matter what shape your body is."

She relaxed and tried to think of more pleasant things. She worried about the coming baby. Would she be able to safely deliver a healthy infant? Of course, why not. Just relax and let God have control. Put you fears away, Irene.

"We've a warrant for the arrest of three brothers, Abe, William and Frank Lewis, on a charge of assault with intent to kill. " Charley handed the paperwork to Abe who scanned the complaint for particulars.

"Will we be back in time to hear the Louis Burrow's sentence?"

"We've a week. We'll be back."

The road to the Lewis' family home south of Skullyville was just a rutted pig trail. Charley had dug so many outlaws out of this section of the Indian Territory, he could not keep track of them. Must be a few hundred by now he thought as they picked their way up the hillside toward a spacious log cabin nestled against a tree line. A pack of barking curs challenged them at the path about fifty yards out. A man stepped from the cabin, rifle held down beside his leg.

The man yelled through clenched teeth. "Gee on out of here, you doags!" To emphasize his command, he chucked a large stone at the leader, catching him right behind the ear. The dog yelped and the whole pack turned tail to dive under the porch.

"Good throw, there, mister. Appreciate you callin' them off. Our horses might've kicked one in the head." Charley smiled but kept his eyes on the rifle that was still held down. "I'm United States Deputy Marshal Charles Barnhill and this is my brother, United States Deputy Marshal Abe Barnhill. We're looking for the Lewis brothers."

"I'm their Pa. They're here about somewhere. We knew you'd be lookin' for them They won't cause you no trouble."

The man went to the door and hollered. "Ma, call them youngster out of the barn. The deputies are here to take them in. They'll be safe now."

Charley dismounted and tied his reins to a porch pillar. Abe stayed mounted, his hand resting near his rifle against his right leg. His stiff left leg made it better to stay put unless he had to get down. From there he could cover Charley if anything went wrong.

Three young men came around the side of the house, their hands already up in the air. "Don't shoot, deputy. We're all here," said the tallest one as he craned his neck to look around the yard. He was about twenty-five, with long uncut ringlets sticking out from behind his ears. A mustache covered his uneven teeth, but the smile was pleasant and his tone cooperative. "Where's your posse men?"

"It's just the two of us. Why?"

"The fellas we tangled with are right mean. Bushwhacking is not beyond them."

"Why did they file a complaint instead of bushwhack you?"

"The complaint came from a friend they sent to Fort Smith. They're still hanging around waiting for us to come out. That's why we're hiding in the barn just now. Wasn't sure who it was coming when we spied you down the hill."

"Alright, put your hands out for these cuffs. You'll have to walk down the hill to our wagon out on the main road. Have your ma get what you want to take with you. You may be in jail a day, a month or a year." Charley chained them together in line, the rope leading to his saddle horn. Abe fell in behind, shotgun resting lightly across the saddle.

Appearing from around the wagon that was parked along the main road, Jimmy met the prisoners, securing their chains to the wagon rungs with practiced ease. The peaceful country side suddenly erupted in gun fire. The first bullet hit a wagon wheel, sending splinters into his face.

"Get under the wagon," Charley ordered. Dust flew as the prisoners crawled under the wagon bed on their bellies. Jimmy knelt down behind the wheel and returned fired with his Winchester, covering Charley and Abe as they kicked their horses and rode into the trees. Dismounting and surveying the road, Charley could see muzzle blasts coming from two locations.

"Abe, you stay here We gotta get these shooters on the run and quick." He ran low, his rifle held down by his left leg, maneuvering his way around the road to the west. Abe's fire increased, covering his approach. He picked out two men, one kneeling behind a tree to his left and one on his belly to the right, both about seventy yards. Not having a clear shot at either one of them, he fired and saw the dirt kick up near the legs of the figure to his left. The man turned and tried to conceal himself behind the tree. Charley pumped four shots into the area as quickly as he could, not trying to aim. The intent was to run the bushwhackers off.

The outlaw yelled to his partner and gestured with a wide sweep of his arm. They sprinted for their horses, Charley's rifle shots kicking up dirt at their heels. The Winchester was getting hot when he heard the click of an empty chamber. Keeping in the shelter of the trees, he moved forward, his Peacemaker in his hand. The barrel of his pistol rose with each discharge. The fleeing men threw two shots his way that went wild over his head.

Dust was all he saw as they disappeared over the ridge into the forest. He refilled the chamber of his pistol as he walked back to the wagon, his rifle tucked under his left arm.

He surveyed the battle ground. "Is everyone alright?" Notches of wood were shot out of the wagon bed and the water barrel leaked around a bottom band. Jimmy was picking slivers out of his left hand.

"We're OK. Who were those hombres?" Jimmy asked.

The oldest Lewis brother answered. "The men we had the fight with, more than likely. They're not scared of deputy marshals unless they're outnumbered. You sure got them on the run."

Charley's ears still rang from the shoot out, his pulse racing and his hands limp as he grasped the bridle reins. That was too close. He was glad those guys were not better shots.

"Did you hear the latest on Sam Wingo?" Chief Deputy Barnes took Charley's warrant for the Wilsons and went into his explanation without taking a breath. "The Paris,Texas jury where the trial was sent to prevent conflict of interest found him guilty of assault with a deadly weapon in shooting the fugitive, Lyons. He was sentenced to sixty days in jail and a $250 fine."

"What? That's crooked. Why do local judges try to pull down Judge Parker's men with such frivolous charges? Wingo's a good deputy and wouldn't shoot unless he was forced to."

"That's not the end of the story. Wingo decided he wasn't going to take that kind of treatment, and escaped from custody before he could be locked up. The shoot out was pretty hot but no one was hurt and he's still at large."

"What about his hearing with Tyne on the murder charge from January?"

"It's scheduled for November 8th."

Charley pointed to the roster laying on the desk. "I notice you have an entry there for Ann Martin."

"She was charged with larceny after the murder charge was dropped and sentenced to six months in Little Rock. Her lawyer appealed to Judge Parker to take another look at the case. He changed the sentence to sixty days in the Fort Smith jail· She is a lucky young lady. The judge has a heart for women in jail."

"I hope she learns something from all this."

"Not likely with that kind." Barnes turned back to his desk duties as Charley disappeared.

It was Saturday, November 3, 1888 as they sat in Judge Parker's court room once more. The high-windowed room was filled to overflowing, the crowd anticipating the sentencing of three murderers: Louis Burrow, William Sorder and Richard Smith. Louis sat with his attorney at the front table, his young face pale and solemn. His little wife, Janey, clung to the arm of his father, Lorenzo Burrow, the two of them seated a few rows back near the door. Beside them sat Mrs. Burrow, son Reuben and daughters, Luvinia and Francis. The other two defendants were seated with their lawyers behind Louis. Charley sent up a silent prayer. *Dear Lord, have mercy on this young man. He deserves to die under the law, but he is so young. Give him time for his lawyers to appeal to the President.*

The assembly rose as the esteemed judge walked to the platform at the front of the court room. He settled into the high-backed oak chair and swung himself into position. His desk was covered with the court work scheduled for the day, everything neatly arranged according to the order in which each case would be heard. He picked up the top file.

"Louis Burrow, have you anything to say why sentence should not be passed on you?" the kindly voice of the judge asked.

Louis and his lawyers stood. "I have something to say before you pass sentence." The young man spoke in a voice so low that Charley strained to hear. "There are only two things I regret in my case. I wish I had not placed any of my family on the stand during my trial though I know they did it out of love and concern for me. The other is that my father raised a family of six boys and up to the time of my unfortunate difficulty, none of us have ever gotten into trouble. I regret exceedingly that I should be the one to place a blot on the pages of the family history. That's all, your honor."

Judge Parker held the sentencing document in his hands. "With nothing else to be offered, having been found guilty of murder, I sentence you, the defendant, Louis Burrow, to the mandatory sentence to be hanged by the neck until dead, date of the execution scheduled for the 25th of January 1889. However, many citizens of Fort Smith along with myself and District Attorney Sandels support the petition of your sentence to President Cleveland for his consideration. That is the only recourse allowed under the law."

Judge Isaac Parker, the year he was appointed 1876

A sigh ran through the court at the death sentence. The possibility of commutation or dismissal seemed to be the popular sentiment of the citizens of Fort Smith. Janey's face was grim as she looked at her young husband but now there was a light of hope in those eyes which had been so dull since the September day he had been found guilty of murder.

The Barnhill brothers rose and walked to the Burrows. Charley offered his hand to Mr. Burrow. "I pray the appeal will be granted. He deserves it. I hope there is no hard feelings about me and Abe arresting him that day. It was our duty."

The gray-haired patriarch, his head bowed in grief and despair, mumbled, "There is none, Deputy Barnhill. You are an honorable and honest man. You must do your duty as sworn under the law. Louis' fate is in the hands of the Lord, as it has been all along." He placed his arm around his sobbing wife and beckoned to the children.

Charley walked outside with his brothers. "We have two prisoners to pick up. You go home and rest, Jimmy. Abe can go with me. I want to be back for Tyne's grand jury hearing scheduled for the 8th."

Charley put his hat on and watched Jimmy took the steps two at a time. *That boy must have a girl? What else would make a young man run home?*

Chapter 43

Tyner's Day in Court

The November 1888 session of court for the Western District of Arkansas had already started when Charley entered the courthouse. Leaves had long since left the trees with barren limbs spreading into the gray overcast. The wind kicked the dry piles around the bottom steps of the white porch as he ascended and opened the door leading down the hall to the courtroom.

His slap on the shoulder caught Tyne's attention. "Howdy, Mrs. Hughes, partner. Where's Sam Wingo?" Tyne sat with his wife on the bench outside the grand jury room, his lawyer beside him, busy looking over the notes from the commissioner's hearing.

Tyne's face crisped up into a smile, but his eyes were solemn. "I hope he appears. He's already in contempt of the Paris circuit court. Marshal Carroll will have to dismiss him from the deputy force; he's too good of a man for that." He looked toward the door in anticipation.

Charley frowned at the thought. "He should come. The longer he's out, the harder it will be on him. As soon as this is over, I have to head home. Irene is due to have our baby real soon."

Charley recognized Little Charley, the owner of the home where Long George had been killed. Little Charley's wife and sister-in-law pulled their shawls around their shoulders, shy eyes peering from under their bonnets. Everyone jumped when the doors opened and the bailiff called Little Charley. An interpreter who sat near by escorted him into the hearing room. The interpreter played a key role and Judge Parker was patient to allow all the time needed for Indians to speak in such a manner.

He tried to offer comfort to his friend. "I hope that Creek Indian has a long memory. Since Black Tiger killed his brother for helping you, I'm sure he wants justice."

Tyne scratched at his chin. "The Creeks are reliable and honest. However, when it comes to talking in a white man's court, they are intimidated by the unfamiliar customs. A simple grunt to them conveys multiple meanings."

Was there a faint glimmer of hope in his friend's eyes, the first that he had seen since this case had begun? "Well, partner, this will be over soon and you have right and truth on your side. Remember that."

The dilemma his friend faced, charged with murder in an attempted arrest that had turned into a gunfight, could happen to any deputy. He knew he could take another's life to defend himself, but shied away from pulling leather like Deputy Bud Ledbetter and other trigger-happy lawmen. So far he had been shot three times. How much longer could he avoid the fatal error of complacency that cost so many deputies their lives?

The door remained closed for nearly half an hour. The attorney began to fidget with his watch fob, but stopped when he noticed Charley's glance. He cleared his throat and spoke. "Deputy Hughes, I feel that this case will fall through. The commissioner should never have passed it on to the grand jury. If these witnesses tell the truth, you will be cleared before the day is out."

"What if they don't?" Tyne asked. Matttie grasped her husband's hand and clung to it. Tears pushed at the sides of her eyes.

"We will petition for other witnesses to be brought in to back up your position. I feel it won't be necessary."

They turned as the door opened. Charley caught a glimpse of the grand jury through the door frame. They looked tired. How long had they been trapped in that room? The interpreter beckoned for Mrs. Little Charley to come in as her husband slipped out. The little Indian sat down without a glance at anyone in the hall, leaned his back against the wall, and tipped his hat down over his face.

Mrs. Little Charley was in the room only a few minutes before she was ushered out and her sister called in. She mimicked her husband, sitting down quietly and propping her body against the wall in a relaxed manner. She bent her head down allowing her bonnet to shield her face from any further inspection.

Charley was anxious to know what they had said, but knew he could not ask. He prayed silently under his breath as he tried to relax. *Lord, you know my partner, Tyner Hughes. He is a hard-working, honest man with the courage of a lion. He goes out every day and risks his life for truth, honesty, and justice. Help him against false witnesses. Let your promise of an honest man being a savior to his neighbor be granted. Amen.*

Tyne sat unmoving, his eyes riveted on the hearing room door, his normally tanned features pale. Mattie suppressed her sobs with a kerchief.

The other woman came out of the hearing room and sat down beside her family. They talked briefly with the interpreter, who indicated through hand gestures that they were free to leave. They rose together and walked out single file. Charley knew it would be a long trip home for them, taking several days to get back to Stonewall in the Creek Nation.

Tyne looked at his lawyer. "Well, what do you think?"

"I'm confident it will be dismissed. I had a long talk with the District Attorney before the hearing and that was his take on the case," the man answered.

Before the words had cleared his lips, the door opened. The foreman of the grand jury came out and beckoned to the lawyer. As they stepped back into the room, Charley knew the firm hand of justice was about to be revealed. Would it weigh in the favor of truth or in the favor of libelous men who used every opportunity to discredit the court and its officers?

They got the answer when the smiling face of the lawyer reappeared as he hurried through the door. He walked briskly up to Tyne and pumped his hand up and down. "You're free to go. The grand jury ignored the case as having no merit. The witnesses testified to the same facts as your posse members - that you never even took your gun out of the holster and that Long George was firing on the posse when he was shot."

Tyne grasped his lawyer's hand, a smile spreading across his handsome face. "Thank you very much," He winked at Charley as he helped his wife to her feet. They strolled out of the court house arm in arm, free from the threat that had hung over them for nine months.

Charley went upstairs to Carroll's office. He found Chief Deputy Barnes staring out the window at gathering storm clouds. "Looks like winter's coming early." He gestured at the piles of warrants spilling out of his in-box. "How many of these can you handle?"

"None. I need the rest of the month off. My wife's expecting our first baby any time now."

"It's a cold time of year for a new-born. I hear you have a house here in town. Does it have gas heat?"

"Yes, Irene will be spoiled while she's here. I couldn't see her staying out in Krebs, a hundred miles away from a decent doctor. We've never lived in town and I like the amenities, but its too noisy."

Barnes chuckled. "Well, enjoy what you do like while you're here. The grand jury is looking at those sisters you brought in, the McCanns. They've been out on bail for some time, but it looks like they'll probably be indicted and have to surrender."

"Don't give me that job again. Those two are a handful for any deputy. They tried to seduce me and Jimmy with their talents, if you know what I mean."

"Wow. If I was a young fella' again, that would be a tempting offer. What was wrong with Abe's appeal to those women?"

"Guess they don't like shot-up deputies."

Barnes lowered his eyes, his throat filling with a hoarseness uncharacteristic of him. "On another matter, I have unpleasant news. Abe will be disappointed. President Cleveland has unconditionally pardoned Bill Frazier."

Charley felt his throat constrict and his fists tighten.

"What? Though he tried to murder me, Lee and Williams and shot Abe twice. I guess they don't consider him much of a threat with his injuries. But he has his gang and can still order them around as his arms."

"I know, but everyone felt sorry for his loyal wife."

"Abe and I have loyal wives, too. Where's the consideration for them when they were almost made widows by Frazier?"

"I know, Charley. Let's hope he stays out of trouble now."

"Time will tell. I just hope no one dies at his hand, in the meantime." He hitched up his gun belt and stomped out the door. *Frazier on the loose again. Who would be his next victim?*

Trying to shake the unpleasant news from his brain, he rolled a twig between his teeth and stared at the low winter sun in the southwest. Another year would soon be upon him and his brothers. Would it be filled with suffering, pain and danger for his fellow lawmen or would the tide of criminal aggression be beaten back? Then a familiar scripture entered his thoughts.

> *Matthew 6:34 - But seek first his kingdom and his righteousness, and all these things will be given to you as well. Therefore do not worry about tomorrow, for tomorrow will worry about itself. Each day has enough trouble of its own.*

He knew if he should meet Frazier again, it would be by God's design and he had nothing to fear of the future. His responsibility was to go home and live each day with the knowledge that his future was in God's hands, not man's.

Chapter 44

God's Blessing

Billie's rhythmic gait ushered his rider through the silence of a midday Sunday along Garrison Avenue. Fort Smithites on the way to or from church paused to stare in shop windows, the holiday colors drawing them to contemplate a silver turkey serving tray or a colorful rocking horse with braided mane and glistening leather saddle. Deputy Charley Barnhill shifted his weight and raised his hat in response to a few friendly waves.

The big horse was thirteen years old but still as strong as a three year-old, despite nine years of negotiating steep hills and brush-shrouded ravines. What type of mount would he get when Billie got too old for riding these trails? A youngster, fifteen hands at least, that he could train to suit his needs. Comanches taught their horses to stand stock still when a rifle was fired from between their ears. A gun shy horse could get his rider killed.

"Well, ole' boy, let's go home. You deserve a bucket of oats. I think a couple more years of this and Henry can have you."

1888 had been a tiring year in the marshal's service. Most deputies only survived two or three years, driven away by low pay, hard field conditions and the constant threat of being killed. Would another ten years bring peace and prosperity for his friends and neighbors? He prayed it would be so.

He had many blessings including a young wife about to present him with a new son or daughter. Child birth was natural and usually without complications, but the anxiety he felt in his chest made him pray for her and the unborn child as he rode.

It was Sunday, November 18th. The Baptist church yard held numerous buggies and saddle horses. He could hear hymns as he rode by. The Methodists worshiped in a similar-looking church a few blocks to the east. He reflected on the devotion of men who had dedicated their lives to missionary service among the Choctaws and had moved with them into the wilderness of the Indian Territory in the 1830's. They had chosen to live and die with their beloved congregations. Fifty years later these were a temperate, peaceable people who fought daily against the whiskey runners and their ruinous drink.

He turned his eyes down the road to the west, catching a glimpse of the roof of his rented two story house which lay off the main road on the west side of town near the Frisco railroad. Smoke ascended from the chimney in the still air. Billie pricked up his ears as his nose caught the familiar scent of home.

"Come on, boy, we're almost there," he said, more to himself than to the horse. He rode into the back yard and pulled the saddle off Billie, leaving him to graze with just the bridle. Throwing his saddle bags on one shoulder and his Winchester and shotgun under each arm, he opened the door with a free hand. As he laid the bags on the floor and the weapons on a bench by the front door, a squeal of delight greeted him. Minnie had caught sight of her father standing in the doorway.

"Pa, I'm so glad to see you." Minnie was growing into a beautiful young woman, the strong resemblance to her mother evident in her long hair and curved lips.

Before he could hug her in response, Irene appeared at the kitchen door. "Darlin', you're home." She ran to him and threw her arms around his neck. With a child present and watching, she chose to give him a tender kiss on the cheek, rather than the passionate one he was yearning for.

He held her at arm's length. The baby had grown and now took up most of Irene's front, discretely concealed under a maternity smock. She was not tall and the size of the baby made her appear wider than her lithe teenage form suggested. He ran his hand over her apron, feeling the tenseness of the muscles and the moving baby underneath. "Wow, that baby is ready to come out."

"The doctor was by yesterday and says any time."

"How's the good doctor doing? Only time I see a doctor is when I'm shot."

"He gives you his regards and will come by again tomorrow. Come look at the size of the chicken that's baking. I figured your Sunday home-coming deserved a chicken since we have plenty. I sold some to a neighbor last week."

He sniffed the pleasant aroma as Irene opened the oven door. Hot coals kept the kitchen toasty this time of year. The past summer in Krebs she had cooked on a fire pit in the lean-to behind the house that opened to a sun arbor.

"Beautiful. Where's Henry?" He looked around the room.

"At church with some friends. I think he has his eye on a girl in his Sunday school class."

"Thirteen is the age boys start to tolerate girls and quit pulling their pigtails."

"Is that what you did?" Irene laughed.

"Of course. A preacher's kid has to show courtesy towards all members of the church, especially the young, pretty girls." He pinched her cheek. "I'm going to wash up and then have a nap in front of the fireplace while dinner is fixing."

He sighed as he unstrapped his .45 and hung the belt and pistol above the bed. He shrugged off his boots next struggling against the stiffness of his old wounds. Thirty-seven and he felt fifty. How long could he keep this up?

After dinner, the family sat before the fireplace in the front room. Irene tended to the knitting in her lap. "Look honey. I'm making a baby blanket. It's just about done. " She held up a pale yellow blanket just about the size of her lap.

"It looks warm. I've an offer to make you. I saved all the baby clothes Salina made for our babies stored in her trunk. Would you like to use them for our baby?"

"Of course. I didn't know you still had them. It would be a wonderful memory of Salina to use something her hands made in love."

He rose to locate the trunk. "It's in the loft above the bedroom." He had placed it there when they moved back from Krebs and had forgotten about it until now.

As Irene squealed with delight at the new treasures, he watched her hands move over the tiny pieces of cloth. The trunk revealed a little laying- in blanket, tiny booties knit out of soft white thread, thin cotton gowns trimmed with tying ribbons, a white bonnet, a long christening gown and much, much more. She hesitated briefly and grabbed involuntarily at her stomach.

"It's just a sharp pain; I've been having them intermittently for the past week." Irene smiled, reassurance in her eye.

He lit up his pipe and relaxed. It was a rare day when he could just relax.

"I told Barnes I want the rest of the month off so I can be here while you have the baby." He tapped his pipe on the heel of his boot dislodging the burnt tobacco into his hand.

Irene paused in her examination of the tiny clothes. "I received a letter from Janey. She is most grateful that you were present for Louis' sentencing. She has exciting news. While his lawyer has appealed to the President for a pardon or change in sentence, something good has come out of that execution date. As the wife of a prisoner awaiting execution, she will be allowed to stay over night with their husband in the jail any time she wants to before the execution date. They have a special room back by the jailer's office for such purposes. It has solid walls and a locking door that allows privacy for the occupants."

"I've seen it many times. In fact, Mrs. Frazier used it for weeks when William Frazier needed nursing. Now that he's been pardoned, it's empty."

"That evil man who tired to kill you and Abe? It should be disinfected before using it after the likes of those."

He put his arm around her. "Now, Irene, don't be petulant. Frazier will get his proper reward one day."

"I know God doesn't always work on my schedule. I think I'll go rest for a while," Irene sighed as she arose from the floor and put the soft little baby things away in the trunk. She clung to the railing as she climbed the stairs to the second floor bedrooms.

He let his thoughts wander as he watched Henry and Minnie play checkers in front of the fire in the fading evening light. This time of year it was dark well before supper time so they usually had a cold supper of gruel, left over ham or chicken and bread. He prayed for their future. Would he die in his own bed or in the dirt of some lonely cabin? Soon or twenty years from now? He was grateful God hid the future from him.

He was stirred out of his thoughts by Irene's sharp shout from the top of the stairs. "Charley, it's time. Get the doctor." He jumped to the stairs, dropping his pipe on the rug.

Irene stood in the bedroom doorway holding her abdomen. "I've been fighting labor pains all day. I can't contain them any longer. Send Henry for the doctor and start some water heating"

Oh, brother. How do women manage to do this year after year?

The doctor arrived from his residence within the hour, his shirt hastily stuffed into his pants and his vest unbuttoned. His wife, who was an experienced midwife, stood close behind him carrying a bag and several bundles of cloth. He looked at Charley and winked. "Don't worry, Dad. This is as natural as falling off a stool for the womenfolk." Charley followed them into the bedroom.

His young wife lay still, the bed clothes in disarray, her hair loosened from its hair pins. She looked at the doctor, relief sweeping the fear from her face. "I've never had a baby before. I hope I'm doing alright."

The doctor pulled the covers from her abdomen and pressed gently on the area."Just relax and we will help all we can. How frequent are the pains?"

"Every few minutes, but they seem to last longer."

"Mr. Barnhill, get the hot water you have prepared so we clean her up and get the area sterilized." He turned to his assistant who pulled the side table toward the bed and covered it with a clean white cloth pulled from her bag. Charley's face whitened as she started laying out sharp-looking instruments. He did not want to think about their use.

After delivering the pot of boiling water to the pair, he kissed Irene on the cheek and stepped to the door like a prisoner bolting for freedom. He could hardly wait to get away.

Henry and Minnie sat in front of the fire, both of them trying to concentrate on their school work. Minnie looked up. "Dad, is she alright? She won't go away like Ma, will she?"

"No, the doctor and his wife will take good care of her. We can help by bowing our heads and praying for Irene and the baby." The little family gathered their hands together in prayer as he talked to the Mighty One, who gives life and takes it away.

Dozing in the armchair outside the bedroom several hours later, Charley roused with a start as the doctor opened the door.

"You are the proud father of a healthy baby boy. Young Mrs. Barnhill did just fine and is resting now. You may go in and see them."

He rose to his feet and brushed pass the doctor. Irene lay in the feather bed, a quilt pulled up around her cheeks, a tiny head poking out from the covers. She opened her eyes as he approached.

"It's a boy. What shall we name him?" She offered the tiny bundle and he picked the baby up with care, his hands trembling under the light weight of the little fella who weighed less than his six-gun.

"It's been a while since I've held something this little. Is he alright, I mean, is he all there, fingers, toes, everything in place?"

"Yes. The doctor can find nothing wrong. He's normal."

"I think we should name him Tony. You pick his middle name."

"What about Harrison after our new President? "

"Well, that's better than Jefferson Davis or Ulysses Simpson Grant," he said.

Irene lowered her eyes after he passed the baby back to her. "I feel kind of tired. The doctor says I can get up as soon as I feel like it."

He leaned down and kissed her check. "I'll send telegrams to everyone first thing in the morning."

Irene smiled, the soft features of her face blending into the pillow. "Amanda and Abe are going to have a baby soon, too. I hope it goes well."

He brushed Irene's cheek with another tender kiss as she closed her eyes. Her smile faded only after her soft breathing indicated she was asleep. The baby nestled quietly in her arms, his little face pressed against her bosom. He tip-toed out of the room and closed the door. A wonderful blessing of life. Another son. He could only imagine the future he would have in this great country.

Chapter 45

Christmas in the Deputy Force

Winter marched into Arkansas from the Indian Territory, rattling the door of Charley's comfortable home in Ft. Smith. One of the newer houses, it had four bedrooms on the top floor, running water, in-door bathrooms, gas heat and a full basement. He could only afford it on a deputy's pay because it belonged to a friend who needed to rent it. He would miss these modern city conveniences when they returned to Krebs in the spring.

His mind wandered and his hand fidgeted with his gun belt as he cleaned and oiled the leather. At home since little Tony's birth three weeks ago, he knew he would have to make a trip soon, but the rest had revitalized his mind, soul and body. Billie wanted an outing. Every time he went to feed the big horse, it nuzzled his bridle, which hung alongside the corral gate.

"I'm going to the office. Do you need anything from downtown?" He spoke to Irene who sat across the room in front of the fireplace, the infant nestled in her arms.

"I need 2 yards of white ribbon to finish the dress I'm making for Minnie for Christmas. Just tell the clerk it must be one-half inch wide."

"Alright, I won't be gone long." He put on his coat and stepped to the door. Blowing her a kiss, he went out into the brisk morning air.

Billie nickered a greeting. His ears twitched back and forth as he watched his master's every move, like a dog waiting for a bone. The big roan pranced to the gate and pushed against it with his muzzle.

Charley inspected his saddle as he buckled down the straps, noticing the worn leather seat; he needed to get it to the saddle maker before he went on any long trips.

The pile of papers on the desk was an obstruction between him and Marshal Carroll. The chair squeaked as Charley sat down and shifted his boots underneath the legs. "I came as soon as I could. I appreciate the time off with my new son."

Carroll smoothed down his long gray beard and shifted his gaze. "A lot has happened over the weeks you've been off. Deputies Salmon and Rusk cornered the Barnett gang. One of the young men in the posse, Moses McIntosh, was killed in the confrontation. Even though he was an Indian and was killed by an Indian, it has become our jurisdiction because he was a duly sworn posse man."

"I read about that at the barber shop," Charley said. "Creeks get mean when they mix with the Cherokees."

"Four of the gang members are behind bars, but the worst ones are still in hiding with a $400 reward for each of them. But I need you on another case. Here is a writ for William Harding who surrendered himself after a fight. He was released on bond because the wounds seemed minor, but the attacker just died. Bring him in."

"Yes, sir. " Charley stuffed the paperwork into his vest and started for the door. The sooner he got this one, the sooner he could enjoy Christmas at home.

As he rode home, he wondered how best to tell Irene that he had to leave. Some men were born with a wanderlust that drew them to far places, but he felt torn away from his hearth each time he had to leave. On guard always analyzing the dangers to himself and his posse, he needed the respite of home.

Billie stuck his nose in the bag of oats measured out for him. The young palomino colt that Charley had bought to start training trotted up for his ear-scratching. It knew better than to try to horn in on Billie's feeding. Billie had travelled many a mile. How many horse shoes had he worn out in his years of marshaling?

After hanging his hat on the rack in the hall, he moved across the front room to place a kiss on the top of his wife's head and to nuzzle the cheek of the sleeping infant. Before the fireplace warming his hands, he took time to pack and light his pipe as he watched the older children through the door to the kitchen. Henry filled up the wood box in preparation for cooking supper, stacking the evenly cut logs across each other in layers. Though the house had gas heat, it had a wood cook stove. Maybe one day, gas stoves would be affordable and safe. Henry flicked a piece of bark at Minnie as she peeled potatoes and turnips. She stuck out her tongue.

"Is there anything you need from the basement?" Charley asked.

"No, darlin'. I'm making venison stew and I have all the fixin's close by."

She was an excellent cook for one so recently married. Young girls acquired the skill at their mother's side feeding large families. Her bread was the best he had ever tasted with flour from a local mill run by a friend.

He paused. "I picked up some arrest papers while I was in town. I have to leave tomorrow morning. I should be back by Christmas Day." He expected a negative response, but Irene smiled.

"I knew you would have to leave soon. Tony is old enough now and I can do more. My mother and sister want to come up and stay for Christmas week," she said.

Charley gave her hand a soft squeeze and looked into her eyes. They were beautifully formed pools of gray flint. He knew he would never get tired of looking into those eyes.

Jimmy Barnhill held the reins of the horse as Charley assisted the prisoner to dismount. It had taken them only two days to make the thirty miles pver and back from Cowlington northwest of Spiro with their cooperative prisoner. Sunday, December 23rd, 1888, was rainy and overcast, most folks staying in doors. He mounted with the reins of the other horse tight in hand and made his way across the yard to the stable where prisoner's horses were held there for family to pick up.

Jimmy did not like to be in a hurry because hurrying could get you killed, but he had a yearning to get home to his soon to be fiancee, Alice Bowers. He had purchased a simple engagement ring at the jeweler down on Garrison Avenue on his last trip to Fort Smith. If she gave her consent, he would announce their engagement at the New Year.

Her father had already given his blessing. The Bowers were an old family in Fort Smith and knew the character of most of the young men in the area. Even though he lived in Krebs, his work with the marshal's service brought him here monthly.

Riding back to the front of the jail building, he wondered what was delaying Charley. A quick turn in of paperwork and then out the door should have been all there was to it.

His older brother finally came out of the door that led through to Marshal Carroll's office. His face was rigid with thought. Jimmy's anxiety got the best of him and he blurted, "What now?"

"The Marshal wants as many prisoners rounded up as possible before the end of the year so he leaves his replacement with a full jail. We're to be on the look out for any liquor violators who are taking advantage of Christmas celebrations. He's interested, in particular, in one fella in Poteau who buys enough liquor for his whole town to celebrate Christmas. We'll head there tomorrow."

Jimmy shook his head. "Supper and a good night's rest will make me feel better about all this. I need to pick up Alice a Christmas present." He was startled by the gold piece that flipped out of Charley's hand towards him. He caught it in midair.

"What's this?"

"Get a present for Alice."

"Alright!" Jimmy kicked his heels into his horse's flanks and sped out of the court yard down Garrison Avenue.

Under umbrellas the few citizens braving the driving rain watched the two lawmen ride by. They waved and smiled. "Merry Christmas, deputies."

A good part of Fort Smith's economy was derived from the esteemed court who offered employment as guards, deputies and posse men and required the services of livery, hotel, stores, lawyers' offices and clerks. Though the good citizens decried the public spectacle of the executions, it was generally understood that the court brought much-needed government money to the growing community.

When they reached Poteau on Christmas Eve, the citizens were celebrating in full force. Long lines of Indians jammed the main street waiting for an old Indian who was unloading six gallons of whiskey. Seeing the deputy's badge on Charley's chest, he flung a tarp over the gallon jugs, but not before they had spied the incriminating evidence.

"Hello Uncle Ike. What you got there?" Charley said.

"Just some fixing for the holidays."

"Looks like whiskey to me. I have no choice but to arrest you. You go on home and spend the night with your family. I know where you live so don't try to run."

"I won't, Deputy Barnhill. My wife's going to take a skillet to me for this." The old man grumbled and shifted his weight. "I guess the good Lord knowed what I was up to."

Christmas Day presented the same drizzly sky. Jimmy spread his yellow slicker over his horse's haunches in a vain effort to keep his back dry. His thoughts were self-centered at the moment, unlike him. Why was he here and not on a parlor sofa with his intended? He shook his head and said a quick prayer, "Forgive me, Lord. I know I am not the center of the Christmas season. Your Son is."

The old Indian had appeared promptly at day break in front of their hotel. Indians were as good as their word, not making promises lightly. They had him delivered to Fort Smith by noon.

"Alright, Little Brother, let's go home." Charley smiled at him and kicked Billie into a steady gait.

Jimmy hoped New Year's would be quieter as he thought about Christmas and the life of a lawman. Crime never stops; it was around when the Holy Babe was born in a manger so long ago, the Holy One who came to save the criminal from his sinful deeds. The efforts of modern men to rehabilitate the criminal were a failure. Only Christ could do that. He knew of prisoners who had been sentenced to Little Rock or Detroit and had come back changed physically. But the outside still covered a sinful heart. His father's ministerial efforts and those of the local pastors who visited the prisoners in their cells were what counted in this fight against crime, teaching neighbors to love one another as Christ loves mankind.

May Your Life shine out in me and my family this Christmas Day and throughout the year to come. God Bless Us Everyone.

Chapter 46

A President's Mercy

Marshal John Carroll sat at his desk in the Old Jail, not really focusing on the pile of writs. He liked this part of his job, one of the few rewards amongst the somber tasks he faced every day. His gaze shifted to the yellow form in front of him. Held loosely in his hand, the telegram was good news for two men who faced a hanging on a cold January day. President Cleveland had commuted the death sentences of Louis Burrow and William Sorder; Burrow to ten years and Sorder to life. He smiled as he stroked his long gray beard.

He turned in his chair to gaze out the window of his office at the broad yard of the Old Jail overlooking the Arkansas River. In the four years he had held this office, he had spent countless hours wrestling with problems and analyzing the activity in the jail yard. Today, the rain kept sensible people indoors. Yesterday had been the beginning of the New Year of 1889, one celebrated with particular enthusiasm by the Fort Smithites. The city was now a metropolitan center with modern sewer facilities and bricked roads. Jay Gould, the railroad tycoon, planned to build a double bridge across the wide Arkansas River, the upper level for his railroad and the lower for wagons, horses and pedestrians. The current population of 18,000 was expected to double in five years. He turned from the window and chuckled to himself as he picked up and read The Elevators' description of the Christmas celebrations in Fort Smith last week:

> *"Christmas Festivities - The Christmas festivities came and went just as of old, except that this year, instead of a frosty morning and bright, clear day, rain fell heavily from sunrise till sundown. The dampness had the effect to keep a majority of our people indoors, and many spent the day at home in peace and quiet, when otherwise they would have ventured 'down town to see what was going on' and came home with tottering steps and thick tongues."*

His thoughts turned to the newly-elected Republican President Benjamin Harrison. As a Democrat appointed by Cleveland, he knew his Republican replacement would be named shortly. He prided himself on the efficient office he had run for four years, keeping expenses down while his clerk maintained an accurate record in his accounting book. Tragically, eighteen deputy marshals, posse or guards had been killed in the line of duty in those four years. He sighed heavily as he heard footsteps approach the door to his office. Could he end his term without another deputy being murdered?

At the sharp rap on the door, he called, "Come in." He smiled as he faced the two tall men that entered his office. They were dressed in the typical deputy garb, yellow rain slicker over a wool jacket displaying a badge that said 'Deputy Marshal I.T. United States', shirt and vest, trousers, knee-high boots with spurs, a Colt .45 on a waist belt and a broad-brimmed hat. Each man had a handle-bar mustache that hung down either side of their mouth. Similar in age and facial features, these were some of his best, the Barnhill brothers. He stood up and greeted the two men with a handshake. "Thank you for coming in to see me, men."

"What can we do for you, sir?" Charley asked.

"Since you were the arresting officers for Louis Burrow and you, Charley, are also his brother-in-law, I felt you should be the one to escort him to my office. I've notified the jailer to get him ready for an appointment here in fifteen minutes. Here's my instructions for his removal."

"Good news, sir?" Charley asked, pointing at the telegram on the desk.

"Let's say, it's a belated Christmas present."

He watched the two men turn and start out the door in eagerness. He chuckled as he met the eyes of Chief Deputy Barnes seated at his desk in the outer office.

Charley addressed the Chief Deputy as they stepped out of the Marshal's office. "We're to pick up Louis Burrow and bring him up here."

"Turn in your Colts. I'll give Abe a shotgun to back you up." Barnes turned to the rack of rifles and shotguns behind him and picked one, handing it to Abe.

"I've got my own on my saddle outside," Abe said.

"Take this one. You don't need to go out for yours."

Charley was in front as they descended the flight to the lower level of the new jail wing. Completed in 1888, the welcomed addition had space for twice as many prisoners. He paused at the main door to "Murderer's Row" on the lowest level.

A three story steel cage in the center of the building rose from the ground level where they stood. On each level twenty-four cells, twelve on each side of a brick wall, faced onto a four foot wide corridor called the "bull run" that went around the cells. Each cell, five by eight feet, contained two cots, one above the other. Outside the cage a seven foot space between the cage and the exterior walls allowed visitors and guards to walk around the cage without having to enter it. No one entered the "bull run" except unarmed guards and prisoners.

Outside the lower level gate, the jailer's desk was tunneled on either side with rows of pegs hung with leg and wrist manacles. No prisoner left the cage without shackles on wrists and legs.

He addressed the two armed attendants at the main door. "How many you got on Murderer's Row now?"

The senior guard answered. "Over thirty. We've had to put three to a cell."

Charley's nerves tightened at this. These were rough, desperate men who would resort to anything to escape. Bribery of a guard was not unheard of. "It looks pretty secure. Any jail break attempts yet?"

The attendant's face was placid. "Naw, this set up is escape proof."

"I'm here to pick up Louis Burrow. The marshal wants to see him." Charley handed the hand-written order to Jailer Pettigrew.

"We have him ready," said Pettigrew. "Most of the prisoners are in the bull run."

Charley turned to the senior guard. "Fetch him for us, please. "

The second guard unlocked the big door and let the other pass in and locked it behind him.

The deputies and the jailer walked along the outside corridor, Abe with his shotgun at ready, until they came abreast of Louis' cell.

"Louis, you ready?" Jailer Pettigrew asked.

"Yes, sir." Louis Burrow stepped out of his cell and faced the three men through the cage. "Hello, Charley, Abe. Good to see you."

"Let's go." The guard led him back to the main door.

As they passed the cells Charley saw some of the murders he had brought in. Shannon Foster and Pastor Joseph White played checkers in their cell. These church-going men had faced down a bully who had paid the ultimate price for his murderous gun play around them. They looked up and gave him a "howdy".

Nudging Abe, he said, "There's White and Foster."

"I hope they get mercy and not the gallows. They've been in prison long enough," Abe said.

The attendant unlocked the door and allowed Louis and his escort through, Abe standing by. No one opened or closed that door without two men present, one armed and standing away from the attendant.

Pettigrew affixed the hand cuff on Louis' right wrist which was then shackled to Charley's left hand. Next came the leg shackles on the prisoner.

"Sign him out on the jail log, then he's all yours."

Charley signed the log. "We'll have him back shortly. Thanks."

The two deputies stopped outside the marshal's office to catch their breath.

"You ready?" Charley asked the young prisoner.

Louis's faint smile showed hope. "Yes, sir. I'm ready to get the news, good or bad. Can I just pray for a second?"

The three men bowed their heads as the words came forth. "Whatever my fate, Lord, I am yours. Give me your peace. Amen."

Charley knocked on the door and waited for a response. He rolled his eyes at Abe and nodded at the shotgun. "We don't need that inside the Marshal's office. Leave it with Barnes."

"Alright." Abe handed the shotgun to the Chief Deputy and took a position beside the prisoner.

"Enter" came the command from the interior.

Carroll looked up from his desk as the three men entered the office, all wearing serious but hopeful looks. His gaze focused on the prisoner: Louis Burrow, age twenty-three, in jail two years and four months, model prisoner, helpful and obedient. Prisoner Burrow appeared pale but well-nourished and well-built without physical problems. This young man should live to a ripe old age now that the hangman's noose was removed. He cleared his throat as he began to speak.

"Prisoner Louis Burrow, I've asked you to come in response to a telegram I received from President Cleveland. He reviewed your case. It is my great pleasure to tell you that you will not hang on January 25th."

Louis sucked in his breath and let out a mumbled "Thank you."

"You are commuted to ten years at Little Rock prison. You will transfer there with the other prisoners in two weeks. In the meantime, you'll be allowed normal visitation from family and friends. Do you have anything to say?"

Louis dropped his head and wiped a tear from his cheek with his shackled hands. "Yes, I want to thank President Cleveland, and Judge Parker and Mr. Sandels who wrote letters on my behalf. I'd like to see my lawyers also to thank them for their efforts."

Marshal Carroll chuckled and extended his hand to the prisoner. "My congratulations to you." He nodded to the two deputies, who had grins as wide as their faces. "Alright, deputies, return him to his cell. Tell the jailer to give him an extra helping of dinner tonight. I'm sure he wants to celebrate."

As he watched the door close, he turned to the window and examined the beauty of the grounds. Though winter's grip lay on the grass and bare trees that reached into the gray sky, his heart was light. Another soul spared a terrible death.

His commission would soon expire. In the meantime, he swore he would use every breath to get the department into exceptional condition. His deputies continued to bring in prisoners as indictments came out of the grand jury. The Republican appointee, whoever it was, would find a well-run, efficient office.

Abe Barnhill turned to his brother and smiled. "Well, what do you think of that? Irene and Janey will be overjoyed."

"We've been praying for this for months. Irene's been so distraught that she can't sleep or eat. She wrote Janey and offered to be with her during the last week before the execution, even with a newborn babe in arms. I can hardly wait to let her know. " Abe saw his brother's eyes sparkling with joy. He prayed that '89 would be a year to redeem the Bloody Summer of 1888.

Arkansas River at Fort Smith

Chapter 47

Devilment in the Borderland

Abe and Charley negotiated their horses on the icy path in an effort to keep footing. Broken trees made the trail a frozen obstacle, branches covered with inch-thick transparent ice which clung to every twig, transforming the thick forest into a massive fortification. Winter was hard on United States deputy marshals and the men they hunted.

Abe pulled his collar up to near eye level. "Hope to see that ferry real soon. Wonder if the river is still flowing?" He felt the cold fingers of the wind whipping around his face and ears penetrating under his hat which was held on with a wool scarf.

A woolen Christmas scarf from Irene muffled Charley's answer. "Don't know. This time of year it could be frozen over. If it's ice-bound, we'll find a crossing farther down. Getting wet in this temperature would turn us into icicles."

Each man led pack mules loaded with camping equipment. Jimmy followed close behind the four prisoners held in their saddles by leather girdles with chains that affixed to each ankle and ran under the horse's belly. It left the prisoner at the mercy of the horse and thwarted all attempts to dismount and run.

Approaching the Arkansas River, Abe could see it flowing and the ferry making its way across from the city. Charley dismounted and unlocked the belly chains allowing the prisoners to move their legs in case of an upset into the water though their hands were still hand-cuffed.

He watched as Jimmy led the prisoners onto the ferry. They were responsible for their safety. If a prisoner bolted at this critical moment, the icy waters of the Arkansas River would kill him in minutes. A prisoner had recently attempted to escape from the Fort Smith jail and swim to freedom. He had drowned.

On reaching the other side, the four prisoners, eager to enter the warm confines of the jail, moved swiftly up the steps to the jail-house. The attendant met Abe at the main entrance to the cage. "What you got for me?"

Abe examined the faces of the two prisoners in front as they went through the door. They were familiar faces, boys he had known since they were too young to talk. "Elisha and James Harris, murder." He pointed to a bandage on Elisha's left hand and a bandage on the back of Jim's head. "See that the prison surgeon looks at their wounds." He jerked his thumb at the other two standing behind. "William Fillmore and Joseph Johnson, whiskey."

Pettigrew nodded at the whiskey runners. "Those go up on the third floor. I'll take these two to Murderer's Row. I don't know where I'm going to put them. We're already full and have been for months."

Charley listened to the tolling of the church bells as he walked into the Marshal's office. As soon as the new courthouse was finished later in the year, the Marshal would be relocated there and the jail staff would take over the empty space.

He dropped the writs on the Chief Deputy's desk. "We brought in the Harris boys from the fight over at Poteau and a couple of bootleggers. The two Harris boys are members of my Pa's church. They wouldn't kill a man in cold blood. There must be more to the story. They haven't talked much, but their pa says it was self-defense. Their other brother, Tommy, is in a bad way, shot through the back."

Barnes looked up from his writing. "It'll get sorted out at the hearing. I swear, the end of a marshal's term can be real trying for a man. Your four prisoners makes seventeen booked in three days."

"We're trying our best to clean up the Territory for the new boss."

"I guess you heard Salmon and Rusk cornered the Barnett gang near Okmulgee and killed the leader, Wes Barnett. Wiley Bear is still at large."

"That's a good way to start a new year."

Abe and Jimmy came stomping in the door.

Barnes spat into a tobacco can at his feet "You boys look like a couple of frozen rats. Warm up some before you leave. If you're in no hurry to get home, you can catch the trial of Pastor White and Shannon Foster."

Charley rubbed his hands before the pot-bellied stove. "We plan to stay around to see how that finishes and the Harris hearing."

As they walked out the door Jimmy hesitated at the porch. "I'd rather spend my time with Alice."

"We understand." Abe winked at him. "See you tomorrow."

The men started down the steps of the jail. A familiar figure appeared from the direction of the livery across the street.

Charley called out to the man. "Zack Moody, how you-all doing?"

The face of the approaching deputy lit up in recognition. Charley remembered the sad day so many years ago when they had buried Zack's brother-in-law, Deputy Marshal Willard Ayers, killed in Cherokeetown in 1880.

"Charley and Abe, howdy. I'm doing well. Got an arrest warrant for Saint

Lopka, one of the remaining Barnett gang. I figure I can flush him out of the Creek Nation if any one can."

"Well, take a good deputy to ride with you," Abe said.

"I'm hitching up with Grat Dalton. Ever since his brother, Frank, and I were involved in the shoot-out that killed him, Grat and his brother, Bill, have tried to fill Frank's boots."

"Well, good luck on your hunt." Charley said.

The commissioner's court was crowded. Hearings ran non-stop trying to keep pace with the trials in the courtroom next door. Deputy James Lee sat in the front row behind the prosecutor's side of the room, his gaze fixed on the commissioner's desk. He rose and greeted the Barnhills as they sat down. Abe found a place at the end of the row where he could extend his left leg, Charley and Jimmy beside him.

"How are you, Jim?" Abe asked.

"Thought I better see what was going on before I head out," Lee said.

Abe looked around the room before he replied. "It's not been a week since the murder and all the prosecuting witnesses are present. That's strange."

At the rapping of the gavel, all spectators sat down and the bailiff announced commencement of the hearing.

A finely dressed man sitting by the Harris brothers rose and bowed to the commissioner and the prosecuting attorney, Mr. Sandels. "I'm George Grace, representing the two defendants." The prisoners seated beside him wore plain white shirts and trousers tucked into boots. Their short brown hair fell over tanned faces.

Abe looked around the hearing room and nodded in the direction of the back row. "Mr. Harris is in the back," he said to Jimmy who turned around and peered at the spectators until he found him.

The commissioner commenced. "The charge is the murder of William Webb on January 15, 1889, a complaint filed by John J. Webb, father of the deceased, on January 16. Mr. Sandels, call your first witness, please."

"I call John J. Webb to the stand."

A thin middle-aged man rose from the bench and walked to the witness chair. After being sworn in, he sat down and squinted at the District Attorney. By the condition of his hands, he appeared to be hard-working. His clothes were a jumble, his tie loosely knotted at the collar of a rumpled white-tinged shirt. His jacket sleeves stopped two inches above the wrist and his pants barely reached to the top of his boots. His speech carried an Arkansas twang.

Abe listened to his testimony, watching his body movements. A fidgety disposition might be nervousness or covering a liar. The old man fixed his gaze on the prosecutor as he described how he and his four sons and two neighbors had met the defendants along the railroad track near Poteau Station. The man's eyes shifted to the defendants as he spoke, the hard glitter of hatred there for all to see. White knuckles grasping at the edge of his trousers bespoke an inner tension.

He pointed his finger at Elisha Harris and told how Elisha had pulled his pistol and fired three shots after which Jim Harris had jumped him to wrestle away his shotgun. His sons, Aaron and Willie, had gotten the pistol away from the attacker who then came at Willie with a knife as Tommy Harris stabbed Aaron in the shoulder. After his other sons got Jim off him, Elisha and Tommy ran away down the railroad track. It was then he noticed Willie was hurt. His son died within ten minutes.

"What happened to Jim Harris?" Sandels asked.

"I don't know which way he went as I was tending my son. I got my neighbor, Westfall, to go after a doctor, who said he was stabbed in the heart just one time."

"That is all I have for this witness." Sandels sat down.

Attorney Grace stepped up to the chair and looked into Webb's eyes. He stayed in that position for several long moments, examining the man from head to foot.

"Was anyone else injured?"

"Tommy Harris was shot by Elisha when he was firing. Afterwards, I went and picked up my shotgun, still loaded. My friend, Kitchen, got Elisha's gun."

"That sounds pretty bad," Abe muttered to Charley sitting to his right.

The District Attorney then called the sons, Charles, Aaron and Samuel Webb. Abe grew suspicious as he listened. Multiple witnesses often revealed discrepancies or omissions. The last brother to testify, Aaron, appeared unsettled. He spoke in clipped phrases, the words filled with emotion, eyes roving, hands clasping and unclasping in his lap. When finished, he rose from the witness chair and walked back the few rows to sit directly behind Abe.

A break in the one-sided testimony came with the first defense witness, Bill Westfall. He was about the same age as the defendants, early twenties. The bailiff approached him with a Bible which Bill covered with his long-fingers, the tips curling around the edges of the cover. After swearing his oath, he placed both hands on the chair arms as he settled into the hard wood bottom and then rested them in his lap.

Abe studied this young man's face, tan with a white forehead, a relaxed disposition of his lips, eyes roving the audience before settling on the defendants with a nod of his head. Abe had heard many witnesses testify and knew the other side of the story would come out. Which one was true? Only a jury could decide.

Bill Westfall refuted the Webbs' testimony explaining that Elisha had only drawn his pistol after Mr. Webb had fired at him with his shotgun, striking Elisha in the left hand, whereupon Aaron and Willie Webb had jumped him, wrestling the pistol loose. He could not tell that Willie had been stabbed or by whom during the fight. Jim Harris had been set upon by the other two brothers, one of them brandishing a claw hammer on his head.

When they quit beating on Elisha, he had run off. Aaron Webb then picked up Elisha's pistol and fired two shots at Elisha and Tom who was hit in the right side, the ball coming out two or three inches below the navel. He explained that Jacob Westfall, his uncle, and Samuel Webb later accosted him asking him to swear that Aaron did not shoot at the Harrises.

"Finally, we're getting to the truth," Abe said under his breath to Charley. Jimmy and James Lee nodded in agreement.

The District Attorney glanced at a paper on his desk and stepped across the floor to the witness. "When did this request to swear occur?"

"It was the evening of the difficulty outside the house just at dark."

"That is all for this redirect," D. A. Sandels said as he sat down.

Mr. Grace rose with a document in his hands. "I have the sworn statement of Thomas Harris. He is currently under the care of three doctors who wrote down and witnessed his statement. I request it be read in this hearing."

"Go ahead, Mr. Grace," the commissioner replied.

> *I, Thomas Wm. Harris, state and affirm that this is a true statement of the case which occurred between James Webb, Aaron Webb, William Webb, and Charley Webb and E.M. Harris and J.W. Harris. James Webb came up with a double-barreled shotgun and said 'Elisha, drop that pistol and drop it right now or I will kill you. You have been blowing around as long as I am going to stand it.' He drew his gun up in a shooting position and James Harris grabbed the gun and they both went rolling down the dump. Then William and Aaron Webb jumped on Elisha Harris and they got him down on his hands and knees. I started down the dump to help Elisha and Jack Westfall threw a rock at me and missed. He got another rock up but did not throw it. I did not see who shot me. I was shot when Jack Westfall threw the rock at me.*
>
> *Thomas Harris, his mark X*
> *J.B. Jones, M.D.*
> *R.H. Green, M.D.*
> *F.D. Askill*
>
> *Witnesses that heard Thomas Harris make statement."*

"Thank you. The statement will be entered into the written file," the commissioner said. "Does either attorney have further witnesses to call at this time?"

"None, sir," both parties replied.

"In that case, I order that James and Elisha Harris be remanded over for trial."

At the sound of the gavel closing the hearing, Abe heard a garbled shout from his left.

"You murdered my brother. I'll kill you!"

Catching sight of a rushing figure out of the corner of his eye, Abe raised his extended left leg catching the attacker just above the ankles. The man tripped, sliding on his chest, face striking the bottom of the railing that separated the spectators from the court.

Abe jumped on the straggler before he could rise. Fighting and struggling with the man, he recognized Aaron Webb. His strength was surprising for someone who had been stabbed in the shoulder a week ago.

Coming to his aid, Charley placed his knee in the middle of Webb's back, while Deputy Lee held down his thrashing legs. His grip straining against the attacker's shoulders and arms, Jimmy forced the prisoner's clenched hands together and slipped on handcuffs. Charley and Jimmy grabbed each arm as the man swerved and ducked his head. Without pausing for balance, the shackled prisoner lashed out with both feet at the men behind him.

A descending boot caught Abe just above the left knee. Immediate searing pain ran through his body. He didn't remember hitting the floor. He grabbed for the bench on his right and tried to rise.

"Are you alright, Abe?" Deputy Lee had both hands under his arm trying to lift him from the floor.

Felled by a hand-cuffed prisoner. How embarrassing. "Just let me get to my feet." As he put weight on his leg, he gasped at the biting surge of pain. He bent down to clear his head of dazzling stars and gritted his teeth to suppress the nausea rushing up from his stomach. "I think I'll be alright."

He glanced at the spectators bunched up in the far corner of the hearing room trying to stay out of harm's way. The commissioner and attorneys watched, surprise and concern on their faces. The Harris brothers sat unmoved at the table, their chairs turned toward the ruckus

The prisoner attempted to kick out again. Jimmy stepped behind him using his six feet four frame and put him in a head lock. Within a minute, the man ceased to struggle.

Abe limped after the other three who dragged the man out of the hearing room and turned down the hall that led to the second floor jail entrance.

His eyes wide with alarm, the guard at the door laid his finger along the trigger of his shotgun. "What happened?"

"This fella' wanted to add his opinion to the case and take care of the defendants himself," Abe explained.

The jailer opened the steel cage and followed the party through the door as the second attendant locked it behind them. The guard covered the group from outside the steel framework.

At the first empty cell, it took all of them grabbing the bars to hold the door shut as the prisoner lunged against it with his whole body. He rebounded back and attacked again with his feet.

His frantic eyes roved over the cell. "Let me out of here. I'll kill 'em."

Abe turned to the jailer. "Keep him hand-cuffed until he settles down. He'll likely be charged with interference with a court officer."

Outside the cage, the four men dusted themselves off. Jimmy had a bruise and scratches on his hands from struggling with the handcuffs. He sucked on the wound. Charley tucked in his shirt tail. James Lee ran his hands through his hair.

"I want to say good-by to Alice before we leave," Jimmy said.

Abe's head swirled as he heard Charley. "Alright. Meet us back here by two p.m. We need to get to Tyne's place by dark. He's waiting supper for us."

Chapter 48

Old Wounds and Good Friends

Charley and Abe had entered the courtroom after dinner to find the defense in summation. Pastor White appeared much debilitated. His once brown hair was streaked with gray and his beard patchy and ragged, sharply contrasting with his new white shirt and pin-striped pants. Shannon Foster, being a younger man, had weathered the jail confinement with less effect.

Their attorney had one hand hooked in his vest pocket, while the other pointed to the jury box. "Gentlemen of the jury, you have heard three days of testimony from two dozen witnesses in this case. Two vicious no-goods singled out for assault these quiet, shy men who interfere in no one's business. You should ask why? Joseph White is a preacher of God's word. Shannon Foster is an elder in his church. These devil's advocates were provoked by the good hearts of righteous man."

The lawyer paused for emphasis and gestured to the defendants. "What was their offense? Nothing. The renegade Holmes teamed up with a known outlaw, Sam Wells, to harass these two men beyond reason. On a quiet Sunday in July the fiends laughed as they fired at women and children. Relief came only when the drunken men ambled off down the lane, promising to come back and finish the job another day. What would you do?"

The defense counsel allowed the words to settle. His eyes moved down the row of men sitting in the jury box. "They sought the help of the local Indian policeman, Officer Ellis, who had already had a run-in with Wells, but Officer Ellis could not intervene. Next they sought the aid of United States Deputy Marshals Abe and Charley Barnhill."

He bent over and peered directly into the eyes of each member of the jury as he walked the length of the jury box. "They could cower in their homes or defend themselves when Holmes and Wells, armed with pistols, came to their house and demanded to talk. Wisely, the defendants ordered the men to put down their weapons. They knew that if they let Wells get to his gun, they would likely be killed.

"Well, you say, both men were unarmed. Yes, but they would not have been for long. These Bible-believing men fought for their lives against two professional toughs who had no qualms over who they might kill."

The men in the jury box shifted their eyes from the him to the defendants as the lawyer reached the end of their chairs and stopped in front of his clients.

"Would you shoot a rattle snake as soon as it rattles or wait until it strikes? They either had to shoot or be shot. The only fair verdict in this case is not guilty of murder. Thank you."

As he listened to Judge Parker's instructions to the jury, Charley wondered how many cases of murder Parker had instructed in his thirteen years on this bench? Hundreds?

"Let's pick up Jimmy and head for home," he said. He was startled at Abe's face, gray with pain. "What's wrong?"

"It's that mule kick from Webb - I can't walk."

"You can't ride home in this condition. Let's go to the hospital."

"Cracked femur just above the old break." The doctor's tone indicated he thought that was good news.

Abe groaned. "How long this time?"

"Six weeks in a splint. A doctor in Sallisaw can take the splint off so you don't have to ride back here. I'm sorry."

Abe tried to find something good in this. " Look's like I'll be home for the birth of our baby next month."

He came out of the hospital on crutches. Charley and Jimmy helped him on his horse and strapped the crutches on the pack mule.

"What'd the doctor say?" Charley asked. He had been over at the courthouse picking up arrest writs.

"Down and out for six weeks."

"Can you ride?"

"I'm full of laudanum. Just don't let me fall off my horse."

Charley scratched his head and thought for a moment. "I'll send Jimmy home for a rest after we pick up Rome Foyil for assault. John Phillips arrested him for horse-stealing back in '87. He hasn't been out of prison more than a month and he's at his old ways again. It's sad. He's only eighteen. "

"What about Foster and White?" Abe asked

"Hung jury, ten for acquittal and two for manslaughter. Their lawyer has changed their plea to guilty of manslaughter at the suggestion of the district attorney. Judge Parker is delaying sentencing in hopes of a pardon. They have been released on bail."

"I'm glad. They are law-abiding and just did what they had to do to protect themselves and their families," Abe said.

"Justice is supposed to be blind and it worked out this time. I'm ready for a home-cooked meal. Tyne is still expecting us for supper." Charley turned

Billie's head and urged him into a lope. Abe followed, his stomach growling at the thought of Mattie's peach cobbler.

Spiro, Choctaw Nation was just a grouping of houses near the more important community of Skullyville. A few sparsely placed dwellings lined the road that came from Fort Smith and then turned south into the interior of the Choctaw Nation. Tyne's house was near the center of the settlement.

A dog barked in the distance and a cow lowed to her calf in the darkening light of evening. With relief Abe saw the familiar dwelling. Every movement of his mare sent pain up his leg into his thigh. His jaw was sore from clenching his teeth.

"Hello, the house," Charley shouted as he reined in.

Tyne poked his head out the door.

"It's about time. Mattie was worried you wouldn't get here, but I told her you never miss a home-cooked meal."

Abe stifled a groan as Charley and Jimmy eased him down from the saddle. Tyne eyed the splint and pursed his lips together.

"What happened to you?"

"I was standing in the wrong place at the wrong time."

"A good plate of fried chicken with gravy and potatoes will fix you right up."

Tyne's son, Freddie, came scurrying in from his room, his eyes widening as he saw his father's friends. He ran to Abe's side and stared at the splint.

"Wow. Uncle Abe, how'd you get that thing?"

"It's a long story, but the short version is a sure-footed prisoner with long legs who kicks like a mule."

The young boy helped Tyne make a place for Abe near the fireplace, carrying in a crate from the wood shed to prop his splinted leg. His hostess fretted over him as she placed a pillow behind his back. "Now, Abe. Just make yourself comfortable. I'll get you a plate of food and you can eat right here." She was a kind woman and Abe could tell she loved to nurse those who needed it.

After the plates had been cleared and Mattie was busy in the kitchen, the men sat down for an evening before the fire to catch up on news.

Abe's eyes began to grow heavy as he watched the embers in the fireplace. He half-listened as Tyne spoke.

"I got a telegram from a sheriff friend of mine in Texas where Sam Wingo escaped after his conviction. He was picked up in Indian Territory and brought back to serve a two month sentence in a Texas jail away from his enemies in Van Buren."

Abe roused himself enough to speak. "I hope he gets that behind him. He was a good deputy."

Charley found time between puffs on his pipe to give his opinion. "Sam is an Indian and he didn't appreciate being tried and convicted in a white man's court for shooting a white man in self-defense while trying to make a legal arrest. And then to be sentenced to be held in a Texas jail for two months. He knew how he would be treated by Texans who are not disposed to any Indians. That's why he ran."

"He saved my life a number of times," Tyne said. "Hope he doesn't become bitter. Some lawmen, when unfairly treated, turn to the life of crime they fought."

Their hostess came in from the kitchen carrying a pile of quilts which she handed to Charley and Jimmy.

"You can make yourselves comfortable in front of the fire. Abe will sleep in Freddie's bed. He's too excited to sleep unless he is out here with you. He worships everything you say and do."

Abe appreciated the offer of the bed but felt embarrassed to kick out Tyne's boy.

"I'll be alright here, ma'am," he said.

"Freddie would consider it an honor if you would accept his bed. He probably won't let me wash the linen for a month afterwards."

"I can't let the boy be disappointed then. Hand me those crutches please, Jimmy."

Abe rose and hobbled into the small bedroom at the back of the house. It was simple but comfortable. He thought about all the nights he and Charley had slept on the ground and how many more were to come. He was grateful for the hospitality and hoped he could repay it in the future. In this wild country, travelers sought refuge with family and friends. Only the largest towns had hotels or inns. He vowed to keep his home available to all who came to his door.

Chapter 49

Death For Friend and Foe

The baying of blood hounds in the cold February morning sent shivers down Charley's spine. His eyes roved the Winding Stairs mountains for movement, missing nothing in their search. What was up there that required blood hounds?

"Could be a wild boar hunt," he said to Jimmy at his elbow. He guided Billie off the main road into the brush toward a group of men, one of whom he recognized as the Indian policeman from Skullyville County.

"Hello, sheriff. How're you doing, today?"

The leader waved his hand toward the hills. "Good day, deputy. We're tracking an escapee, Jesse Lewis."

"Jesse Lewis? I brought him in last summer charged with murder. How'd he get away?"

"When he was let out to exercise in the prison yard, he ran the instant the guard turned his head. Dogs couldn't find his scent after he swam the Kiamichi River. We'll search along the banks until dark."

"Well, good luck. I'll keep my eyes open as we head over the mountains toward Poteau." Charley tipped his hat and watched the armed horsemen move down the road.

Rome Foyil didn't look like a convicted felon. The youngster with a scar at the corner of his mouth which gave his lips a venomous twist stared at his grim-faced parents. His glittering eyes reminded Charley of the constant roving of a hungry coyote. Searching him for weapons, he could feel the firm muscles of a young warrior in his torso and limbs.

"Let's go, son."

The boy pulled away turning his back on his mother who dabbed the corners of her eyes with her apron. The old man kept his lips pressed tight, finally spitting out, "You mind the marshal, now, son."

Jimmy boosted the prisoner up into the back of the wagon. Foyil's family was too poor to own more than one horse; government transportation would suffice. The roads in the vicinity of Fort Smith were well- maintained and reinforced with rock by the local communities to attract commerce. This one skirted along the new rail line the New York millionaire, Jay Gould, had laid from Fort Smith west and south into Indian Territory. Reminiscent of the inter-tribal warfare caused by previous treaties, the Choctaw tribe's approval of the right of way had caused opposing faction violence at the recent county elections. The prisoner had used that disruption to steal himself a horse from a white storekeeper who was selling booze to the voters. Another man that needed hunting down.

The familiar hills around Skullyville appeared as the party came around on the main road to Fort Smith. Charley's eyes swept the landscape. Jesse Lewis was still loose and this was his territory. He may have doubled back and headed for home.

Jimmy pointed to a column of smoke that rose in a clearing ahead. "What do you make of that?"

Charley could see it was not chimney smoke, maybe a brush fire or a building. They approached a crowd assembled around a large mound of rubble, the structural beams of a large building still standing erect, without walls and roof - a type of destruction he had witnessed many times during the War of Rebellion as both sides had burned railroad stations, court houses and commercial buildings. It was unrecognizable as the fine building it had been.

His heart sank as he realized it was the Skullyville County Court House where he had been witness to so many trials and executions.

"What happened?" he asked a man standing on the outskirts of the crowds.

"Someone lit the court house off last night."

"Who would do such a thing?"

"The faction opposing the railroad had threatened to do this. Everything is gone: records, furniture, evidence."

"Wow! So how will the judge and sheriff pick up the pieces?"

"Outstanding cases will have to be reconstructed from memory. In the meantime, they will use the Girl's Academy."

"That's tough. Hope they catch'em," Charley muttered. The grin on his prisoner's face - was it "a job well done" salute to his friends?

Charley sensed it the moment he stepped into Chief Barnes office. A grim face, an air of depression. "Every time I come in here, I get bad news. What's it now?" He tried to judge the seriousness of the coming disclosure.

Barnes rolled a cigarette and placed it on his lips then patted at his vest pocket for matches. "Someone ambushed Belle Starr on the 3rd. Shot her in the back with a shotgun and then finished her off while she lay in the road. Her new husband, Jim Starr, brought in a neighbor claiming he did it."

"That's too bad. She was a wild woman and led a rough gang, but no one deserves that. You could never tell if she was going to run or fight. But she was always obliging to us when we did catch her."

Belle Starr's grave at Youngers Bend

"There's more." Barnes took a deep draft of his cigarette, exhaling the smoke through his nose. "Deputy John McAlister was shot in Purcell while he and his partner, Deputy Swain, were entertaining ladies. His wound was thought to be survivable, but we got a telegram from Heck Thomas that he died yesterday."

"And the shooter?"

"Swain and a posse chased him 70 miles onto the prairie and killed him when he tried to shoot it out."

Charley tallied up in his head what the loss of another deputy meant. Every vacancy put more pressure on the rest. Would the new marshal be given the funds by Congress to beef up the force? "McAlister will be missed. How's his family taking it?"

The edges of Barnes' lips twitched. "Pretty rough. There is no compensation, not even burial expenses when a deputy goes down."

In an effort to give Barnes some news of his own, he recalled the encounter near the Winding Stairs mountains. "I ran across the sheriff from Skullyville

County who was looking for Jesse Lewis. Has he turned up?"

Barnes tapped a newspaper in front of him. "Yep, he was found by a couple of hunters in the mountains north of where he was last seen, frozen to death after swimming the river."

"He was an old man who let his hatred overcome him. I feel sorry for his family. A woman without the support of her husband usually winds up having to find a family member to live with."

Barnes searched through the pile on his desk. "Here's a writ of arrest for three men wanted for assault. You should be able to get them all at once."

He stuffed it in his vest pocket. "See you next week."

Barnes pulled out his desk drawer and searched through it. "Hold it. I have something else for you. Here is the new style badge, proposed for use. Judge Parker has seen it. I just need the approval of the new marshal. What do you think?"

Badge of the 1880's

Badge for the Indian Territory

Charley turned the shiny piece of metal over in his hand. It was a round badge with the letters I.T. UNITED STATES in the center. Around the outside were the words Deputy Marshal.

"That looks good. The badges we wear now are too small to be seen at a distance. Maybe that's a good thing, preventing a target on our chest. But it is often confused with the badges worn by the Indian sheriffs."

'I'll get them ordered as soon as they're approved. Have a good trip," Barnes said.

Outside the building, Jimmy waited on his horse. He had a fresh scratch extending across his cheek.

"Can't you keep out of trouble for a few minutes?" Charley teased.

"That Rome boy. He fought like a tiger when I loosened his chains, tried to claw my eyes out. Claimed he wasn't going back to prison for nothing. The jailer had to give him a lick with his fist even after I settled him down in the wagon bed."

"Let's stop by and see Abe and Amanda so she can clean up your face; Irene isn't expecting me back for a week yet."

"I'd like that very much. I need a home-cooked meal right now."

"What about Alice?"

"She's gone to visit her sister for a week."

Charley chuckled. "How will you manage?"

Abe used his cane to move to the front window. Lightening played on the clouds as two horsemen rode up to the hitching post. He smiled as he saw his brothers coming into the yard. He met them at the porch.

"Come in and warm up. Amanda has the coffee on."

Charley and Jimmy dismounted at the hitching rail. In the cold morning air, the horses gave off steam from their sweat.

Jimmy took the reins. "I'll take our mounts back to the barn and unsaddle them. We're in no hurry, right?"

"Only to get your faced tended," Charley chuckled.

"Amanda, look who's here," Abe said.

The attractive woman with high cheek bones looked up and smiled as her visitor came through the door. She instinctively replaced a strand of hair behind her ear.

"Welcome, come in and sit. You look like you need some coffee." She rose to lay the bundle in her arms in the cradle beside the fireplace, but Abe put his hand on her arm.

"Let me hold the baby while you go in the kitchen. I would just spill the coffee."

He held the baby wrapped in a pink blanket. All that could be seen was a fuzzy pink scalp. He lifted the end of the blanket to check her status.

"We've named her Effie. The doctor says she is healthy and normal. After losing little Abel Jr. last year, God has answered our prayers."

Charley hunkered over the small form and took hold of a little pink hand.

"She'll have a fine playmate in Tony; he is only three months old. You'll have to move closer to Krebs so they can play."

"I've been thinking about moving over by Sam near Whitefield. This area is too close to Fort Smith for me," Abe said.

"Well, the area around Sam with the Starr families is still a hot bed of violence and rustling. Heard in Fort Smith that Belle Starr has been murdered,"

Abe thought about the woman who had saved Charley's life from her gang. "Saw that in the paper. She was a tough woman who lived to the extreme and died too young as so many outlaws do." If he continued wearing a badge, would he die the same way, shot down from ambush?

Amanda came in with a tray, placing it on the table and seating herself on the sofa beside it.

Jim opened the front door and stomped his boots off on the rag rug at the threshold.

She gasped and stood to examine his face. The scratch was deep and turning red. "You sit right down and let me clean that." Her small frame disappeared into the bedroom and returned with a tray of cotton, iodine and bandages.

He tried not to wince as she applied the soap and water and then the iodine. When she was finished, he looked around the room. "Where are the girls?"

Abe took the coffee from Amanda in exchange for the pink bundle. "Mollie finished the eighth grade last year," he explained, "and works as the teacher's assistant three days a week." Jimmy, soon to be married, loved children and Abe hoped he would be blessed with many.

"I can't believe she's grown up so fast." Jimmy persisted in his inventory of the children. "And little Jenette?"

Amanda laughed. "Mollie took her to school. She's been so cooped up because of the weather. How's the courting going?"

Women-folk always seemed to know when a young man was smitten. Abe figured it was a look in their eyes or the fact that they tried to clean up and present themselves in their best manner. Jimmy was a young man of twenty-two and certainly of marriageable age.

His face reddening darker than the scratch, Jimmy gulped. "Alice's only sixteen and her folks want her to wait until she is legally of age."

"That sounds wise to me," Amanda said. "However, when I met Abe, I could hardly stand being away from him and the sooner we married the better."

As Charley sipped his coffee, he stared at the splint on Abe's left leg. Abe knew what was coming.

"How's your leg?"

"The splint comes off next week and then two more weeks before I can ride."

"We need you as soon as you can get back. After these arrests, I'm going home to see my family."

Amanda turned in his direction. "I have a little sweater I knitted to send to Tony." She laid the baby aside, stepped into the bedroom and then came back carrying a blue bundle of yarn. "Hope it fits."

Abe got up and went to the window, pulling back the curtain. The front yard was drenched by heavy rain showers mixed with snow.

"It looks like the weather is turning bad. Why don't you stay here for the night? It's better than being out in a camp under a tent somewhere."

Charley slapped Abe on the shoulder as he stood. "My thoughts exactly. I'll get my gear from the barn. I have some paperwork to do for the marshal and I need to clean my pistol before it rusts out."

Jimmy had already taken off his boots to toast his feet in front of the fireplace.

Abe sat back down in front of the fireplace. He was so glad he had his family. What would life be like when they quit carrying a badge and a gun? He couldn't get his mind around that concept, but he knew God would provide for them at each stage in their life. His hand slipped down to massage the ache he could not reach through the splint.

Chapter 50

Marshal Carroll's Legacy

Water gushed down the sides of his wagon in a torrent. Much more rain and we'll have to leave this wagon behind Jimmy Barnhill thought. He pulled his collar up and his hat down, leaving just a slit for his eyes as he negotiated the team on the slippery surface. His slicker was doing its job except at the boot line. Three men chained inside the wagon growled as the wagon tipped. They were charged with assault which, in most instances, just meant the victim got away before they could kill him.

He could just make out the outline of his brother riding ahead of the wagon. Billie, his horse, looked miserable, his ears bent back and his head down as he forced his way through the sheets of rain. All he could think of now was a hot meal and a warm fire. Following the motion of Charley's left arm, he swung the wagon off the road into a clearing that already was occupied by two wagons parked end to end and several horses tethered on a line. The markings on the wagons were identical to his own, "U.S. MARSHAL". *Wonder who that is?*

He pulled to a halt beside the other two and set the brake. "Look's like we're making camp," he said more to himself than to the three prisoners behind him.

As he walked toward the cook wagon, he discovered a familiar face: long handle-bar mustache, short hair, wide-brimmed hat, well-hung wool overcoat over corduroy pants tucked into knee-high boots. Charley was already pumping the man's hand.

"Heck Thomas, how you doing?" Charley said.

Heck Thomas was one of the most resourceful and active deputies in the Western District of Arkansas. Like Charley and Bass Reeves, he went out for weeks at a time to haul in two or three wagon loads of prisoners. One letter to the editor of the Fort Smith Elevator, signed by some of the prisoners Heck had brought in, had complained that he was "bringing in too many prisoners at one time, over crowding the jail." Judge Parker had answered the petition by sentencing the complainers to heavy terms. It sent a clear message to the dissidents. Intimidation of his deputies would not be tolerated.

"I didn't recognize the horses when I came up. Where are your two grays?" Jimmy asked.

Heck frowned and shook his head in disgust. "They were stolen at Ardmore two days ago. I can't believe someone would be so bold as to take my horses out of the livery."

Jimmy's hand moved across his chin. "Sounds like revenge to me."

"If I get within 200 yards of them, they'll be mighty sorry. Are you headed for Fort Smith?"

"Yes," Charley said.

Heck handed him an envelope. "Would you take this ad to the newspaper for me? I want my horses back."

Charley stuffed it in his vest. "Be glad to. Do you mind sharing your camp with us tonight?"

"Be my guest. Cookie has already started some supper. Where's Abe?"

"Mending his leg. He got it broken again last month wrestling down an unruly family member at the Harris murder hearing."

"That man is lucky to be alive. Fortunately, he's a real go-getter."

After supper, the campers settled down to the challenge of keeping dry. Jimmy took a cup of coffee from Cookie and went to Heck's tent.

The host sipped his coffee and nodded at Charley. "Who do you think will take over for Marshal Carroll now that he's been offered the position of warden at Little Rock?"

"I don't know," Charley said. "Whether we keep our jobs will depend on the new marshal. Carroll was a good choice, but who knows what we will get next?"

Heck smoothed his moustache. "I hope we don't lose more deputies. If it hadn't been for those deputies that have been killed, this place would be worse than when we started."

"Let's drink to our health, then," Charley said as he lifted his tin cup.

Jimmy drained his. "I'm ready to put the prisoners away for the night."

Charley grabbed the keys and helped him unlock the men from the steel rings inside the wagon. Those who needed a nature break were escorted into the brush.

Jimmy turned his attention to his sleeping tent and had it up in a few minutes. The wet soil made it easy to pound in tent pegs. The trouble was keeping them from pulling loose. He settled onto his cot and drew off his wet boots and socks. His thoughts wandered to his up-coming marriage to Alice Bowers. Twenty-one months until shet was eighteen gave him time to save up and fix the place he was leasing down in Krebs.

Jimmy began to relax. He felt Charley's touch on his shoulder.

"That boy sure goes out fast," he heard him say as he slipped into sleep.

John Carroll stared at the calender hanging just below the portrait of the newly sworn President Harrison. The photograph told little of the characteristics behind the politician. Grandson of President William Henry Harrison, he had made a career of law and became an active Republican before the War serving as a Union brigadier general who had marched with Sherman on Atlanta. General opinion was that he had won a narrow victory over Grover Cleveland by corruption. Though he had made no political bargains, his supporters had made many pledges on his behalf.

Carroll shook his head as he read the newspaper. One supporter boasted Harrison would never know "how close a number of men were compelled to approach . . . the penitentiary to make him President."

The first Civil Service Act had been passed under Cleveland and promised to stabilize the bureaucracy. Carroll, a Cleveland appointee, was proud that his management of the marshal's office had shown that political appointees could be efficient, in spite of the process.

He shifted his attention to a description of a fugitive being held in Texas. The local sheriff claimed it was Oscar Coulter who had killed a young man in Logan County. *Hope he's right. The sheriff'll get the reward if it's him.* He cleared his throat as he called to his chief deputy through the open door of his office.

"Who do you plan to send to Texas to pick up Coulter?"

"I think I'll send Barnhill. It's his turn for a trip out of state. I've sent so many of the others, they're getting tired of traveling."

A few days later in Krebs, Charley opened a telegram from Marshal Carroll. He had moved his family back the first of March and found everything in it's place at the house and the office. Neighbors, who were invaluable in this sparsely settled country, had kept a sharp eye on everything while he was gone.

"Proceed to Denison, Texas and pick up Oscar Coulter, being held by the marshal of the Eastern District of Texas. Reward will go to the local sheriff who took him into custody from descriptions sent to him."

His brow crinkled as he read the order. Out of state pick ups were touchy. Technically, each United States marshal had jurisdiction in his own area and cooperated with other marshals in moving wanted men amongst the districts. The Eastern Texas and Western Arkansas Districts were hard to sort out because the men arrested sometimes had offenses overlapping into the Indian Territory. The question was often who had the case? Separate judges in each district could, and did, rule opposite each other; then the mess had to be sorted out by the Attorney General. It was a legal tight rope.

Krebs Train Depot

After he boarded at McAlester, he thought about the train ride, hoping it would be quick. Since the first of the year, he had been on four trips and this was the second week in March. As the train pulled into Denison he could see a big man standing beside an even taller man outside the terminal. He stepped down to verify a United States deputy marshal's badge on the big man's jacket.

Displaying his badge to the official, he spoke first. "I'm Deputy Barnhill, here to pick up Oscar Coulter." He eyed the prisoner cuffed to the deputy and wearing leg shackles. He was taller than his brother, Jimmy, maybe six foot six or seven. Pale blue eyes peered out of a young wind-burned face, the stamp of time spent in the weather.

The Texan said, "This is him, according to the sheriff that arrested him. His identity will have to be verified by someone who knows him personally. All the sheriff went on was general description. Just sign the paper showing transfer of custody and he's all yours."

He released the handcuffs and waited for Charley to put his on the prisoner. Next came the transfer of the leg shackles. These necessary tools were furnished by the deputy, so each one took their own supply with them when in the field.

"Thanks. How's his behavior?"

"No problem. He claims he's not Coulter, but he had no one around to identify him."

"How'd he get tagged?" This sounded more and more like a wild goose chase.

"He was drinking pretty heavily in a local saloon and boasted he knew about a man named Massey killed up in Arkansas. When he sobered up in jail, he claimed his information had come from a cowboy he had been herding with and that he's never been to Arkansas."

Charley shook hands with the lawman. "You hear every long tale in the world in this job. We'll sort this out when we get to Fort Smith." He headed to the ticket booth, the lanky young cowboy in tow. The next train north would be coming through within the hour.

The ticket agent looked up in surprise as he noticed the handcuffed and shackled prisoner.

"Oh, sorry marshal, didn't see you? What can I do for you?" His eyes roved the platform for other passengers.

"Two tickets to as close to Fort Smith as you can get me, please."

"That's Sallisaw until Mr. Gould gets that bridge across the Arkansas River completed," the agent replied. He stamped and handed him the tickets. "Do you need a receipt?"

"Yes, please." He stuffed the receipt into his vest and the tickets into his coat pocket. "Let's go Coulter."

"I'm not Coulter," the prisoner growled.

On board the train, he thought about the rest of the month. Marshall Carroll had turned in his resignation effective May 1st. Rumor was that Judge Boles, the marshal previous to John Carroll, was vying for reappointment. He hoped it would be someone who knew law enforcement and not a political payoff.

He tried to rest as he kept one eye fixed on the prisoner sitting across from him. The fellow appeared to be asleep, his head nodding on his chest. Even shackled prisoners had been known to overpower deputies and force their freedom with the law man's own pistol. *I better get off in McAlester and stay the night.*

When the conductor came back through to announce that was the next stop, he detained him with a hand on his arm.

"I need to change our tickets so we can stay overnight in McAlester," he said.

"No problem, marshal. I'll just punch your tickets for a lay over. The next train out is 8 am," the man replied.

As the engineer started applying brakes, Charley reached over and shook the prisoner awake.

"Get up. We're getting off for the night."

He guided the him through the few passengers waiting on the platform then to the stairs which led to the street. At the jail the Indian deputy rested with his feet propped up on the desk. The man quickly lowered his boots. "Hello, Charley. Who you got there?"

"A federal prisoner. I'll pick him up at 7:30 in the morning. Give me a bill for his keep."

"He'll be as warm and comfortable as if his own mama was here to tuck him in," the man said. "You hear about Sam Wingo being arrested in the Territory? I don't like seeing Choctaw lawmen go bad like that. His brother, Ed, is real upset."

"If he serves his sentence and keeps himself clean after all this, he'll be alright," Charley said.

"I hope he does. We have hard enough time keeping our own people out of trouble without our lawmen getting in trouble too."

He found Billie in the livery where he had left him and rode home to Krebs. Irene would be surprised to see him.

Despite the fringe outlaws that hid amongst them, he liked this area filled with Choctaws who had lived here for over fifty years and with newcomers that had filtered in on the MK&T Railroad to work in the coal mines. It was a mix of people who supported progress and law enforcement

Smoke rose from the chimney as he topped the ridge west of his house. Henry's dog, a basset hound named Roy, came baying out from under the front porch. He wagged his tail as he recognized the master of the house.

Henry appeared at the door. Now fourteen, he was the man of the house, when Charley was gone. Irene depended on him for chopping wood and milking the cow among other duties.

"Pa! What you doing home so soon?"

"It's just for the night. Take Billie to the barn and feed him."

In the front room, he hung his hat and coat on the rack by the door. He slipped his gun belt off and walked to the bedroom, hanging it on the bedpost within easy reach. As he turned, Irene's arms caught him around the neck.

"What a pleasant surprise. I didn't expect to see you for several days." She nuzzled her face against his cheek.

He felt the warmth of her breath and hugged her tight. He did not feel tired now. One day when he gave up man-hunting, he would not tell her good-bye anymore.

"I didn't want to handle the prisoner alone on a train overnight. So here I am until morning. Where's Tony?"

"He's asleep in the cradle by the fireplace. I just fed and changed him. Minnie's in the kitchen helping prepare supper."

Charley walked to the cradle and looked down at his sleeping son, so tiny and so perfect. *God, you are so great. Help me give my family the same love you have given me.*

After supper, he sat in front of the fire, watching the flames. The warmth filled his body and relaxed his mind. Irene came and sat down beside him.

"I got a letter from my sister, Janey. She and Louis are going to be parents in August. The visits she was allowed with Louis while he was awaiting execution made it all possible."

"What kind of life will it be for a child whose father is in jail for ten years?" Charley asked. Louis would be helpless to care for his family in any way.

"The Burrows will tend to her, I'm sure. They are devoted church people and will do whatever it takes to help raise their grandchild."

"Yes, I suspect so. My parents were a great help to me in caring for my children after Salina died. God will bless them for their efforts." He hugged her tight and closed his eyes. The picture of Louis' face when he had heard the commuted sentence would never be erased from his memory. It was the same look Charley would have on his face one day, standing before the Great Judge of the Universe.

"Look's like we'll have to let him go," the chief deputy said, his tone matter-of-fact. His words caught Charley by surprise.

"What do you mean?"

"Witnesses came up from Logan County. He's not Coulter."

"The whole trip he was moaning about not being Coulter. That sheriff in Texas must've been thinking of the reward."

"This happens occasionally."

Charley spat out his words before he could think. "The Indian Territory is full of men who need to be hunted down and I wasted three days on a loser."

The older man shifted in his chair. "Go home and rest. The grand jury's backed up again."

"Thanks. I need a few days off." Charley noticed the chief deputy was looking a mite older than when he took his position five years ago. *Does this job wear us all down like that?*

After he had been home a few days, he rode to his office - a tiny room stuck between a barbershop and a butcher shop on main street - a place to keep his case files and supplies needed for long trips. He allowed other deputies traveling through to use it. The people of Krebs liked to see the marshal's symbol in the window though he was seldom in residence. A citizen could leave a message for him through the mail slot.

He unlocked the door and picked up an envelope that had been pushed through the mail slot. He opened it and stared at it, blood draining from his face.

A telegram from the marshal's office dated that morning instructed: "Be on the look out for Jeff Berryhill and Saint Lopka of the Barnett gang. Zack Moody killed Mar. 15th ten miles west of Tulsa, Creek Nation."

This message was so important it should have been delivered to him at home. He would have to talk to the telegraph clerk and ask that all telegrams be brought to his home from now on.

He sat down at his desk and stared at the paper. Zack had been one of the first men he had ridden with and the fourth law men to be killed by this gang in just nine months. When would it end? The fugitives were likely hiding out in the new Oklahoma Territory that would open for settlers within the month.

He rubbed his eyes and set the paper on the desk. 19 lawmen and posse killed in the past four years out of a deputy force of 46. His job was high risk with low pay, and though it was in his blood, his motivation seemed less than it had been ten years ago. He had a young wife and a new son, treasures too precious to jeopardize if he was the next lawman killed or hurt. Maybe it was time to consider turning in his badge. He would discuss it with Irene before he went to Fort Smith.

Carroll smoothed out his long beard and stared at the dwindling stacks of cases on his desk. He had only six weeks to finish everything: witness subpoenas, deputies' vouchers, vendors' statements, and, most importantly, prisoners to be released or transported to Little Rock.

He peered into the outer office. "Barnes, do you have the release for the McCann sisters and Ann Martin?"

"Yes, sir. Right here," Barnes said.

"After I sign them, take them down to the jailer. All I've heard from the women's matron since they've been here is complaints. She's tried to get them to help with the women's sewing jobs, but they make such a mess of the projects, it has to be thrown out. I thought all women knew how to sew."

Barnes blurted out and then reddened. "I guess being a woman of the night, you only need to know one thing." He tried to disguise his discomfort by fiddling with his ash tray. "You know what my little girl asked me the other day? She said, 'Papa, what do people do over at those pretty houses along the river? They are so fancy and the women who live there are so pretty.'"

"What did you tell her?"

"I told her that it was a great secret and only special people get to go there."

Carroll chuckled and signed the documents. "Life's never dull around here. Get these women on their way as soon as possible."

Charley had no thought of work as he rode into Fort Smith. He had a shopping list from Irene that covered both sides of the paper. Abe was there to have his leg checked at the hospital and, Jimmy, of course, to visit Alice.

Succumbing to his old habit, he stopped and stared at the jail. "Let's go by the marshal's office and check in."

The three started for the stairs then halted at the spectacle of three colorful females descending the stairs, arms locked and heads thrown high. Their laughter was loud and unrestrained. The rouge on their cheeks stood out against their pale faces.

Julia McCann's eyes fixed on Jimmy, the delight of her discovery displayed in her tone. "Well, lookee here, Lou. Isn't this the cute little ole guard we had such fun with last summer?"

Charley watched Jimmy blush and then realized he was reddening too. Men did not speak to prostitutes in broad daylight on a public street. His hand went to his back pocket, feeling for what? His handcuffs? These women were evidently free to go. His memory flashed to the scene in the tent with Ann Martin. People would never understand the temptations that the deputies faced every day - a feisty woman, an offered bribe, crooked officials who claimed amnesty for their friends. Judge Parker kept the reputation of his court spotless and compromised officials were dismissed without recourse. Charley knew his reputation was on the line every day he rode out looking for trouble-makers.

"Ma'am," Jimmy touched his hat.

Lou McCann giggled and waved her fan at him in a beckoning manner. "Just remember our offer, you cute little ole thing, We'll be right over yonder in the houses along Front Street. Come by any time, now, you-all hear."

With a flurry of petticoats and feathers, they turned and walked northeast toward the Red Light district. Their laughter and chatter could be heard for two blocks. Pedestrians on the street turned to stare and men riding by covered their grins with gloved hands. A man turned his head in an effort to see the source of the noise, the woman beside him in the buckboard tapping his arm with her fan.

Then he thought of Proverbs 5:3: "For the lips of the adulteress drip honey and her speech is smoother than oil, but in the end she is bitter as gall, and sharp as a double-edged sword. Her feet go down to death."

Jimmy pulled his hat down and tucked his hands in his pockets. "If Alice knew I was seen with such women, she would skin me alive."

Abe put his arm around the younger man and gave him a squeeze. "That's part of our job, bringing in all kinds of offenders, even women. There aren't many women who commit crimes of such a violent nature as these three did."

As they entered the office, Barnes looked up. "Did you see the McCanns outside?"

Charley answered. "As a matter of fact, we did. They found Jimmy particularly appealing. There's not been that much feminine attraction around here since I arrested Belle Starr a couple years ago."

The chief deputy nodded in agreement. "The women's matron is glad they're gone. She had her hands full with them."

Charley let his eyes move to the window to rest on the lilacs just coming out on the jail square. "We'll be in town overnight picking up supplies. If you need us, we'll be at the hotel,

"Marshal Carroll is trying to finish up all outstanding writs before he resigns. You boys want to stay on under the new marshal?" Barnes was being polite. It was up to the new marshal to pick his own deputies, but if he were smart, he would keep a core of the most experienced personnel.

"Who is going to be appointed?" Abe asked.

"Judge Boles is the popular local favorite, but it's still up to the President. We'll know by May 1st.

When Charley did not answer, Abe looked at him and then poked him in the ribs. "Come on, what better things do we have to do?"

Charley finally answered. "I don't want to work for a bureaucrat who is only interested in his political reputation."

Miss Laura's Social Club, North B Street, Fort Smih

Chapter 51

Self-Defense

Charley grimaced from the bitter taste of the pencil tip. He tried to concentrate on his trip ledger in an effort to write the numbers. Like most deputies, he kept every detail of expense for his report. He looked from the little tally book across the table at Abe. "OK, I've got it all down. You put in for ten days as posse with me. I've heard once the new Marshal takes over, a deputy can only take one posse and a guard. They can take another deputy only if they have more than four men to arrest."

"What's the purpose of that?" Abe asked.

"It'll spread the deputies around and allow them to cover more ground."

"What if we come up against a hard case like the Barnett gang?" Abe sucked in his breathe as a dark shadow fell across their table and reflexively reached for the pistol that was not there. No guns carried in Fort Smith while a deputy is off duty. What a stupid rule. He hoped this wasn't a disgruntled ex-prisoner.

The shadow spoke from behind Charley. "There you are, Charley, Abe, you sluggards. Only two prisoners this trip. You getting old?"

Charley recognized the voice. "George Williams, how you been?" He offered his hand to the deputy who had backed him up on the first shoot out with Bill Frazier and had fought Frazier again when Abe had been wounded.

Abe rose and shook the man's hand.

"How's the leg?" Williams asked.

"Mended for now."

He slapped a familiar form on the table. "It's a subpoena to appear as witness at the Harris trial. Since you're already here, you can just stick around. The subpoena says "forthwith."

"Why do they need me to testify?" Charley said. "We just picked them up."

"Something about what you might have seen or heard from the Harris boys and the Webbs when you went to Poteau."

Charley shrugged and slid the paper into his vest pocket. "It's a family feud that's been going on since these two families lived down in Logan County. It will continue until one side kills the other off."

The tall deputy sat down and removed his hat. "I remember one in my end of the county right after the War. Two families that had fought on opposite sides came home and harsh words flew whenever they met. Finally, the leader of one family was ambushed and the survivors took revenge on the other family. It ended with five widows, twelve orphans and three men in jail charged with murder."

"Tough to let your pride get the best of your judgment and then leave your family unprotected. But we see it all the time in the men we bring in. Some call it *The Rule of the Winchester.*" Charley lifted his cup in salute and drank. "Here's to the new Marshal, whoever he'll be."

Only photograph of Judge Parker's vcourtroom in new courthouse 1894

The Harris trial was in summation. During Judge Parker's fourteen years, the great court had averaged seven hundred cases a year with 10% of those being capital offenses. Only 10% of the murderers had been brought to trial with a 50% conviction rate. Fort Smithites and the whole civilized world stood aghast at the number of hangings. As one expert pointed out, none of those hanged had committed crimes in Fort Smith or in Arkansas. They had all occurred in the Indian Territory. The court had no jurisdiction on capital crimes committed in the state of Arkansas.

Charley felt the tension in the courtroom. The Webbs sat on one side and the Harris family on the other. During the testimony, Judge Parker had to call for order on several occasions when one side or the other shouted insults at a witness or a spectator. The young man Charley and Abe had subdued at the commissioner's hearing sat nearby scowling at the defendants. *I better keep an eye on him.*

The District Attorney peered at the jury over his glasses.

"Gentlemen of the jury, the evidence in this trial has shown that the defendants did, as charged in the indictment, participate in the killing of William Webb. Surely, he was not stabbed by his own brothers. Your duty is to find the Harris brothers guilty as charged."

Mr. Sandels sat down and turned to observe the defendants seated with their lawyers. The senior partner rose and cleared his throat.

Charley tried to concentrate on the lawyer's words but he found his eyes drawn to the faces of the jurors. Each man stared at the defense lawyer, some with slack mouths, others twisting the ends of their mousaches. One man relieved his nervous energy with a tapping boot.

The defense lawyer spoke in a clear, confident tone. "This case has had many turns and details brought out through the testimony of two dozen witnesses. One thing is clear. The Webb family was armed with a shotgun and a claw hammer that fateful day in January. Why the need for the arms? This undermines the Webbs' claim of peaceful intentions."

As several witnesses testified, Elisha Harris fired only one shot into the air. The other shots came from his own gun after it was wrestled from him by the Webbs. A man has a right to defend himself in the face of such aggression. If a knife is all you have left to defend yourself, you use it. They could not out run a pistol. The charge of murder must be dropped in face of the obvious self-defense of these two defendants. Thank you."

The man sat down and all attention turned to Judge Parker. He went through his charge to the jury who listened with keen attention. Summing up the difference between murder and self-defense, Judge Parker addressed the always present question of necessity. Could the defendants have done something to prevent the killing?

The jury left the room as the spectators filed out. Charley watched the young Webb boys. One of them turned and stared at him with brown eyes, fixed and unblinking.

If they wanted trouble, the lawmen in the room would be ready for them. He walked up to the bailiff, a stout man with a double chin hanging over a muscular chest. His uniform was spotless and his appearance serious.

"I think there might be trouble. It's going to be unwelcome no matter which way the verdict goes. I'd recommend a group of deputies in the court room," he said. The bailiff nodded in agreement.

Charley stepped into the hall. He caught sight of one of his friends, Deputy James N. Cole, talking to another deputy. He walked swiftly down the hall towards them.

James turned. "Howdy, Charley. I see you got roped into this trial. It's a hard one to call."

"That's why I'm here. I want you two to come with me to be ready for any problems when the verdict is given."

He led them down the hall to the benches and sat down. He turned his attention to the spectators that were standing around. The number had thinned out, many going across the street to get supper.

"Watch who comes back in the courtroom. When the spectators are seated, we'll stand at the door."

A couple of hours passed. Charley sent a runner to the restaurant for sandwiches and coffee which they consumed seated on the benches. Cole took the time to fill Charley in on his plans.

"I've about had it with marshalin'. I think I'll take the money I've saved and start using my peddler's wagon full-time. The Cherokees are mighty fine people and I think I could make a good living taking goods around in their nation. I know the area like my own back yard," he explained.

Charley nodded. "I think you would make a good store keeper. Just keep your .45 and Winchester handy."

That is when Charley heard the sound of the bell. It was tolled outside the courthouse whenever a jury was coming in to render a verdict. Clang, Clang, Clang a five second pause and then Clang, Clang Clang again. That also gave Judge Parker time to come across the grounds from the Commissary Building where he had his main office. He went there to await the jury, having something to eat brought to him while he worked on signing document. If a jury was still out late in the evening and had not reached a verdict, he would call them in and dismiss them until morning.

The courtroom filled up fast. The three deputies watched the faces of the spectators as they filed back in and found seats. The Webbs were silent and glaring as they sat down. One of them pointed to the door and nodded his head toward the deputies standing there. At least they knew the deputies were here and ready for them.

The Harris family sat in silent resignation, bracing for the worst. Charley noticed their old father fold his hands in prayer. *Now is the time to pray for your sons, ole man. And never stop praying.*

The foreman of the jury stepped forward and handed the paper to the bailiff. After reading the verdict, the judge handed it back. The foreman, still standing, held it in front of his face and then lifted his eyes to the courtroom.

"We, the jury, find the defendants not guilty by reason of self-defense."

A cry of appreciation went up from the crowd. However, the harsh cries of the Webbs filled the room. They rose as a group and pushed their way toward the door. They were in a mighty big hurry to get out of there, disappointment evident on their faces, teeth and fists clinched.

Charley stepped to the defendants' table. The two boys embraced their family who stood around them. The grateful family parted to allow him through. He gazed at the young men who had just found mercy at the hands of a jury. His father would be pleased that two of his parishioners had escaped the rope.

"Deputy Barnhill, thank you for your help," Elisha said. He was the oldest and stood a head above his brother, James.

"Just watch your backs as you go home. I would suggest you get out of Poteau. There's going to be plenty of room with the opening of the Cherokee Outlet. The next time your adversaries may not allow you a chance to escape."

"We've discussed this. I think it's time we moved on," ole man Harris answered.

Charley turned away and walked outside. The cool evening air revived his mind as he headed for the stable. He noticed a man come out of the jail with a prisoner chained to his wrist. The man tipped his hat. Charley recognized the prisoner, Gunter, whom he had brought in last week.

"How are you?" Charley asked as he drew near. He saw the badge on the man's chest, a U.S. deputy marshal, no one he knew though.

"Fine, and yourself, sir?" the man replied.

"It looks like the people of Kansas get their fugitive back," Charley said. "I picked Gunter up last week not far from here."

"The federal court there appreciates your help. Hope we can return the favor sometime," the man said.

I hope you can, too. Charley thought as he crossed the street.

Chapter 51

Search for a Corpse

It was Thursday, May 9th, 1889. The morning air, warm and sultry, proclaimed spring in the bloom of the trees that lined Garrison Avenue and the clumps of foliage along the Arkansas River. The brightness of the colors went unnoticed by the three prisoners whose hand cuffs and leg irons testified to their dismal position. Jimmy Barnhill sighed as he pulled the team to a halt in front of the jail at Fort Smith. His hand went to the brake handle and his foot to the wooden pedal which he set with a hard push, wrapping the reins around the handle.

He watched Charley disappear into the Marshal's office. The newly painted white trim around the windows and roof of the Old Jail and Courthouse contrasted nicely with the big red brick building. He had seen several paintings of this prominent landmark hanging in local businesses that depended on the presence of the court.

Abe dismounted and stood along side the wagon, shotgun tucked under his right arm. "Alright, fellas. Stand up and move to the back of the wagon." Each prisoner came to the wagon tailgate, sat down and waited as Jimmy removed the leg shackles. He threw the heavy irons into the wooden box attached just inside the wagon bed.

"Let's go," he said.

He led the three men up the stairs to the main jail entrance, Abe bringing up the end. They were met by a new jailer.

"Hello, Mr. Conway. What happened to Jailer Pettigrew?" Jimmy asked.

"He was moved to second chief deputy when Marshal Carroll left May 1st."

"Good for him. Pettigrew is a dependable hard worker."

Conway, a middle-aged man with the girth of a sedentary life, led the procession to the main jail door. Jimmy handed him the temporary mittimus, the paperwork that allowed each prisoner to be held until a hearing determined whether they would be allowed bond.

"Here you go. We found these three with a little bit of luck and a lot of tracking. The Winding Stair Mountains around Talihina has so many whiskey runners and bootleggers, it couldn't possibly get worse and the Frisco railroad coming in last fall has made it even more of a hotbed. We're glad to get out of there with these three."

Conway turned the key in the door. It creaked slightly as he opened it and poked the three prisoners through. "That's what I'm hearing from every deputy that travels down there. It's more violent than the Creek Nation in some ways." He watched the turnkey escort the prisoners to the first available jail cell which was at the back of the row. The jail was full.

"Well, see you next time," Jimmy said.

He and Abe returned to the wagon just as Charley stepped out. Taking the steps two at a time, he met them on the ground level.

"Looks like we have a tough assignment." Charley's normal tone of voice was clipped and brisk. What's wrong now? Jimmy thought.

"When have we ever had an easy assignment?" Abe asked.

"We're to look for an old man named Henry Wilson who has been missing for almost two months. His family and neighbors have searched for him to no avail. Tyner Hughes is already in the area. We're to search every house along Wilson's planned route."

"When do we leave?" Jimmy asked.

"As soon as you go over to the commissary building and get supplies. We'll use the pack mule and leave the wagon here."

There went his chance to see Alice.

James Barnhill

They arrived at LeFlore Station late on the fourth day, one hundred and ten miles of fast riding to cover that distance. This little community had a few houses, livery, and general store. The yard in front of the store was filled with horses, carrying bed rolls and filled saddle bags, the search party waiting for them.

The Winding Stair Mountain, part of the Oachita Mountains that extended almost to Little Rock, Arkansas, stood visible in the distance to the southeast. Charley remembered his and Abe's trip through there from Talihina a few years before with more than twenty prisoners. This was a rough area of the Choctaw Nation, just far enough from Fort Smith to be a hide out for the lawless , white or Indian, who took what he wanted.

Oachita Mountains of Oklahoma

A young man with red hair and mustache and a face of granite came out of the store followed by six others. He was unarmed but, the men behind the redhead carried Winchesters or shotguns. Two were Choctaw.

Charley did not hesitate to take charge of the group. "I'm United States Deputy Marshal Charley Barnhill. This is my brother, Deputy Abe Barnhill, and my other brother there, Jimmy, is our guard."

The young man stepped up and shook hands with of them.

"Howdy. I'm George Wilson; my Dad is the one who is missing." He pointed to the Choctaws. "Enoch Davis is a friend and neighbor and Jerry White will act as interpreter since none of us speak the language. We've been expecting you since I sent that telegram to the Marshal last week."

Charley's heart sank at the thought of a man missing in these hills for two months. All tracks would have disappeared. Back tracking to his last known sighting would be the only thing to do. "What brought him out here?"

"He went to fetch a horse from Cove, Polk County, Arkansas, just over the line. We've searched with no luck."

"His route of travel?" Charley asked.

"Across the Winding Stair Mountain on a direct line toward the southeast. He stayed the first night at a friend's house about fourteen miles from here. The next stop was to be another friend farther south the other side of the mountains. He never made it."

"So he was crossing the mountains using trails and not the public road?"

"Yes, he thought it would be shorter to cross into Arkansas just east of Cove."

"Alright, let's start where he was last seen."

"That'll be Mr. Winton's place. These men with me are neighbors and friends."

"The more the better if we have to spread out. We will search every house along the road from where he was last seen." Charley mounted and tickled Billie's ribs with a gentle spur. This could be tedious and they had brought only a week's grub.

The two room cabin in the trees had a porch furnished with a rocking chair and bench. A man came out as the search party rode up. His clothes were the common style worn by everyone in these parts, pants tucked into boots, suspenders over a light blue work shirt, neckerchief around the collar.

Charley dismounted and tied Billie to the railing in front.

Two youngsters poked their heads out the door to stare at the search party with wide eyes. A passel of lawmen in someone's front yard usually meant trouble. "Glad you're here. I'm Ike Winton. We've searched high and low for Henry for over a month now without a sign or clue."

"Tell me what you know."

"He came to my house on March 12 and stayed the night, said he was going to spend the next night at George Myers' place the other side of the mountains."

"Did he have a gun?"

"Yes, a single shot .50 caliber calvary gun. He had three or four cartridges, says he borrowed it from a friend."

"How about money?"

"He was carrying $6.50 to pay for food and lodging along the way. That's all I saw."

"Anything else?"

"I gave him directions on how to get to George Myers' house on the public road, to take the left break where the trail splits about seven miles from here. It heads southeast in the direction he wanted to go. The right break takes you more southerly. His son, George, came by about five days later looking for him. We searched for a couple of weeks and then decided we needed help."

"Any houses between here and Myers' place?"

"Two that belong to Choctaws, names of James Beams and Jimison Jones.

Beams is about eleven miles from here and Jones about fourteen, both along the left fork. There's nothing much along the right fork until you get to Black Fork Mountain."

"Thanks. Alright, men. It's getting late. We'll camp here tonight and then resume the search in the morning."

Abe stared at the split in the trail. Left to the houses along the road to the southeast or right to the south? The left side seemed less traveled, brush growing right up to the beaten path.

"What do you think? The left side seems just a cow path," Abe said.

Charley did not answer, but swerved his mount to the right.

Good move. Abe watched the narrow trail ahead as they rode. This was a vast wilderness with only a few occupants who resided in little valleys and ravines. The houses were placed far back from the trail which prevented unhindered access.

They moved swiftly along the ridges and into the canyons, the seven men in the search party behind them pushing their horses to keep up. No houses were seen after covering five miles.

Swiveling his head around, Charley pulled Billie to an abrupt halt, the dust rising from the trail. He rested both hands on the saddle horn as he peered into the distance. "If we keep going along this road, we'll come out at Black Fork Mountain and have to face Bill Frazier and his gang. Robbery of a traveler does not seem to be their type of crime. Let's head back and check the other fork." Abe sighed in relief. He did not want to give Frazier a second chance to kill him.

After an hour of methodical searching along the left break in the trail, Abe picked up a house in the distance. Placed slightly off the passage, shrouded by trees and bush, it appeared to be a Choctaw dwelling with out buildings, a brush corral, and a small chicken coop. It sported a single window in front and a wooden door on leather hinges.

Abe took a guess. "This must be James Beams' place."

"Yes, he's usually around somewhere," Enoch Davis said.

Abe watched Charley and Jimmy dismount about fifty yards from the place, motioning for them do the same. He swung his unbending left leg back behind the saddle, holding on to the saddle horn to slide to the ground. He moved up to stand beside his brothers who were staring at the lay out.

Charley gestured to a stand of trees behind them, well off the trail. "A couple of you men take the horses and tie them up out of sight. Stay with them until we call you."

They walked to the front of the house keeping to the cover of the trees.

Charley cupped his hand around his mouth. "*Halito* (Hello) in the house. Anyone home?" Receiving no reply, he motioned the men to move up.

Typical Indian cabin of the IndianTerritory

"You men search the grounds," he said pointing to three of the men standing behind him. "We'll have a look inside. Jimmy, you stand watch out here."

Abe followed Charley and George Wilson up on the porch, motioning Wilson to stay back since he had no weapon. As Charley stopped along the left side of the door, Abe took the right side, knocked and then pulled on the leather strap to release the wooden bar. Charley stepped forward as it swung open, using the door as a shield, his pistol gripped in both hands. To fire a seven pound piece of iron accurately, a tight grip with both hands was best. Even then, the recoil could kick the pistol up into the air above his head. He crossed the room and prodded at a rumpled corn husk mattress on the floor.

Abe peered into the dim interior, his hands full of his Colt .45. It gave him goose bumps to move into a dimly lit room with his form outlined in the door. He looked up to the rafters toward a ladder and loft on the right side. The house appeared to be the humble dwelling of a family that had few items worth stealing. Indians never locked their doors. It was a matter of honor that a house was left open for all to use. They expected the same from their white neighbors.

Wilson moved into the room behind him and rummaged through the contents of a wooden chest filled with pots, pans and kitchen ware. He moved to examine the back wall underneath the loft.

Abe turned over a rug on the floor. Indians were very particular about covering their floors with rugs or skins. A bare floor was an embarrassment, an indication of an uncivilized family. They marveled at the white farmers who settled among them never thinking twice about the bare floor in their homes.

He looked for a possible trap door or other opening beneath the rug. He saw none.

Charley pointed to the loft. "George, head up the ladder and check it out. He poked amongst a pile of traps and fish cages stacked against the back wall. A deer hide covered a pile which turned out to be folded bedding.

"Nothing here. What about up there?" Charley called up the ladder.

"I've found something." Wilson held out a pistol.

"Bring it down."

"Looks like the pistol that Ike Winton described. I don't see any cartridges though. It's unloaded." George held the pistol out to Charley as he descended.

He grabbed it and turned it over in his hands. "Alright, get outside and station the men around the house. We'll wait and see who comes along. Tell the men with the horses what we're doing and to stay out of sight."

Abe went out the door to secure a place in the brush with Jimmy. Charley joined them after he checked the positioning of the party.

"There are two men in back and three dispersed along the sides. We'll watch the front. I've given them orders not to move if someone approaches. I don't want them in the way if we have to move fast."

A half hour passed in silence, Abe watching for the slightest movement and straining for any sound. The silence was broken only by the call of a black bird. The late afternoon sun seemed suspended in the western sky, being about an hour until dark. This stake out could last for days if the residents had decided to go on the scout.

Abe placed his hand on Charley's shoulder as two figures appeared in the distance, a man walking along the narrow trail followed by a woman. He heard their words as they approached, Choctaws. He wished he had spent more time learning the language. He caught a phrase or two. The man sang in a happy voice, the beautiful rolling sound of Chatha spilling from his lips. He was always amazed by the harmonious lyrics of the Choctaw people.

The woman entered the house and the man sat down on a large boulder placed strategically under a shade tree. The slanting rays of the sun now at his back, he took off his hat and laid it on the rock. His hair was braided with long leather thongs twined into an intricate pattern, decorated with feathers and beads. After a few minutes he took out a pocket knife and began to whittle on a stick, singing as his hands turned the wood and carved it into a form.

The woman reappeared at the porch and closed the door behind her. She spoke to the man as she stepped off the porch. Her hair was similarly braided, a long turkey feather protruding from above her ear.

Not waiting for Charley's signal, the men behind the cabin began to move. Abe knew this would spook Beams. As quickly as he could, he moved into the clearing as he heard Charley shout, *Issa* ("Stop). That was not good, a frightened rabbit always runs. The man let out a whistle and sprinted toward the trail.

Charley halted him again with a shout which made the man run even harder. Holstering his pistol, Charley ran after the fugitive with Jimmy hard on his heels. Enoch Davis fired a warning shot into the air as did other members of the party. No one dared fire close to the unarmed man with the deputy in pursuit.

Knowing he couldn't keep up with the chase, Abe turned his attention to the startled woman. She shrieked and cried in a loud wail, throwing her long apron over her face. She settled into the dust of the yard and rocked back and forth as the anguished sounds spilled from her lips.

Dusk began to settle while Abe waited. He knew that if Charley didn't get the man in the first fifty yards, he would lose him. The thick undergrowth would slowed down the pursuers and Beams would be lost in the twilight.

Charley returned to the front yard and, through an interpreter, attempted to question the woman. Abe listened to the conversation as his eyes roved over the scene, ten men, all heavily armed, and a despairing woman.

"She says she knows nothing about the pistol except Jefferson Jones came by sometime in March and gave it to her husband," Jerry White, the interpreter, explained.

"Is there a Choctaw deputy sheriff close by who may know where Beams would hide?" Charley asked.

"Yes, Bob Willis lives half a mile from Mrs. Woods' place down the trail toward Black Fork Mountain."

"We'll camp at Mrs. Woods' while you fetch Deputy Willis," Charley said.

Three of the men went to locate the deputy. The rest gathered up their mounts and started down the hill to the west. It was completely dark when they arrived at the Wood's home.

Mrs. Woods prepared supper for the hungry men. After a hard day of riding in the hills, anything tasted good. Abe particularly enjoyed the corn mush that the Choctaws prepared called Tom Fuller. It was fermented and then baked in a hollowed-out log.

Willis appeared about the time they were finishing the meal. The Choctaws were fairly short in stature; he was about 5 feet 4 inches in his boots. Abe tried not to peer down at him. Choctaws considered face to face encounters as confrontational.

"We need you to find James Beams and bring him in. We just want to question him about this pistol we found at his house. It belongs to a white man named Henry Wilson who's been missing for two months," Charley explained. He showed the deputy sheriff the pistol.

"Huh," the man grunted. "I think I know where he would hide. I'll search for him at first light." He pulled his hat down over his eyes and turned toward the door.

"Much obliged," Charley said.

Abe moved his hand across his face, feeling the dirt of the day's ride. "I think I'll go wash up and get some rest. Jimmy's outside with the other men, having a cup of coffee. This is a break in this case, but what happened to Wilson?"

"Someone did him in. This country isn't safe for a lone traveler, no matter how much we ride through it. The Indians have citizens who don't think twice about killing a man for a few dollars, just like the whites do."

"Tomorrow will tell," Abe said. His leg ached and he wanted a bedroll by a fire.

Charley sipped his coffee and squinted into the morning sun, his boot resting on the bottom log of the corral fence. The spring air was fresh and cool, a slight breeze fanning his bandanna. His hand went to the holster at his hip as a rider and a man walking appeared on the hill crest. Focusing his eyes, he recognized the Indian deputy sheriff. The man on foot was unshackled and walked quietly beside the deputy.

"Here is James Beams. I found him at his brother's house, hiding in the wood shed," Willis explained. "He's all yours."

"Would you mind waiting around while we question him?" Charley asked.

Willis stepped down and ground tied his mount. "I'll have a cup of coffee while you talk to him."

"Bring the interpreter over," Charley said.

Abe stepped to the porch of the house and called, " Jerry White, *Minti* (Come here).

White came to the yard and gazed at the prisoner. He walked up and stopped in front of Beams, whose his eyes were aloof and unconcerned.

"Ask him where he got this pistol?" Charley held out the gun they had found the night before.

"He says Jefferson Jones gave it to him in March. He doesn't know where he got it."

"Where's Jefferson Jones now?"

"He says he hasn't seen him since last month sometime," White said.

"Deputy Willis, do you think you can find this Jefferson Jones for us?"

"Huh," grunted the deputy. "I can find him pretty quick. I saw him yesterday at his folks about six miles from here."

"Please fetch him for us. We need to question him." Charley said. "I'm placing James Beams under arrest."

While the search party waited for the return of the deputy, they talked amongst themselves. Charley listened without comment.

"What do you think happened to Wilson?" one asked.

George Wilson did not hesitate. "I figure Dad's somewhere out in the forest. Probably will never find him," His face showed the tension of the past two months, lips set in a tight line, eyes blurry from the lack of sleep. Charley knew the tension of the chase wore everyone down, but they had to know what happened to the old man.

Charley turned as he heard a crowd approaching. A group of 8 or 9 Choctaws appeared moving down the trail toward the house. Charley noted they were unarmed, a good thing. It was against Indian law for a man to carry a pistol, though rifles were allowed for hunting purposes. Most disregarded the law and carried whatever they felt they needed for protection.

The interpreter stepped forward and spoke to the lead man. He was young, wearing rough trousers, a cotton shirt and work boots. White turned away from the group and addressed Charley.

"This is Jimison Jones, brother of Jefferson Jones. He heard you had Beams under arrest after finding a gun at his house. He says he owns a gun that he loaned him. He wants to see it."

Charley held out the weapon to the young man who fingered it and turned it around in his hand. He gave it back, muttering a few words to the interpreter.

"He says it's not his."

"Does he know where Jefferson got this pistol?"

"He doesn't know."

"Tell him he is being taken into custody for questioning until this matter is sorted out."

The young man stepped forward and lifted his hands to Charley.

The men ate the breakfast kindly prepared for them by Mrs. Woods and tried to keep occupied. Two or three pulled out pistols and commenced to clean them. Charley noted several different makes, a Colt. 45 single action, an army .38, even an old cap and ball, whatever they could afford. A pistol like he carried was priced above what the average man could pay. Second-hand weapons left over from the War were still plentiful. However, professional lawmen carried the best and the newest.

The deputy sheriff reappeared with another man walking alongside his horse. He dismounted and escorted the man forward. The prisoner's head was down, his eyes fixed on the ground.

Willis' voice was soft and low. "This is Jefferson Jones."

"Good work. You saved us a lot of wasted riding," Charley said. "Ask him about this gun and how he got it."

"He claims he took it from an old man after he killed him in self-defense. The white man came to Beams' house and asked for directions to the public road. When he showed him the way, the man asked if he could change a $5 bill. When he said no, the old man got mad at him. As he turned back he heard a pistol cock and he ducked behind a post oak. The bullet went between his body and his arm. The man started to run and he shot him in the back, underneath the shoulder. The ole man ran on down a creek about 60 or 70 yards and then fell down. Jones got scared and ran off, leaving him there."

"Will he lead us to the spot where he left him?"

"He will," White said. His eyes were silent and his face impassive waiting for the next instruction from Charley. Indians would set for hours and not speak other than a grunt or two.

"How far is it from here?"

"He says about four miles."

"Ask him if his brother had anything to do with this?"

'He says no, he was alone when he killed the old man."

"Get him something to eat first, then we head out."

Charley's head was full of questions that needed answers, but they could wait. The big one had been answered. "Abe, you stay here and guard Beams and Jimison Jones. I'll take Jimmy with me."

Placing Jones on a mule that belonged to one of the men, they began the trip to the murder site. The mule's owner walked beside him. About 2 1/2 miles past Beams' place, the prisoner halted and pointed to a spot along the trail.

Jerry White indicated a small disturbance in the undergrowth. "He says this is where they left the trail."

Charley stepped forward to take a look. "Get him down and we'll continue on foot."

The prisoner led them off the path a half mile to a little creek coming out of the Winding Stairs Mountain. He pointed to a spot along the creek.

"He says this is where Wilson fell in the middle of the creek."

"There's nothing here. Ask him if he's sure."

"Yes, he remembers it by the odd-shaped boulder on the edge of the creek."

We are close now, Charley thought, his heart at the same time sinking in dread at what they may find. "Spread out and search both sides of the creek."

A few minutes of searching was broken by the cry, "Over here." George Wilson raised his hand and waved. He stood one hundred yards down stream, pointing toward the creek. There was evidence of a dim trail leading from the spot the prisoner had identified to where Wilson stood.

Charley reached the spot in a few seconds. He immediately recognized human remains, rather bones and clothing in the edge of the water. On closer examination he picked out most of the body parts. One hand, one foot and the jaw bone were missing. It looked like the head had been chewed by a wild beast, probably, wild hogs which were plentiful in this area.

"Can you identify any of the clothing?" Charley asked Wilson.

"Yes, there's his shirt, under shirt, pants and drawers, vest and socks. I don't see his hat, coat or shoes." Wilson's voice cracked and he fell down in a sobbing heap beside the bleached bones of his old father.

"The right pocket on his pants is cut out." Charley picked up the vest, which had several holes in it. "This looks like a bullet hole."" He pointed to a torn area under the right shoulder.

He brought the prisoner and the interpreter over to the bones. "Ask him how the pocket got cut out?"

"He says he came back the next day and decided to take the man's pocketbook and gun. He cut the money out of the pants and picked up the pistol where it had fallen. "

"Place the prisoner on the ground and guard him. We'll bury the remains here. Mr. Wilson, is there a particular place you would like your father's grave?"

George Wilson looked up from where he was still kneeling. His face was no longer drawn in anxiety, but shadowed with grief and anger. "What?"

"Where do you want the grave?" Charley asked again, trying to keep his tone gentle and soft.

The man blinked his eyes, stood up and looked around the area. It was a beautiful site, the little creek tumbling down from the mountain above, trees along the bank, a natural place for a grave. "I guess over under that big hickory tree. Then, I can find it when I bring my family back here. I'm sure they will want to place a proper marker."

Jimmy came up with two shovels. He handed one to Wilson and they began to dig. The soil was rich and soft, covered in a bed of leaves and mulch. It took about an hour to dig a proper grave. It had to be deep enough to keep out wild hogs, coyotes and other predators.

While they were busy with the digging, Charley directed a couple of the men on how to gather the remains. "Go back to the trail and get the canvas roll off my horse," he said. "In the meantime, we'll look around for any personal articles of clothing that might have been drug off."

It was not the first grave he had dug out in the field, but he hoped it would be his last. His mind went back to his friends, Deputy Ayers, buried at Cherokeetown and Ayers' brother-in-law, Deputy Bill Moody, buried at Tulsa. The Indian Territory was littered with the graves of brave lawmen, resistant ruffians who had died in gun battles and innocent travelers like this old man.

With the canvas rolled out on the ground next to the body, they gathered the bones and articles of clothing with reverence and care, placing them on the canvas. Charley could not help noticing how small the heap of bones seemed compared to the man they represented. The clothing was badly decayed, some of it only shreds. He rolled the bones and clothing securely in the canvas and tied the ends with rope.

"Jimmy, you take one end and I'll take the other." Charley lifted his end and they lowered it into the grave laying it flat on the bottom. Jimmy and Wilson began to fill in the grave. After the task was complete, Charley called the men together.

"No one should be buried out here without a proper ceremony. Please join with me in a prayer. Dear Lord, we give back to the earth your brother, Henry Wilson. He was taken unexpectedly and his family grieves for his death. Be with them and comfort them with this verse. John 14:6 - 'I am the way, and the truth and the light. No one comes to the Father except through me.' If Henry Wilson was your sheep, he is now home in your sheep fold. And we can take comfort in that promise. Amen."

The party got back to their camp by mid-afternoon. Charley turned Jefferson over to Abe to secure with the other two. "We'll head for LeFlore Station in the morning and talk to Charles Murray. He can say for sure if this is his gun."

Reaching LeFlore Station the next day, Murray positively identified the pistol. "It's mine alright, except the handle has been scraped clean of finish and there's a dent in the barrel that wasn't there before."

"Ask Jefferson if his brother helped him in this plot?" Charley instructed Jerry White.

"He says no, he was alone when he killed the old man."

"Alright. Abe, release Jimison Jones to return to his home."

The search party was dispersed. Most lived in the area and were glad to get home. Charley recognized a familiar horse at the general store as he turned his attention to the care and feeding of the prisoners.

Tyner Hughes stepped out of the store and walked to where the three brothers stood. "Howdy, I see you had a successful hunt. The store keeper told me all about it."

"We're ready to camp for the night. Where's your camp?" Charley asked.

"Over there about a hundred yards. There's plenty of room for you."

"We'll be over as soon as I pay for the livery charges."

After supper, the marshals attempted to talk to Jefferson Jones again. Charley knew that this man had been hiding a terrible secret for almost two months and would freely talk about it now. A killer did this out of pride or out of remorse. Jones seemed too matter-of-fact in his demeanor. He had no remorse.

The interpreter pointed at the prisoner. "How much money did you take off of Wilson's body? Where's his pocketbook?"

"I took $20 off him and buried it at my brother's house under the floor near the door. I gave him the pocket book."

"Did you tell him where you got the money?"

"Not then. I told him about a month later."

"So, he knows that you killed this old white man."

"Yes, he even went and seen the body."

"Tyne, it seems I let a prisoner go that I'll have to re-arrest. Can you take these two to Fort Smith with your prisoner? Abe and I'll head back over the mountain to search Jimison Jones' place for the money and pocketbook."

"Sure enough. I should be there by Wednesday."

A smaller search party consisting of George Wilson and two others reassembled to accompany the deputies. It took them most of the day to reach the location 25 miles from LeFlore Station.

As they approached the cabin which was three miles on the other side of the little creek where Wilson's body had been found, a pack of hounds came out from under the porch, trumpeting their challenge to the six riders. Jimison Jones came out on the porch.

The interpreter spoke to Jimison. "Call off your dogs. We need to talk to you some."

A *thunk* into the side of a hound with a rock sent the culprit to his hideout with a yelp and a whimper. The others followed with their tails tucked underneath their bellies.

"Sorry. These are for my security. Never know who might be coming up on me. My nearest neighbor is six miles away," Jimison said.

Charley got down and tied Billie to the hitching post. "Sit your saddles a minute while I talk to him."

He beckoned the interpreter to come to the porch with him. Charley stepped up and faced the man who was visibly shaking. His hands trembled so bad he stuck them in his pants pockets.

"We've been informed by your brother that he gave you some money in a pocketbook sometime in March. Do you remember that?"

"Yes, sir. It had a five dollar note in it."

Charley stared back at the young Choctaw. "He claims it contained $20. That's two months wages for a good cowhand. Did he say where he got it?"

"No, and I didn't want to know. My brother is wild sometimes and steals money from people. He told me to hide the money under the floor until he came back for it."

"What did you do then?"

"I hid it under the floor while he watched me."

"Show us where." Charley beckoned to the search party to dismount and follow him into the house.

The young man walked to the door and lifted up a loose board in front of the door. Charley stepped up and looked inside. He put his hand down and felt through the loose dirt. Nothing.

"What happened to the money?"

"I took it and spent it in Talihina after Jefferson didn't come back for it.

"Where's the pocketbook?"

The young man drew something out of his pocket and handed it to Charley.

George Wilson jumped forward and grabbed the leather pouch. "That's my Dad's. I recognize it."

Jimison hung his head. His voice was soft. The interpreter listened carefully and then spoke. "He says he preaches the Gospel and did not intend to tell any lies but got into this by reason of accepting this pocketbook from his brother."

Charley looked at the cowhide wallet in his hands. A man killed for a few dollars. How little money was enough to make it worth killing a man? This young man was remorseful only after he was caught being an accomplice. "Did your brother tell you about killing Wilson?"

"Yes, he told me a month or so ago. I then looked for the body. It was where he told me I would find it."

"Why didn't you tell someone about this?" Charley asked.

"I didn't want to see him hang on the white man's gallows."

Charley placed handcuffs on Jimison's wrists. The healthy muscles in the young man's arms would soon weaken as he languished for months in a five by six foot cell. "Because of your silence, you may join him there." A tragic mystery had been solved with no good to come of it for anyone.

We the Jury find the defendant, Jefferson Jones, Guilty of Murder as Charged in this Indictment.
W.J. Weaver, Foreman
And We find the defendants, Jimison Jones and James Beams, Not Guilty as charged in this Indictment.
W.J. Weaver, Foreman
10/14/89

Guilty verdict of murder by Jefferson Jones who was hanged at Fort Smith, Arkansas on January 16, 1890, the 64th man hung by sentence of Judge Parker, the second time 6 were hung together.

Chapter 53

New Boss, New Rules

May 29th, 1889 - the changing of the guard had begun at Fort Smith. Jacob Yoes, appointed by President Harrison, would fill the Marshal's office with his own appointees. Thunderous applause and cheers from the floor above tumbled down the stair case. It seemed to go on forever, ceased and then just as abruptly rose to a crescendo a few minutes later. The three deputies waiting quietly on the hard bench outside the Marshal's office raised their heads. Would the floor hold? Charley wondered.

The furor drowned out the ticking of the clock above the chief deputy's desk which normally sounded like the Tower of London in the quiet office. A painter stopped his task of removing the lettering of Marshal Carroll's name off the frosted glass to wipe his rag, a simple flick of his wrist removing the symbol of four good years of service.

Charley sat on the bench, elbows on his knees. He rotated his black felt hat, suspended between his knees. Tyner Hughes' right hand twirled the rowel of his spur. Deputies who were constantly riding and fighting could not sit still for long.

Charley looked at the ceiling as if checking for broken beams. "I'm glad I'm not involved in politics. This is hard on my hearing."

Tyne smiled and rubbed his chin. "I never think much of politics. We either go to war or sue for peace according to who's in charge. The War taught me to be suspicious of all government leaders until I get to know them. Judge Parker is the exception and a man worth following."

The man on Charley's right cleared his throat. James Lee, the deputy who had helped him pursue Bill Frazier in 86, sent a stream of tobacco juice expertly into the spittoon at his right foot before he grumbled. "I wonder why we're sitting here and not upstairs."

Tyne stopped fiddling with his spur to pick at his trousers. "Yoes wants us to meet him here promptly at noon. Either we're going to be the first ones to be let go or the first ones to be recommissioned. I'd like to think it's a swearing in ceremony."

Heavy foot steps coming down the stairs caused them to rise and stand, each man's quiet face hiding any thoughts or concerns for their future. The door to the office swung open, filling the room instantly with well-wishers and the new appointee. Carroll opened the door to his old office and held it while his replacement walked in. "You'll find everything in perfect order, Marshal Yoes."

Jacob Yoes had been a compromise choice over the imminently popular Judge Boles who had served before Marshal Carroll. His beardless, pleasant expression conveyed a sense of confidence. He smiled as he surveyed the office's neatly arranged shelves and file cabinets. A Republican in politics, he was a successful businessman and former Union Army soldier who had led aggressive raids against the Confederate bushwhackers during the War and had served in the state legislature in recent years.

"Most certainly, Mr. Carroll," replied the bellicose Yoes. "I wish you well as the new warden of the Arkansas State Prison. I'm sure I will see you on many occasions."

"My pleasure, now if you will excuse me, I've a train to board."

The three deputies stood quietly watching the departure of their old boss. Carroll's good-by speech had already been made to his deputy force. The new one turned to them and motioned them into his office.

"I've gone over the deputy roster with Mr. Carroll and he recommends you as the first appointees to my deputy force. If you consent to stay with me for the next four years, I will be happy to administer the oath to you at once."

In unison, the men said, "Yes."

"Then raise you right hand and swear after me:

> *I do solemnly swear that I will faithfully execute all lawful precepts, directed to the Marshal of the United States for the Western District of Arkansas, under the authority of the United States, and true returns make, and in all things will and truly, without malice or partiality, perform the duties of Deputy Marshal of the Western District of Arkansas, during my continuance in said office, and take only my lawful fees, so help me God."*

Charley repeated the oath which he had taken several times before, most recently under Marshal Boles in 1884 and Marshal Carroll in 1886. Each time he listened to the words, he reflected on the awesome responsibility it put on each deputy.

Yoes interrupted his thoughts when he handed him a pamphlet. "Here is the written summary of the Rules for Deputies for my administration. Read it in your spare time. If you have any questions, I'll be available in my office the rest of the day."

Charley glanced at it before tucking it inside his vest. He would read it before he left Ft. Smith tomorrow.

The new marshal continued. "I've persuaded the new President to grant an increase in the food rate for prisoners. It has been increased to 85 cents a day. Everything else stays the same. Good luck."

Charley shook hands with his rookie boss. The man's grip was firm but not aggressive. Maybe this change would not be as disruptive as he feared. Criminals always challenged a new marshal with increased violence and mayhem. Could this man handle it?

Outside the office, he glanced around at the new faces. A pleasant man in a business suit extended his hand. "I'm the new chief deputy, Sam Williams. This is my second, R.B. Creekmore." He had met both men previously. They were old friends of the court and Judge Parker, having served on several juries.

"Pleased to serve with you," Charley said. "When do the new guards come on duty?"

"Later today. We will relieve the old guards about six p.m. The only one being retained is the old hangman, George Maledon. No one wants his job."

"I'd like to come back and meet them later."

"That'll be fine," said Williams.

Charley returned in the evening to the Old Jail, now on duty with arrest warrants in his pocket and wearing his Colt Peacemaker. Two shifts of personnel crowded the main floor. The old guards handed equipment over to their replacements, a new jailer, deputy jailer, turnkey, three day guards and three night guards. The out-going men shook hands and slipped out quietly, their four years on duty finished. Most would have to look for new positions in the growing city of Fort Smith.

He noticed the new night guards carrying pistols or shot guns. A bright eye and a steady hand characterized the eager new hires.

The new marshal handed the keys to the main doors to the new jailer. "Jailer Pape will be ably assisted by Deputy Jailer Roberts. I've given each of you written policies for the administration of this jail. It goes without saying that when someone enters the cell compound, an armed guard will be present on the outside of the cage. The guards are the only ones allowed to carry weapons and are to cover the outside corridors that encircle the steel cage. When the prisoners are confined to their cells at night or to be released in the morning, only then will the turnkey enter the main cage to lock or unlock the cell doors. Any questions?"

All shook their heads except one man who raised his hand.

"How many people will be on duty at any one time?" he asked.

"The schedule will be set by the jailer according to the inmate population on each floor. Right now we are 90% full with 131 prisoners. The ideal is at least one turnkey and one guard on each floor at all times until the prisoners are locked in for the night. After that one man should be sufficient on each floor. Let's break for dinner."

Charley introduced himself to each man as they filed past him toward the exit. Personal relationships went a long way when working together. He didn't consider the jailers and guards as less qualified political appointees as did some deputies. They had to work together as a team to successfully maintain the great court and jail.

"I'm glad to meet you all. I try to bring in prisoners with undue harm. Take good care of them." They smiled and shook his hand. Deputies were a critical part of the arrest process, but confinement until trial was equally important.

The lull after the general crowd had been dismissed was welcome. It had been a busy day for everyone. Deciding to take a break before heading out, he sat down on the bench in the hall outside the main jail entrance and pulled the writs out of his pocket and studied them. The names were not familiar, larceny and introducing whiskey cases. Bring them in and then head home? He hoped it would be easier than the hunt for the corpse.

He pulled out the pamphlet titled, "Laws Governing U.S. Marshal and His Deputies." One of the sentences in the first paragraph caught his attention.

> "For violations of the revenue law and for introducing ardent spirits into the Indian Country, the Deputy can not make an arrest without warrant, unless the offender is caught in the act, when he can arrest for these offenses without a warrant."

Well, that's what they had been doing all along. Two more caught his eye. "No Deputy shall ever use the horses or other property of any prisoner in his charge." This had been abused and caused unpopularity, but what if he lost his horse? Lastly, "A deputy will be discharged promptly for conduct unbecoming an officer and gentleman while on duty." What's the interpretation of conduct unbecoming an officer and a gentleman? Sounded mighty arbitrary to him. He knew these petty regulations would anger many of the older experienced deputies.

He turned his head at a faint unfamiliar sound in the jail compound. Was a prisoner sick? He listened more intently then heard it again - a muffled, but clearly audible cry. *Help!*. He jumped from the bench and rushed to the outside door of the steel cage on the first floor.

A group of prisoners clustered together on the other side of the locked door, six or seven. One man, a rough, burly figure holding an iron bar, stood over the prostrate form of Deputy Jailer Roberts, blood oozing from a long gash in the top of his head. The escapee was searching his pockets. Charley recognized him as a prisoner named Reynolds in for assault.

"Where is it? Where's the key, old man? I'll kill you! Give it to me."

Roberts moaned but did not move.

"Drop that piece of iron and step back from the door!" Charley ordered.

The ring leader looked up from his struggle with the clothing and found he was staring down the barrel of Charley's large pistol and the steady hand that held it.

"Get out of our way, Barnhill," he demanded "Or I'll kill the old man, here." He raised the bar in a menacing manner over the still form. "We're getting out of here and you ain't stopping us."

Charley cocked his revolver and held it level, two feet from the Reynold's head. "I said drop that iron and step back."

"Everybody knows you won't kill nobody, Barnhill," muttered the determined inmate as he started prying at the locked door with the iron bar, "and you ain't likely to kill an unarmed man."

The other prisoners had already backed away and were watching wide-eyed pressed up against the bars of the holding cell just inside the main entrance.

This prisoner was calling his hand. Charley knew he could and would fire if necessary, but he had to try once more before firing. He made his tone serious. "You haven't had your trial yet. Jailer Roberts looks dead from here. I'll just have to carry out your execution a little early. I'm sure the judge won't mind."

Reynolds swore on oath and dropped the iron bar.

"Back away from the door." Charley unlocked the front door with the spare keys kept in the jailer's desk. Waving his pistol at the group, he herded them into the holding cell and locked the door.

"You just added a charge of attempted murder to your assault charge, Reynolds. That should be good for ten years at Little Rock."

His attention fell on the injured jailer. As he turned him over, Roberts' eyes fluttered open.

"What happened? Did they get away?"

"No, you put up enough of a fight to slow them down and allow me to throw down on them."

Charley wrapped his bandanna around the man's bleeding head and laid him back down. He pulled a blanket from a cot in an empty cell and placed it over the injured man.

"You just rest while I get help."

He rose and went out to the front hall. Stepping out on the front porch, he summoned a man walking by on Garrison Avenue.

"There's been an attempted jail break and the jailer is injured. Fetch the prison doctor and Marshal Yoes who are over eating dinner at the Silver Bell Restaurant."

The startled man hurried away at a run, his coat tails flapping in the breeze.

Charley returned and started up the stairs to the third floor, where the three night guards were having dinner. He burst in on their jovial meal making them all jump to their feet.

Hangman Maledon growled under his breath, "I should've known. The night was too quiet."

Hangman George Maledon

On the first floor, Charley and the guards met the Marshal and the prison doctor. Charley described the events to Marshal Yoes as they walked into the prison cage.

"I was resting in the hall and heard a ruckus coming from the jail. Found Roberts down and seven prisoners trying to get through the main door."

"Mighty glad you happened to be here still, Barnhill. It's obvious they've been planning an escape for just this time, the changing of the new guards. We'll question Reynolds and the others. Someone smuggled that iron bar in to them. From now on, everyone will have to be searched before going in to visit the prisoners."

"I agree, but women will pose a problem with their long skirts."

"I'll have the women's matron take care of that. Maybe the thought of a search will scare off some of the busybodies who like to gloat over the prisoners. You're a hero for stopping this dastardly jail break. I'll see to it that you get proper credit for your timely action."

"I just did my duty, sir. If you need me for anything further, I'll be at the hotel. Good night."

It was only after he had crossed the street headed for the hotel that he realized his pistol was still cocked and ready to fire, resting in his holster. Taking it out, he slid the hammer down on an empty chamber.

Resting in his room, he closed his eyes and visualized the scene he had just experienced. Why had Roberts entered the cage without another guard present? The overlooking of one simple procedure could lead to a jail break. Though an old man, he had put up a brave resistance. Charley wondered at the human will power for self-preservation when in a life or death situation. Unfortunately, the fugitives he tracked had the same fierce self-preservation instincts. Out-witting them was the best way. Sleep crept in as he saw the face of his little son and his young wife waiting for him at home.

Chapter 54

Betrayal

Lightening sparked out in all directions causing the clouds to look like a giant mushroom. The horses flinched with each crash. Abe pulled his slicker tighter as he watched Jimmy struggling with the wagon through the mud. He had his hands full keeping his team going. Charley rode in the lead barely visible in the heavy downpour.

Marshal Yoes had appointed thirty-six deputies in the past month, many of them experienced men from previous administrations, but also some new faces. One new face was Cal Whitson, the father of the young man, Billy Whitson, who had been killed with Deputy Phillips by the Barnett gang. He was returning to law enforcement because of a desire to help tame the lawlessness in the Indian country which had taken his son's life. Every man was needed for the task ahead.

Abe wondered if he would be retained. His commission was over two and a half years old. He managed to hang on to his duties, but some days, like today, it was tough. He felt the ache shoot up his left leg aggravated by the wet weather.

The arrest writs flowed from the grand jury in unprecedented numbers. They had arrested two the first two weeks in June, five last week on June 17th and now seven more on board the jail wagon. It was a relief that none of them were wanted for murder. He had reached his tolerance of hunting murders after finding the body of Old Man Wilson last month. Liquor violations could still get you shot in the back though.

One of the seven prisoners in the wagon was a repeat offender. Tyner Hughes had arrested Lafayette Hudson twice before for the same offense, hog stealing. He had been one of the defendants in the hog-stealing scheme with John Morgan in January of '88 and had been arrested again in January of this year but discharged for lack of evidence. Either he was an unrepentant hog-thief or had a running feud going with his neighbors. He was easy enough to find out in Bokoshe, Choctaw Nation.

As the Arkansas River came into view, Abe could see the new bridge being built to span the river. What a blessing that would be to the Indian Territory and Fort Smith. The ferry would be replaced by the most modern structure carrying both Jay Gould's Union Pacific Railroad and wagon and horse traffic separated on the lower level. It would be a headache for deputies who would have to patrol the passenger trains for illicit spirits.

He gave his horse a moment to snatch at a clump of grass at the bank as they waited for the ferry to pull ashore then watched the heavy wagons loaded with merchandise come off the ferry headed for the new Oklahoma Territory which had opened up in April. Merchants in Fort Smith and surrounding areas were selling stoves, shovels, plows, and barrels of nails as fast as they could be shipped in from St. Louis or New Orleans. The trains that ran inside the Indian Territory were also stuffed with cargo.

At the jail, the prisoners were released to the jailer, who had two guards standing outside, armed with shotguns. The scare they had received from the attempted jail break made everyone extra cautious.

Jimmy clicked to his team and waved to his brothers. "I'll meet you at the hotel when I'm done," he said.

They gathered at the round dining table in the hotel, discussing recent events. Always ready to enjoy time at home with their families, the time together was just as valuable.

"How's the little one, Effie?" Charley asked Abe. They were both new papas, yet seasoned veterans.

"She's growing and thriving. Jenette loves her dearly just as Mollie doted on Jenette when she was born. A young man from Milton named Pearly Robbins is courting Mollie. I won't allow her to marry until she is seventeen, though, two more years."

Charley felt a pang of sadness. Their children were growing up and would soon be living in their own households. "Well, if the boy really fancies her, two years will be worth the wait."

Jimmy shook his head. "I just want to get married and see what its like to be a husband and father."

"You've plenty of time for that," Charley said. "I plan on going out next week with one of the new deputies, Tom Shelbourne. We both cover the territory around McAlester. He's asked me to go with him on some of his first trips, just to teach him the terrain, the trails and the people he can trust."

A familiar figure appeared in the dining room, Heck Thomas dressed in a suit holding his signature white hat in his hand. "Can I join you fellas?"

Charley moved his chair around the table to let Heck sit down. "Sure, have a seat. We're just finishing supper. Where you been? Haven't seen you in a couple of months?"

"I've been over working with Marshal Needles in Oklahoma Territory."

Abe swallowed back his coffee and nodded. "I hear that's been some mad house."

"It took three hundred temporary deputies to keep things in order. Even then, it was murder, mayhem and robbery unchecked. I've been appointed also for the Eastern District of Texas. But I really want to work in the northern Oklahoma Territory."

"You have your work cut out for you if you take that district, right in the heart of the Cherokee country. There are some really rough citizens out there," Charley said.

"I know. I like the challenge."

Charley knew the exodus of experienced deputies was starting. "James White has turned in his resignation too. That eight page pamphlet of rules seems to have overwhelmed a lot of the older deputies."

Heck stood up and pitched his I.T. badge on the table. "You can turn that in for me. I think Fort Smith has become too civilized."

In silence they watched him walk away, hat still in hand.

Abe contemplated his brothers. "I feel he has made the right choice. This jurisdiction is going to get torn apart by politics from Washington.". He felt a certain uneasiness at the change, but knew it meant civilization and the taming of the Indian country.

Talihina, a little town deep in the Choctaw Nation, sat heavy in the heat of summer. It was the center of illicit whiskey sales for the whole of the Choctaw Nation, made worse by the arrival of the railroad the year before. The town was particularly busy since it was the 4th of July, 1889. Even in the Indian country, this auspicious day was celebrated with extra vigor.

Abe held a warrant for larceny against one William Bomine. He and Jimmy had found him hiding in a barn south of town. Now hand-cuffed and shackled to his horse, he rode without speaking, his eyes roving over the street and the many people about town. A young Indian boy pointed to the horsemen as his mother hurried him toward the general store.

Abe's eyes swept the throngs on the street. "All this celebration may encourage some people to use liquor right in front of us. The smugglers are hard to shut down. Keep you eyes open. We're going to camp near a man who's a leading citizen here. According to my informers, he may have procured some liquor to sell for the celebration."

After dinner, the brothers sipped at their coffee. The prisoner had his cup and drained it with one gulp.

"Hello the camp," a voice cried from the trees.

Abe stood up and stepped away from the fire to focus his eyes. "Who goes there?"

"A neighbor, come to celebrate the 4th with you." A man stepped into the light of the campfire. He appeared to be well-dressed and was unarmed. A well-trimmed beard covered his face. "My name is Ben Hare, live in that house yonder."

Abe extended his hand and indicated a seat by the fire. "I'm Abe Barnhill and this is my brother, James." He didn't mention his title as the badge was evident on his chest. If his informer was right, this man would offer him a drink if he acted like he wanted one.

Jimmy raised his hat to his head. "I'll go check on the horses."

The visitor seemed cordial enough when he spoke, his gaze drifting to the prisoner sitting alone in the shadows."The folks are sure happy about the 4th, and any excuse to whoop it up," the visitor said.

"I guess on a night like this a man feels he needs a little liquor just to celebrate."

"We want to keep you deputies happy when you travel through here."

Abe eyed the man's features. Was he making conversation or leading up to something? "What do you mean?"

"Some of the businesses here depend on bootleg sales, if you know what I mean. A cooperative gesture would make your travels through here a lot safer."

"I feel pretty safe right now," Abe said. Where was this going? Sounded like a good ole boy offer to make it worth his while to turn his head.

"It's in your interest to be friends with the leading citizens of this town."

"I can't say my interests rest with this town. My oath ties me to the citizens of the United States."

"If you want to make a little extra money, we could arrange that. Let me go up to the house and bring back something to seal the understanding."

"I don't have an understanding but you're welcome to come back to the camp fire if you've a mind," Abe said. He hoped he did not bring any friends back with him to seal the *understanding*.

As the man disappeared into the dusk, Abe turned to Jimmy who had just returned from the horses. "I've just been offered a bribe."

"I was too far away to hear the conversation. What's he want?" Jimmy said.

"Some kind of favorable treatment. Be on the look out for trouble." Abe noticed the prisoner was sitting real still and listening intently. "Hope this prisoner doesn't have friends figuring to help him out tonight. Keep a tight watch."

In less than half an hour, Hare reappeared. He was carrying a half gallon whiskey jug.

Jimmy sat silent watching the visitor.

"I reckon we can seal this understanding with a drink." He offered the jug to Abe.

Now what? He did not drink and he could not let this fella think he was interested in anything crooked.

"Sorry, Mr. Hare. I don't drink. And I can't ignore your possession of liquor in the territory. I'm placing you under arrest."

The man's face reddened. "There must be some misunderstanding. You asked me for this drink."

It was Abe's turn to be taken back. "You must have misunderstood. I said nothing of the sort. Do I have your promise to appear here in the morning to go to Fort Smith?"

"Yes, I'll be here, but the marshal is going to hear of this outrage."

Abe could not rid himself of a feeling of concern as he rode into town to send a telegram for the arrest warrant. Had he been set up? Was his informer working with this fella?

At the telegraph office, he scrawled a short message for Fort Smith. It read:

> *Sent to: Fort Smith, Ark. 4:40 p. 7/4/1889*
> *Dated: Talihina, I.T.*
> *To: Jacob Yoes*
> *Fort Smith, Ark.*
> *Caught man named Ben Hare with half a gallon whiskey issue writ near Talihina. Will be here till morning.*
> *A. Barnhill, Dep. Marshal*

He had done his duty. The prisoner could take up his complaint with the marshal.

Abe couldn't believe what he was hearing. Yoes faced him across his desk.

"I've been informed by the prisoner you brought in on Monday that you tricked him into bringing out his whiskey. He says he has several prominent friends in Talihina who will testify to that fact."

"Marshal Yoes, the charge is completely false. In fact, the man offered me the drink as a bribe."

"Well, he has had to procure $100 bail and await the hearing of the grand jury on the charge at a great inconvenience to him. He has to reappear on the 12th. His complaint is serious and I can't have my officers charged in such a manner."

"Marshal Carroll had enough sense to know when someone is lying to get an officer in trouble."

Now it was Marshal Yoes' turn to get red in the face. "Consider yourself relieved. Turn in your badge now. I don't need a deputy who is not fully fit physically anyway. I've plenty of able-bodied men waiting to take any vacancies I get."

Abe's lip curled as he answered. "It doesn't seem to matter to this office if a deputy is seriously wounded in the line of duty. He's just no longer fit for duty. What about Deputy Slusher who was waylaid down on the Black Fork last week? That's some of the same bunch that shot me."

"You can still work as a posse to your brother. I just need your badge to give to someone more fit."

"Your hiring practices have run off some mighty good men. You'll regret their loss when the toughs make their next stand in Indian country. The Barnetts are gone now, but someone else will be along to take their place."

Abe watched in silence as the two prison wagons rumbled up to the jail compound. After being dismissed earlier that morning, he had waited for Charley's arrival to break the news to him before he heard it from the jail gossip. They confided in each other and discussed life events on a level only brothers could understand. He dreaded the scene and felt he had let Charley down somehow. How could he have been so stupid?

Charley dismounted and threw the reins over the bar. He smiled and walked toward him.

"Howdy, brother. Shelbourne and I have a good haul here, ten prisoners. He's going to do alright. What are you doing hanging around?"

Abe swallowed in an effort to suppress the gall that rose up in his throat as he pulled Charley aside.

"I've been dismissed."

Blood rushed to Charley's face as he heard the word. *Dismissed.*

"What does this Marshal think he's doing? Carroll stood behind his deputies. I think I'll turn in my badge and join you."

"I made a mistake in trusting an informant and got set up. It's my fault for not checking my sources more carefully."

"Well, he didn't have to fire you over it." Charley gritted his teeth as he spit out the words.

Abe fought his bitterness in an effort to encourage his life-long best friend. "Keep your badge and see what the rest of the year will bring. Don't make a hasty decision because of me."

"I don't know if I have the stomach for it, working for a man who fired my brother. Will you posse for me?"

"I need to go home and tell Amanda what has happened. She will be sorely distressed. I've been pressing pretty hard since my wound and re-injury, trying to show the other men I could keep up. Maybe I can't. It'll be good to go home and not have to worry about chasing outlaws for a while. I may even have time to enjoy my baby daughter, Effie."

Charley spat into the dirt in disgust. "Maybe this marshalin' isn't for me anymore. I used to love the challenge of the tracking and apprehending, but now it seems like it never ends. Bring in one man and two takes his place."

"Do your duty and love it, Charley. Don't fret about me." Abe turned and limped to his horse. A family, a comfortable house and a good home-cooked meal, what more could a man ask for? Maybe he'd take up farming again.

Marshal Jacob Yoes

Chapter 55

Uncle Johnny

The new town of Sallisaw, Cherokee Nation was born when the Arkansas Valley Railroad had been laid through last year. The increased businesses with eating establishments and stores around the rail stop had made the old stage stop at Childers Station obsolete. The post office, still a mile and a half out of town on the stage line, would be moved eventually when the railroad started carrying the mail.

Charley eased up beside his assistant deputy, John Yoes, relative of the new marshal. He seemed an alright sort and Charley didn't mind riding with him.

"You ever met Uncle Johnny Childers who runs the post office?" "No, I've heard he is quite the personality."

"This post office established in 85' was the first between Fort Smith and Muskogee. The people gather for hours before the stage's arrival to whittle and chew. We should be just in time to observe the show."

A crowd of about a hundred of all ages and sizes stood around the post office: mothers with little children, some carrying a little one on their back in a blanket, old couples sharing a blanket on the grass, younger men and women in their going to town clothes. It had the appearance of a tribal ceremony.

The stage coach had already arrived and the mail bags stood on the ground. The younger boys grabbed a pouch apiece and scrambled for the door so as to be the first to grab the mail bag key off the peg hook. As they unloosened each sack, it was poured onto a large square table in the middle of the room. It reminded Charley of the old corn husking tables from Arkansas.

After the large mound of mail rested in a pile, the postmaster stepped up, somewhat unsteady on his feet. "Well, boys, I thank you for helping me, but you must stand back now while I let the older folks hunt for their mail. Come on you older folks now and see for yourselves if you have a letter or something - now stand back you children." His words, though coherent, were run together.

Yoes observed the goings-on from the door. "Can they all read? Whose to make sure no one takes someone else's mail?"

"Most can read due to the efficiency of the Indian schools. Everybody expects everybody else to be honest and especially to tell the truth. The myth of the stealing Indian does not exist here, only amongst the Plains Indians who see stealing from their neighbor as a badge of honor."

"I wish my neighbors were so honest. The War certainly put our nation back with its destruction of normal society and rules."

"What a nation loses so quickly is hard to regain. Same with this culture during the War when Cherokee fought against Cherokee. Let's say hello to Uncle Johnny. I've had complaints about his drinking while on duty and he hides a few gallons behind the counter of his store."

Charley walked across the small room to the postmaster who sat behind the store counter, a slumped heap of vest, long sleeved shirt, a double strand of yellow beads around his neck and bandana in his pocket. The old gentleman got up when they approached and held up his hand in greeting. He had gray hair, full length to his shoulders, grayer than the last time Charley had seen him.

"Marshal Barnhill, greetings." He tried to stand but tottered back and sat down hard on the bench.

"Uncle Johnny, have you been drinking?" Charley asked.

"Why, yes. Do you expect me to lie to you?"

"I guess I have to take you to Fort Smith, then," Charley said as gently as he could. This old man was an icon of the community and loved by everyone. "I'll have to search your store for liquor."

Charley located what he suspected, 2 1/2 gallons of whiskey behind the counter. "Who brought this to you?"

"My partner, Charles Starr."

"Where is he?"

"At his house."

"We'll pick him up too."

"You bet, marshal. I'll be right with you." Uncle Johnny put on his hat and coat and took the door key off the peg. As they exited the post office, he locked the door and gave the key to one of the older boys.

"See to it that no one bothers the mail 'til I get back."

"I, Do Solemnly Swear and believe from reliable information in my possession that JOHN CHILDERS AND CHARLES STARR did, within the Western District of Arkansas, on or about the 14th day of July, 1889, and at various other times within three years last past, unlawfully introduce into the Indian Country a large quantity of spirituous liquors, to-wit 2 1/2 gallons of whiskey, and did also, at or about the same time, violate the Internal Revenue laws of the United States by engaging in and carrying on the business of a Retail Liquor Dealer without first hav-

ing paid the special tax provided for and required by law, against the peace and dignity of the United States of America and I pray a warrant for his apprehension."

CHARLES BARNHILL
Subscribed and sworn to before me this 15th day of July, 1889.
STEPHEN WHEELER
United States Clerk
WITNESSES: C. BARNHILL and JNO. YOES

Charley signed the document and handed it back to the court clerk.

Clerk Wheeler examined it for completeness. "I'll give this to the district attorney. I'm sure both men will give bond and be home by tomorrow. How'd you happen onto this?

"Just riding through and stopped to show John Yoes the mail scramble that goes on out there."

"You used to live there, didn't you?"

"Yes, I consider Old Uncle Johnny a dear friend."

"Then, why did you bring him in?" Wheeler asked.

"I've had complaints about his increasing drinking problem. It's getting worse. Thought this might get his attention and straighten him out. He's lived too long to die like that."

The next day the courtroom was full, as usual. The two defendants, Johnny Childers and Charles Starr, stood up to make their pleas. Witnesses, friends, newspaper reporters and lawyers all filed in and sought seating. The bailiff read the complaint.

Charley and John went to the stand to describe the discovery of the whiskey and the subsequent arrest of the defendants.

"Deputy Barnhill, did you have a writ of arrest of John Childers at the time you went to his store?" the defense attorney asked.

"No, sir. I did not."

"Under what authority did you arrest him?"

"Both Deputy Yoes and I witnessed that he appeared to be drunk, searched his store and found two and a half gallons of whiskey behind the counter, in pint canning jars. I arrested him and brought him to Fort Smith where we filed a complaint against him."

"Have you ever seen the defendant drunk before?"

"No, sir."

"That'll be all. Your Honor, the defendant, John Childers, would like to testify."

"Alright call him to the stand and swear him in. Does he need an interpreter?" Judge Parker asked.

"No, I don't think so."

The old man rose and stepped to the witness box, great dignity apparent in his clothing, his braided hair, his steady eyes and set lips. He looked around at the sea of faces watching him.

"Mr. Childers, did you import this whiskey that the deputies found?," his attorney directed.

"I did not 'port it."

"I want to talk to this Indian, myself" Judge Parker interrupted. "Mr. Childers, did you say you didn't import this whiskey?"

"I don't know the 'port of it, but I got whiskey."

"Say you did it."

"Yes, you bet, I did it."

Laughter filled the courtroom as the spectators were drawn into the drama of the great judge questioning a noble and revered Indian leader.

"How much whiskey did you get?"

Uncle Johnny sat there a long time.

"Don't understand how much. Don't know how to tell it."

"Tell it in your own words or you can have an interpreter," Judge Parker said.

"'Bout three hundred barrels, guess so," blurted out Uncle Johnny.

Judge Parker burst out laughing. "I will decide tomorrow what the sentence shall be on this confession."

The next day, the court room was filled again. What would the judge give the old Indian? He had been charged in the same offense several years ago in 1883. He had gotten off when witnesses who knew him vouched for his good character. Would he be punished this time?

The people stood as the judge came in. Silence. Charley looked around and noticed smiles on faces, eager to hear the verdict.

"John Childers, Charles Starr, please stand for your sentencing." Judge Parker cleared his throat before his full voice echoed around the courtroom.

"John Childers and Charles Starr, since you have confessed so honestly to your charge, I hereby sentence you each to one hour in jail and a twenty dollar fine." The judge rapped his gavel as the courtroom burst into laughter.

"Marshal Yoes, the prisoners are released having met the one hour in jail part of the sentence when they were brought in and made bond. Collect their money and send them to the stage depot for home."

Charley arose and walked to Marshal Yoes.

"I'd like to be the one to escort them, since I brought them in."

"That'll be fine. Hope your friend has learned his lesson. He got off scot-free on this charge that could have cost him a lot of money and time in jail."

"He's an old man and will surely meditate on the error of his ways, Marshal."

Charley walked to the prisoners and released their handcuffs.

"I'll take you to the clerk to pay your fine and then to the depot."

"Thank you, Deputy Barnhill," the old man said. "I've learned my lesson. Don't like to come to Fort Smith and face the Great White Judge."

Charley thought about the simple honesty of these people, that most white men did not understand. They were grand examples of a fine civilization which had ruled one third of the whole East Coast, from the Mississippi River to the Atlantic Ocean.

Chapter 56

The Muskogee Court

If the wisdom of Solomon could be imparted to men, Charley wished it to be given to the Congress of the United States of America. Politicians tried to make rules for a country they did not understand, listening to the land grabber interests who had greedy eyes on millions of acres in the Indian country. The beginning of the end of the separate Indian Nations came in 1889.

Charley turned the newspaper and read more, skimming the court notes. He was still too upset over Abe's dismissal to take much interest in the other deputies' activities. He would concentrate on his own work and leave everything else alone.

As the Washington interests stripped away the land from the Indians, they also removed power from the Fort Smith court. The first court for white men established in the Indian Territory would have complete civil jurisdiction and jurisdiction over criminal offenses that did not hold a sentence of death or hard labor. Judge Parker would keep that for a few more years. Both jurisdictions would mutually share charges involving liquor violations. A judge, marshal and juries to hear the cases would convene at Muskogee in the Cherokee Nation.

A further weakening of the great court had occurred when "the right of appeal to the Supreme Court of the United States should be allowed in all cases of conviction of crime where the punishment provided for death." Judge Parker's' death sentences could now be over-turned by the Supreme Court. That's all the country needed, murderers that deserved to die crying to the Supreme Court, which had never heard a criminal case in its history.

The Chickasaw Nation and the southern half of the Choctaw Nation were now placed under the jurisdiction of the Northern District of Texas with the court meeting at Paris. To Charley's relief, he noticed that all penalties had been raised with mandatory sentences and fines for most offenses much higher. He guessed he would not be going south anymore.

One item did catch his attention. Another killer of a deputy marshal would face his doom. Frank Cogburn, moonshiner from Montgomery County, Arkansas had been tried and convicted of Deputy Trammel's murder during the bloody summer of '88.

He hoped he would never see things that bad again. The incremental arrests and convictions were having an effect on the violence of "Hell on the Border", as one newspaper called the Indian territory.

The newspaper finished, he laid it aside and took up the paper work the chief deputy had sent him, eight arrest warrants for violent crimes, rape, larceny, and introducing illicit spirits into the Indian Territory. He could not go after all these men without a reliable posse. He would need Abe by his side. Maybe he had rested enough to consider going out again.

Taking his hat off the rack he stepped out to find Irene in the back of the house hanging wash. One day each week she set aside for her and Minnie to do the wash. It was hard work and took all day, but when it was done, they rewarded themselves with a cup of tea and cookies she had baked special the night before. The clothes line sagged with the weight of the wet articles. An extra long pole placed in the middle kept the line well above Irene's head, just within arm's reach. Minnie scrubbed the clothing at the wash board, placing items aside in the rinse water as she finished them. He'd seen a picture of a hand-turned washing machine in the Sears Catalog. They ranged in priced from $2 to $8. He would order her one the next time he was in Fort Smith.

Charley kissed her on the back of the neck. "I've got to send a telegram to Abe. Do you need anything from town?" Her hair was pinned up and her skin felt warm and moist to his lips.

"No, I don't think so. I have to stop and feed Tony in a few minutes after his nap."

He found Henry in the barn repairing the stirrup on his saddle. He rode Billie now that a younger horse had been trained for Charley's use. Billie deserved his last years in a comfortable pasture.

"You want to ride with me to McAlester?" His son already stood a head above Billie's sixteen hands shoulder height (64 inches). His red hair and freckles shown in the summer sun.

"Okay, Pa. I'll saddle up and be right with you."

The ride into South McAlester took only a few minutes. The telegraph office at the train depot was manned twenty-four hours a day, the operator also acting as ticket clerk and baggage handler for the passengers and freight. Three men rotated around the clock to cover the station.

A balding man wearing the uniform of the MK&T Railroad stepped up to the window. "Howdy, Deputy Barnhill. What can I do for you?"

"Please send this telegram as soon as possible. When I get an answer, send it out to my place right away."

"Sure thing, Deputy."

"Come on, son. Let's celebrate by getting something at the general store. We'll surprise the women."

"What's the occasion?"

"My ten year anniversary of riding for Fort Smith and I'm still breathing."

"But you gotta remember all the holes you've had shot in you."

"I do, and I thank the Lord every time I look at my old scars. I've used up a lot of guardian angels."

Charley looked in the candy case for a peppermint stick for Minnie and some brown sugar drops for Irene. "That should do it. What do you want, Henry?"

"I'll try the horehound drops. They're my favorite."

"Give me two sugar cubes for the horses, too."

Charley paid for the purchases and stuffed the paper sack into his vest pocket.

As they rode home, Henry was unusually quiet. When Charley was home he usually talked his ear off.

"What's on your mind, son?"

"Pa, I've been thinking about what I want to do when I get old enough."

"What's that?"

"I want to go hunting outlaws' just like you and Uncle Abe."

"I don't think so. By that time, I'll have caught all the bad guys and you won't have to worry about them." Charley laughed as he said it. *Wish that were true.*

Abe stared at the message.

August 9, 1889, McAlester, C.N. Need your help right away, eight men to bring in. Meet me in McAlester if you can come. Charley

The three weeks he had been at home had not removed the bitter feelings every time he thought of a deputy's badge. He was a Christian and the Lord commanded him to love his enemies. Was this the opportunity to put aside disappointment and hurt and step out in obedience?

Amanda had sat down in the rocking chair and cried when he told her. "Well, at least I don't have to worry about your safety anymore. I always fret when you got out on a trip. The Lord knows best." She had gathered little Effie in her arms and begun to rock her, singing softly to the drowsy baby.

Now, he had to tell her he was taking one more trip for Charley's benefit. He rode home with the message tucked in his pocket. He would wait until he talked to her to send a reply.

Five year-old Jenette was playing in the yard with the neighbor boy. Kick the can, a favorite sport, kept children occupied for long hours in the summer sun. Her long hair flowing down her back, she ran to her father as he came in the gate.

"Papa, Rodney's here to play. Can we go swimming later?"

"I'll talk to your mother about it after dinner." He picked her up and gave her a kiss on the cheek and let her back down. She got embarrassed if he tried to pick her up in front of her friends, something about not being a baby anymore.

As he stepped in the house, he could smell the wonderful aroma of fried chicken. What was the occasion? Amanda usually reserved chicken for Sunday dinner and the parson coming over.

Amanda came from the kitchen, wiping her hands on her apron. She kissed his cheek and stepped to the cradle where the baby napped in the coolness of the back porch. With both the front and back doors open, the wonderful morning breeze kept the outside kitchen where she cooked in the summer moderate and cool. They actually moved the wood stove outside on the back lean-to during the summer months.

"I've got a telegram from Charley. He wants me to take a trip with him to pick up eight fugitives. I wanted to talk to you before I send him a reply."

"Are you sure you want to keep helping out after your dismissal? You'll have to face all your friends who'll know what happened."

"I'll do it if Charley needs me."

"Honey, don't overlook your opportunities for a great life without a gun and a badge, when you do decide to quit completely." She kissed him and hugged his neck.

The slap of harness against chain, the creaking of the wagon wheels, the snort and wheeze of the team signaled all living creatures that the prison wagon was passing. The town of McAlester, busier now than ever before, did not even notice the two lawmen and the eight prisoners, riding in the wagon behind the guard. The cook wagon brought up the rear of the procession.

Charley stopped his horse in front of the deputy's office which had been moved from Krebs to McAlester on the appointment of the new court in Indian country. He and Deputy Shelbourne were the main tenants but the facility was shared with other deputies that patrolled the Indian Territory as they came through.

"Find a camp spot along the river, and I'll join you after I check in at home." His eyes ran over the prisoners, assessing their condition. Most were young men who had made unfortunate life choices, landing them in the prison wagon in chains. Two men charged with rape, two charged with running a horse stealing ring, two brothers running a whiskey still and two other liquor sellers. They had covered a good portion of the Creek territory to catch most of these men.

The evening fire flies came out in thick flocks that lit up the meadows and fields. How many beautiful sun sets had he watched from beside a campfire?

As he rode up to his home, his eyes searched for anything amiss. All seemed as he had left it. Billie grazed in the pasture beside the house, swishing his tail rhythmically. The family cow munched at the grain in the trough, her young calf attempting to stick his nose in beside hers. Lightning cut the sky to the west bringing a smell of rain. Tornado season caused the more cautious citizens to build underground rooms for protection. His was behind the house, the small hill with a metal stove pipe marking its roof.

Irene met him at the door, her hair tied in a ribbon. He was always amazed at this slip of a girl who shared his bed and his fortune. Motherhood made her more radiant.

"What a pleasant surprise. I've got supper about ready. How'd things go?"

"Abe and Jimmy are guarding eight men. I'll join them after supper."

"You've a letter on the lamp table by the door. It came today."

The letter was written in a familiar hand. He noted the return address, H. Thomas, Vinita, Cherokee Nation, Indian Territory.

He sat down and began to read, the three short paragraphs.

"Dear Charley,

I brought my last prisoner to Fort Smith on July 24th and heard the news about Abe. It's a real shame a good deputy can be dismissed over such a charge. I hope he continues to help you. Offer him, please, my concerns.

The territory here is filling up with men of bad character as expected. Seems all I do is run from one case to another for the tribe. I had the pleasure of arresting a lunatic recently who managed to escape from the chains the town marshal had put on him. I moved him and chained him to the post office safe, but then he stripped naked to the horror of the patrons. Had to take him to an empty warehouse and watch him all night.

If you want to take a position in McAlester working for the Muskogee court, I'm sure you could help out.

Your Most Sincere Friend, Heck Thomas"

As he ate supper, he tried to concentrate on his family and their supper table conversation, only half-listening as Henry told a funny story of a porcupine and his hound dog. His thoughts returned to the letter, offered at a time when his duty as a deputy seemed to be challenged by circumstances out of his control. He'd continue to think things over between now and the end of the year, as he had promised Abe.

Heck Thomas in new Oklahoma Territory, 1889

Chapter 57

The Christmas Train

Two days before Christmas the streets of Fort Smith displayed holiday cheer. Carolers on corners sang tunes with unusual gusto. Store windows glowed with bright colors and selections that bulged the displays to their limits. The town on the Arkansas river was no longer on the frontier; commerce thrived as did its citizens. Smartly dressed women in bonnets and caps covering long skirts tugged children along as they threaded through the crowded sidewalks. Townsmen carried brightly wrapped packages tucked under arms. Men stopped and tipped hats to any acquaintance they chanced to meet.

Charley stepped out of C.C. Ayer's general store, a package under each arm, and headed for his hotel room. Earlier in the day he had brought in John Ogelsby, charged with murder of his own cousin. He planned to get home for Christmas by catching the afternoon train to McAlester.

The hustle and bustle of Garrison Avenue was a comfortable reminder of the progress of the city. Maybe Heck was right, it had become too civilized. He dodged a hack in the middle of the street and entered the hotel lobby. Assistant Chief Deputy Creekmore rested in a comfortable parlor chair, a newspaper held to his face, which he lowered when he saw Charley.

He rose and folded the newspaper under his arm, "You're just the man I've been waiting for."

Charley extended his hand while balancing the packages. "Howdy, I thought all you fellas from the jail would be home with your families today."

"The chief deputy asked me to track you down, knowing you were in town. He has an assignment for you."

"Let's go to the dining room and talk about it over some dinner."

After he ordered, the man turned in his seat and rested folded hands on the table.

"I guess you saw the newspaper editorial in The Elevator from November first." The man pushed the paper towards him.

Charley read the article in its entirety before he looked up.

DEPUTY MARSHALS

Poorly Paid and Poorly Protected Servants of the Government.

Few people are aware when they read in the papers of the arrival of deputy marshal So-and-So from the Indian country with a lot of prisoners how much hardship the officer has encountered on his trip and how little the compensation allowed him by this great government or care for the trials and dangers he had endured. His trip of from two to six weeks is made up of long night rides, hard living and much expense, which comes out of his own pocket. When he makes his report, if he had not succeeded in bringing two or three hard cases - murder, assault, or larceny - remarks will be in order that too much attention is given by him to trifling whiskey cases and the next inquiry is "Why don't they arrest some of those hard cases out there instead of pulling so many of those light offenders,"etc. There are several reasons for deputy marshals being very careful about trying to capture big game. In the first place, if they run down a murderer and happen to kill him to save their own lives, they get no compensation for time lost, time and money spent in their pursuit of this bad man. If they wound him, then they must necessarily give him proper medical attention and keep him as best they can until they can bring him to jail and all this time he is an expense to them for which the government allows them nothing in return. On the other hand, if he gets wounded himself in his endeavors to enforce the law, then he is in for it, as he is perhaps laid up for several weeks among strangers and makes no return of his trip and must defray his own expenses. Frequently they get killed and as a rule their remains must be buried wherever they chance to fall, at the expense of themselves or comrades, in many instances leaving large families on the cold charity of the world.

We think it high time that congress adopted some measure allowing deputy marshals in the Indian country better compensation by fixing their fees in such a way as to enable them to make proper efforts to pursue and arrest the many desperate characters in that country without risking the loss of their time and private means as well as their lives."

He folded the paper and handed it back to his companion. "Yes, I did see this. There's been much talk among the deputies about this problem. What has that got to do with me?"

"The Marshal wants to make a point about the importance of liquor violations and that they are not small stuff when it comes to putting down the violence in Indian country."

Where was this leading he wondered?"What do you mean?"

"The Frisco Railroad has been running through Indian Territory for two and a half years now. It runs through some of the worst whiskey peddling country in the Choctaw Nation. The train actually invites even more liquor smuggling. It's not popular, but he feels searching the passengers has to be stepped up to discourage such activity."

"Where do I fit in?"

"Yoes wants a deputy who is above criticism, one who does not drink and is known to be honest in all his dealings. He's picked you, '*the Bible-believing deputy.*'"

Charley had a sinking feeling he was not getting home for Christmas. "What does he want me to do?"

"Pick another deputy and two posse men and be on the train when it leaves Fort Smith on Christmas Day. Discreetly but forcefully search all passengers' grips, no exception."

"And if this causes an uproar, who gets blamed?"

"Not you. He will defend your actions to the fullest. Searches on the Valley trains have caused some complaints, but they must continue."

" I'd rather be home for Christmas, but I'll help." Charley knew this would not be easy, too many holiday travelers.

Abe and Jimmy watched the passengers board the two coaches, one for general use and the second one a smoking coach for men. It had the amenity of card tables to pass the time. Of course, all liquor would be locked up until the train passed out of Indian Territory into Texas. Abe knew the festive nature of the day would dissipate as their presence and purpose were revealed.

They stood with Deputy Ben Cantrell who had agreed to go along. Ben had also arrived in Fort Smith on Monday shortly after Charley, with five prisoners in tow, all charged with introducing and selling liquor in the Indian Territory. The men had been briefed on the exact purpose of the trip. Charley would explain the touchy parts to them after they got on board.

The conductor observed the badged men and waved them aboard.

"Take any seat that's empty. We should have a full car today."

Abe followed Charley to a seat. The four sat facing each other. Charley removed his hat and ran his fingers through his hair.

"I'm glad you're all here. Here is the plan. As soon as the train crosses into Indian Territory, we have been instructed to search all passengers' personal baggage for whiskey. No exceptions."

Oh, great. He gave up Christmas at home to get in more trouble for whiskey arrests. Abe knew this could be a trap that would entangle them in controversy if they were not careful. As the Indian Territory marched closer and closer to statehood, people were less tolerant of being denied their liquor. They viewed it as a personal right, regardless of the law.

Ben Cantrell spoke. "Whiskey searches will be a real affront to most of these holiday travelers. Why today? Let's ride to Paris and do it on the way back out of Texas."

"Our instructions are to do the search on the train that left Fort Smith. This is to get Fort Smithites to realize the seriousness of transporting illicit spirits for any use including personal. The law says it is illegal to possess any illicit spirits in Indian Territory. You know that."

The trip began with a great belch of smoke and the furious churning of metal against rails until the friction of the heated wheel grabbed the rails. A slight lurch and they were underway. The coach was full as the conductor had advised them. Most of the passengers were men though Abe noticed two women in the crowd. He hated to put women to such an embarrassment.

Then, he remembered the time the jailers searched Belle Starr after Charley and Tyner Hughes brought her in and found a great big .45 pistol hidden in her petticoats. Women had places to hide all sorts of bulky items. He also knew that the curtains tied back from the windows were favorite hiding places for people carrying on bottles. They would hide them there as they boarded then retrieve them as they got off. If any lawman accosted them in a search, they would come up clean.

After the train moved away from the depot stop at Rock Island, Abe watched Charley stand up. Before he moved away from them, he instructed them.

"Ben, we'll start in the middle of the car and work towards the doors. I'll have Abe and Jimmy seated at each door in case anyone attempts to leave the car. Don't show your pistols unless someone tries to leave."

Abe moved to the front of the car as Jimmy took the opposite door, nodding to Charley that he was in position. Charley approached four men seated on two facing benches, each one wearing big fur hats, heavy wool overcoats and knee-high hunting boots. The cars had no heat and passengers dressed accordingly.

Charley spoke to the first man, who looked up and eyed his deputy's badge.

"Sir, I have to take a look in your grip to make sure you're not carrying whiskey," Charley said. His tone was direct but polite.

The man's face purpled. Oh, no. This could mean trouble. Abe's hand went to his pistol, resting his fingers lightly on the grip.

The passenger drew himself to his full height and gestured toward his satchel. "Sir, I protest your search of my private possessions without proper papers. My friends and I are prominent citizens of Fort Smith. We're on a hunting trip."

"Then, you should be aware that deputies routinely search passengers on the trains," Charley said.

"If you're to open that grip, you'll have to cut it open."

"Sir, that is a very nice and, I am sure, expensive case. I would hate to ruin it. Just tell me if you are carrying whiskey and I won't pry it open."

The man thought for a moment and then shrugged his shoulders.

"Yes, we all are. I give you our word that we'll report to Marshal Yoes when we get back. We are his friends and supporters."

"Give me your names and I will turn in the complaint when I get back to Fort Smith."

Charley wrote down their names making sure to spell them correctly.

"I demand to know your name, sir," the first man said.

"Why?" Charley asked.

"I should inform you that as soon as we get back, I'm going to lodge a complaint with the Marshal about this outrageous search. And the editor of The Elevator will also be informed."

"My name's Barnhill, United States Deputy Marshal Charles Barnhill, spelled B.A.R.N.H.I.L.L."

A bad taste filled Abe's mouth. Why did prosperous, influential men think they were above the law? His eyes roved over the faces of the passengers who had grown silent at the confrontation in the middle of the car.

The next passenger was an older woman dressed in gray with a white fur collar on her cape. She had gray hair pulled into a bun and wore black gloves.

'Ma'am. I notice you have a paper box there beside you on the seat. May I look in it?"

"I assure you, Deputy, all that is in there are six quarts of peaches for my grandson."

Charley picked up the box and shook it. It rattled of glass and liquid. Abe could tell from his vantage point that Charley was squirming. This could be his own mother.

"Sorry, Ma'am." He carefully pulled out his hunting knife from its sheath and cut the strings around the box. He peered inside and glanced up at Abe. Their eyes met. Must have been peaches.

"My apologies, but I had to be sure." Charley tied the string back up and laid the box gently beside her on the seat.

The next passenger appeared to be a traveling salesman with a sample case at his feet beside his grip.

"Sir, you need to open your grip and your sample case for inspection."

"Alright, Deputy." The man opened both. They were free of any suspicious liquors.

"Thank you." Charley moved on. Ben Cantrell, moving in the opposite direction, had covered five rows of seats. Charley had three left to the end of the car.

The next passenger was an old Indian, asleep in his seat. His coat was open revealing a suspicious bulge in his front pocket. Charley shook the man awake. "Halito. (Hello) Chi hohchifo nanta? (What's your name?)"

"Sa hohchifo ut (My name is) Tom Bushyhead," the old man said, his voice slurred with sleep or liquor.

"Whiskey?" Charley pointed to the pocket.

"A,(yes). You want drink?"

"You're under arrest, no whiskey," Charley pulled the bottle from the old man's pocket and put it in his coat pocket. He had cuffs on him before he could fully understand what had happened. The old man shook his head as if trying to clear a fog before his eyes.

"Ugh." His head sunk on his chest and he fell back asleep, as Charley attached the cuffs to the bench arm.

Abe watched the last two rows which held two men who had observed the searches. One of them had become fidgety as Charley grew closer in the search process. He rose and started toward the door. Abe stood up and pulled his coat back to reveal his Colt Peacemaker; the man plopped down quickly in the nearest seat.

"Is this your bag, sir?" Charley asked him, pointing to a leather grip under the seat where he had been riding.

"No, it's not mine," the man said.

"Why is it under your seat, then?" Charley asked. He noticed the initials PH on the front carved in the fine leather of the flap. "What's your name?"

"Paul Henderson."

"What's your destination, Mr. Henderson?"

"Paris, Texas. I'm traveling to visit family for Christmas."

"I need you to open this bag."

"I told you, it's not mine."

Charley tugged at the locked latch. "I'll have to cut it open if you don't unlock it for me."

The man said nothing but watched intently as Charley carved open the flap. Abe stepped forward from his position at the door and stood behind the seated passenger, just in case he intended to bolt. Charley reached his hand in and pulled up a large heavy bundle wrapped in newspaper.

Unwrapping it while Charley held it, Abe saw it was a gallon jug of something. He uncorked it and sniffed. Whiskey.

"Sir, you're under arrest for having whiskey in your possession," Charley said.

After the handcuffs were placed on him, the man spoke.

"I'm a stranger to this part, didn't know about such a law."

"There are signs posted at the ticket counter where you purchased your ticket. You should have taken note of the warning."

"What'll happen to me now?"

"You'll be taken back on the return train to Fort Smith to plead your case and pay the appropriate fine. First offenses are usually a twenty-five dollar fine."

"I can't afford that and my wife is expecting me home by tomorrow night.

Could I just pay you the fine money and you turn it in for me?"

"No, you must appear before the commissioner in person to plead your case. You can send your wife a telegram from the depot at Poteau, the next stop."

Abe stepped back and sat down behind the prisoner as Charley secured the cuffs to the seat handle. The traveler began to wring his hands and then attempted to jam them in his pockets.

"Damn" Abe heard him say under his breath.

Their side of the car searched, Abe relaxed as Charley meet Cantrell at the back of the car. He also had two men handcuffed to seats. Jimmy settled in the seat across from them and relaxed his gun belt to move the Navy Colt from its cross draw position to the center of his lap.

"When the train gets to the next stop which is Poteau, we'll take these men off and wait for the northbound train from Paris," Charley said.

Abe did not relish spending Christmas night sleeping in the railroad depot. But it was better than the time they slept in the snow at Christmas in front of Jackson Crow's cabin and about froze to death.

Fort Smith Federal Court House built in 1889

Sure enough, as he suspected The Elevator made a great noise about the search. Charley's jaw muscles tightened as he read the inflammatory description.

> *"Many complaints have reached us of late condemning the conduct of deputy marshals on railroad trains running out of this city through the Indian country. It is said that they simply capture trains, forcing the passengers to open up their grips for examination to see if they may have whiskey in them, acting more like a parcel of train robbers than like officers of this great government of ours."*

He folded the paper and stuffed it in his coat. Walking out the front door of the hotel, he paused and then turned right toward the new courthouse that housed the marshal's office. He stopped at the outer office of Chief Deputy Williams.

"Is Marshal Yoes in?" Charley asked as he removed his hat and coat and placed them on the rack beside the door.

"Yes. What do you need to see him about?"

"This," Charley said as he laid the paper's editorial diatribe on William's desk.

The chief deputy tried to suppress a smile. "Oh, let me tell him you're here." Williams got up and knocked on the door with a glass panel labeled, Jacob Yoes, United States Marshal, Western District of Arkansas. He entered and came back promptly leaving the door ajar.

"He'll see you. Go right in."

Marshal Yoes, a prominent businessman, was popular with the commercial business owners and had many friends. I hope these fellas I tangled with are not close friends of his, Charley thought as he rehearsed his speech in his mind.

"Deputy Barnhill, please have a seat." said Yoes. "What can I do for you?"

The paper still gripped in his hand, he laid it in front of the Marshal before taking his seat.

Yoes glanced at it and flipped the paper back across the desk. "I'm really sorry about this editorial, Deputy Barnhill. You were just doing your duty. I hand-picked you for this assignment because I know you are above reproach and can take comments from the press."

Charley began his rehearsed speech. "I appreciate your confidence, but I don't like being set up as the target of criticism you knew would come. I feel my time as a deputy here in Fort Smith is not helpful to the court. I live in McAlester and I would prefer to stay there and help out the Paris and the Muskogee courts."

Yoes' face clouded. "I understand. I will notify both of those marshals that you are available as needed. Can I still send you important writs of arrest if I'm in a bind for help?"

"Certainly. I can make a trip up here a few times a year, if needed. Thank you for your understanding."

His boss, a true politician, placed his elbows on his chair arms and clasped his hands before speaking. "How's your brother, Abe, getting along? I hated to let him go, but his handicap was just too much of a risk and I feel it endangered his life as a deputy."

Charley knew that was an attempt to smooth over hard feelings. He'd take it. "He's making out alright. He was with me as posse on that Frisco train."

Charley stepped into the cold January air. In a few days, January 16, 1890, one of the last murder suspects he had brought in, Jefferson Jones, was scheduled to hang on the gallows along with six other men. It would be sensational because that was the most men to ever be hanged on the same day. Well, he would not be around to watch that. His mouth filled with bitter gaul as he remembered the humiliation of Abe's dismissal and now the attack on him personally in the newsaper. Good-by, Fort Smith.

Chapter 58

Family Matters

Headlines announced the opening of yet another part of Indian Territory for settlement. Since the first land rush of April 1889 which had established the Oklahoma Territory, other Indian lands had been opened in Sept. of 1891 and now a third, even larger, the Cheyenne and Arapahoe lands would be opened on April 19, 1892, two days hence.

Irene sat at the kitchen table dying wool for spinning.

Charley folded the newspaper and set it aside. "They're whittling this territory down piece by piece."

"I know. But I'm glad the number of outlaws is decreasing too."

"They're not decreasing, honey, just being squeezed into a smaller area where they can hide. The newly settled areas with families living on farms don't tolerate their robbing and murdering for very long. Neck tie parties are common where the marshals don't ride."

"I'm relieved you don't have to ride so much anymore." Irene said.

He was glad too. He had taken only a dozen men to jail since his falling out with Marshal Yoes two years ago. Instead of chasing outlaws, he now farmed a prosperous lease and worked as posse with other deputies for extra income. He was relieved at the peaceful turn his life had taken, just when he had thought there was no hope for a normalcy. He was surprised at the amount of tension between him and Irene that had dissipated once he was home for more than a few days. She was still a very young woman and loved his presence. He had not realized the toll his life style had taken on his family.

"Heck Thomas is hard on the heels of the Dalton gang. It's sad to see two good deputies turn to lawlessness for the shear fun of it. Heck pleaded with Bill and Grat to turn back and mend their ways. He carried a thousand dollars from their mother to pay them to quit. They just laughed in his face."

"Are you going to help him?"

"No, he has enough good men to keep them running. I think I'll check on the animals. It feels like thunderstorm weather today."

Charley put on his farming hat, a wide-brimmed object with leather band and ties. A hard rain began before he finished penning the cows in the corral. As he returned to the house, he sloshed off his hat and hung it on the peg by the back door. The fire in the kitchen stove felt good.

Minnie and Henry came in about the same time. Minnie was fourteen and still attending the local school. Seventeen year-old Henry wanted to be a cowboy as soon as he turned eighteen. Two year-old Tony came in the house with a whoop, a pussy willow in one hand and a frog in the other. He had red hair like his older brother, Henry whom he adored and followed around everywhere he went.

"Everyone get dry and warm in front of the fireplace while I fix dinner," Irene said. She was going to have another baby in October, her still slim figure concealed behind a long apron.

After dinner, the rain subsided. Henry left shortly afterward to visit a friend on the next farm. Minnie helped Irene with the dishes as Charley tried to teach Tony how to count.

"Say it again son, one, two three." Charley extended Tony's pudgy fingers as he counted.

"Just keep trying." Charley rose and went to the kitchen where Irene stood, her hands in the dishpan. She dried them off and sat down at the table.

"I've something to discuss with you, darlin'," she said. She patted the bench beside her.

Charley sat and waited patiently while she unstrung her apron ties. He had found Irene explained things in her own way and at her own pace. She placed the apron on the bench and folded her hands.

"Henry brought a letter from my mother this morning. She needs to have new guardians appointed for my brother, John, and sister, Laura. Her brother, who has been their guardian, is moving away from Indian Territory. She asks if you would consider taking on that responsibility."

Charley was completely surprised by this request. "I'll have to think about it. I had not expected this." If he was the proper person to take on this task, the Lord would give him peace. He'd talk to Abe too.

Abe looked up from his field of young corn, ankle high now, but growing fast. He pushed his hat back and wiped his forehead with his handkerchief. His eyes focused on a rider in the distance, approaching at a leisurely pace, the hooves of the horse barely disturbing the dust of the road. The figure took on a familiar shape. Charley.

He wiped his hands as he walked to the road, the smile on his face as wide as the Arkansas River.

"What brings you out of the lower realms of Choctaw land?" Abe had moved from Sallisaw to a farm a few miles east of Whitefield shortly after Mollie married Pearly Robbins last year. The area was a little quieter now that Jim Starr (Belle Starr's last husband) had been killed by Bud Trainor.

Mollie Barnhill with her engagement ring

"Irene could tell I was getting restless, so here I am."

"Come on up to the house. We're delighted to see you."

Amanda appeared on the porch as the dogs raised a ruckus. She had a rolling pin in her left hand and flour smeared on her cheek. On seeing Charley she attempted to push her hair back inside the ribbon that held it out of her face.

"Still as beautiful as ever." Charley smiled at her efforts.

"What a pleasant surprise." She hugged him and took his hat. "Sit on the porch where it's cool. I've got the kitchen so hot with baking."

"Where're my favorite girls?" Charley asked.

On hearing his voice, Janette and Effie burst out of the house. "You girls look just like your mother, long brown hair and all."

"Uncle Charley, Uncle Charley," they chimed. He gave them each a hug, lifting them off the ground and twirling them around. They giggled and squealed in delight. He sat them down and they flounced off, chasing the dog across the yard.

Abe offered Charley a pipe. It was good just to be alive, safe and well, living in peace, Charley thought as he smoked, enjoying the beauty of the day.

"How's Sam and his family?" he asked.

"He just moved a few miles further up the road toward Porum on the opposite side of the South Canadian River. His daughter, Elizabeth and her little baby, Lily, are living with them since her husband, John Cooper, was killed last year in that lumbering accident."

"That was terrible. They had been married only a couple of years. I think lumbering is more dangerous than chasing outlaws."

"What brings you up here?" Abe searched for clues in Charley's face, whose eyebrows arched into a fight with his tanned nose.

"I've a few things to discuss with you face-to-face."

"Go ahead." Face-to-face was mighty important. What had happened?

"I've been asked to take over the guardianship of Irene's brother and sister. It won't be for long for John Henry who is sixteen. It'll be longer for Laura who is almost thirteen."

"I see no reason why you can't," Abe said. He knew Charley could handle that responsibility better than anyone in the Morgan family. John Morgan had disappeared after he got out of jail.

"What else is on your mind?" Abe could feel Charley's worries as if they were his own.

"It's the deputy duties I've turned my back on. I feel like the Indian Territory is getting ready to explode, what with the crush of white settlers all around, and outlaws looking in desperation for places to hide. This peace won't last long."

Abe had struggled with the same feelings of anxiety every since he had laid his pistol aside and took up the plow. "There's a Presidential election this fall; maybe things will change in Washington and we'll get a new marshal. Until then, I'd say take it easy and keep your guns oiled."

Charley relaxed his eyebrows. "Heck Thomas keeps asking me to ride with him. I don't want to leave McAlester. The few cases I get are enough for me right now."

Abe tried to voice his thoughts. "The Indian Territory will soon disappear before our very eyes. It's sad to see a whole culture of people who are fine as any in the world being taken apart before our eyes. What will we tell our children about them?"

"That we knew them and lived with them admiring their customs and ways. Sam's children are quarter-bloods as are yours. I pray they never feel the sting of that in their lives," Charley said.

***

He sat on the front porch waiting for a sound from inside the house. Tony played in the yard, drawing a play fort in the dirt with his stick. Make-believe soldiers fired on his troops from behind a barricade of rocks. His pet hound dog, tied to the opposite barricade of small logs, barked in hopes of winning his freedom. Charley jumped as the front door opened. The doctor came out, rolling down his shirt sleeves.

"Congratulations, Charley. You are the father of a healthy, bouncing baby girl," he said. His kind face and smile made the news even more welcome.

"Thank you, Dr. Barnes. How's my wife?"

"She'll be fine, just needs to rest for a few days until she gets stronger. You can see her in a few minutes."

A healthy daughter. Minnie would be so excited.

Irene's head lay on her pillow, her eyes closed, a slight smile on her face. She opened her eyes and turned her head when she heard him enter the bedroom.

"Darlin', it's a beautiful little girl. What shall we name her?" Irene asked.

"You should pick the name for the daughter," Charley said as he kissed her cheek.

"I think, Cecilia and we can call her Celia, my mother's nick name."

"Cecilia it will be." His family was growing. Glad he was to love them and tend to their needs, rather than chasing around the Territory.

***

Charley with John and Laura Morgan at his side stood before the judge of the Second Judicial Division, James M. Shackelford who had been appointed Federal judge of the Muskogee court in 1889. The court also held sessions at McAlester and Vinita during the judicial year. Judge Shackelford had seen Charley more than once in his position of United States deputy marshal.

"I find that the application for guardianship of John Henry Morgan and Laura Elizabeth Morgan, both minor children of William H. Morgan, deceased, is in order. Charles Barnhill is appointed the principal in this assignment with John C. Foster and James L. Evans surety. You may sign these papers before the clerk of the court. Congratulations, Deputy Barnhill."

As he signed the guardianship papers, Charley's eye was caught by one line. "We bind ourselves, our heirs, executors and administrators, firmly by these present. . . if the said Guardian shall in all things faithfully perform and fulfill his duty as guardian as aforesaid, then this obligation shall be void and of no effect; otherwise to be and remain in full force and virtue. Subscribed and sworn to before me this 21st day of November, 1892."

He put his arms around the youngsters. John looked like his father. Charley's thoughts flashed back to that fateful day six years ago when he first saw the body of Billie Morgan on the ground, a bloody ax laying beside him. The families had been torn asunder. Would time mend the pain and the hurt?

"Come on, you two. Let's go home."

"Alright, Charley," they replied in unison. Each youngster bowed to the honorable Judge and exited the courtroom.

"Fine young people, you have there," The Judge remarked.

"Yes, sir, I think so."

He might need to move into a bigger house now to accommodate three teenagers, an adolescent and two babies. Suddenly, that deputy's pay looked mighty attractive. He would contact Heck Thomas.

Chapter 59

Shoot Out at Halfway House

The Cherokee outlet, a strip of land 58 miles wide and 220 miles long on the northern border of the Cherokee Nation, had been purchased from the Cherokees at a price of $1.40 per acre. This part of the seven million acres granted to the Cherokee Nation in the treaties of 1828 and 1835 had been carved out for sale because of complaints against cattlemen getting rich from leased lands. Land hungry speculators had put enough pressure on Congress to make the sale happen.

Congress eventually paid the eight million dollar price tag and announced the opening along with surplus Pawnee and Tonkawa lands on September 16, 1893. The eating away of the Indian Territory continued. The *run* for 6,000,000 acres, brought 100,000 land hungry people from all over the world, gathered by horse, train, wagon and even on foot.

One-third of the eight million dollar price tag went to the Cherokee National Council. The remaining $6,640,000 would be paid to anyone proving to be one-eighth Cherokee by blood or greater. The Cherokee Nation treasurer, E.E. Starr, started the pay out to individual Cherokees in May of 1894. Each person got an allotment of $265.70·. Cherokees of the Going Snake District had to come to Tahlequah to receive payment by June 16, 1894.

In the weeks before the distribution, hordes of unscrupulous salesmen swarmed over the Cherokee Nation, selling the Indians items they did not know how to operate, all on credit at inflated prices. At the payment locations gamblers and bootleggers reinforced with pickpockets and thugs thrived. The Cherokees didn't have a chance of getting home with their money still in their pockets.

Charley held his Winchester up and sighted the barrel toward a target fifty yards away. He needed to make sure the sight was accurate. He fired and saw a puff of dirt kick up a foot above the line of bottles. He lowered his muzzle slightly and fired again. Right on. Glass flew as the bullet took out the middle set.

His ears ringing from the muzzle blast, he heard a faint cry. "Charley." He looked around.

Irene called to him from the back door of their home. "There's a telegram here for you."

He had spent the past four years working for the other courts in Paris and Muskogee trying to stay away from Fort Smith. He knew eventually they would call him back. Yoes was gone now, replaced by George Crump, a Cleveland appointee. The Marshal's office was beginning to clean up the last of the villains in the Indian Territory who were violent enough to kill for what they wanted. They seemed to swell in number, rather than decline, each man out for what he could grab from the Indians who were rich with cash. As $265 was paid to each family member, a father could easily walk away with $2000.

The rifle to his side, he walked through the tall grass of the pasture to the back porch. The sun was high, causing a trickle of sweat to run down his face. He wiped at it with his sleeve before reaching for the yellow paper.

"June 10, 1894 Meet me in Ft. Gibson at the payment office as soon as possible. Heck Thomas."

He tucked the paper inside his shirt pocket and hefted the rifle to his shoulder to ascend the steps. "I need to make a trip. Can you help me pack my saddlebags?"

"What is it this time?" She laid aside her needlework. "How long will you be gone?"

"I don't know. I have to meet Heck Thomas in Fort Gibson as soon as possible."

"I'll have Minnie and Laura bring the clean shirts off the clothes line. I haven't had time to iron them."

"It doesn't matter. They'll just get wrinkled in my saddle bags." He was startled to see a tiny tear at the corner of her eye.

"What is it?"

"I wish you could just give up your commission. I can't count on you being home." She sniffed as she picked up the baby from the cradle. Little Dora was seven months old and her sister, Cecilia, only thirteen months older. He realized she had her hands full with five year-old Tony and two babies.

He tried without much success to soften the impatience in his voice. "Do you want me to refuse to help Heck?"

"No, of course not. I just wish we could live a normal life like everyone else." She dried her nose on her apron and shifted the baby to her shoulder for burping. "I'll be alright once you leave. It's just the good-bye I can't stand".

"Now that Louis Burrow has been paroled for over a year, maybe Janey can come for a visit."

"Her new son is only three months old. I'll be alright." She smiled and kissed him on the cheek. "Henry and John will take good care of things."

Charley looked around at the small town of Fort Gibson as he rode in. It reminded him of the land runs. Hundreds, maybe thousands of people, milled about - Indians and their families, white settlers, government workers and soldiers. The whine of barkers on the corners, tent shows of every description and a merry-go-round filled with laughing children added to the carnival atmosphere. Most of the unsophisticated Cherokees would go home with empty pockets after loosing at roulette and faro tables what they had not spent on useless goods.

He dismounted at the payment office which was set up in the town's largest building, the former guardhouse for the fort which had been abandoned in 1890 and sold to private citizens. The building, holding the six million dollars that was transported to the site in one million dollar shipments, was surrounded on all sides by Cherokee Light Horse and United States deputy marshals. No one was taking a chance at a robbery of the huge payment.

"Hello, Sheriff." He greeted Sheriff Ellis Rattling Gourd, Chief of the Cherokee police. "I'm looking for Deputy Heck Thomas. Have you seen him?"

"Yes. How are you, Deputy Barnhill?" The sheriff shook his hand and pointed to the front door. "He's inside conferring with the military guard that brought the last shipment. They didn't have any trouble, but reported their train being followed by a band of men for several miles just outside of town."

"Thanks." Charley removed his hat and stepped inside the building shouldering his way through the solid line of policemen, standing with Winchesters held at the ready.

The familiar form of the famous lawmen who had chased the Dalton gang all over Oklahoma Territory two years prior was bent over a map. He turned to the troop commander, a young lieutenant. "Was it here you saw the gang?"

"Yes, sir. At a place called Fourteen Mile Creek."

"Alright. I'll take a look."

Charley nodded at the broad smile that covered Heck's face as he turned and spied him standing at the front door. "Glad you could come. Let's go get a cup of coffee in the back room and talk."

He glanced at the payment table and the lines formed in front of it as he walked to the back. Each agent had a pile of bills in front of him, the $267.50 already counted out and put into piles of five payments. When a family came in and their names were checked, the agent counted out the proper number of payments and placed it in a cotton bag and handed it to the recipient who signed the log verifying payment received. Some families with multiple children went out with more than one bag.

Thinking of the dark-eyed hawkers he had seen on the way in, he asked, "How's the crime rate?"

Heck took a sip of his coffee before answering. "So far, several robberies and two murders including a woman on her way to town in a buggy. Most of the suspects are in custody already. The payment moves to Tahlequah tomorrow to finish up the last round. Anyone not paid by June sixteenth forfeits his payment and the left over money goes into the Cherokee National Council treasury."

Charley removed his hat and smoothed down his hair. "What do you want me to do?"

"Several Cherokees with warrants on their heads have come out of hiding for their payments. Help me ferret them out if they pop up. Talk to the people coming in and see if they know anything." Heck handed him several writs of arrest.

Charley scanned through them, mostly larceny, alcohol violations, no murderers. "When do we leave for Tahlequah?"

"First thing in the morning. Take my interpreter, Long Braids, with you for the remainder of the day." He pointed to a tall Cherokee standing silently with a Winchester grasped with both hands, his eyes roving over the faces of his people as they came in the door. "I'll be here watching the allotments handed out."

Cherokee State Capitol, Tahlequah, Indian Territory

How could he find anyone in the mass of people? It seemed that everyone in the Cherokee Nation had descended on this little settlement. Charley raised his hands to cover his eyes from the sun. The brim of his hat was pulled down as far as possible, and the bright rays of the sum still penetrated his vision.

Tahlequah, the county seat for the Going Snake District of the Cherokee Nation held, among other things, the Cherokee Tribal Prison. Most punishment was in the form of whippings or executions in the case of murder. However, a number of prisoners from all over the Indian Territory were sent to this prison for sentences of from six months to several years. The grounds were attractive with shaded trees and benches for the use of visitors inside the prison compound. Charley had picked up a few prisoners here to take to Fort Smith. Now, he watched as the lines formed in front of the courthouse.

Heck stood in the shade of a tree assessing the crowd. He walked over to Charley and shifted his attention to the Indian police force, standing attentive guard over the last piles of money.

"Sheriff Rattling Gourd informs me a woman has come in requesting the allotment for three men of interest. She has a written document authorizing her to pick up their money."

Charley followed Heck into the court house. The sheriff sat at a bench to the side of the room, his attention directed to a woman who had just gathered up her pay.

Rattling Gourd rose and pointed toward the woman. "Well, Deputies. Luck has come our way. That woman is going to take money to three men I know have been on the scout. Two are wanted by us and the third is a brother."

"What names?" Charley asked.

"Jim and Bill Cook, the brothers, and Crawford Goldsby, all Cherokees of bad reputation."

Charley looked at the papers he had pulled from his vest. "I have a writ of arrest here for Jim Cook for assault with intent to kill. It's been open since January twenty-third and not served. Know anything about him?"

"He's just a kid, seventeen, but a kid prone to get in trouble. He was arrested in '92 and '93 on charges of introducing and selling liquor. His brother, Bill, served as posse for a United States deputy marshal just last year."

Heck took the warrant from Charley and scanned it. "Sounds like the Daltons recreated, good man goes bad."

The sheriff turned his attention back to the woman who was seven people away from the counter. "My deputy and I will follow this woman back to her place and stake it out for the night. You want to join me?"

Heck answered for them both. "Yes, give us a few minutes to get our gear and horses."

Charley dashed across the compound to his horse tied at the railing in front of the livery stable. The young roan backed away in fright and then stood still while he took the reins and mounted to join his companions in front of the court house.

Rattling Gourd spoke in the low guttural of his people. "I sent an officer on ahead to trail the woman. She owns a place called Halfway House, a hotel and eating establishment for travelers between Tahlequah and Fort Gibson."

Two hours later, the three men joined the scout on an embankment looking down on a ridge fifty feet below. Beyond the ridge sat a house, clearly visible from their vantage point. The only problem Charley could see in the layout was the approach to the simple structure. Scrub oak and brush extended to within seventy-five feet of the house. The approach from there on was devoid of protection.

After watching for a few minutes in the warm afternoon sun, Charley felt his eyes beginning to burn. He took his hat off and ran his handkerchief over his face. Heck, who always looked dapper even when on the trail, pulled his hat off and moistened the inside of the band with water from his canteen.

"There he is," pointed the sheriff at a man as he exited the house and went to the outhouse in back.

"There's who?" asked Heck.

"Goldsby. Let's see who else comes out." All three men were identified as they took turns coming out to visit the outhouse or smoke a cigarette.

The sheriff had seen enough. "I'll go into town and round up a posse. How many men do you think we need? "

"Bring as many as you can that are reliable and not trigger-happy, men you've had on posses before."

As Charley watched the sheriff and his deputy ride out of sight, he looked around for a suitable place to rest. He chose a spot some fifty yards back in heavy timber. "Let's eat something. This may be a long watch."

Heck stifled a yawn with the back of his hand. "I've some dried beef in my saddlebags and coffee in a canteen. I'll take the first watch then you can take over. It shouldn't be hard to keep them in sight."

The reinforcements returned in the late evening, ten men all total. Charley recognized a few, Sequoyah Houston, local police man, and two gunslingers who worked for the Fort Smith court on occasion, Zeke and Dick Crittenden. They left their horses in the trees and waded Fourteen Mile Creek flowing through the meadow.

Charley turned to Heck who was loading extra cartridges in his belt. "The sheriff must know something about these three men that we don't. It looks like he's expecting a fight, The Crittendens alone could whip a dozen men." His return to deputy work with Heck was turning out to be more than he had expected.

His partner just spat into the grass and peered at the men. "We might as well be prepared for the worst. You never know how they're going to react."

As the sheriff put his men in position, some reeking of liquor imbibed to reinforce their courage, the two deputies moved to the sides of the group, putting themselves into a flanking position on the house. The man next to Charley let out a loud whoop, loud enough to alert the men in the cabin. *I thought these were seasoned posse men?* Charley knew their surprise approach was now compromised. The sheriff waved the posse forward, the men moving in a line in the protection of the trees and the ridge. The sheriff and Houston, the tallest of the bunch, were in the center.

Just as the lead men topped the ridge, a shot rang out. Charley reflexively ducked and looked for the direction of fire. At the same moment, Houston was hurtled backwards by the force of the bullet, his wide-brimmed black hat tossed into the sky by the force of his fall. The whole line crouched down behind whatever protection they could find and returned fire towards the house.

He aimed his Winchester at the front door and poured several rounds through it. The men around him did the same, riddling the structure with bullets. Wood chips flew as the bullets found their mark. Anyone inside would be flat on their bellies by now.

The sheriff waved for them to hold their fire. In the silence of the brief interlude, he shouted," Hello in the house. Come out with yours hands up and you won't be harmed."

The answer was another round of shooting from the side window and door which was now ajar from the force of the onslaught.

Zeke Crittenden lay beside him. Charley pointed at the cabin. "Who's in there besides those three? It feels like we're facing an army."

"I don't know, but they won't get out alive." Zeke fired another round into the cabin.

The stand off continued- both sides not giving ground, the lawmen having to cling to the rocks and dirt to avoid the deadly fire.

The sheriff crawled over to where Charley lay sprawled on his belly.

"I'm going to take some of my men and carry Sequoyah down the hill. He's in a bad way, probably won't' make it to town."

Charley spit out a mouthful of dirt so he could answer. "Alright, leave us whoever you can spare."

"The Crittendens are worth all the men I have. I'll leave them and a couple others."

Just before dark, Charley moved over to Heck. "Let's see if we can burn them out."

"I'll get a torch made." Heck returned shortly with two pine knot torches ready to be lit.

Zeke hollered to them."Some one's trying to crawl out the side window."

A figure pushed it's way out the window, Winchester tightly gripped in his hand, the other hand on the window sill, leg partly out the window. A desperate outlaw was like a caged animal, willing to do anything to get free.

Heck dropped the torch and aimed at the moving mass. The dark figure fell on the ground, pumping his rifle at the hip as he lay, flames from the barrel lighting up the ground at his side. Several more shots from the lawmen kicked up dirt around him until he finally lay still and ceased firing.

Two more men came out the window firing rapidly. They moved to the still form and picked him up under the arms, dragging him around the side of the house. The lawmen could not move away from their protection to approach the house.

Charley heard horses leaving in the darkness. "They're making a break. Get to your horses."

Heck and Charley sprinted for the trees where the horses were tied, the Crittendens close behind.

Charley could not tell the direction of the fleeing outlaws. He guessed it had to be down hill toward the river. In the darkness the men picked their way down the trail until reaching the Grand River.

"We can't do anymore until daylight. Make camp," Heck said.

Zeke turned his horse around. "We'll just head back to town and see how Sequoyah is doing."

Sequoyah Houston, Cherokee policeman

At first light they were on the move, back tracking to Half Way House to pick up the tracks of the outlaws. Charley inspected the interior of the cabin, riddled with bullet holes in every corner. Blood on the ground outside the window marked where the outlaw had fallen. Horse tracks led down to the Grand River through a canyon as they had suspected then entered the river and disappeared.

Most of the morning searching the banks revealed nothing more. Charley knew something was wrong. A seriously wounded man could not get far in this heat and rough terrain. He had to be hiding somewhere close to where the tracks entered the water. "Heck, let's stake out the river edge. You go up the river about a fifty yards and I'll go down. If the wounded man can walk, he'll crawl down here for water sooner or later."

The afternoon passed without a trace of movement except for deer coming to drink and birds flying overhead. Charley dozed, his head resting on a stump. His hand laid lightly on the stock of his Winchester, which he hugged like a pillow, the barrel extending up past his ear. The coolness of the metal on his face was pleasant.

An almost unnoticeable change in the stillness of the afternoon heat caused him to sit up and squint out from his shade toward the river edge, fifty yards away. He could just make out the shelter where Heck sat on the other side of the river bend. He saw the glint of his rifle as Heck shifted and moved to his feet. Something was happening.

A head appeared at the edge of the brush, closer to Heck than to him. The now visible form moved his head slowly from side to side scouring the river bank. It was the teenager, Jim Cook. He gripped his rifle stalk with a bandaged hand and hopped on his right leg as he eased toward the river.

Heck waited until the young man bent down to put his hand in the water, then he stepped out and ran toward him, Winchester held firmly in front.

"Hands up, Jim. You're under arrest."

Startled, Cook attempted to rise, then fell back on the ground in pain. Charley covered him while Heck took out his handcuffs. Charley moved his gaze quickly from side to side to make sure the other two outlaws were not crashing in on this scene.

"Where's your brother? Where's Goldsby?" he asked.

"I don't know. They left me here because I couldn't ride."

Heck helped him to his feet and placed the cuffs on his wrists. "Sit down and let me look at your wounds." He unwound the bandage on his hand. The shotgun blast had taken away a couple of fingers, leaving the remainder in shreds. The upper arm was peppered with buckshot. Heck bathed the wounds and applied a fresh bandage. Next, the knee wound appeared minor but painful. Jim had several more wounds, two in the chest, two in the thigh, and two in the groin.

Heck motioned the boy to lay still. "We'll take you to a doctor in Fort Gibson."

Charley led his horse up and helped the one hundred twenty-five pound stripling into the saddle. He secured the cuffs to the saddle horn and then mounted behind him. It was a slow go riding double, but they reached Fort Gibson by dark.

A crowd pressed around them as they rode in, people gawking at the wounded prisoner. At the doctor's office, Charley helped the wounded boy down while Heck went to the telegraph office to send word to Fort Smith.

A reporter from the Indian Chieftain appeared, wanting a run down of the events. Charley gave him the details as best he remembered them, wishing he could just get a hot meal and a soft bed. *Wish we had caught the other two. Now we'll have to track them all over the Indian Territory. These young hoodlums cause so much pain and loss.*

Post Script:

Crawford Goldsby was nicknamed Cherokee Bill after this incident. He and Bill Cook then formed the notorious Cook gang with several other outlaws, which terrorized the Indian Territory for almost a year. The following quote explains their history well:

Cherokee Bill - Crawford Goldsby when captured

"In one week short of three months, they successfully committed ten assorted stagecoach, store, bank and railroad holdups. It is a record unmatched by the James-Younger Gang or any other. In the course of it, they killed only one man, which is another record. . . Even when it was flourishing, it grabbed very few headlines, principally because it was running competition with the Bill Doolin Gang, which was operating in the western part of the Territory. Doolin, in his own right, and because of his connection with the Dalton brothers, was known to newspaper readers the country over; few people had ever heard of Bill Cook. Among those whom the law tabbed as members of the Cook Gang were the Cook brothers, Sam McWilliams, alias the Verdigris Kid, Lon Gordon, Thurtan Baldwin, alias Skeeter Baldwin, Elmer Lucas, alias Chicken Lucas, Curt Dayson, Hank Munson, Jim French (of Starr gang association,) . . . George Sanders, Will Farris and Jess Snyder. Eventually, Judge Parker got some of them. The Creek and Cherokee police and U.S. deputy marshals snuffed out the rest. . . Though it came late in Judge Parker's career, it was, in many ways, his greatest victory. His certainty of punishment had never been so potently expressed."

Bill Cook

Bill Cook was eventually caught in New Mexico and sentenced to forty years in prison by Judge Parker. He died in prison while attempting an escape by jumping down onto a roof top two stories below. Cherokee Bill, who was responsible for the one murder, was hung at Fort Smith. Jim Cook was turned over to the Cherokee authorities and sentenced to eight years at Tahlequah. He subsequently escaped several times and was eventually left to roam free by the Indian authorities. He was killed by a frightened citizen who thought Cook was armed and dangerous.

Chapter 60

An Outlaw's Revenge

Bill Frazier looked down at his breakfast plate, scrambled eggs in the middle, pancakes along the side. What was left of his mangled right hand attempted to grasp the food between thumb and ring and little finger. He cursed softly under his breath as the lumps of eggs slipped into his lap. *A damn invalid, that's what I am thanks to those damn marshals. I can't take this any longer. I'm going to get even and I'm starting with Erwin Justice, the double-crossing, backstabber.*

His neighbor and store-owner Justice had loaned a Winchester to Deputy Williams the first time the lawmen had tried to tree him over a simple little horse trade gone bad in '86. That stand-off during which he had wounded Charley Barnhill got him three charges of assualt with attempt to kill and had branded him a fugitive. Over a year later he had another gunfight with the deputies - outnumbered four to one that time. Too bad he had only wounded Abe Barnhill, Charley's brother. Those Barnhills were a nuisance. Next time he had one of them in his sights he would not miss. Seven years since his trial in '88, he had waited to get even with someone. Now Justice was a prosperous store-owner, he no longer responded to Bill's requests for supplies on credit.

He looked at his wife across the kitchen. With a swipe of his hand he sent the plate hurtling against the wall. "I can't eat this slop. Bring me some whiskey. And where's Harris?"

"He's feeding the hogs, Bill," his wife answered from her stooped position on the floor, attempting to clean up what was left of his breakfast.

"Get him in here, now!"

She placed a gallon jug on the table in front of her husband "I'll fetch him right away. Here's your jug. Now, Bill, don't start drinking and thinking. You know that only leads to trouble."

"I have a heap of thinking to do before this jug is finished."

His wife turned and went out the back door. He could hear her calling Charley Harris. Since the marshals had crippled him, he had to have hired help around the farm. In a few minutes , the tall young man came in the door, wiping his hands on his jeans legs.

"What you need, Bill?" His face was smooth and unshaven, no promise of a beard except for the fine hair above his upper lip. He wore a wide-brimmed hat pushed back on his head. His eyes, clear blue, were quick and piercing.

"I want you to ride over to get Charley Perry and John Gregory. Tell'em to be here by four o'clock for supper. I've got an assignment for you."

As Harris rode off, Frazier headed into the house. Stopping at the rack beside the door where his revolvers were gathering dust, he selected his favorite, a Colt .45 Peacemaker, just like what the marshals carried. Tucking the weapon in his waistband, he picked up the whiskey jug and headed to his neighbor's house, three hundred yards down the hill. *Looks like it's going to be a good day, the day Erwin Justice pays.*

Charley Perry looked up from the lunch he was enjoying with his friend, John Gregory. His normal good nature was displayed in his ease of manner, slow talking, slow walking, slow thinking. He did not like to be rushed. They had spent the morning looking for one of his father's horses down on the Black Fork Creek which ran out of the Black Fork Mountain. He had been successful in locating it at a farm. The owner had recognized the horse and penned it up for the rightful owner to come looking for it.

"Let's get going. The sun's getting high and I want to be back by mid-afternoon." He stuffed the last piece of the bread into his mouth and brushed off his hands.

His companion grumbled something about finishing his meal. "Alright, I'm ready to get home. I hear there's a dance at Peter Conser's tonight. You want to go?"

Gregory was a follower, not a leader, and seemed more a shadow to Perry whose eyes sparkled at the thought of pretty girls in flowing skirts and scarves. "Yup! His dances are always great fun. That's part of his politicking and elections are coming up."

As the two young men came off the mountain onto the public road, they saw a rider approaching. It was Charley Harris, Bill Frazier's hired man.

"Glad I found you," he said as he reined in his horse. "Mr. Frazier wants us at his house by four o'clock for supper."

"What about the dance at Conser's?" Perry asked. He was not one to miss entertainment of any kind.

"That can wait. This is more important."

It better be important, Perry thought. His hopes were on the evening's entertainment and he did not want to be put to a task before the dance. But Frazier was a man he could not disrespect at his own peril. The local gang leader held influence over the farmers in the area who feared his temper and his acts of spite.

Perry watched Frazier's wife, Mollie, place the last plate on the table and indicate to them to commence. She ate in silence as the men talked about things that interested them, horses, crops, politics, the neighbors. After supper, she cleared the table and commenced washing the dishes. Most of her and Bill's children were grown now, though one son still slept overnight when he was not working for Erwin Justice at his store.

The four men stepped outside on the porch. Frazier handed the tobacco paper and can to Harris.

"Roll me a smoke." Harris obliged with deft fingers, shaking a small amount of tobacco onto the paper he held in a V-shape. Rolling the paper around the tobacco, he licked the edge and sealed it to the perfect size.

"Here you go." He handed it to his boss and then lit it for him.

"Harris, Gregory, come with me. I've something to speak to you about." Frazier looked at Charley Perry, his eyes commanding him to stay put.

A hushed council was held by the three men, just out of hearing range. After five minutes of animated conversation during which Perry caught the phrase, "finish the work" spoken by Frazier , they rejoined him at the porch.

Frazier opened the door. "Wait here. I've something for you." He walked into the house and returned holding his .45 by the stubs of his fingers on his right hand. Perry tried to keep his eyes off the empty left sleeve, the long cuff tucked into Frazier's waist band.

"You'll need this," he said as he handed the revolver to John Gregory. "Remember, don't come back until the work is done."

Perry noticed that Harris also carried a revolver, a .44. He shrugged it off. Going to a dance in the Indian Territory, it was routine to carry weapons.

He mounted his horse and followed the other two who rode double on a stout bay gelding. It took them two hours to reach Conser, I.T. , some fifteen miles. The two men in the lead rode on through town failing to take the trail to Conser's house.

"What's going on?" Perry asked. "Where we going?"

"To have some fun at Justice's place," Harris said.

A faint sense of alarm went through Perry's mind. What type of fun? He did not like this. He better stop right now, before he got more involved. "If that's the case, I'm not going on with you two. I'm going to the dance."

Harris spoke sharply. ""You stay here and watch the horses." He guided the horse up and tied it to a sapling. "This won't take long then we'll all go to the dance."

Perry waited in the dark, the spring evening chill penetrating through his jacket. He rubbed his hands together then stuck them in his pockets for warmth. Several minutes passed as he tried to reason out being stuck there. If they were not back in half an hour, he was going to Conser's. He wondered why they had gone to Justice's, the old man never bothered anyone. Why have fun with a solid citizen?

✪

Sarah Jane Justice held the dish towel in her hand. Her neighbor, Mrs. Norman, passed her a dinner plate. Sarah's hand stopped in mid-air as she heard stomping on the front porch. She started from the kitchen to the front room. John Frazier, a clerk from her husband's store who had been there for supper, appeared in front of her and grabbed her arms, pulling her back into the kitchen.

"Don't go in there," he ordered, his voice betraying the urgency of his words.

She heard the front door crash open and a voice shout, "Hands up." She screamed as the command was followed by rapid firing of a revolver. She covered her ears and sank to the floor, sobbing in fear, trying to press herself into the protection of the kitchen cabinets. Two or three bullets hit the walls of the kitchen. The clerk had bolted out the back door. Mrs. Norman lay flat on the floor praying fervently. *Help us, Oh, God.*

As quickly as it had started, the firing stopped and the foot steps of the assailants left the porch. She let out the breath she had been holding and tried to rise from the floor. Mrs. Norman was still praying, her head covered with her apron, her cheek on the wood floor.

"Erwin, Erwin," she screamed, the shrill, high-pitched wail of women over the ages who knew they were now widows. She crawled into the front room. Only the faint light of the pine burning in the fireplace lit up the scene. The black shadow-covered form of her husband lay by the door.

In an instant she knew he was dead. Two bullets had entered his shirt just to the right of the breast bone. His right shoulder and both arms seeped blood which spread over the wood floor. She knelt beside him and put her head on his chest. Sobbing his name over and over, she felt the life warmth seeping out of him, his flesh still soft but lifeless. As she lay on his still form, Mrs. Norman's hands reached for her shoulders.

"Come, my dear. Sit down by the fire. There's nothing we can do for him. He's gone."

Their other hired man, Caleb Kinslow, entered from the back door. He approached surveying the scene with wide, fear-filled eyes. His hands shook as he examined his employer, laying dead on the floor.

"Who would do this? Who?"

Sarah heard herself speak, the shock of the killing muting her words to a whisper. "Caleb, please go to Mr. Jones' and bring help. Maybe they can track the murderers before they get too far." She wrapped herself in her shawl and began to moan and cry, the funeral cry of the ancient people she lived amongst.

Charley Perry heard the shots from a quarter of a mile away. They were rapid, too rapid to count. He started up and caught his horse. *What's going on? Those fools, what have they done now?*

A few minutes later Gregory and Harris burst through the brush, breathless and giddy.

"We did it. We did it," Harris gulped between breaths.

"What did you do?" Perry asked.

"We finished the work Frazier gave us to do. Let's go."

The two men mounted up on the single horse and trotted away in the dark searching for the main road back to town. Perry followed cursing under his breath. *What have I got myself into now? I should've left them.*

His breathing labored and fast, John Frazier ran for his horse in the corral, its saddle still on. He had seen the faces of the killers and knew in an instant that his father had sent the assasins. Why? After all these years? He had heard his father grumble often and bitterly about Erwin Justice and the complaint he had against him. But to go this far? He could not believe it! With eyes filled with tears, he forced his mount the fifteen miles to his father's cabin, sitting back in the forest at the foot of Black Fork Mountain.

Not stopping to secure his horse, he burst through the front door. A lamp on the entry way table outlined his father sitting deep in the shadows behind.

"What have you done, Papa? Why?"

The older man leaned forward into the light and smiled. "No one ever goes against me and lives. Remember that, boy."

John placed his hands on his father's shoulders, a gesture he had never had the courage to make. "Papa, you will hang for this."

"Not if you and your Ma keep your mouths shut. Those boys I sent to do the job will disappear. They can't hang a man if there are no witnesses."

John Frazier knew he could not and would not speak of this to anyone. The deputies would have to find the killers without his help.

***

Marshal Crump looked at the complaint: William Frazier, Charles Harris, Charles Perry, and John Gregory wanted for murder in LeFlore County, Choctaw Nation. Since he had been appointed in April of 1893, the violence and complaints flowing from the Indian Territory had not abated. He looked up from his desk and handed the arrest writ to Deputy John Salmon.

"John, see if you can locate these men."

John Salmon looked at the paper. "It seems Frazier's got his gang back. I'll need help on this one."

"Who do you want?"

"The only deputies that every successfully brought him in, the Barnhills."

"Alright, send a telegram to Charley in McAlester. He's not done much since the shoot out with the Cooks last summer, but he'll probably help."

Charley tightened the cinch strap on his mount. The telegram he had received about noon was tucked in his shirt.

March 21, 1895, Fort Smith, Arkansas: Get Abe and meet me at Conser, I.T. as soon as you can. Bill Frazier's holed up in the area and wanted for murder. John Salmon, Deputy Marshal.

He had sent a telegram to Abe and started his preparations immediately. It would take two days of fast riding to get there, 70 miles for Abe and 83 miles for him.

He lashed down the last strap on his bedroll and turned to face his family. His two little girls, Dora and Celia, clung to Irene's long skirt tail. They were cute little things, two and three years old, long hair to their waists. He lifted them up together in his arms and kissed them.

"Be good and mind your ma. I'll be back soon." Their little eyes pooled with tears as he sat them on the ground.

Irene went to the back of the house and called Tony who was playing in the old oak tree. "Tony, your father's leaving. Come say good-bye to him."

"Is Uncle Abe going with you?" Tony asked.

"Yes, I'm meeting him on the way."

Minnie stood on the porch with Laura Morgan. They were similar in age and build. Many people took them for sisters.

Irene gave him a hug around the neck, her arms lingering, reluctant to let him go.

"God bless you and protect you, my husband."

"Bye" they chorused, waving at him as he mounted and swung his horse toward the gate. Henry and John Morgan were plowing in the field along side the road. They stopped and stepped to the fence as Charley rode up.

"Bye, Pa," Henry said, "Have a good trip."

John stuck out his hand. "Be careful, sir."

"You fellas' keep a watch on the women. I'll be home as soon as possible."

He hoped he would be home as soon as possible. Hunting Frazier was always a challenge. The man had unlimited ways to avoid capture and knew every crag and cave on Black Fork Mountain.

Two days later, the three lawmen converged on Justice's general stone in

Conser, LeFlore County, Indian Territory. The store had been owned by the victim who had been a prominent man in the community. Several men in full fighting garb stood on the porch, carbines held at their sides.

"I'm United States Deputy Marshal John Salmon and this is Deputy Charley Barnhill and his brother, Abe, our posse man. Who's in charge here?"

"I guess I am," a man said as he stepped down from the porch. "I'm John Harrell. I led the first search party when Justice was killed last Friday night."

"I've got a writ of arrest for Frazier and three others."

"We followed the tracks of the murderers. They led from Justice's house to Charley Perry's house to Frazier's. Perry's already admitted that he went with the killers, but refused to go all the way to Justice's place, because he did not know what was planned. He claims Frazier gave the order for the killing.

"Where're they now?"

"The men here wanted to give Frazier a necktie party, but he got word of us coming and took to Black Fork Mountain. Peter Conser, the Indian sheriff, arrested Charles Perry at his father's home. Gregory and Harris are on the scout. "

"Got any idea where Frazier might be hiding?"

"No, sorry. There are too many places to hide in the Black Fork Mountain. I've had people watching to see if he returns."

"Thanks," Salmon said. "We'll take it from here."

Mollie Frazier stared at the lawmen. "My Bill's innocent; he had nothing to do with this murder. You and your brother just have it in for him. "

Charley thrust a paper in her direction. "We've a writ of arrest from Fort Smith signed by the grand jury. Why'd he run if he's innocent?"

"He was afraid of being lynched."

"If he's innocent, he'll get a fair trial. If he runs, we'll have to hunt him like an animal."

"I don't know if he'll surrender to you; maybe he will to Deputy Salmon. He won't come out unless he feels safe. I'll have you an answer by noon."

"Alright, we'll give you that time to decide. Then we'll start the hunt and he'll be *shot on sight* by any citizen that sees him."

At the front gate, Charley explained the conversation to Abe.

"We know Frazier. He's not to be trusted. Maybe he'll come in and maybe not," Charley said.

Salmon glanced at the sun, measuring how long until dark. "In that case, we will guarantee he comes in. We'll watch the place and see if she sends a messenger."

Abe stared at the back of the house. It was quiet, the sun heading toward the straight up position. HE could see Charley covering the main trail with Salmon in the front. A figure approached across the plowed field behind him. He knew Frazier, but this figure was unfamiliar. The man went to the back door and knocked. Mrs. Frazier opened the door, looked around as he entered and then closed it quickly.

Waving his hat in the air, Abe signaled to Charley who sent the same signal to John Salmon. The two men hunkered down and ran to Abe's position.

"What's up?" John asked.

"Someone just slipped in the back door real secret-like. It wasn't Frazier."

Charley moved away. "I'll cover the trail at the edge of the forest."

Salmon peered at Abe in the shadows. "If he tries to leave, we'll intercept him if he doesn't appear to be armed and find out what he's up to. "

In the shadows of a great white sycamore, Abe tried to pick his spot so he could see the house and the trail leading across the plowed field. A few minutes later the stranger appeared, carrying a small bundle tied in a cloth. He slipped out and back-tracked through the field.

Charley popped out from his hiding spot. The young man stopped and turned to run. Abe and John blocked his route as the young man sprinted back down the path. He dodged off the trail when he saw he was surrounded.

John pulled his Colt. "Hold up there, gent. We just want to talk to you."

The young man stopped at the sight of the six-shooter pointed at his chest.

Salmon grabbed the bundle. "What'cha doing out here? What's your name?"

"Frank Young from Wilburton. Just getting me some dinner from Mrs. Frazier. I have a camp over yonder in the meadow. I'm here to buy cattle." His words came out halting and chopped.

"You sure you aren't taking that to someone else?" John pulled open the knotted scarf. Inside was a modest meal, underneath which was hidden three boxes of 44.40 shells.

"What's with the shells?"

"I need those for my rifle and pistol."

John turned the man by the arm and pushed him down the trail behind Abe who led the way to the back door of the cabin. Charley caught up and stepped in beside John.

Abe knocked on the back door, the others gathered close behind. In an instant, Mrs. Frazier's face turned from surprise to recognition of the figures standing before her door.

"What are you doing back here?" Her eyes moved from face to face.

Salmon's tone hardened. "We caught this young fella slipping in and out of your place. Claims he was just picking up a meal. Mrs. Frazier, you must lead us to Bill. His life hangs by a thread if the vigilantes find him before us."

"Alright, if you promise you'll take him straight to Fort Smith and not leave him in jail here. I want Frank to go with us."

She came out a few minutes later in a riding skirt, a Winchester tucked under her arm.

Salmon rubbed his face. "What do you need that for?"

"Just in case any of those vigilantes get too close." Her eyes were unblinking and her lips set in a faint grimace. "I fight for my man, no matter what."

The men mounted and fell in line behind the woman and her cohort. Abe noticed her path was straight forward; she lead the way without looking about for the trail. His head moving from side to side as if searching for an escape route, Young followed her riding a borrowed mule. Abe wondered what hold Frazier had on this young fella. He was tangled up in a murder now.

The course moved up and down ravines filled with brambles and thistles that pulled at Abe's clothing, but it seemed to follow a previously used path. Two hours into the ride, Mrs. Frazier and her companion stopped, turned off the trail and headed straight toward what seemed to be a sheer rock face. She dismounted and pointed above their heads.

"He's up there, has a stone fort he built back in '86 when you-all were pursuing him."

Abe spotted an opening in the rock, almost hidden behind the brush. Mrs. Frazier bent her head a little to clear the overhanging ledge and went through the cleft in the rock. John motioned them to stop, hesitated a few seconds and then peeked around the upright granite face. Abe followed Charley to Salmon's position.

The deputy pointed to the cleft. "It's a cave entrance opening up into a tunnel. We'll go in, but be ready for anything. Try not to make any noise."

Abe followed them through the tight wedge into the cavern forged out of the hillside by large boulders which had settled in ancient times. The far wall exposed a tunnel through piled rocks leading back into the mountain side.

As the lawmen shifted their weapons and took off their hats, Mrs. Frazier pointed to the tunnel. Young stood beside her, his face a pasty white, fear etched on his features. Was he afraid of the law or Frazier? Abe wondered.

The woman moved along the cliff wall to the tunnel. "That leads up the back of this cliff to his fort on top of the ridge."

"Go up and tell him we want to parley," John Salmon commanded.

She turned and scurried into the opening leaving little wisps of dust in her haste.

Salmon shifted his attention to the surroundings. "Be ready for anything. I'd hate to shoot it out in this small enclosure."

Charley burst out. "If there's any shooting, make your first shot in the heart. Frazier'll never give up once he starts fighting."

Abe pulled his .45 and checked for a full chamber, inserting a shell into the one that lay under the hammer. He cocked it to the firing position and waited, his heart beating a thunderous pulse in his temples. Would this end peacefully? Never could tell with Frazier. He could prop a Winchester on his stub of an arm and fire with the remaining fingers of his right hand.

The three men spread out into the interior trying to pick spots that would provide protection but not present a cross fire. The seconds ticked away in Abe's head, his sense of hearing acutely tuned for the returning messenger. He looked at the tunnel and tried to focus his vision against the dim light.

Hearing the scattering of loose rocks on the tunnel floor, he pointed his revolver in that direction. A white handkerchief appeared stuck to the end of a willow branch. It fluttered frantically in the air, backed up by a hoarse voice. "I give up. Don't shoot."

Frazier appeared from the crevice, his hair in disarray under his hat, a Winchester hanging at the end of his intact right arm, the three remaining fingers holding tightly to the stock of the heavy weapon. He had two six shooters on his right hip and two shell belts around his shoulders. His dedicated wife stepped out of the crevice behind him, her eyes full of relief.

Abe caught his breath and eased the hammer down on his .45 as his eyes fixed on the face that had lived for so long in his nightmares, the face of the man who had wanted to kill him and had almost succeed. Charley and John Salmon stepped out from their shelter.

"You're under arrest for murder," John said as he took the man's Winchester from his maimed hand and slipped the handcuff on the single wrist.

Bill Frazier looked around and then growled. "I might've know - the Barnhills. I've never been able to out run you two. Should've killed you both when I had the chance."

Abe put his .45 away and stepped up to Frazier. "You won't have to worry about that where you're going this time. No more pardons from the President for a poor helpless outlaw." His mind reeling from the proximity to his old enemy, he clenched his fists and strode away before he hit an unarmed cripple. A cripple, just like him.

Charley poked Frazier in the back with his Winchester. "Let's go."

The man who had brought the provisions to Frazier stood near by. He was silent, his eyes full of fear.

"Frank Young, you're under arrest for aiding and abetting a fugitive," John said. "You'll have to explain yourself to the commissioner in Fort Smith."

"But I've got cattle to herd over to Wilburton tomorrow."

"You should've kept your nose out of this business."

Post Script:

William Frazier, Frank Young and Charley Perry were charged before the commissioner at Fort Smith on March 25, 1895. After the testimony of more than a dozen witnesses, they were committed to jail and bound over for trial on

April 9, 1895. Charles Perry and Frank Young testified for the government and were removed from the indictment for murder against Bill Frazier that was issued on June 3, 1895. Charles Harris and John Gregory were never found, Gregory's father suspected that he was killed by his cohorts.

On Oct. 9, 1895, after more than six months in jail, Frazier was acquitted from the box by the jury with the consent of the district attorney. Insufficient evidence against him was cited as the reason since the real killers had never been found.

Frank Young got into more trouble and was charged with larceny in the same month as Frazier's acquittal after being arrested at Hartshorne, Indian Territory.

Chapter 61

Death of a Legend

The impressive justice building loomed over him as he climbed the steps. It stood on the same block as the Sebastian County Courthouse, both three story buildings of red brick and white brick trim on the roof edges and corners. Inside the building was heated by the modern radiator system that had been installed when built six years prior. He looked around and took the stairs to the Marshal's office. The assistant marshal sat at his desk in the foyer. His eyes lit up when he spied Charley.

"Howdy, Charley. We've been expecting you." The man knocked on Marshal Crump's door and opened it to announce the visitor.

"Come in, Charley. Good to see you. How you been?" Crump was a dignified man in a white shirt and navy blue trousers held up with suspenders. His medium-length beard surrounded a firmly set mouth. A renowned lawyer and legislator, he made the marshal's office a symbol of efficiency and justice, a partnership that matched Parker's reputation. "I'm glad you could come on such short notice." He motioned him to a chair beside his desk.

"Your telegram sounded urgent, so I dropped everything and came on the first train."

Crump thumped his desk with a clenched fist. "I've got over two hundred prisoners in jail and piles of arrest writs yet to be served. I need the help of every experienced deputy I can call up."

"How long do you figure to need me?" Charley asked.

"Until this court's criminal jurisdiction in the Indian territory ends on September 1st."

"Alright. I'll give you my best effort."

"You know the oath by heart now, you've taken it so many times. Just sign it for me."

He grasped the pen and wrote his signature as carefully as he could filling in the date, Feby. 6th, 1896. Judge Parker would sign it later. His spelling wasn't the best, but his penmanship was clear and artistic. He took the writs the marshal stuck in his hands.

"The one on top is a very sad case A woman and her son have been charged in the death of a newborn baby. I'll send more to you in McAlester."

Sitting on his horse with Abe beside him, Charley observed the little frame house behind the trees. They had brought in a dozen prisoners since February, spread all over the Choctaw Nation, mostly one man at a time. Charley was amazed that it took almost as much work to track down and arrest one fugitive as it did a half-dozen. It was now June and the jail still held over two hundred prisoners, so far the busiest month it had ever had. With this trip, God-willing, they would add the occupants of the house to it's total.

"Look's pretty quiet," he said. "I'll approach and hail them. You cover me from the trees just in case."

"Alright, but don't take any chances," Abe replied.

Charley tightened the leather thongs of his hat under his neck and stepped out into the clearing, about twenty yards from the porch.

"Hello in the house," he called, cupping his hands to improve the sound. He kept his eyes on the front door, watching for movement. A crude blanket hung without care over the single window.

"Who are you and what do you want?" a female voice came from inside, its tone weak and desperate.

"I'm looking for Lamuel White."

" I'll get him."

The door opened and a man stepped out. As he did so, Charley heard the click of Abe's Winchester behind him in the trees. He stepped back into the tree cover.

"I'm White. Who are you?"

"United States Deputy Marshal Charles Barnhill. I've a writ for your arrest."

The man made a sudden start for the door. Abe sent a shot crashing into the porch overhang, sending splinters into his face. Charley heard a startled cry from inside the house.

"Stand still and put your hands up," Charley commanded, his revolver held firmly in his hand.

The man turned with his hands in the air. Charley approached with caution, still not knowing for sure how many were in the house. "Who's in the house?"

"Just my woman and baby."

"What's her name?"

"Mary Olive."

"Call her out." Charley secured handcuffs around the man's wrists. He was a sorry looking specimen, unshaven face, tangled dirty hair, blood-shot eyes, and no front teeth.

"Mary, come on out. I need your help."

Charley heard Abe crossing the clearing at a hop.

A woman stepped through the door. Her appearance was just as bad, dirty skirt, hair that hadn't seen a brush in months, and eyes bulging with fear. "What's wrong, Lam?" It was the weak, whining voice he had heard from the window.

"Marshal got me caught," the man said, rubbing his crotch with his manacled hands.

"Ma'am, I've got a writ of arrest for both of you for the murder of Mrs. White. I must handcuff you." Charley attempted to put the cuffs around her wrists. She screamed and rushed for the door.

Abe stepped in front of her. "Now, ma'am, let's not make this hard." He placed his Winchester down behind him and stepped toward her.

She backed away, screaming, "My baby, I can't leave my baby."

"Your baby will be alright. You can bring it with you, no problem." Charley watched as Abe tried to reason with her. While she was distracted looking at Abe, he slipped up behind her and grabbed her arms, pinning them behind her. Holding his breath so as not to smell the stink of her hair, Charley tightened his grip. "If you won't resist, I'll secure your hands in front. Otherwise, you'll be handcuffed with them behind you. What'll it be?"

She wiggled and fought to get loose for several seconds, but he held her hard and firm. She gave up and started crying.

"Alright, but don't hurt my baby. My baby needs me."

Charley motioned Abe to take her in the house.

"See that she gets their personal gear packed and the baby ready to go. I'll take Mr. White and find his horse, if he has one."

Abe stepped in the door pushing the woman ahead of him. Charley turned to his prisoner.

"Where's your horse?"

"Don't got one."

"How do you get around?"

"If I have to, I pull Mary in the buggy with the milk cow."

He secured the man to the porch and went to find the milk cow. It was better than having them ride double on one of their horses. After several minutes, he found the cow in the back of the pasture and led it to the barn where the buggy was parked. Before he could get it harnessed, he heard a call from the house.

"Charley, you better come here and take a look," Abe said as he walked around the back of the house.

"What's wrong?"

"The baby, it don't look too good to me," Abe explained.

They went to the front of the house. The woman stood on the porch, a little bundle held tightly in her arms. Pathetic cries came from underneath the dirty blanket. Charley attempted to turn the blanket back. The woman cringed and pulled away.

"That's my baby. You can't have it."

"If you don't let me see it, I'll have to take it from you and you won't get it back."

The woman whimpered as she held out the little bundle. Charley pulled back the blanket - he was shocked at the sight. It was a very small baby, apparently not newborn, but so frail and under-nourished it looked like a skeleton. "What's happened to this baby?"

"I don't have no milk to give it and we can't afford canned milk. I been trying to feed it with cow's milk, and then the cow dried up last week."

"What's it had since then?"

"Just some corn syrup water and corn meal gruel."

"As soon as we get to Fort Smith, the baby will have to go to the prison hospital to be examined."

"I can't let no one take my baby from me," the woman wailed.

Charley turned to Abe. "Keep them here while I finish harnessing the milk cow. What a mess."

After he led the cow-drawn buggy to the front of the house, the prisoners were placed in it and shackled to the sides. Charley mounted his horse and tied the cow's halter lead to his saddle horn.

"Let's go."

The party started out the trail to the main road. As they moved into the meadow opening onto the public road, a man rode up. He moved quickly to the buggy. His eyes were unfriendly as he spoke.

"White, you scoundrel. I hope you get the noose for what you did to your poor wife. Killed her, you did. Starved her to death after that baby was born."

Charley was relieved to see the man was unarmed. Sometimes neighbors had other ideas about justice in a particularly bad case.

"What do you mean?" Charley asked.

"After his poor wife had her baby, she was laid up. He just let her starve and took up with this hussy."

"You mean, this isn't her baby?"

"No, it ain't. I offered to take it and care for it, poor little thing."

"No one's going to take my baby away," the woman wailed again, clutching the little bundle even tighter.

Attempting to assure the neighbor, he explained, "We'll get them to Fort Smith and sort out the baby's fate there. The judge will make a decision on what to do with it. The Salvation Army takes in orphans to raise and does a good job of it."

Heat held sway in the Indian Territory. Every living thing sought shelter in the shade. Men stayed out of the fields; women cooked only early in the morning or late in the evening, offering cold dinners at midday to their families; children were forced to nap on pallets under shade trees to avoid the feared polio season. Several had already succumbed to the terrible disease during the past two months. A mother's fear was fever which signaled the onset.

The jail had been inspected in August by the grand jury and found wanting only in the bedding which was described as filthy beyond reason. Half of the cells with the more than two hundred prisoners had no mattresses and only a few ragged old blankets which had not been washed or aired since issued to the inmates. Vermin ruled in the ticking and bedding that did exist.

Outside the Marshals' office Charley chuckled as he read this description in the newspaper. It was about time someone did something to get those prisoners to clean up. The society they were used to did not require them to bathe.

Their recommendations included ice water for the prisoners in summer, fresh hay for the mattresses every three months and everything washed every 90 days. If a prisoner could not furnish a change of clothes for washing, the jail would provide them a uniform. Prisoners who came in would be bathed thoroughly and old clothes burned if vermin-infested. They were to whitewash their cells monthly and put down powder for the lice, and keep their persons clean by use of the plumbing facilities.

The assistant marshal had asked him to come in and be sworn in again. He had already taken a new oath on July 7 and now it was August 12. *What's going on?*

The assistant chief deputy came out of the marshal's office and instructed him to come in.

Marshal Crump extended a sheet of paper. "Since the jurisdiction of this court over the Indian Territory ceases the end of this month, I want all my deputies who are willing to stay on and serve in the Western District of Arkansas to take new oaths of allegiance. The wording has been changed in accordance with the new jurisdiction. Here's you oath to sign, if you're willing."

Charley looked at the paper. The oath was now 8 lines long versus 4. The new wording included:

> *and that I will support and defend the Constitution of the United States against all enemies foreign and domestic; that I will bear true faith and allegiance to the same; and I take this obligation freely, without any mental reservations or purpose of evasion; and that I will well and faithfully discharge the duties of the office on which I am about to inter. SO HELP ME GOD.*

"Why the new wording?"

Crump pointed to the portrait of President Cleveland. "Congress wanted to add to the oath for all federal offices to reinforce dedication to our founding values. Too much foreign influence out there these days."

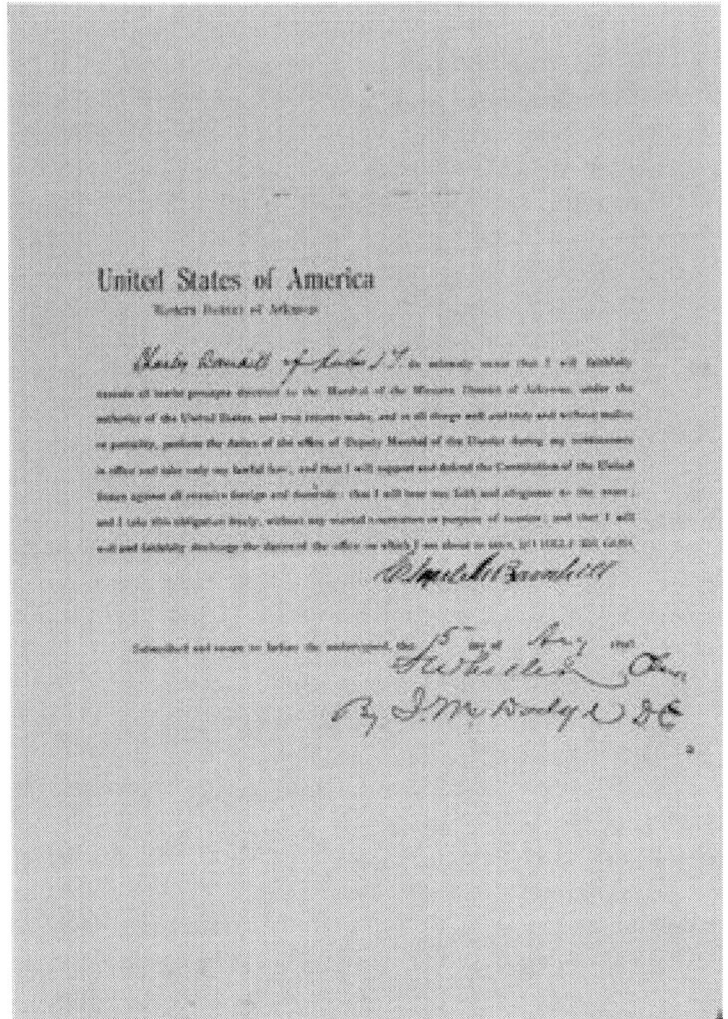

United States of America

Charley's new oath of office, August 15, 1896

"I guess that makes sense. Some people say our government is too old fashion. I'll be available for as long as you need me, Mr. Crump." Charley liked this marshal as did most folks. He was very popular and an easy man for which to work. "Just send any writs to McAlester when you need me."

"Thanks, Charley. I'm glad to see the violence subsiding, but Judge Parker has been the energy behind all that made it a success."

"I don't think any other judge in the world could have accomplished what he did, even though he was not perfect. I've worked for him for seventeen years, with the assurance that the men I brought in would get their just and fair day in court." An era was closing, one that may soon be forgotten by the next generation. He would see to it that his grandchildren would know and understand what he, Abe and James and all the other deputies, posse man and guards had done for this great country.

Marshal Crump offered his hand. "I'm honored to have served with you and all the other brave men that have made up the deputy force."

Charley shook it and smiled. "Your job hasn't been easy, either. Under your guidance, we brought in the Cook gang, Cherokee Bill and the Rufus Buck gang."

The marshal's face became thoughtful as he walked Charley to the door. "Yes, I did, with your help."

Pretty Ada Patterson, a professional reporter of some notoriety from a St. Louis newspaper, sat outside Judge Parker's bedroom. She had been sent to get a last interview with the famous judge. She squirmed in her seat, anxious at having to face the stern man who had sent so many men to the gallows. It was October 29, 1896. The famous judge had been too ill since the middle of August to hold court. She was fortunate to have arranged this interview.

The doctor came to the door. "You may come in now, Miss Patterson."

She entered the sick room, her eyes adjusting to the dimly lit room, with drawn curtains on the windows. Her eyes focused on a stately figure sitting propped up by pillows in the bed.

"Thank you for seeing me, sir." She offered him her hand. His hand shake was gentle though trembling.

"Please sit down, Miss Patterson," Judge Parker said. "I must apologize for my condition. I haven't been sick in forty-five years. My physician says I have over worked myself to this state."

She observed him as she began the interview. His blue eyes still sparkled with energy and his whole countenance appeared to have a vigor of youth, though his hair and beard were now silver. Knowing the encounter must be brief, she plunged in to the accusation that was always on his critics' lips.

Hoping not to offend him, she put forth the question that was on every reader's mind. "My readers think you have been too harsh in sentencing so many men to death. What do you have to say to their charges?"

"My dear, that is an old complaint against me. I favor the abolition of capital punishment, but punishment must deter a man's further slid into evil. In the uncertainty of punishment following a crime lies the weakness of our halting justice. I have not hung these men. It is the law that has hung them."

"Some say you oppose a court of appeals as infringing on you authority," Miss Patterson stated, glancing at her notebook.

"I do not oppose the court of appeals but I would reorganize it instead of sending cases straight to the Supreme Court. I feel courts of appeal should be made up of judges learned in criminal law, not civil law. This would help restore the public's confidence in the court system. And appeals should be handled at once."

"Some call you cruel, Judge Parker. What do you say to them?"

"Such critics forget the hardened criminal I dealt with and the sixty-five deputy marshals, one third of the total who served, who were murdered in the discharge of their duties. They forget the crime he perpetrated and the family he made fatherless by his assassin's work." Judge Parker paused and took a drink from a glass by his bedside.

"What I say of these ruffians is not directed against the Indians. Twenty-one years experience with the Indians has taught me that the race is not one of criminals, but of law-abiding members."

Miss Patterson paused as a woman entered the room.

"This is my dear wife, Miss Patterson. She is here to make sure I take my medicine. Excuse me a moment."

She watched as the elegant lady in the lace and broach-decorated dress tucked the pillows under her husband's back and handed him a tray that held a glass of milk and several pills.

"Now where were we?"

Ada looked at her notes. "What about the Supreme Court?"

The judge smiled and began. "They said Judge Parker is too rigid, but cannot point to any one case and say, 'He was too severe in this.' I have ever had the single aim of justice and have often said to the grand jury, 'Permit no

Old Fort Smith Jail, 1897
Courtesy of Fort Smith National Historic Site

innocent man to be punished, but let no guilty man escape.' We have had as fine juries at Fort Smith as could be found in the land."

Miss Patterson rose and bowed to the famous man in the bed. "I thank you for allowing me to take your time. I wish you the best of health in you recuperation. I know my readers will be pleasantly surprised, as am I, at your gentleness and kindness." She held her breath as she tiptoed out of the room and shut the door.

The next day she went to interview the attorneys who had worked with Judge Parker. In her room that night, she summarized their comments.

One lawyer had told her, "Judge Parker's was a court in which there was a certainty of arrest and surety of punishment. It is what saved the Indian Territory from its threatened fate of becoming a barren waste. He was a man of unimpeachable integrity. No Judge was ever more revered by the bar."

She looked down at the story she had written, her concluding paragraph a flourish of sentiment.

> *He is a good man. What a tribute that is from one man of the world to another! What music to the ears of the woman who loves that man! I am glad I have the honor of knowing this alleged cruel Judge. It is darkly indeed the press and people view him through the glass of distance. He is a Twentieth Century hero, worthy of the fame of the most just of Romans. More than all, as the old lawyer said to me, while a moisture he was not ashamed of made the office belongings and the face of the visitor look misty and far away, more than all, "He is a good man."*

Post Script:

Judge Parker lingered until November 17, 1896. The day of the Judge's death was hailed as a gala day by the prisoners in the jail awaiting trial. The jailer promptly and forcefully quelled the disturbance and made them to understand that open contempt for Judge Parker, even when dead, would not be tolerated in the Federal Jail·

However, in Fort Smith, and throughout the Indian Territory there was great mourning. His funeral the next day was the largest that Fort Smith had ever seen. Hundred of Indians came to walk in the mourning procession escorting the casket to the Fort Smith National Cemetery. As Theodore Roosevelt's Attorney General, Philander C. Know, observed

> *Many of them (Parker's trials) were conducted without the regard to the rights of defendants which prevails in more settled and law abiding communities, and . . . many convictions were obtained which could not have been obtained elsewhere. . . . But, this condition was perhaps the almost necessary result of the state of affairs which ex-*

isted in the Indian Territory in the days when the Territory was infested with outlaws, and desperadoes, and murder and robbery were every day occurrences.

Judge Isaac Parker 1895

Chapter 62

Epidemic

The yellow sign on the front door bore an ominous warning.

> **Meningitis: Until this notice is legally removed, all persons not occupants of these premises are forbidden to enter.**

It was signed by the local county judge of the Indian Territory and dated, January 4, 1899. Abe knocked on the door and then stepped back off the porch. He had come the few miles from his place as soon as Sam, his oldest brother, had sent his neighbor to fetch him. It concerned Emeline Lish, (Emmy as they called her) Sam's oldest daughter. The door creaked as it opened a crack and then wide enough for Sam to step out. His reddened eyes stared at the sign.

"I knew if I sent a messenger, you would come help us," he said as he ran his fingers through his hair. "No one can leave the house and I've livestock to feed. William and Pearl are stuck in here with us."

"Well, I'm here now. What's the news on Emmy?" Abe asked.

"The doctor was here this morning. He confirmed the diagnosis, meningitis. It came on quite suddenly. She was over here yesterday helping Mary with a quilt when she developed a terrible headache, then fever. She wanted to go home, but her mother compelled her to stay overnight. By morning she was confused and delirious."

Abe was alarmed at this news. Sickness that severe in onset usually meant something dire. "What do you want me to do?"

"Feed the livestock and then go to Emmy's house and check on her husband and son. I sent him a message last night and he came over, but had to go home to care for Johnny. That was before we knew it was something contagious and the doctor put on the quarantine."

"Do you need anything from the general store?"

"No, the doctor left us the medication to give her, pain relief for the headache and fever is about all. He says we'll know in a day or so if she is going to recover. She's sleeping now. Oh, please send a telegram to Charley and Jimmy so Mom and Dad are informed."

Abe finished the chores and rode the couple of miles to his niece's home. It was a pleasant little structure of finished boards and a wood shingled roof.

As he rode up, her husband, Bill Lish, came out. His face showed the anxiety he felt. "How's Emmy?"

"Sleeping. The doctor says it will be a day or two before she starts to recover."

"I appreciate you coming over. I'm going to take Johnny over to my folks, and then go over to her parents and stay, until I know how she's doing."

Abe rode home to report to Amanda what was happening. Her eyes filled with tears as she heard the news. "Meningitis, they're under quarantine."

William H. Lish and Emeline at their marriage in 1894

Charley took the train to Eufaula as soon as he got the news. He rented a horse from the livery and rode the twenty-four miles to Sam's farm, south of Porum. As he approached the simple farmhouse, he saw Abe's horse in the barn. He found him looking through lumber piled up against the back of the barn.

"What's the news?" Charley asked.

Abe turned and stared at his brother before answering.

"Emmy died an hour ago. The doctor just left. I'm making a coffin."

"Where's her husband?"

"Out in the woods there, crying his heart out to God."

"Let me go speak to Sam and I'll come back and help you."

He tired to compose his feelings as he stepped up to the door. How terrible to lose a daughter so suddenly without warning. The memory of Salina's death from the same disease came back with all its raw emotions. Would the Lord give him words of comfort for Sam and Mary, Bill and little Johnny.? He noticed the black wreath on the door that now hung just below the quarantine sign. He knocked and waited.

Sam's face appeared in the door and when he saw his brother, he stepped out and stood with his eyes cast to the ground.

Charley spoke through the hoarseness in his throat."Sam, I'm so sorry. I wish I could have been here to comfort you. Mom and Dad send their love and prayers."

"I'm glad you're here. We need to get Emmy buried as soon as possible because of the disease. We can't have a regular funeral. It'll be just you, Abe and her husband, Bill. I've already sent my neighbors over to the graveyard to start digging the grave. Mary is wrapping her body now."

Charley returned to the barn. It took them most of the afternoon to finish the simple pine wood coffin. He hitched up the team and backed the wagon to the porch. Young Bill Lish had returned from his sojourn in the woods with tear-stained cheeks and vacant eyes.

The door opened and Sam beckoned. Charley peered through the doorway. Emeline Barnhill Lish's mummy-wrapped body lay on a wooden plank supported between two kitchen chairs. Her mother, Mary, stood over her daughter's still form, crying and moaning, speaking in Cherokee, the old cry of her people. Sam and his son, William, lifted the lithe woman's body and moved the burden to the porch.

"Let's give Bill some time alone with her," Sam said as he pulled his wife into the kitchen. The young widower approached his wife's corpse. Her unwrapped face was covered with a lace hankie. He reached down and removed it to view his beloved's face and to touch it for the last time. Charley could not bear the sight and turned away in sorrow. Minutes passed in silence disturbed only by a sob from the bent form.

"I'm ready," he said.

The four men picked up the planking at each corner and carried it's burden to the wagon. As they lowered the lifeless form into the coffin in the back of the wagon bed, the team snorted and stomped, smelling death. Charley rushed to the front and quieted them with pats and words of comfort.

The family stood on the porch and watched in silence as he guided the team out the front gate, Abe beside him on the wagon seat. The grieving husband rode in the back, his head resting in his arms, hugging the cold pine boards that enshrined the one he had sworn to love and cherish until death parted them.

The winter sun was low on the horizon as they pulled into the Briartown graveyard and found the location of the newly dug grave. It was on the hill side just beyond the graves of Sam and Mary's two sons who had died as children, Earl and James. Their sister would now join them in this place of peace and solitude.

The old Indian cemetery lay shadowed in the fading light, hallowed ground with old stones scattered beneath bare-branched trees. Some of the people they had known for so many years now rested here. It was a place of beauty and reverence.

The two neighbors who had dug the grave stepped forward to help them carry the coffin the few yards to its final resting place, Bill Lish following behind in silence. The gravediggers stepped forward with shovels to quickly fill in the hole. The light was almost gone when the last shovel of dirt was tapped into place atop the grave.

Charley stepped over to the young man and took his hand.

"Bill, do you want to pray for Emmy?"

"I can't find the strength. Will you do me the honor of offering her final words?" The young man looked at him with pleading red-rimmed eyes.

"Yes, of course, I will." He moved to the front of the grave and the rest approached and bowed their heads, hats held in front of them in mute respect. The silence of the graveyard was broken only by the distant call of a loon.

> "Dear Lord, We give you the body of your faithful servant, Emeline Barnhill Lish, as it returns to the dirt from which it was created. Ashes to ashes, dust to dust are your words. We are reminded that you are the Great Creator and Redeemer. I ask for comfort for Emmy's family, her husband and son, her parents and sisters and brother, and her extended family. May the glorious angels who took her to you rejoice at her life. In your Son's Name, we pray. Amen."

Charley put his hat on and shook hands with the grave-diggers. "Thank you for your help. May God bless you."

The two brothers stepped away from the grave site a discreet distance to give the husband time alone. While they were waiting, Charley turned to Abe. "If you need me from now on, I'll be at Jimmy's place." He saw the startled look on Abe's face. Before he could comment, he tried to explain. "Now that Irene's brother, John Henry, and sister, Laura, are grown and on their own, she doesn't want to stay with me anymore. She says since I quit the Marshal Service, I'm hard to live with. I did it for her. She wanted me home more but now we seem to get on each others nerves."

"But Charley, what about the children? How's Minnie taking it?"

"I'll live near by for a year and then she can file for divorce on grounds of desertion. At that time, we will let the children decide who they want to stay with. Minnie is leaving to take a secretarial job in Texas."

"I'm so sorry to hear that. I'll pray for you. Do Ma and Pa know yet?"

"No, I haven't told them because Dad has been so weak lately. He can't hardly walk across the room anymore. When Henry joined the Army last year during the Spanish-American War it almost did Pa in to have to say good-bye."

Abe patted his brother on the shoulder. "Amanda and I will help with the children, if you need anything. Janette and Effie are big girls now and good with children."

"Thanks, I'll let you know. I'm not going to tell Sam and Mary until later. They're going through enough."

The two brothers rode back to Sam's in silence. They dropped Bill off at his house where a crowd of family and friends had already gathered to offer him comfort.

He'll be comforted with all that love and care, Charley thought. That's how God ministers to us in our time of need, through his earthly disciples. *Who will minister to me, Lord? An old warhorse that has spent his life for a cause bigger than himself.*

William Harrison Lish

Post Script:

1899 was a difficult year for the Barnhill family. In March the Lord took home the family patriarch, Alford Barnhill. Meningitis continued to spread through the Indian population. Sam and Mary's second to youngest daughter, Margaret Barnhill Phillips, died in June of the same disease.

Charley and Irene divorced in 1900. Henry chose to live with his father and Irene took the two girls. She remarried within eighteen months to a man her own age.

Chapter 63

A New Century

Charley shifted his position in the saddle. He had been called by the local deputy's office to take a prisoner to Fort Smith for them. He did not do much marshallin' now, but he did not mind doing an old friend a favor now and then. The familiar sight of the city by the Arkansas River came into view as he and the prisoner passed under the railroad trestle south of town. It was the same railroad on which he had made the whiskey search on Christmas Day so many years ago. He chuckled to himself as he thought of the surprised look on those business men's faces as his posse had covered the doors to start the search. Too bad he had not chuckled at the ruckus that it had caused in the newspapers and had made him retreat home to McAlester.

After depositing the prisoner to the jailer, he rode up the street to see an old friend, C.C. Ayers. Buggies and the new- fangled automobiles that made horses bolt in fear filled the streets. When he opened the door to the store and walked in, the man behind the counter jumped up and ran around the edge and clasped him in a bear hug. "Charley, you old gun-totin', run down deputy, how you been?" The grin on his face seemed to spread from ear to ear. "I heard you were about retired now?"

"I still make a few runs for the younger fella's in the Indian Territory who don't like the long ride to Fort Smith when they have a federal prisoner. They don't want to go anywhere they have to ride a horse very far. They use automobiles to scour the county. Of course, there's not many roads they can get through with that gadget. A horse never fails you."

"Come on, I'll buy you a cup of coffee."

The two men stepped out into the spring air. 1905 was a year that held a lot of promise for the Indian Territory. The allotments were almost done and the surveying of the land to be sold to the public progressing. Charley knew a lot of men who were leasing land in the Indian Territory that would be put out of business because they did not have the money to buy what was needed to continue their enterprises, old ranchers who had leased the land for twenty or thirty years. Fortunately, Jimmy, his brother, had saved up his profits over the years as he saw this day coming. He had his eye on a good piece of land in Pittsburg county.

As the two men chatted over the pie and coffee, Charley surveyed the restaurant. Electric light fixtures replaced the gas lights. Pretty girls in long skirts and aprons, their hair pinned up and fixed with colorful ribbons, replaced the waiters.

"What do you think will happen to the crime rate when Oklahoma becomes a state? Ayers asked.

"Who can tell? The three districts of the Indian Territory courts have done a fine job since they took over. State officials might not be as honest and upright as the Indians. The voters will have to be particularly vigilant the first few years. Arkansas had the same trouble a few years back and had to clean out the graft and greed of the politicians."

The merchant scratched his whiskers and shrugged his shoulders. "I just hope my brother, Will, didn't die in vain and we didn't ride all over hell for nothing."

He did not like to think about the bad days gone by. He wanted to look to the future for his children and his granddaughter, Katie, with promises of more to come.

Charley patted his friend on the shoulder. "Just look at the difference now compared to twenty years ago. A man can walk the streets in most towns in the Indian Territory now without the fear of being robbed or assaulted. The carrying of personal hand guns is less popular because people can rely on the law to do their fighting for them. That's progress." He would be glad when he could put up his Peacemaker forever.

"How's Abe doing?" Ayers asked.

"He's fine. He moved to Pittsburg County a couple of years ago to be near the rest of the family. All his daughters are married and have growing families. How about your family?"

"The same. The next generation of children is coming along with privileges we never foresaw for them. Thank God, the Almighty, doesn't let us see the future. We would want to take all the credit for our blessings."

A few lines of sun-darkened wrinkles around his eyes and a chin covered with a thin beard were all that was visible beneath Abe's hat, the round brim protecting his face from the sunlight as he peered towards the camera. It would take the photographer a few minutes to get everyone posed with more than thirty people in this family group. He glanced over at Amanda in her summer bonnet standing beside him, her pretty blue eyes sparkling in the afternoon light.

He was amazed how his family had grown over the years. It was already the end of the first decade of the new century, the summer of 1910. He now had three son-in-laws and eight grandchildren. Only one daughter was here today; Effie who had married Albert Selby sat in front of them with her three children, Archie, Mae and baby Tonie, her husband standing dutifully behind her. Mollie's family had moved to Baylor County, Texas along with Sam and his family right after Jenette had died.

Standing in front of them with Amanda's hands on his shoulders was six year-old Andy Bounds, Jenette's son. It was two years since they had buried her and her stillborn baby together in a common grave at Arpelar, just west of McAlester. Her husband, Mort Bounds, and young Andy lived with them. Amanda excelled in caring for Andy while his father worked with Abe at the saw mill.

In fact, most of the men in this group worked at the saw mill in Blue, Bryan County, the county just to the south of McAlester: Albert Selby, the saw mill operator and his three brothers, and Darwin Mann and three of his sons. Darwin Mann was one of his father's fellow clergymen. The Selby family was headed by John Selby, also a preacher. Preachers were as common as farmers in this family, it seemed.

Mort was now engaged to Bessie Mann Mason, the Mann brothers' little sister. Standing beside Mort Bounds was his brother, Hardy, and his family up from Fannin County, Texas, about forty miles away, to spend a few days with them.

The nineteen children in the group ranged in age from babyhood to thirteen. Since the families all lived side by side along the road leading to the sawmill, they played together and went to school together. The older children were best of friends and helped take care of the little ones when their mothers were busy in the garden or doing the wash. They were like a small village.

He shifted his gaze to the photographer and remembered the few times he had seen a camera and photographer. The old Roeders Brothers' Photography Studio in Fort Smith had been a popular place for the deputies to stop after a particularly important arrest. Tyner Hughes had been photographed with Belle Starr after he and Charley had successfully arrested her in May of 1886. The posse that had captured and killed Ned Christie had posed with rifles and revolvers prominently displayed and the body of the dead Christie propped up for proper viewing.

A popular postcard to sell to tourists featured groups of young Indian prisoners sitting on the Old Jail steps. The grandest of all was the photo of over one hundred people standing in front of the Old Jail. A reunion of the deputies from Judge Parker's court had been held in 1908 just after Jenette had died. He had declined to go to stay and comfort his grieving wife. That photo showed thirty eight of the old deputies, most still in excellent health and form.

Then there was the photograph of his daughter, Mollie, proudly displaying her engagement ring. Twenty years later a roving photographer had come by and taken pictures of Mollie and her three daughters who were dressed in their playing clothes and barefoot. He cherished each photograph he had and hoped this one to be taken shortly would turn out well.

The photographer addressed the crowd. "Ladies and gentlemen. I'll be ready in just a minute. Lets move the littlest children down front to sit on the grass. You men stand in back beside or behind your wives. You older girls come down front and kneel." He was doing his best to make this family photo as grand as possible.

Blue, Oklahoma school, summer 1910
Back row - Martin Bounds, Hardy and Bertha Bounds
Middle row - Archie Selby, Amanda and Abe Barnhill holding Hester Mason, daughter of Bessie Mann Mason
Front row - Effie Barnhill Selby holding son Tony, her son Arthur Selby, her daughter Maybelle Selby, my grandfather Andy Bounds wearing the hat, unidentified boy, Jimmy Bounds

Abe could see the babies in the group starting to squirm and fret. Their mothers rocked them and cooed to them. The little one in her arms, Hester Mason, Bessie's little baby, was a model of manners sucking her thumb and watching the grown-ups. Hardy Bounds' son, Jimmy, stood in front of him. Most of the men wore ties and the older women bonnets, the younger women their heads uncovered. They weren't so afraid of the sun ruining their complexion.

"All right. I think that'll do. I must have you all stand perfectly still so that the faces are not blurred. Put on your best pose. I will count to three. 1...2...3. OK, that one is good. I need to change the film. Don't move and I'll take one more." The photographer unlatched the back of the big camera and removed a framed film. He quickly inserted a second one and latched the back.

"Same thing. I'll count to three. 1...2...3! You did great. Thank you all very much."

The babies and young children squealed in delight as they wriggled free of their parents' arms. Abe exhaled as he felt his lungs straining, not realizing he had been holding his breath. He rocked the baby in his arms and kissed her before handing her to Bessie, an attractive young woman.

"Let's get back to the pie and watermelon," he called to his large family group.

"Hooray!" the little boys shouted. The girls squealed and ran toward the tables laden with the fruits of their labors, God's blessing on this new state of Oklahoma and his growing family of hard working men and women.

Just as he sat down to enjoy the desserts, he heard a horse coming up the road to the meadow. He turned his head and saw ***Charley!***

Excited that his brother was able to make it, he ran to the parking area where the teams, buggies, and saddle horses conglomerated. He grabbed hold of the bridle and held the young roan as Charley dismounted.

"Glad you could come, but you missed the photographer. He just left with his camera and equipment," Abe explained.

Charley brushed the dust off his pants. "That's OK. You know how much I detest *likenesses* as the old Indians call them. What you got to eat?" Abe noticed that his brother had a few gray hairs at his sideburns just like him.

"Everything, fried chicken, biscuits, corn on the cob, pie, tea, watermelon. Whatever you like." Abe patted him on the back and walked with him into the group of people who greeted him with handshakes and shouts of *Howdy.*

Abe sat by his brother as he dug into his heaping plate.

"How's it going working for Abner Pusley?"

Charley answered between bites. "Abner has a pretty big farm from his allotment and he needs all the help he can get. He's a good friend and I owe him a lot for giving me a steady job. Not many people want an old broken down lawman working for them." He was kidding but his words had a lot of truth to them.

Abe pointed down the table at his son-in-law, Albert. "Yes. We're fortunate to have Albert and his sawmill to employ all of us. How's Henry doing?"

"Very well, he's farming and raising a good family. Tony is living and working with him for now."

"And the girls?" Abe asked, his mind visualizing young girls in ribbons and bows.

That vision was shattered at Charley's answer. "Celia is engaged to be married to Gerald Dunlap in February of next year. She turns eighteen in October. Dora is sixteen and trying to copy her older sister in every way she can, hair style, clothes, mannerisms, suitors. They sure grow up fast."

Abe's mind turned to law enforcement in the state he loved. "I hear Oklahoma has a new state prison going up at McAlester to be done next spring."

Charley took a healthy bite at a corn cob before commenting. "They already have almost a thousand prisoners living in make shift buildings with barbed wire fences. Tyne gave up his job as town marshal at Spiro to take a job as prison guard. He really likes it. He says its a piece of cake compared to tracking murderers all over the Indian Territory."

"Well, enough talking. I'm glad you could come. Let's go challenge these young fellas to a game of baseball. That's all the rage now. I can't run, but I can hit a homer as they call it." Abe got up and walked to the batting mound, kicking at the dirt with his toes.

Only a few months hence from this happy gathering, Abe tried to focus as he listened to Pastor Selby's familiar words, "Ashes to ashes, dust to dust." It was the first week of May, 1911, Most of the same family members that had been at the summer picnic gathered around an open grave. Friends and neighbors stood in clumps of black mourning joining old friends from the marshals' force: Tyner Hughes and his wife, James Cole, now a merchant in McAlester, and James White. Abe thought of the four faces that were missing, dead at the hands of an assassin's bullet: Willard Ayers, John Phillips, Zack Moody, and George Williams. The location in the new graveyard brought back the memory of three years ago. The grave of his dear daughter, Jenette, unmarked except for a simple wooden cross engraved with her name and dates, lay there beside the open hole. He hoped one day before he died, he and her husband, Mort, could arrange a more proper marker for her. He grasped Amanda's hand and squeezed it tight. She stifled a sob and dabbed at her eyes with her hankie. His mother, Sarah, sat in a chair beside them, too infirm to stand for long.

Two pretty young women and a mature thirtyish one just as pretty stepped forward and addressed the crowd, Minnie, Dora and Celia Barnhill (now Dunlap), Charley's daughters.

Minnie cleared her throat and fought back sobs. "My sisters and I have written an epitaph for our father. We want to share it with you. This will be engraved on his marker."

The younger sister, Dora, took the paper and began to read the few simple words. "The pains of death are past. Labor and sorrow cease and life's long warfare closed at last. His soul's found in peace." She began to cry and buried her face in her sister's shoulder.

Their brother, Tony, stepped up beside them and cleared his throat. "I was born in Fort Smith at the time when our father was the busiest working for the famous Judge Parker. He was a committed lawman and loved his job, but he loved his family more. He never let us forget that even when he was gone most of the time. I hope to be as good a father as he was."

Henry, the oldest son, moved to the front. His voice was clear and strong, reminiscent of his Grandfather Alford's preaching voice. "As we say good-bye to our father, your brother, your uncle, your brother-in-law, I want to share with you something I heard him say often. He said, 'Whatever you do, be honest and don't lie. Make peace with all men and give God the glory for everything you achieve.' He lived by this creed and it has served as an example for us all. A century from now maybe no one will know this man and what he accomplished, but I feel that a person is not truly gone as long as his memory and his life are talked about and followed in his family. I pray that our great-grandchildren will be able to tell their children about him and what he meant to this family. "

He stepped away from the open grave and guided his sisters to the chairs along side. They sat down and sobbed as the grave diggers began to fill in the grave. When it was done they arose and placed a single bouquet on top of the fresh dirt.

Abe escorted his wife to the young people and gave the girls a hug. He shook hands with Henry and Tony, kissed Ruby, Henry's wife who held baby Nellie and ruffled Katie's hair. "Your Dad would be real proud of you today." His voice grew husky with emotion.

He turned and greeted Jimmy, Alice and their son, Alva and daughter, Myrtle. Jimmy could only stare at the dirt and shake his head. "I can't believe he's gone. I thought he would live forever. He was so healthy until last week. Why does pneumonia fell the strong? He died in my bed, quietly and without suffering."

Abe hugged his brother. "Jimmy, you've always been the caretaker for this family. Whenever anyone needed something you were there to help. He knew that and came to you when he was sick. God will bless you mightily for that."

Tyner and the others came to Abe's side. They all had graying at the temples, thinning on top and a few crow's feet around the eyes. The graveyard. was only a few years old, with a sparse number of graves - a peaceful place situated behind a beautiful native stone church. Trees provided shade intermittently amongst the stones.

He grabbed Abe's hand. "When did we get to this? Seems like only yesterday we were trailing and arresting all the outlaws we could locate. This new state has softened us up. Don't even need federal deputies any more."

Alice, Myrtle and James Alfred Barnhill about 1893

Abe's eyes, filled with moisture, peered into his face, the smile of a lifelong friend. Tyner knew he was fortunate to have known such men as these. Abe's voice, when he spoke, held a tremor, a mixture of age and emotion. "Will our grandchildren even understand what we have accomplished?"

Tyner smiled back. "Yes, they will, I am sure."

Cole and White stood near by nodding these heads at their remarks. Cole, always the hungry one, glanced at the crowd moving toward the church. "Let's get some of that friend chicken the good ladies of the Nazarene Church has prepared for us. Charley wouldn't want us to miss a meal on his account."

As the old friends gathered with the family inside the stone church, Abe's grandson, Andy Bounds, ran up and grabbed him around the middle and squeezed as hard as he could. "Papaw, there you are. Grandma was looking all over for you."

Ruffling his hair, Abe bent done to his level. "Tell her I will be right over. "

Cole chuckled as the youngster ran off. "That one of yours?"

"Yup, we're fishing and hunting buddies. I'm going to take him over to the White Chimney Cemetery when it gets cooler. That's the best squirrel hunting area around."

Abe scanned the cemetery as they walked away. It was a peaceful place situated behind a beautiful native stone church. Trees provided shade intermittently amongst the stones. He would speak to Sam and Jimmy later about buying a family plot. Now that there were two Barnhills here, the rest of the family would want to be buried as close to them as possible. Only God knew who would be next to have a home-coming.

Arpelar Church of the Nazarene

He resolved to go home and enjoy every minute the Lord would allow him to have, loving his family, his friends, his neighbors, and most of all, His God. His life was swiftly headed toward the same fate, the grave. But with his grandsons, Andy and Archie, to cheer him up and share hunting and fishing adventures, he would be greatly blessed in what time he had left.

He would tell them tales of tracking and fighting outlaws, of terrible tragedies and wonderful triumphs, of courageous men and cowards, of loss and reward, of the brave Indians and their customs and the many friends they had among them, and lastly of the contributions their family had made in the conquest of a violent land so that they could benefit from it and pass the blessings on to their children. Life was bestowed by God and he and Charley had experienced a great adventure while living it.

Charley's tombstone at Arpelar Cemetery, Oklahoma

Chapter 64

James Cole's Memories

The old man shielded his eyes from the sun with a hand that was skeletal and shaky. The stains on his lips indicated he had just eaten something gooey and blue. Thve berry cobbler sat in the bowl beckoning him to finish his dinner. It was forgotten in an instant when he recognized the face of his neighbor, Wyly Thornton. Tahlequah, the capital of the Cherokee district, had been his home for the past five years and Thornton, a full blood Cherokee, shared his love of the land and the people. Wyly drove him to the celebration dances at the community center when the people got together for festivals and weddings.

As Thornton approached the porch, James Cole knew it was more than a friendly visit. His friend held a clipboard thick with papers. He turned the top page back and then spoke."Howdy, Mr. Cole. Do you have some time to talk?"

"Why, sure. Come on up. If you don't mind, we can stay right here, cooler than inside."

Thornton sat down on the porch swing just a few feet from his host. His face was lined with weathered wrinkles, the face of a hard-working man who was not afraid to get outside. "Since this Depression thing has hit, as you know, many in the community including myself have lost our jobs. Now the government hires people to work on public works projects to help the economy and themselves I don't like taking a handout but with this I can work for pay and keep my family going."

"What kind of project?"

"Interviewing old pioneers. I can usually get in two interviews a day and I get paid $1 apiece. Would you be willing to help me out?"

"I don't know what I can tell you but go ahead."

The interviewer turned to the first page of his form. "I will take you information down in pencil and then retype it on the government form to send in the end of the week. Give me your birth date, location, name of parents."

The old man spoke in a brisk monotone reciting the technical part of his identity. He figured this might not be so bad after all. At least he could still remember things.

"I'm a Illinois boy from McComb, born in 1852, lived there until I was twenty years old when my family moved. We pulled our wagons across

Indian Territory - a rough haul - no roads to speak of and hills that strained our mules and horses to their limit. The Indians didn't bother us but they sure looked at us funny like, made me real nervous."

Stayed only one crop year in Denison, Texas and then came back to through the Territory to Kansas. Finally, in 1879 I moved to Fort Smith. Became a deputy in and traveled with some fine lawmen, but the best and the shrewdest were Charley Barnhill and Tyner Hughes."

Wyly stopped his pencil and studied his interviewee."Why do you say that?"

"Well, they were the only ones who could track down and haul in Belle Starr without getting killed. One time they snuck right up to her place before she even knew it. Of course, ole Sam, her husband, had us in his sights half way to Fort Smith. Only thing that saved us was Belle herself calling them off. She was the brains of the outfit, for sure."

"Did you stay in contact with your old buddies over the years?"

"Yes, there was a couple of deputy reunions over at Fort Smith after statehood. I went to one of them, but only about forty of the one hundred or so still alive came. Out of two hundred deputies that served Judge Parker, over one-third were killed in the line of duty. I visited the Barnhills any time I was passing through McAlester where they lived. Went to Charley's funeral back in 1911. That was a bad year for the family."

"Why do you say that?"

"Well, Charley's daughter who had just been married and was expecting a little one got killed in a runaway buggy accident not two months later. Their oldest brother, David, got sick and died right after that. But the hardest to take was Abe. He went down to Wichita Falls, Texas for Christmas with his daughter, Mollie's family and got pneumonia and died. All that happened in 1911."

"Wow! How can a family live through such losses?"

"They did. James lived in McAlester until about 1930 when he went to Wharton, Texas to live with his kids. He died of pneumonia too just year before last. They're all buried over at Arpelar."

"What about Tyner?"

"Lost track of him after he quit working at the Oklahoma State Prison. His son, Freddie, is still around. All the old timers are dying off; that's why it's good to have these interviews. Maybe one day someone will read them and learn something about the old life in Indian Territory."

Wyly smiled and nodded his head. "My kids are the same way. When I start to say, *Now when I was a little boy. . . .*they all seem to find something else to do. Any other prominent lawmen you knew?"

"Bass Reeves, Heck Thomas,. Reeves served law enforcement so long I can't remember anyone else surviving against such odds and dying with their boots off. He was so big in the saddle he had to ride the biggest mule he could find and that just made him more identifiable. So he had to go in disguise sometimes to get close to his prey. One time he even put on rags and walked around acting like an old beggar with his six guns strapped under his shirt. It worked - no one suspected an old darkie of being a lawman. Then the white lawmen made such a fuss since he was outperforming them that they got him demoted to local law enforcement positions in his last years."

Bass Reeves, United States Deputy Marshal

"What about Heck Thomas?"

"He got tired of the politics at Fort Smith and the new marshal that took Carroll's place so he went to the new Oklahoma Territory and had such a mess on his hand out there. He rode down the Daltons and the Cooks and other gangs that seemed to spring up overnight with the first land rushes. He died just a couple years after the Barnhills. I think the reason I have lived so long is I got out of law enforcement before it ruined my health."

Cole studied the strip of land across the street from his place. " I've only lived in Tahlequah for five years, but the changes I've seen are startling. I remember when the Indian prison tried to hold the outlaw, Jim Cook, after Charley and Heck Thomas arrested him. He ran away so often that they finally let him have free reign in the town until someone killed him. Those violent men usually met a violent death. None lived to die of old age except someone like Zeke Proctor. He outlived three or four wives."

Thornton passed a hand across his jaw and dropped it to the clipboard once again."Only one or two things left to ask..What about law enforcement practices back then?"

"I saw nine men hanged at Fort Smith and most of them were Negroes and two men killed by firing squad. It wasn't a pretty sight but the worst was the whippings. No white man could stand up against such punishment and had to be revived with water after each application of the lash. Tyner, Charley and I saw an Indian boy withstand thirty lashes one time without a whimper."

The interviewer placed his pencil in his shirt pocket and sighed."You sure led a mighty interesting life, sir. Off the record, do you have any memorabilia from those days as a deputy?"

The old man did not answer but instead shuffled to his feet and disappeared into the house. Thornton did not know whether to follow him or just wait on the porch. Old folks were like that sometimes. After a respectable time interval he was about to rise and go hunting for his friend, when the slight figure appeared, carrying a shoe box.

"Seen one of these before?" Cole handed him a Colt .45, freshly oiled and wrapped in a soft cloth.

"Dad had one of these, never left home without it on his hip."

"Deputies carried pistols but the main gun was the Winchester. Pistols were only good for close in fighting, fifty feet or less. A good deputy would aim for the belt buckle. Too easy to miss otherwise."

He dipped back into the shoe box and brought out a badge, still shiny and polished as the day he had bought it. He pinned it on his shirt front and laughed. "We used to kid each other that the only good thing about this badge was the target it made on our chests, so lots of deputies wore them inside their vests and just displayed them when needed. But most folks could spot a deputy a mile away, just by the way they rode, their rigging and clothes. We were pretty much distinct in our dress - most men would not wear what we wore unless they were man-hunting

To bring a conclusion to the visit, Thornton handed the sixshooter back to Cole. "How did you get through those years?"

Cole thought about that for a moment. "I was just living - never even gave it a thought. Certainly never expected to live to be eighty-five and still have most of my teeth."

With that Wyly stood up and shook his hand."Thanks, Mr. Cole. They're having a tribal dance next week. I can pick you up if you want to go." He waved as he went out the gate toward his car.

James Cole watched the middle-aged man drive away then turned to his newspaper. It irritated him to have to wear glasses to read it. The headlines were not good - war was coming, the Japs were attacking our ships in Asia and Amelia Earhart was missing. Oh - for the good old days when all he read about was gunfights, cattle thieves, train robbers and labor strikes.

Deputy Marshal Reunion, Immaculate Conception Church, Fort Smith, Arkansas

Made in the USA
San Bernardino, CA
25 September 2016